12/03

HUNTING
MIDNIGHT

HUNTING MIDNIGHT

RICHARD ZIMLER

DELACORTE PRESS

Published by
Delacorte Press
Random House, Inc.
New York, New York

Book design by Lynn Newmark

Delacorte Press® is a registered trademark of Random House, Inc.,
and the colophon is a trademark of Random House, Inc.

Library of Congress Cataloging-in-Publication Data
Zimler, Richard.
Hunting midnight / Richard Zimler.
p. cm.
ISBN 0-385-33644-6
1. South Carolina—History—1775–1865—Fiction. 2. Porto
(Portugal)—Fiction. 3. Africans—Portugal—Fiction. 4. Jews—
Portugal—Fiction. 5. Slave trade—Fiction. I. Title.
PS3576.I464 H86 2003
813'.54—dc21
2002073963

Manufactured in the United States of America
Published simultaneously in Canada

July 2003

BVG   10   9   8   7   6   5   4   3   2   1

To all those who fought to end the abomination of
slavery in the United States and southern Africa.
And to Midnight and his people.

ACKNOWLEDGMENTS

Grateful thanks to my editor, Samantha Bruce-Benjamin, for her extraordinary passion, intelligence, generosity, and hard work.

Thanks, too, to Cynthia Cannell for her loyalty and enthusiasm, and to Kate Miciak for her faith and support.

It is sometimes a difficult job reading an early draft of a novel, and I am grateful to Douglas Herring, Ruth G. Zimler, Michael Rakusin, and Alexandre Quintanilha for their invaluable comments.

I am also forever in debt to authors too numerous to name for their wonderful historical research.

Special thanks to Alex, who—like this book—links three continents.

HUNTING MIDNIGHT

PREFACE

A FIERCE WIND WAS DRIVING THE RAIN IN OFF the sea as I made my way home across the slippery cobblestone streets of my beloved city of Porto.

It was May of 1798, a month after my seventh birthday. Carefully tucked away inside my cane basket were two scrolls of indigo muslin that I had agreed to fetch for my mother—but only in exchange for a favor, I have to confess. If this rain were to splash so much as an inch of her fabric, she would grumble to herself all evening and refuse to make me my favorite sweet. Hence, not so much for the continued protection of the goods themselves as for the sake of my sweet tooth, I sought out shelter.

A certain inherited distrust of all things religious prompted me to choose Senhor David's old bookshop, rather than the whitewashed chapel next door, as a place to wait out the storm. As I entered through the low doorway, David encouraged me to leave my basket behind his writing desk and to remove my sodden boots, which he dangled over the iron railing by his fireplace.

"Senhor David," I asked, "may I go to the British Isles?"

"Off with you, lad!" he said, smiling.

I dashed over the creaking wooden floor to the musty

back room where he kept his treasure trove of English books, which Father and I had referred to as the British Isles for as long as I could remember.

I ought to explain that although I was born in Porto, a provincial city of sixty-five thousand souls in the north of Portugal, Father had had the honor—as he so often referred to it—of having been born a Scotsman. I was not yet aware of it, but when I spoke English, I had a distinctly Scottish accent.

Of tightly packed shelving, mildew, and thread-legged spiders these British Isles were blessed in abundance but, alas, they boasted nary a decent window save for the small octagonal skylight in the low, sagging ceiling. The rain was pelting down on its yellowing glass, creating a pattering din, rather like mice scampering.

It was so dark that I could barely see my own hands, and I was just considering asking for a candle when the sun suddenly peeked through the clouds, illuminating a bookshelf against the wall. Stepping closer, I could see that one of the titles was embossed in glittering gold letters—*The Fox Fables*. As no author's name was printed on the binding and since I was given to flights of fancy, I imagined that a clever fox had written them himself.

I shooed away Hercules, the calico cat whom Senhor David kept to chase off rats, plopped down on the sawdust of the floor, and opened the book. Inside, thick yellowing pages bore colorful drawings of dogs, cats, monkeys, elephants, and many other animals—a Noah's Ark of sorts. I was so excited by my find that I could read only the opening sentences of each story. Wishing to inquire its price of Senhor David, yet dreading the prospect of a sum beyond my means, I stood up to consider my options. That was when a single sheet of blue-tinted paper, delicate as a butterfly's wing, fell from the book's pages, fluttering down to finally settle on my right foot.

I picked it up and glanced around surreptitiously. Senhor David was sitting at his desk, smoking his pipe, absentmindedly rubbing his hand over his bald head while studying a large map. Hercules had curled up in his lap.

I crept into the darkest corner of the room and saw that I held a letter written in elegant script, addressed to a woman named Lúcia. It began, *My beloved, will you think me too bold if I were to say that I fall into the arms of slumber each and every night imagining your hand over my heart?*

Next I read of moist lips, moonlight, fainting spells, and orange blossoms. I recognized the word *seios*—breasts.... What glorious, heart-stopping wickedness that portended! Many other words were unfamiliar to me, however. I'd need a dictionary to know how daringly shocking this letter might be. It was signed with a swirling flourish by a man named Joaquim. He even dotted the *i* with a wee heart.

I wondered if *The Fox Fables* had been a present from Joaquim to Lúcia. Perhaps it had displeased her and she had sold it to Senhor David, forgetting she had concealed her suitor's letter inside. Since it bore no date, the two lovers might very well be grandparents by now. Though it was possible they were still unmarried and were at that very moment planning their next forbidden tryst at the top of the Clerics Tower, two hundred feet above the city's streets.

I tucked the letter into the pocket of my breeches, took a snootful of musty air into my lungs to rouse my courage, and marched to Senhor David. Handing him the book as innocently as my racing heart would allow, I dropped into his large palm all the copper coinage then in my possession: precisely four five-*reis* pieces. Judging from his wrinkled nose, this grand sum of twenty *reis* was not nearly enough. I begged him to let me pay for the book a little each week, giving him a helpless look, as was my wont when entreating an adult.

"I simply can't, John," he said, shaking his head. "Were I to conduct business on credit, I would soon be a pauper."

"Please, please, *please*—I shall have the rest of the payment for you in one month," I whined, clueless as to how I might fulfill such a promise but unwilling to see the beautifully illustrated fables escape my possession.

I might have simply left with the letter, of course, but I could not imagine owning it without the book. That would have been robbery.

Knowing he was about to refuse again, I called upon my theatrical gifts and assumed the air of a destitute orphan. Senhor David laughed, since he had seen this coming. As recompense for my effort, however, he agreed to my offer with a pat on my head, though by way of a warning he said, "Should you fail to abide by our agreement, I shall take *you* as payment, whereupon, make no mistake, I shall have my wife boil you in a stew for supper!"

"Being mostly bones and beak, I'd taste like a seagull," came my reply, which pleased David so much for some reason that he laughed again and pulled up a stool for me, instructing me to examine my new purchase while waiting for the storm to pass.

And so I began to read the first few fables, most memorably "Mouse, Frog, and Eagle," whose moral is: *He that pursueth evil pursueth it to his own death.*

When the sun returned for good half an hour later, I thanked Senhor David, slipped on my boots, and raced home. After receiving high praise from Mother for taking such good care of her cloth, I took the stairs two at a time to my room, where I and the letter could be alone.

I paid for my treasures one month later, just as I had promised, with coins earned helping Papa to clean his study and our storeroom.

I slept with the book and the letter under my mattress for months. The two objects became as inseparable in my mind as Joaquim and Lúcia themselves.

It is more than likely that my mother and father discovered the letter while tidying my room, but they never mentioned it. Years later, I gave it to my bride—along with *The Fox Fables*—as my wedding gift.

Upon her death, I clung to them as though they might save me from a shipwreck. I have them with me still.

SINCE MY PURCHASE of *The Fox Fables,* I have jeopardized my eyesight with thousands of evenings spent reading by my hearth or in bed by the light of a candle. Long acquaintance with the art of storytelling has made me aware that a tale such as the one I am about to tell ought to have a man or woman of universal sympathy or special bravery at its heart. And yet I feel myself wholly lacking for such a role. Furthermore, I am unsure of my own talents in giving an accurate account of the events that brought me from Portugal to America.

I therefore feel that the proper and most honest way to begin is with a lad of twelve named Daniel, whom I had the good fortune to meet by accident some twenty-four years ago. It was he who would set in motion the ripples that would later carry me across the Atlantic Ocean to America. If I am worthy of the central place in this story that I shall come to occupy later on, then it is, in part, due to the courageous example he set.

As I prepare to write of Daniel and many other things besides, I find myself speculating on what secret messages may flutter out of the pages of this tale of mine and fall at your feet. I can only hope that whatever reaches your hands encounters a receptive heart and an unbiased soul.

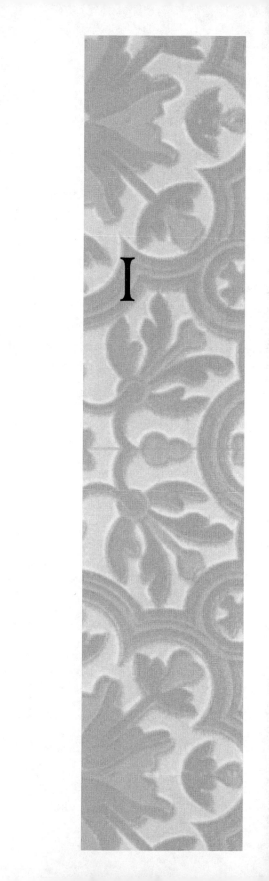

I

THOUGH A CHILD OF TATTERED CLOTHING and bad manners, Daniel has always held a special place in my heart. Had our life together been an adventure novel, he would have continued to train himself through many hours of candlelit study to become a great sculptor, revered far and wide, by the last page. But life, as Father used to say, is at best a game of Pope Joan played on a slanted table with the dealer hiding all the best cards up his ruffled sleeve. And so my friend was prevented from accomplishing such wonders.

Had fortune smiled upon him, or more importantly, had I, John Zarco Stewart, greater strength in my arms, then my own life might have gained by proximity as well. After all, we sometimes only realize the effects we have had on our loved ones years later.

I MET DANIEL in June of 1800, when I was nine years old. More than two years had passed since I'd discovered *The Fox Fables* in the British Isles. I was heading out early, fortified only by a cup of tea and a crust of corn bread that I'd smeared with honey and gobbled—to my mother's great displeasure—in an instant.

My destination was a wee lake—or tarn, as Papa called it—far beyond the walls of our city, in the wooded hinterland along the road to Vila do Conde. It was a wondrous spot for watching all manner of birdlife, especially just after the dawn. I was at the time, and still am today, a great lover of those handsome creatures of feather, air, and light—a keen appreciator and imitator of avian song as well. Back then, if I could have begged a beak and wings from God, I surely would have considered becoming one.

I was already approaching the granite steps at the end of our street that led down to the riverside neighborhood when raucous shouting reached me from a nearby alley. Racing there at top speed, I discovered Senhora Beatriz, a widowed washerwoman to whom we gave our soiled sheets every Wednesday, splayed on the cobbles outside her house. Whimpering like a beaten dog, her bony knees were drawn protectively into her belly. A periwigged brute in the livery of a coachman was standing threateningly over her, his countenance distorted by rage.

"You careless bitch!" he shouted, fairly spitting out the words. "You pilfering, lying *Marrana*."

Marrana was a new word to me. Later, my tutor informed me that it meant both swine and converted Jew, an epithet that had confused me, since I had never heard Senhora Beatriz described as anything but a good Christian soul. Indeed, I had only the vaguest idea of what a Jew might be, for though my grandmother had spoken to me of them on two or three occasions, I had not learned anything more than a few legends in which Jewish sorcerers always seemed to be foiling the work of nefarious kings with their magical prayers.

The villainous coach driver now finished his diatribe by snarling, "I'm going to sell you for glue-making, you lazy whore."

Then, after kicking Senhora Beatriz several times, he grabbed hold of her thinning hair, preparing to pound her head against the cobbles.

My heart was battering against my ribs and I began to feel dizzy. I wondered whether I ought to let loose a scream and if it would be able to fly over the rooftops separating my father from me and shake him awake. In those days, I was fully convinced that—at nearly six feet in height—he possessed unsurpassed power to restore order to the entire world.

I would surely have given voice to this bloodcurdling shriek if out of nowhere a rock hadn't caught our brute straight on his cheek. It had been hurled so perfectly and with such righteous force that our evildoer staggered back in shock. Falling to one knee, he seemed puzzled by what had happened, until he spotted the culprit stone sitting innocently at his feet. Looking around for the willful David who had dared to challenge him, he soon fixed me with an enraged stare. In my frilly white shirt, black-and-red-striped breeches, and buckled boots, I was a most unlikely enemy. I even had angelic bangs back then and what my father referred to as "doelike" blue-gray eyes. Nevertheless, I took several steps backward and began to hiccup—a reaction provoked by shattered nerves that I had suffered many times before.

I intended to scurry off if he threatened me, but instead, he turned to gaze at an urchin on the other side of the street. The lad looked at least three years my senior and wore a ragged shirt and soiled breeches. So filthy were his bare feet that they looked like roots pulled from the soil. His head was shaved.

This was the early summer of 1800, and despite the dawn of a new century, it was still a time when children never spoke to adults without first being invited to do so. A rock hurled by a miserably clothed waif at a liveried coach driver in the service of a man of riches was tantamount to heresy.

The injured man stood up with difficulty, dabbing at his cheek with his fingertips. Staring in disbelief at the blood left on his hand, he lurched forward. "You little son of a bitch!" he sputtered. Summoning his flagging strength, he hurled the stone with a grunt.

The weapon sailed over and past its youthful target and rebounded off the granite facade of the house belonging to Senhor Aurelio, the shoemaker. That was the last act our evildoer was going to attempt that day. His eyeballs rolled back in his head and he crumbled to the ground, his head meeting the street with a dry thud that did not sound promising.

I was shivering with fear and anticipation. I had never felt so alive. Imagine—a rock hurled by a filthy urchin felling an ugly brute not two hundred paces from my house!

Senhora Beatriz was sitting up now, her arms clasped around her belly as though protecting an unborn child. She was shaking her head in confusion, plainly trying to understand what had happened. Blood flowed from her bottom lip to her chin; one of her eyes was swollen shut and would later grow infected. It became a milky marble with a cloudy gray center for the rest of her days.

Daniel rushed to her, but she waved a trembling hand to halt his advance. "Go home," she said, wiping her mouth. "We'll talk later. Leave before there's more trouble. Please."

He shook his head. "I will not. At least, not until that shit gets swept into a dung heap," he said, pointing to the villain.

Daniel's accent gave him away as a resident of one of the crumbling riverfront neighborhoods. I was jealous of the way he seemed made for Porto, a city that had its share of gentlemen's clubs and formal gardens but had at its heart a labyrinth of dark alleyways patrolled by peddlers, waifs, and petty thieves.

"Daniel, pay attention to me," Senhora Beatriz replied, drawing determined breaths. "You must leave the city. Two days from now we will meet at your home. *Please,* before there's trouble..."

The senhora would have pleaded further, but neighbors were beginning to gather. Very shortly, a group of men—some still in their night clothes, a few of them bare-chested—had formed a circle around the fallen driver.

"Is he dead?" Senhor Tomás asked his brother-in-law Tiago the roofer, who was holding the back of his hand to the man's nose to see if he could detect breathing.

Various neighborwomen were now rushing to the aid of Senhora Beatriz, lifting her to her feet and making inquiries about the man and what had so incensed him.

I moved closer to the group of men. "No, he's still alive," said Tiago disappointedly—a perfect start to a new day of gossip would have required a murder, of course.

Senhora Maria Mendes, who was built like a bull, pushed her way through the men and spat in the insensible villain's face.

"Pig!" she yelled.

"And you there, son!" shouted Tiago the roofer at Daniel. "What in God's name do you think you're doing throwing stones at people?"

"Now wait a minute," came Senhor Paulo the tinsmith to the lad's defense, "he was only helping Senhora Beatriz."

"But with a stone the size of an orange?" cried Senhor Alberto.

"Had I a knife, I'd have slit the driver's throat!" exclaimed a man hidden from me.

"Gouged his eye out!" declared another.

The men trumpeted their bravery by telling what they would have done to the evil brute had *they* arrived in time. The women scoffed at what precious little use any of them were in times of real need. Alas, none of this was of any help to Senhora Beatriz or Daniel, who were looking at each other as though they were the only two people on the street. She was being led limping into her home, clearly more concerned for the lad's sake than her own. That sight made a solemn impression on me and I wondered how they knew each other.

The men now began demanding that Daniel leave their neighborhood. "You're going to end up flogged if you don't get out of here before I count to five! You don't belong here, son," Tiago the roofer shouted.

This struck me as unjust. As a lad of nine, I did not know that Daniel might have been in real danger. In those days, even a young boy could have his head impaled on an oakwood stake if the villainous driver were to die and if Senhora Beatriz's testimony failed to justify his courage. I was also unaware that a count whose royal-blue damask breeches had not been soaped, scrubbed, ironed, and perfumed in a timely manner, whose wine-stained brocade doublet was still hanging like a rain-drenched bat from a cord in Senhora Beatriz's back garden, was entitled to have his coachman beat the offending laundress near senseless. Anyone dissatisfied with this sort of justice could send his written protest to the Bishop, our mad Queen Maria, or even Pope Pius VII, who, even if he sympathized, would have been far too busy evading capture by Napoleon to open any communiqués from overseas. In short, one could send a letter of indignation to whomever one chose because it would make no difference.

No, I was not aware of these things, and so as I watched Tiago the roofer confronting Daniel, I was outraged.

The lad gazed down at his feet, confused. He had expected praise no less than I.

"Christ, I only wanted to help," he finally said. "I had to. She'd have been deader than a drum otherwise."

Daniel covered his eyes with his hand, unwilling to cry in front of the men, then rubbed his temples with his thumb and forefingers, as though to banish unwanted thoughts—a gesture of distress that I would come to know only too well over the next years. With maturity that I found extraordinary, he then said, "I guess I'll be going now. Good day to you all." Before parting, he went to retrieve his stone.

"Son, leave that be," Tiago advised, pointing a finger of warning. "You've done enough damage for one day."

Daniel picked up his stone nevertheless, eliciting reproaches from Tiago and the others. What added depth to my solidarity with him at that moment was his shorn scalp, plainly an attempt to rid him of head lice. This style was unfortunate, for it made him look ill and poor and might have inspired these men to act more harshly than was appropriate. If he had had blond ringlets of hair falling to the crimson collar of an expensive silken coat, this confrontation might have instead ended with pats on the back.

I ran forward. "Senhor Tiago," I cried. "Senhor Tiago, Senhora Beatriz was being beaten. The lout was *kicking* her!"

"John, go home immediately," he said, furrowing his brow in displeasure.

"She was hurt," I cried, "and her eye was nearly closed. It was big and puffy. Couldn't you see it? It was wrong to have done that to her. The man, he was...he was a *bloody poltroon*." I said these last words in English; it was my father's term for a dastardly wretch, and I could think of nothing in Portuguese to equal it.

Sensing in Tiago's glare that he had not understood me, I frantically sought a worthy translation. He had other plans and grabbed my arm.

"Come, son, I'm taking you back to your mother," he said, his eyes glinting with righteousness.

"If you don't let me go ..." I shouted.

"Then what?" he laughed.

I considered kicking him where the fabric in his tattered trousers hung suggestively forward, but sensed that this would only get me into deeper trouble.

"Make fun of me if you like," I declared, trembling, trying to imitate my father's voice, "but if you don't leave this lad alone ..."

Pity my youth, I couldn't for the life of me think of a way to boldly conclude this exciting start to a sentence. And I still had not freed my arm from Tiago's hairy grip.

Daniel, however, made an end to my threatening sentence unnecessary. Rearing back, he hurled his stone right at Tiago's tyrannical face, but at half speed, so to speak, giving the man ample chance to duck.

The roofer dove to the ground, relinquishing his hold on me.

"Go on!" Daniel shouted at me, waving furiously. "Close your goddamned snout and run, you little mole! You're free!"

11

SOMETIMES I THINK THAT HOPE IS NOT ALL individual in nature, that it exists as an ether that suffuses into us at the moment of birth. Of late, I have even come to the unlikely conclusion that nature bestows upon us hands and feet, eyes and ears, so that we may work as loyal servants to this boundless mist of hope, performing when we can the delicate alchemy of turning it into tangible reality—giving it form and influence, so to speak. So when I found myself free from Tiago's grasp, I served hope as well as my young heart knew how and bolted up the street, full of wild joy, paying no heed to the shouted commands behind me, wishing only to befriend the defiant lad who had helped me.

I caught up to Daniel outside the city gates. "What are you following me for, *caralho!*" he snapped.

Caralho was a rude reference to the male member. Many residents of Porto commonly ended their sentences with such swear words.

At a loss for words, I trudged forlornly behind him. Finally, I piped up that I wished to thank him for freeing me from Tiago the roofer.

"You're a strange little mole," he said.

"No, I'm not," I replied, wounded, because I was not yet aware that he was right.

In a singsong voice, he then said, *"Esquisito e pequenito, corajoso e faladoso..."*

It was a rhyme describing me, I was sure, and it meant, "strange and small, courageous and *talkacious.*" This last word, *faladoso* in Portuguese, was plainly an invention of his own.

I began to believe in that moment that he might be clever. He gave me a wily smile, his tongue darting out. One of his canine teeth was missing and made him look a bit daft. I knew nothing of Shakespeare then, but I can easily imagine now that Puck was penned with an actor of Daniel's temperament in mind.

He then told me of his fisherman father, who was away in Newfoundland. The lad was going to join him at sea in two years, after his fourteenth birthday. He said that his mother was a seamstress at a dressmaking shop on the Rua dos Ingleses, one of our most elegant streets.

"She makes things for all the wives of the wealthiest merchants," he boasted. Sensing my suspicion that this was rather far-fetched given the state of his clothing, he added with assurance, "Ma sewed a dress for Queen Maria once. Long and purple, with lace everywhere. You never saw so much fabric. Shit, you could have clothed two or three cows in it."

I would have wished to learn more about the similarities between dressing Queen Maria and a small herd of cattle, but he forestalled my questions by pointing to his house just ahead—a moss-covered hovel on a narrow dark street by the river. A straggle of honeysuckle snaked up the facade and peaked over the rooftop, bees zooming through the perfumed flowers.

Daniel took a key from his pocket. We entered a tiny square room, no larger than five paces of a man from side to side. The ceiling sagged at its center and was covered by a fuzzy black mold that gave off a sour smell. I worried about being buried alive, but he pushed me inside.

A faded floral rug was spread over the chipped tile floor to the fireplace at the back wall. Fuzzy brown cabbage leaves floated in the water of a wooden basin sitting before it. A granite crucifix above the hearth caught my attention. The Savior's visage was painted over in a ghastly array of colors. I never asked Daniel who did it, but it occurs to me now that he was the likely culprit. We kept neither cross nor rosary at our house, my father dismissing any and all objects of Christianity as tokens of superstition.

Raising his eyebrows mischievously, Daniel led me into a slightly larger room, where a cracked window at the back wall allowed a gloomy light to filter through. Two rude mattresses were wedged into the outside corners.

Daniel hopped around the sprawling mess on the floor with deft little leaps and succeeded in reaching a chest fashioned of old planks. Opening it, he pulled out a roughly carved wooden mask with a bulbous snout and hollows for eyes. Two V-shaped sticks had been inserted in holes in its prominent brow, creating spiky antlers. The mouth was a somber slit.

He placed it over his face and was transformed into a creature of the forest. My heart sank. I said, "You ought to be careful. Changing into animals can be dangerous."

"It's just a mask, silly." He offered it to me.

I took it and stared through the eyes. He told me he'd made it himself. When I asked how, he pulled an iron chisel, two short knives, and mallets of varying sizes from the chest.

"Where'd you get all that?"

"I bought some of them with what I get collecting clothes for Senhora Beatriz to wash. I begged the others from a cooper I know. He gives me what he doesn't need."

"You work for Senhora Beatriz?"

"I do."

I hoisted myself up onto the rim of his chest. A score of masks nestled in among the old clothes. Some had antlers, others horns. A few had serrated mouths, like the teeth of a wolf, and one had the pointed snout of a mosquito.

We decided to bring the masks of a frog and a deer with us to my tarn outside Porto. Daniel also took from beneath his straw pillow a tiny canvas pouch with a drawstring opening. He slipped it over his neck. "There's a charm inside," he explained to me. "A monk wrote it out for Ma to give to me. She says I have to wear it to protect me when I leave the city, because there are lots of witches hiding in the countryside. She says they have hair like horse manes and smell like leeks."

Daniel opened the pouch and lifted out a piece of old brown paper, folded in four. "I can't read nothing—you read it to me," he said, opening it up.

The talisman was written in a rough scrawl and said:

Divine Son of the Virgin Mary, who was born in Bethlehem, a Nazarene, and who was crucified so that we might live, I beseech thee, O Lord, that the body of me be not caught, nor put to death by the hands of destiny. If any evil should wish to track me or watch me, in order to take me or rob me, may its eyes not see me, may its mouth not speak to me, may its ears not hear me, may its hands not seize me, may its feet not overtake me. May I be armed with the sword of St. George, covered with the cloak of Abraham, and sail in the ark of Noah.

I was most impressed and reread it while he slipped on his mildewed leather shoes and grabbed a threadbare quilt in case it got chilly in the woods, since he was planning on spending the night.

Our path out of town took us past the market of wild birds by the São Bento Convent. So moving were the peeps of distress coming from the larks and thrushes caged inside this ramshackle row of wooden stalls that my hands formed fists.

"I'd like to destroy this all!" I declared.

Daniel summoned me ahead with a swear word, and I thought, mistakenly, that he hadn't noticed my anger. By the cattle pens we saw a wiry, long-haired man in a ratty fur-collared cape, a most impractical covering in the June heat. Overturning a wicker basket, the man climbed on top. The skin of his hands and face was bone-white. Crouching as though to do battle with a dragon, he began to shriek that the body of Christ was the only way toward redemption. We stopped to listen and heard him announce that all Jews, Protestants, and pagans would be expelled from Porto. We who were left would come to live in a City of God through the drinking of the Savior's blood.

"Filth, vermin, excrement of the devil!" he shouted. "We must fling all the *Marranos* into the dung heaps and be done with them once and for all!"

There was that word again—*Marranos*. It rankled me that I did not know its meaning. And twice in one day I had heard it.

Daniel shook his head when I asked him what it might mean, and he dragged me away. Just then, the preacher ceased his rant. Made curious by the silence, I turned and found him staring directly at me. Grinning, he motioned for me to come closer to him—or so it seemed at the time. My heart was thumping a warning.

A squat man with a feather in his cap then led a goat at the end of a tether, a noose around its neck, to the preacher.

"In the guise of a goat comes the devil!" the preacher told the crowd. "And in the guise of the devil comes the Jew!"

Taking a blackened knife from his coat, he jumped down from the basket. When he thrust it into the poor creature's side, it shrieked and shuddered, then fell to its knees. Blood sluiced from its wound like water from a spigot. Holding his hands to this living fountain, the preacher smeared his face and hair with blood, raised his arms, and called on the Lord to witness this sacrifice. Cries of terror pierced the air as onlookers scattered in all directions.

Noting my fear, Daniel said, "John, any old bugger with a rusted blade can kill a goat. Come on—let's go."

"But he knows me. He looked at me."

Daniel sighed theatrically, replying that I must have been mistaken. It would be several years before I would see the connection between this hate monger and the beating of Senhora Beatriz.

IN MY YOUTH I thought there could be no greater gift than being able to speak with animals. So as soon as we reached our lake, I stood and imitated the call of a kingfisher I spotted high up in an oak tree. When I ceased my calls, my avian friend contemplated the water thirty feet below. Then, without warning, he hurtled downward like a winged arrow, cutting into the water and disappearing.

"What's happened to him?" exclaimed Daniel.

"You'll see."

Emerging a few seconds later, none the worse for his swim, the bird flew back to his tree, a silvery minnow writhing in his beak. When I turned to share my joy with Daniel, I expected to see his wily smile, but he was sobbing.

I watched him without saying a word, his hands covering his eyes, since I was sure he would not want me to call attention to his display of emotion. When I finally dared to question him, he glared at me viciously. I decided to go on a brief bird-watching expedition in the woods. When I returned, he made me swear to keep a secret, then told me that Senhora Beatriz was his grandmother. "Her daughter gave me up as a baby. She left me on the wheel. The nuns gave me to my adoptive mother and father."

Left on the wheel was the Portuguese expression for placing an unwanted infant on a turntable set inside the window of a charitable institution maintained for just this purpose. The turntable was partitioned by a wooden board to keep the identity of the mother a secret. Babies left there were cared for by nuns and, if possible, given to new parents.

"Why did she give you up?" I asked.

Daniel wiped his nose with his hand, picked up a branch from the ground, and began making fierce cuts in it with a short-bladed knife. "Don't know. She's dead now—the fevers took her a year after she gave me to the nuns. She was just nineteen. She must have been too poor to care for me." He looked off into the distance. "I only found out about her because one day Senhora Beatriz was delivering laundry to a neighbor of ours and saw me in the street. She got a big fright and went all pale. Like she'd seen a ghost. *Bobo de merda, sem cabeçeira, vá-te-embora, vá agora.*"

This was another of the rhymes I would come to associate with Daniel. It meant, *Fool without wit, boy of shit, leave today and go away.*

"See, I looked just like her dead daughter—but I only found that out later."

He fashioned two tiny holes in his wood with the point of his blade, then scored some curving lines. "I secretly followed Senhora Beatriz to her house and began to go there every day at the same time. She'd always look sad, then close her shutters."

I twisted my head to see his work better, but he held it away from me and said he'd clout me if I peeked again.

"John, you can be damned sure I've got a head filled with shit, because the next thing I did was tell my mother about Senhora Beatriz. She never stays at home now—Ma, I mean. I haven't even seen her in a year. The last time I did, the old donkey grabbed me hard"—the lad's eyes shone with rage—"and slapped me right across my face. She told me to beg forgiveness for being born. Everything got broke in her life when she took me in. That's when I found out I was adopted."

Holding his knife like a pen, he made a long circular incision across his design.

"Then, one day, Senhora Beatriz came to our house—maybe two years ago. I invited her inside, but she wouldn't come in. She started crying right in the doorway. I went to her, but she told me to stay back. She said she needed a lad to collect soiled linens and things. She'd pay me."

"What did you say?"

"What do you think I said? I'd never have been able to buy my carving tools without her money. That's how I get all my things, John. So, about six months ago, I was at her house and she sat me down and gave me some biscuits. She showed me a tiny painting with a woman's face. The whole thing wasn't any bigger than my palm. And the woman's face looked like mine. She said that that was why she got a fright the first time she saw me, because I looked so much like her."

"The woman in the painting was your mother?"

He nodded. "Her name was Teresa. Senhora Beatriz told me she'd given up a baby she'd had with a man who'd run off. They weren't married. Senhora Beatriz sure was angry at him for leaving her. She said he was a clothing merchant from Lisbon and that he'd ruined her daughter with his silk and promises. Not that she said the baby they'd had was me, of course. She thinks I haven't figured it out. I haven't told anyone but you, so you've got to keep quiet."

"Why don't you tell Senhora Beatriz you know? She's your grandmother."

"If she wanted me to know," he replied angrily, "she'd say so. *She* has to tell me. I'm not going to say anything otherwise. And you're not either! You hear me?"

"I'll not say a thing to anyone," I agreed, but I didn't understand his reasoning. Now I know he showed a sensitivity for her feelings far beyond his years, and an exemplary capacity for self-denial.

Daniel held up his finished carving. It was a face with questioning eyes, an open, awestruck mouth, and wild hair. It looked like a spooked cat.

"What's that supposed to be?" I asked.

"It's his Scottish lordship himself—it's you."

"Me!" I held out my hand for it, but he stood up, reared back, and threw it into the lake.

I jumped up. "Why'd you do that? I wanted to keep it."

He gave me a defiant look. "'Cause I'm evil. *Fool without wit, boy of shit, leave today and go away!*"

"You ought to have at least let me get a good look. That wasn't fair!"

Daniel's face crumpled as though I'd slapped him. When I reached out for him, he jerked away and said, "Don't touch me, I'm filthy."

AFTER HE'D STOPPED crying, I swam in the cold tarn while Daniel waited on shore. He asked me questions about the bird market we'd seen earlier, which was pitched every Tuesday and Saturday in New Square.

"Listen," he said, "we'll go there on Tuesday. Late afternoon. I want to follow the seller with the most birds as he leaves for home. Also, I want you to get some paints—and brushes."

"Daniel, what are you planning? My parents have warned me—"

"Christ, John, I haven't worked it all out yet. Have a little patience."

What he wouldn't let me say was that my parents had forbidden me from visiting the bird market. This was because once, when I was four, I'd fainted dead away on seeing a goldfinch in a wire prison no bigger than a man's fist. Now that I was older, they surely feared that I'd get my revenge and do something rash, for which I'd end up caged myself.

Quite right, they were, as it turned out. Though I suppose I might even today blame it all on Daniel.

III

ON THE SUNDAY AFTER SENHORA BEATRIZ WAS beaten, Father told me a Scottish tale counseling caution. In this story, a witch transformed Papa into a pimply toad and chained him to a standard in her granite tower. To my delight, Porritch—the dog he'd had as a lad—rescued him by sneaking up on the hag, catching her asleep, and clamping his jaws around her neck. I say *delight* because I had always wished for a dog, though my mother had obliged me to wait until I was a trifle older and more "responsible," as she put it.

"When a witch is killed," Papa explained to me on this occasion, "all the evil spells she's ever uttered are undone in an instant."

I recall he made quite an impression on me that day by explaining that the gold chain on his pocket watch had been the same one the witch had used to tie him to her standard. "It's fixed now, son, but the clasp was broken when I found it. You see, when the evil nighthag was killed, I was transformed from a toad to a lad in an instant. My growth shattered the clasp."

He let me hold the watch and added, "I shall give it to you on the day we celebrate your twenty-first birthday. Do you know why I told you this particular tale, son?" When I shook my head, he said, "It has to do with what happened to Senhora Beatriz and certain other related dangers in the city at the moment. Son, you're a wee thing still and, though you are brave and swift of foot, already a defiant *kelpie,* you cannot do everything yourself." *Kelpie* meant monster of the lochs in Scottish, but Papa used it as a term of endearment. "We all need to be rescued now and again—from all sorts of snares. So you are to race home to me if you ever see anything like that again—any woman, man, or child being hurt. Do you see my point, lad?"

"I understand."

At the time, Papa's worry, and his vague reference to *certain other related dangers,* seemed to have nothing to do with the preacher I'd listened to in New Square. But as I write these memories it is now only too obvious that my parents would have heard a number of terrifying accounts of his hateful activities by then.

TO GET THE paints and brushes that Daniel had asked for, I went early on Monday morning to visit Luna and Graça Oliveira, kindhearted neighbors whom we referred to as the Olive Tree Sisters. They were then halfway into their sixth decade. If asked, however, I would have sworn that they must have been over seventy, since their gray hair and puckered faces indicated to my youthful eyes a withering decrepitude.

Luna and Graça were renowned throughout the city for the lifelike beauty of the wax fruit they molded. Their likenesses were so precise, in fact, it was rumored that our mad-as-a-hatter Queen Maria, while on a visit to Porto before my birth, had taken an ill-advised bite of one of their sunset-colored peaches. As I have it on good authority that the Queen's brown teeth were as precarious in her mouth as tortoiseshell buttons on a ragseller's waistcoat, this must have meant a shattering end to several.

Standing outside the Olive Tree Sisters' home, I tapped the lion's-head knocker against their door. I had not considered the ungodly time—no more than half an hour past sunrise. And even worse, I'd disobeyed my parents by sneaking out, as I was forbidden from leaving our home while they were both asleep. But I was optimistic that I could complete my mission without their finding out—an indication of just how far afield Daniel's friendship had already led me.

Luna peered down from an upstairs window, her head crowned by a scarlet nightcap with a woolen ball tassel. Considering me a figment of the early-morning mist, her gray-green eyes blinked. "John? Is that you, lad?"

I confirmed it was and she shouted, "Codfish cakes! What are you doing here at this hour? What's wrong?"

I started to explain, but my excitement left me tongue-tied.

"I'm coming down, John. Don't move or I'll flatten you!" she said, pointing a stern finger at me.

I was too much of an imp to heed her request and after only a few seconds knocked again, far harder. Placing my ear to the door, I heard her say, "That wee son of a bitch knows nothing of the pains in this old body."

I wasn't offended; Luna was renowned for speaking like a stevedore. She opened the door, frowning. "You are a most impatient little devil!" she declared.

"I'm sorry, Senhora Luna, but . . . but I need your help."

Luna's wiry gray hair was clipped short and she was wearing several slender gold necklaces and earrings of filigree six-pointed stars, which made her look, I thought, beautiful.

"John," she said in a grave whisper, "is something wrong—is your mama or papa ill?" She was convinced that only tragedy could have brought me here so early.

"I need paints," I replied.

She turned and looked behind her, as though I might have been addressing someone else.

"You woke me at this hour for paints? Are you mad, child?" she shrieked.

"I promised Daniel I'd get paints."

"Who in God's name is Daniel?"

Before I had time to answer, she breathed in stiffly and muttered, "Oh, never mind, lad." Grabbing my arm, she dragged me into their sitting room like a hooked fish. Though tiny, she was powerful, with the great knobby hands of a peasant. I had once seen her crush a walnut between her palms—afterward, she told me that all artists need strong fingers in order to strangle their doubts.

She waddled to the base of the stairs, her feet splayed like a duck. With no warning, she gave a deafening screech for her sister. "Graçinha! Move those bones, Sister. Someone left another surprise on our doorstep."

"You're cleaning it this time, Little Sister," Graça called down.

"Too late—it's in the house. We've a sorry spectacle here right on the rug." She grinned at her prank.

"What in God's sweet name are you talking about, Little Sister?"

After a moment, Graça appeared at the top of their stairs, her bony feet wedged into clogs. She was the taller of the two by nearly two inches, though she usually described herself as "a full hand closer to God" to irritate Luna. She smiled more easily than her younger sister, and now, having noticed me, she offered a pixie grin, saying, "A handsome little surprise it is too!"

Once downstairs, Graça bent down and kissed my cheeks. Both sisters reeked of garlic. Luna once told me she slept with a clove around her neck to fend off mosquitoes, flies, and meddling priests.

Upon their insistence, I sat in the red velvet armchair that I'd adored since I was tiny. They dropped down in front of me on a chaise with embroidered cushions. They had the prettiest furniture on our street.

"Speak, child," Luna commanded, "or I shall be forced to get out our instruments of torture."

So it was that I explained about Daniel and a secret plan he had conceived, which had something to do with the bird market.

Graça turned to her sister and smiled wistfully. "Children," she sighed, as though I and all my fellow fledglings were a perpetual mystery. I am not of the opinion that Luna ever regretted her unmarried and childless state, but Graça may have. As to why they never took husbands, I cannot say.

The sisters looked at each other, exchanging shrugs, sighs, and coded phrases. In the end, they agreed to my request and disappeared into the nether regions of their house, where they had their workrooms. Alone and anxious, I lifted up a brass warming pan and began conferring knighthood upon their furniture. While making my rounds I discovered a crystalline green and blue tile, four inches square, bearing the figure of a triton. I'd never seen anything so lovely before.

At that moment the Olive Tree Sisters hurried back into the room, carrying ceramic jars containing red, blue, yellow, and white paint. After learning that I didn't know how to mix colors, Luna remarked disdainfully, "A filthy damnable disgrace that your tutor teaches you nothing of art. I shall be talking to your mother about getting you some proper lessons."

Graça explained that with the three primary colors and white, I could make all the others. While I listened, Luna fetched me brushes and a papier-mâché tray painted with tulips for carrying it all home.

"And I'll dip you up to your nose in wax if you make a mess," she warned me.

On my way out the door, I asked where they had bought the tile of the triton. Graça told me it had been made by their friend, Senhor Gilberto the potter.

Graça looked at Luna, who twisted her lips into a frown. How this expression was interpreted as permission, I do not know, but Graça patted my head and said, "It's yours, then."

"Mine?"

She kissed me on the brow and placed the tile gingerly onto my tray. "Always surround yourself with beautiful things, John, and all will be well."

I BALANCED MY tray in one hand, eased open the front door to our house, and tiptoed inside. Mother was standing by the mirror, brushing her chestnut-brown tresses in a luxurious curtain over her face, as she did every morning. She was wearing her blue day dress, stitched tight just under the bust and falling straight to the floor, hiding her slim waist. Her feet were bare. For a single moment, I believed I still had a chance to slip by her. If I exercised caution, I could retrace my steps and vanish past her upstairs. But on parting her hair in front, she caught a startled glimpse of me and my courage failed.

"Good morning, John," she said. This was the *en garde* before our battle.

"I was just outside for a moment, confirming we shall have sun."

She eyed my tray suspiciously.

"I've also been with the Olive Tree Sisters," I rushed to confess. "They invited me for tea and let me borrow some things."

"Luna and Graça had you for tea at seven o'clock in the morning?" she asked skeptically. "John, you must either think me insane or unconcerned for your welfare. And you are testing my patience yet again. Now, would you mind telling me what it is you are carrying?"

"Paints. Daniel and I shall be painting some things."

"What things?"

"Some masks he's made," I lied.

"Indeed." She came to me and snatched up one of the jars. Peering inside, she sniffed its contents. Satisfied that I was telling the truth, she said, "Now, listen to me: You are not to eat any of this. I'm quite sure it's poisonous."

I gave her a furious look, because imbibing such a paste would never have crossed my mind.

"Promise me," she said, wagging her finger.

"Mother, do you think I am a complete and utter idiot?"

To which she replied, without batting an eyelash, "No, of course not, dear, far from it. We all know only too well how intelligent you are. But I must say that you imitate many things brilliantly, and if you can bear a small criticism, you even do an excellent imitation of an idiot at times."

THAT AFTERNOON, MOTHER and I bid farewell to my father at our door, as he was journeying upriver for one of his two-week sojourns to survey lands for the Douro Wine Company. Trying to cheer me up, he said, "Soon, son, we shall have our own vineyard upriver and I shall not need to part from you."

Leaning down to whisper in my ear, he added that he had spoken again to Mama about getting a dog and that she was softening. Furthermore, his absence would no doubt play on her emotions and render her butter to our wishes. I embraced him very hard. I would have liked to press my little self fully inside him.

Mama and I waved good-bye as he strode down the street, her hand trembling around mine. She brushed away her tears and whispered something to herself that surprised and chilled me: "This life is killing me."

IV

BACK IN 1800, THE BIRD MARKET WAS NOT SO well established as it is today: It consisted of only a single row of wooden stalls pitched haphazardly, eleven in total on the Tuesday of my visit with Daniel. Each stall held between ten and thirty cages, some on the ground, others on tables. The cages were made of wicker, cane, rusted iron, wire mesh, and in one case—for a golden pheasant—glass and gilding. The number of birds per cage proceeded from a low of one, in the case of most hawks, egrets, crows, and herons, to a high of fifteen or more for the wrens, wagtails, and other small birdies. That day, I counted seventeen European goldfinches trapped in a single tunnel of despair fully as long as my arm but no taller and deeper than the width of a man's hand.

Even worse, some birds were kept in direct sunlight with little or no water. A slender parrot with emerald green feathers had plainly been incarcerated in that condition for too long and was lying limp at the bottom of its cage, flies buzzing noisily at its eyes.

I suppose it was merciful that these creatures could not understand the speculations of marketgoers as to how certain red, rose, and yellow feathers would look when stitched to a hat.

Inside the largest of the stalls, a woodpecker was lying belly-up at the bottom of a wire-mesh cage, his scarlet-capped head tilted far to the side, squawking in helplessness. One wing was splayed; likely he had broken it trying to fly. I squatted next to him, and Daniel joined me.

The owner, a bald man with sallow skin and rotting teeth, was calling out to onlookers, "See these beauties of mine! Handsomest birds in Portugal. Step up and get a good look at them!"

When he paused for a drink from his mug, I pleaded with him to let me free the woodpecker—or allow me to take him to someone who cared for animals.

He burst out laughing, spraying wine on me. "That one's ready for the compost heap, son."

"You're the one who belongs in compost, you bastard!" Daniel shouted.

The man grabbed his broom and tried to whack Daniel on the head, but the lad jumped out of his range and cursed him again.

While they traded insults, the woodpecker began to choke, and a slender pinkish worm, like a string, slipped out of his mouth. I jumped back, trampling a lady's foot. She screeched that I was a no-good filthy urchin and described me in a whisper to her lady friend as a worthless mutt. I didn't know why she used this particular expression, but her words clung tight as a tick to me even then. As a child I was not aware of just how many residents of our small city knew that my father was a foreigner.

That worm in the woodpecker's throat is what's made him ill, I reasoned, pushing my face right up to the cage, wishing to be able to extract the hideous thing.

The proprietor had given up on trying to knock Daniel on the head and was explaining the advantages of thrushes over larks to an old man with smallpox scars on his cheeks. I pulled Daniel's sleeve to make him look closer at the bird and said, "See what was inside him?"

While we stared through the mesh, the worm seemed to turn solid—to become a splinter. All this time I had failed to take note of the creature's hesitant breathing, but when it ceased, I remarked its absence easily enough. The woodpecker's eyes remained open but were no longer staring into our world. I called to him, then banged on the cage.

"Hey, stop that now!" the proprietor ordered.

Daniel began exhorting me to leave. Just then I realized that the worm was, in truth, the poor bird's tongue.

Before we left, Daniel asked again if we could have it, now that it was dead. The proprietor told him that if we would leave and never return, Daniel could open the latch and take him.

As Daniel lifted the woodpecker out, he said in his most proper voice, "I hope I may count on your presence here on St. John's Eve. I'll have silver then for buying a healthy bird."

"I'll be here, though I doubt the likes of you will ever save enough coins for one of my beauties. Now, go away!"

We placed the woodpecker in a small sack that we begged at a cobbler's stall. I wished to bury the unfortunate creature, but Daniel said we'd need him to do our painting properly. To my series of ensuing questions, all he'd say was "Hush up, John, I need to think."

We sat for some time on the steps of the São Bento Convent, where he could work out the details of his plan while studying the marketplace.

"Here's what we do, John," he finally announced. "We're going to wait here till that bastard leaves, then follow him."

When I asked why, he leaned toward me menacingly and gave me one of his favorite rhymes: *Raptado, embrulhado, e entregado*...Kidnapped, wrapped, and delivered...

I was unsure if he meant me or the birdseller, but before I could ask, a hand clamped down on my shoulder. I looked up and, to my horror, discovered the preacher whom we'd seen a few days earlier.

Struggling free of his grip, I tumbled down the stairs, banging my elbow hard on the granite. The villain's dark eyes glinted with mirth. Daniel stepped in front of me as my guard. "What the hell do you want?" he demanded.

The villain fixed his gaze on me over my friend's shoulder. So transformed was his appearance from the last time we'd seen him that for a few bewildered moments I believed I had mistakenly identified him. Instead of his ragged fur-collared cape, he now wore an elegant scarlet dress coat with small pearls sewn into the wide lapels. On his head sat a black velvet hat, and his hair, exquisitely styled, cascaded in waves to his shoulders. He carried a silver cane under his arm.

"Blessings unto you, my child," he said with heavy sincerity. He took a pinch of snuff from a silver box and inhaled sharply into both nostrils.

"Go away, you bastard!" Daniel demanded.

"Though we have never met," he said, winking at me, "I am an admirer of yours."

Removing his hat, he displayed its interior to us, then swirled his hand inside and extracted a foot-long indigo feather. Leaning forward, he offered it to me. "I have been watching you for quite some time, little one. So please accept this gift of heartfelt esteem. I, too, am most fond of God's tiny winged creatures."

I shook my head in refusal.

"Ah, what a shame," he said sadly.

He placed the feather back in his hat and smoothed his hair off his brow. His hand was long and thin. It had never known labor.

"Let me explain, little one. There occasionally appears a face in the crowd that represents all those souls one would like to reach—a beautiful face that is symbolic of all in God's creation. Do you understand what I am saying?"

I started to hiccup, which caused him to laugh.

"You are the son of James Stewart and Maria Pereira Zarco, if I'm not in error."

"How . . . how is it that you know my parents?" I asked.

"I know who all the Jews are. That is one of my duties."

"He's not a Jew!" Daniel snarled. "Now leave us be."

As though confiding a secret, he whispered, "It is your devilish soul I desire, little one. Nothing less."

Daniel had had enough. He took a knife from his pocket and brandished it like a sword.

The preacher placed his hat on his head and made a deep purring noise, then meowed.

"I shall just say one more thing," he said with a smile, "and then I shall leave you. Have you never thought of returning with your father to Scotland, dear John? No? Well then, be so kind as to tell your parents from me that that must be your destiny. Let them make plans now, before we meet again. As the Apostle Matthew has told us, *The gate that leads to life is small and the road is narrow.*"

"But I've always lived here. I'm Portuguese. I was born in Porto."

He said nothing, merely crossed himself, then turned around in a slow circle and tapped the ground twice with his cane. His back was to us for a few seconds at least. Turning to face us, he opened his mouth. A bewildered yellow finch peeked into the world, struggling to emerge. The villain held the bird's neck between his teeth, as though in a vise, about to bite down.

"Please don't," I pleaded tearfully. *"Please . . ."* In that very instant, I began to think of him as a *necromancer,* Papa's word for an evil sorcerer.

I was sure he was about to commit an unspeakable act. But he wished to make a different point. Opening his mouth fully, he permitted the bird to fly away.

Daniel took a step back.

"You see what your friend Lourenço can do, little one? It would be unwise to doubt me. Though the holy delight of burning you in the squares of Portugal is no longer an option, I shall not accept the stain of your presence among us any longer." He breathed in deeply to quell his rage. "Never forget, the smoke rising off your body is incense to all those of righteous belief."

He produced a lighted candle from out of his hand. Twisting it in the air, it became a silver *tostão* coin. He held it up before us, then threw it at my feet. I let it clang on the steps, then picked it up. I was going to give it back to him, for I believed I might gain his favor by doing so, but he told me to keep it.

"You see," he said, pointing first at me, then Daniel, "the Jew among us can always be found if we but leave a single coin in view!"

The crowd that had gathered around us howled with delight. An elderly woman stepped forward and threw an apple core at me, and several men began to shout at us.

I cannot say how long they had seen fit to witness this cruel encounter in rapt silence, but when I turned back, the necromancer was striding away from us.

Daniel took the coin from me and whispered, "Never mind, John, we'll see that bastard swinging from a gallows someday."

V

AS A CHILD, I KNEW NOTHING OF CHRISTIAN religious practice, having been strictly forbidden by my atheist father from attending weekly Mass with my mother and grandmother and only having witnessed a formal service on one occasion. Of that single visit to the Church of Mercy in the year of 1791, I confess that I own not a single recollection. This profound ignorance is due to no deliberate act of forgetfulness on my part, but rather to my extreme youth. For the momentous occasion in question was none other than my own rapid-fire Baptism.

Father had opposed my christening vehemently and refused to attend, preferring to sulk inside a cloud of pipe smoke in his study. It was, however, a religious duty insisted upon by my mother, who had fixed her most determined gaze at my father for days on end until, sensing his troops outmanned by this Medusan onslaught, he extended the white flag of surrender. The logic behind her offensive was this: She wished to spare me the unfortunate fate of a German girl with Humanist parents whom she had befriended as a lass and who had for years been referred to as "the infidel" and "the savage" by a good many children and adults for not having had her original sin erased with holy water.

Depending on whom you believe, she had either told my father, "I will hold this against you forever if you prevent it" (my mother's version), or "I will have it done in secret and you will not know a thing until it is over" (my father's).

As it happens, I was not only nearly completely ignorant of the Christian faith as a child but also of Jewish beliefs and history. All I knew for certain was that Moses was a prophet who'd had horns on his head. I owed this latter tidbit of knowledge to the Olive Tree Sisters, who'd shown me—when I was five—an engraving of the Lawgiver with two spikes poking from his brow. Graça had told me that all Jews had such protuberances thousands of years ago but that they had fallen off in successive generations from disuse. Luna swore that a few ancient members of this race had even possessed furry tails.

Soon after that, I learned there were no Jews to be found in Portugal. I discovered this when I asked Professor Raimundo, my tutor, if he could suggest a Jewish person I might follow, as I was eager to spot any sign of a tail or horns.

"Happily, we can no longer observe that stubborn race," he'd replied, rooting in his ear with the long curling nail of his little finger. "There are no Jews left in Portugal, for the wise men of our Church had the foresight to cleanse the monarchy of such heathens long ago."

To my further inquiries, he told me that in 1497 the Jews had been converted upon threat of death and made into so-called New Christians. Beginning in 1536, those New Christians who continued to practice their old religion in secret were arrested and placed in dungeons by Inquisitors, prosecutors sanctioned by both Church and King.

Professor Raimundo had been noticeably put out by my questions and resorted to frequent pinches of snuff to steady his nerves. Sneezing, he had added that the Inquisition had—unfortunately—been stripped of much of its power some fifteen years before my birth. Even so, Jews were still forbidden from founding a community in Portugal. As to what practicing Judaism might entail, he rested his hands on his ample paunch, grimaced in distaste, and replied, "They stubbornly refuse to believe in the divinity of Our Lord Jesus Christ. Hence, the prayers they speak in their temples are nothing more than blasphemies against the Son of God and the Virgin."

In my innocence, this seemed a reasonable assertion. Jews were plainly a disagreeable people.

Being a monstrously insistent young lad, I then asked if there wasn't even one last member of this tribe in Porto whom I might secretly study. Inhaling another dusting of snuff, Raimundo snapped, "Not that I am aware of, but you would do well to ask your mother."

I considered that a strange comment, but since he refused to utter another word on the subject, I resolved to do as he suggested.

When I asked her, she calmly replied, "No, John, there are neither Jews nor New Christians residing in Porto at the present time."

She presumed that Raimundo might have wrongly believed her familiar with such matters since the home we lived in, which had been in her mother's family for generations, was at the heart of what had once been a small Jewish quarter prior to the Inquisition. My father was present for this explanation and puffed on his pipe without saying a word.

IT WAS ATOP these slanders and fanciful images that the necromancer's accusation of my being Jewish now found awkward footing. Giving in to my worst fears, I begged Daniel to search my head and nether regions for indications of unsightly growths of any telltale sort. He took to this task with admirable solemnity. We must have looked a sight with my breeches down and him squatting to gaze at my hindquarters. To my solemn relief, he soon dismissed my fears.

WHILE HUNTING WITH Daniel for discarded bottles and trinkets on the riverbank that afternoon, I began to think that a life without close friends was not an inevitability for me. I remember being quite literally shaken by this knowledge when he grabbed my hand without warning and said, "I've found something, John, hurry!"

He raced ahead, shouting that he'd spotted a tabletop sticking out of some mud and that it was perfect for carving. "Run! Come on! Faster!" His green eyes were aglow with the pleasure of having me share in his discovery.

So excited did he become when we had safely unearthed his treasure that he began flapping his hands as though to brush away bees. A year or so later, he would offer the tabletop, intricately carved with the mischievous faces of children hiding in trees, to a young girl called Violeta. He would place me right at the center, replete with a beaked nose and gaping mouth.

I understand now that Daniel, more than anyone I ever met, saw through the surface of objects to what lay hidden beneath. Would it be an exaggeration to say that he was capable of seeing the potential in me, as well, and that I loved him for it?

I remember when we first pulled the tabletop out of the mud that afternoon, he stomped around as though seeking to create footprints so deep they could never be washed away by the river. Perhaps what he most wished with his carving was to offer a permanent impression of himself to the world.

We were too young to know that he had already—in only a few days—created deep and lasting marks in me. And even if we'd known, I do not believe we'd have spoken of it.

AT THE STROKE of four o'clock we returned to New Square, to follow the bald birdseller to his home. It was nearly an hour later when he and his wife loaded their cages into the back of their wagon and headed off. On the far side of the Gate of Oaks, they turned toward the town of Valongo and soon stopped at the Douro Inn, a grim-looking establishment. When they resumed their journey a half hour later, we continued our eager pursuit. But the birdseller now lashed his mares into a gallop and we were soon left shielding our eyes from the dust they threw up in their wake. Daniel turned this disheartening situation to our advantage by returning to the Douro Inn and making inquiries of the innkeeper, who told us that the birdseller and his wife were in the habit of stopping there for a drink every Tuesday and Saturday, prior to the market and occasionally afterward. The lad made a point of asking about St. John's Eve, and we were told that they generally came to the inn early that morning.

Outside, Daniel put his arm around my shoulder and whispered conspiratorially, "Kidnapped, wrapped, and delivered . . . Now, listen, John. We'll have to come back here at dawn on the Twenty-Third. Which means we have only"—he counted by tapping his fingers on the top of my head—"five days. So starting tomorrow, we paint."

I LATER DISCOVERED that Daniel, on returning home, placed the dead woodpecker on his bed, sat on the floor beside it, and got to work with his tools and pinewood. His goal was to create at least ten carvings before St. John's Eve, which he estimated would occupy him from sunup to dusk on each of the next five days.

That afternoon, Senhora Beatriz interrupted his feverish work with a knock at his door. Her puffy eye was bruised blue and yellow and had nearly closed. She walked with a limp. Two of her ribs had been broken and she breathed with noticeable pain as well. Remaining in the doorway, she thanked Daniel for coming to her rescue. He received her thanks with a downcast gaze, worried that his knowledge of their kinship might overwhelm him should he look her directly in the eye.

He would later tell me, "My heart was thumping so hard I could hardly hear a thing. But you'd have been proud of me, John, I didn't make a single peep. And I didn't ask her for nothing. What would have been the good of asking, anyway? Things'll always be like they are."

When Senhora Beatriz left, he started carving again, using his knife with such force that he made a deep gouge in his woodpecker's tail.

AT HOME I discovered my mother and grandmother embroidering in our sitting room. Grandmother Rosa smothered me in her perfumed bosom, then asked after my new friend's father, plainly intending to evaluate his station in life. Mama gave me a sidelong glance to say, *Let me handle this.* I begged her permission to leave, then ran to my room.

From many such experiences of my childhood, I learned that Mama wished to keep me away from her mother. In addition, I almost never saw her two elder brothers, though they lived only thirty miles away in Aveiro.

When she came to kiss me good night, I asked her to stay for a moment and to close the door. "Grandmother is still here and has fine hearing," I whispered.

Mama covered her mouth to stifle a laugh. After easing the door closed, she sat by me and placed her hand on my chest.

My agitation banished all possibility of tact. "Are we Jews, Mama?"

"Goodness! Where did that little cannonball come from?"

"Something happened today."

"What? Tell me, John."

"There was a man preaching in New Square. He came to talk to Daniel and me. And he said that . . . that we were Jews."

"You and Daniel? He said you and Daniel were Jews? How odd!"

"No, you, Papa, and I. Mama, he knew our names."

She gasped. "Who was he? Did you find out *his* name?"

"Lourenço. He did not tell me his family name. I saw him once before. Then he had long oily hair and wore a horrid cape. But this time he was changed. He wore expensive clothes. And his hair was brushed. I think he's a magician. Or a necromancer. He did tricks."

"John, he didn't hurt you or Daniel, did he?" she asked anxiously.

"No, but he said you ought to take me away from here—to Scotland."

"How perfectly odd. And what did you say?"

"I said I was Portuguese—and that I was born here."

"Good for you. And then?"

I sat up. "And then Daniel told him to leave, but he wouldn't go. He said we would be burnt. He even held out a lighted candle to us."

She sprang up and clasped her cheeks, closing her eyes. "Goodness, oh, my goodness . . ."

"And, Mama, he put a tiny finch in his mouth. He was going to bite its head off."

Taking out her silk scarf, she reached out to the wall, then dabbed at her forehead. I rushed to her and led her back to my bed. After a time, she regained her composure and caressed my hair.

"Mama, we're not going to be burnt, are we?"

"No, of course not." She frowned and shook her head. "He was a silly man. He was trying to frighten you. Some men like scaring children. They are wobbly in the head." She took my hand. "So what's this about a bird in his mouth?"

"He must have bought it at the market. And he put it in his mouth when we weren't looking. He was going to bite its head off, but then he let it fly away."

"Yes, well, it just proves that such men will do anything to frighten a child. Please, John, think no more of this. Let me do the worrying for us both. And if you see him again, you must run directly home, just as your father has told you. Do not dawdle or linger—not for anything. Now come, get back under the covers."

"Are we Jewish?" I asked again.

She was fluffing my pillow. "I have answered that question already, John."

Her abrupt tone made me pout. Placing a kiss on my brow, she apologized.

"John, if you were Jewish, don't you think you'd know? Would it not be obvious that you were different from other people?"

"I looked all over myself, and Daniel did too, but we could not find any scars or anything."

"Scars? What manner of scars?"

"For my horns. And my tail."

She smacked the mattress. "Oh, please. Let's not be silly now. You cannot truly have thought..."

"But you know people think I'm strange—even Daniel thinks so."

"John, you are not in the least strange. You are the same as everyone else. Just as I am the same and your father too. Now, cease with such foolish talk." She kissed my palm, then made it into a fist. "Keep that with you always." She smiled gently. "You are the love of my life, John. You know that?"

After I nodded, she said, "Yes, it's true, you're not like every other child. But you do not have horns, and there will never come a day when I shall care a whit what anyone else thinks of you. Never!" She kissed my lips. "Now go to sleep. When your father returns from up-river, he will handle this Lourenço with the oily hair and canaries in his mouth."

These were the words I'd been waiting for; as I have said previously, I was of the firm opinion that my papa could resolve all problems.

LATER, NEARLY ASLEEP, I plainly heard Grandmother Rosa shout, "He said what to the child?!" I crept to the door to listen more closely, opening it a crack. "It's Napoleon," she continued in an enraged voice. "His victories are causing madness all over Europe. The Church isn't sure how to slither its way into his plans."

After that, I could hear only frantic whispering. Then Grandmother Rosa shrieked, "Jewish, Jewish, Jewish!"

At the time, I believed it the end to a long condemnation she must have made against this odd race.

THE NEXT AFTERNOON, on my mother's invitation, Daniel came to our home for the first time. He met me down the street, carrying a ragged flour sack with something rattling inside. When I asked him what it was, he gave me his wily smile and reached in, lifting out a likeness of the woodpecker that had died the day before. It was crudely carved and sanded only roughly, to be sure, and if asked I could have scripted a long list of its imperfections: wings too stubby, a beak too blunt . . . There was also a gouge on its tail that was clearly a slip, yet I thought it a wondrous thing.

Mother served Daniel and me tea and a custard sponge cake on her blue and white windmill-pattern porcelain from Porto's Massarelos Factory. Daniel had never drunk tea before, nor ever used a cup, by the looks of it. He gripped his in such a firm hand that I feared being hit by shrapnel. He bobbed his mouth into the steaming liquid only to wet his lips.

Mother lifted her cup with her little finger at an aristocratic angle. I was trying to spot in her eyes whether she had yet heard any rumors of kinship between Daniel and Senhora Beatriz, but she was giving nothing away. "I'm so glad you could join us today," Mama began. "John tells me you live in the Miragaia neighborhood—is that so?"

"Yes." Daniel snuck a look at me. He sensed subterfuge and looked eager to flee.

"Your father, I believe, is a fisherman."

"Yes."

"And your mother a seamstress, am I right?"

The lad nodded, then answered her subsequent queries in an equally voluble manner. Mama remained unperturbed. She enjoyed drinking tea with me on any occasion, so this was a treat for her, no matter how thin the conversation.

Every time she looked down or away, Daniel pulled his lips apart so that the tendons on his neck stood out. It made him look like a turtle.

As Mama handed me my cake, I decided to add some substance to our conversation. "Daniel has the best aim of anyone, Mama. You ought to have seen the villain after he got hit with his stone. The blood was running all the way down—"

Her hand went up. "Feel free to omit further details, John." She turned to Daniel. "I should like to tell you that what you did was very brave. I shall not forget it. And I want you to know this: If you are my son's true and loyal friend, you will always be welcome in this house. That I swear to you."

Mama's voice quavered. She took a long sip of tea to compose herself. "I'm sorry if I've embarrassed you," she said sweetly. "Let us eat our cake. I hope you both like it."

The lad held his fork in his fist while he sawed with his knife, concentrating fiercely. Mama gave a quick head shake when I looked at her, a signal for me to remain quiet about his difficulties. "And your grandparents, Daniel, are they living in Porto?" she asked.

The lad looked up and asked, "My grandparents?"

"Yes, do you see them often?"

"No, not often."

"Do they live near you?"

"No."

She let him return to his sawing. Her furtive glances at me indicated that she knew the truth. She'd either been told by Senhora Beatriz herself or had stitched rumors together into a recognizable pattern. I'd have wagered she was wondering if I knew.

Daniel, stymied by his fork and knife, used his hand to lift a gargantuan piece of cake to his mouth, dripping custard on the table. I was about to divert Mama's attention from him with a volley of questions about cake recipes, but she must have thought I was about to criticize him. She caught my attention by tapping the table, warning me with her stern eyes not to shame him. He remarked our coded glances, however, and grew self-conscious, biting his lip and placing his cake back on the plate. Then, for the first time in history, Mama picked up a piece of cake with her fingers and placed it in her mouth. To my utter astonishment, she proceeded to lick her fingertips.

"Yummm," she said. "My, that *is* good, isn't it, Daniel? You can have more when you finish that piece. So eat up."

He smiled, then pulled his turtle face, which made Mama laugh.

I suggested that the time had come for us to begin painting.

"Not in those clothes, you don't," Mama warned, wagging her finger. "You, my son, are to wear your old smock. And I will fetch something for Daniel from the Lookout Tower."

"The Lookout Tower? Are you sure you wish to venture up there?"

It was our storage room, up an ironwork spiral staircase from our second-story corridor. It boasted a huge octagonal skylight of red and yellow glass, through which there was a glorious view of the rooftops of Porto, but several panes leaked piteously. Recently, I'd discovered a dead lizard lying in a puddle.

Mama folded her arms over her chest and glared. "You know, John, you must think me made of lace. I'll have you know that when I was your age I was often just as filthy as you." At that, she stuck out her tongue at me and laughed.

I ought to have been pleased that she felt so at ease with us, but children tend to be shamed by singularity in their parents. When Daniel and I were alone, I apologized for her. He smacked me in the belly and said, "Your mother is the best, you idiot!"

VI

MAMA WATCHED US FOR A TIME FROM THE back door while we painted our carved birds on the patio. Blessedly ignorant of Daniel's plan, she was relieved that we were not up to mischief. Luckily, I knew nothing of his strategy myself or I'd have been tempted to own up to our proposed wickedness.

I had never previously believed that I could be capable of making something lovely with my hands, but after a few hours we had crafted startling likenesses of a falcon, two goldfinches, and a wren.

We applied ourselves happily to this work every afternoon until the evening of the Twenty-Second of June, the night before our secret dawn rendezvous at the Douro Inn with the bald birdseller, by which time we had twelve likenesses. Mother came into the garden to inspect our creations when they were nearly complete. She beamed with astonishment, her hands to her mouth, and made not a single mention of the streaks of paint covering our smocks and hands.

"You two are the cleverest lads I believe I shall ever encounter," she said proudly.

"Only one problem, Senhora Stewart," Daniel observed. "They have to be able to perch."

Mama suggested we hammer two short nails into each belly as feet, then tie a clasp fashioned out of wire to them. Upon receiving our approval, she rushed out to purchase these materials for us.

When we were finished, we tested a jay on her index finger. It gripped perfectly. We gave it to her as a gift, reducing our lot to eleven. She kissed me, then Daniel. From a moment's hesitation, I sensed the lad's soiled face and fingernails rankled her. That his presence might have reminded her of a sorrow in her past never entered my mind for a moment. In any event, it was too late for her to hold herself back, for she was most fond of him already.

THE NEXT MORNING, just after dawn, I slipped into my father's study, took out his inkstand and quill, and wrote a brief note informing my mother that I needed to leave early for my tarn and not to worry. Scripted as adultly as I then knew how, full of elegant curls and loops, I was hoping, of course, to be given credit at the very least for good penmanship. The things I did as a nine-year-old to test Mama's patience... Suffice to say that she could surely have had a winning argument for chaining me permanently to a metal standard in her bedroom, just as the witch had done to my father after he'd been turned into a toad.

I left the note on our tea table, then dashed outside to meet Daniel at the Douro Inn. Ten minutes after my arrival, I spied him trudging up the street, carrying our flour sack of painted birds on his back.

"Hey, there you are!" he hollered when he saw me.

Joy rose up in me, and though he motioned for me to stay put, I could not help myself from running to him. He smacked the top of my head playfully, and when I yelped, he did too.

The hot scent of onion was radiating from him; for breakfast, he sometimes ate one boiled and sliced onto a piece of stale bread. I insisted he eat an apple I'd pilfered from our fruit bowl, but he shook his head. "My stomach's all grumbly," he said, frowning.

Making a circle with his mouth, he blew onion breath in my face. While I held my nose, he began to explain his plan to me in a hushed voice. I immediately had grave doubts, since I believed my parents would be furious, but I didn't speak of them; I was unwilling to spoil things. Then, while I was on the lookout, the birdseller's covered wagon appeared. With a shout, he brought his horses to a halt by the inn, and he and his wife ventured inside.

"Now!" Daniel whispered to me.

We ran to the back of the wagon, where we untied the knots of the canvas flap and jumped inside. The cages were piled one on top of another. Feathers flew as the birds began flapping and chirping, rankled by the disturbance. I was frightened that the parakeets and other exotic species might die if we carried out our plan, but Daniel declared, "Better a death in the forest than jailed."

One by one we opened the doors to the cages and coaxed the birds free. A good many were reticent, and others were plainly fearful. It took much cajoling, but soon fifty-seven birds, by our count, had flown off to their new lives. Daniel's expression was one of fixed determination throughout. He worked with the swift, assured movements one might expect of a wood-carver. Only when all of the birds had been freed did he permit himself to smile and raise his fist in triumph. "Good work, John," he whispered.

Covered with feathers, feeling the golden weight of freedom in my hands, I smiled back. Yet a pulse of worry was throbbing at the back of my head. If we were caught, the birdseller would cane us to our knees, and my mother would never live down the shame. I could already hear the lecture my father would give me upon his return: *I thought that any son of mine would know better. . . .* I'd likely never be allowed a dog.

The astounding thing was that I truly did not care a damn. I didn't regret my rash behavior, even if it meant my demise.

Though the birds were now free, we did not rush away, for there was still the last part of our plan to bring to fruition. Daniel handed me five of our painted birds, keeping six for himself. We began placing them in the cages, twisting the wire feet of each wooden creature around its perch so that it posed in a lifelike position.

Most people would have considered it a waste of time to carve and paint our birds only to give them away, but gift-giving was Daniel's unspoken motivation; he wished not only to right a terrible wrong but also to create for the world something beautiful.

As he was fixing the last carving in place, we heard the birdseller and his wife coming.

"Hurry!" I said.

In his haste, Daniel dropped the woodpecker. It fell with a dull thud to the bottom of a wicker cage.

"*Merda!* Shit!"

"It will be a good selling day," the wife said. "No fog this morning."

By the time Daniel had a firm grip on the bird, they were stepping up to their seat in the front of the wagon. The birdseller shouted an obscenity at his horses and lashed them away. I fell back against the wooden frame of the wagon and grabbed hold of the canvas in order to steady myself. Daniel was making wild, incomprehensible hand gestures.

"What do we do now?" I mouthed.

"Depenados e prontos para a panela!" he mouthed back. We are plucked and ready for the pot!

Had I been thinking clearly, I could have simply jumped out of the wagon at that moment, for it had not yet reached full speed. As for Daniel, he was not about to end this adventure just yet; he thrived on danger, after all.

On we rattled, now at a full gallop. Daniel motioned for me to crawl as quietly as I could to the back of the wagon. I did as he commanded, and together we reached the edge. After a few moments, he lifted up the flap and peered out.

"What are you doing?" I whispered.

"We have to jump."

"Jump?"

The cobbles were flowing away from us like a cascading river of stone. I shook my head vehemently. There was a carriage about fifty feet behind us that would undoubtedly crush us under its wheels.

"Go!"

"No!"

Daniel grabbed my arm. "Now!"

We landed hard. I lurched to my left and tumbled over, skinning my knee badly and banging my shoulder. I regained my wits just in time to see the bald birdseller's wagon trundling down the street.

I heard a shout. A horse with a white patch over its nose was huffing at me, plainly just drawn to a halt. A driver in a red and blue uniform, gripping his reins with fists, was screaming. "You there, beanhead, what d'ya think you're doing? You could've been killed."

"I'm sorry," I squeaked, rushing to the side of the road.

Spinning around in search of Daniel, I found him sitting by a stone fountain on the other side of the road. Though he had twisted his ankle badly, he was grinning like a fool.

"That was insane," I said, brushing dirt and blood from my skinned knee.

Daniel spat in his hand and rubbed my wound. Wincing along with me in my pain, he said, "Does it hurt much?"

"No, not so badly."

"You're more hardy than you let on." He smiled, then he did something strange: He held my shoulders and kissed me on the cheek as though he had just received me as a present, almost as if I were his wee brother.

I could not speak after that.

DANIEL AND I limped on to the stalls of the bird market. The bird-seller, in a plumed green cap and festive waistcoat of rose-colored velvet, was standing by his wagon, outraged, surrounded by a growing crowd. His wife stood by in tears as he lifted one cage after another, offering proof of our robbery.

"What else can I believe?" asked his wife in a trembling voice to one of the women in the crowd. "All our beauties have been turned to wood."

"Woman, you're pissing mad," snapped her husband, banging a cage down. "They're carved and painted. Anyone with bloody eyes can see that!"

"This very jay," she replied, holding up the carving she gripped in her gnarled hand, "this jay turned to wood as I reached in for him. You explain that if you can!"

Daniel gave me a gleeful look; proof of supernatural intervention was far better than we could have hoped for.

"It is a miracle given to us by St. John himself," called out a slender lass in the crowd. "A miracle!"

Daniel stared at her in astonishment and took a step toward her, as though tugged by an invisible lead. But she crossed her arms over her chest defensively and raised her eyebrows, as though daring him to disagree with her, and he immediately retreated.

A tall man with a mangled ear then lifted up a cage with a wooden goldfinch perched inside, held it high over his head, and addressed the crowd. "The lass speaks the truth! St. John has changed feather to wood."

It was shameful to let this talk continue, but I didn't have the courage to confess our hoax.

The birdseller spit. "It's your head that's been changed to wood, my friend. Someone has hoodwinked me"—he raised both his hands like angry claws—"but I shall find out who and then I will strangle him. Those beauties were my silver and gold. I've lost everything!"

His wife licked her lips and spoke in a vengeful whisper. "You choose your words more carefully, you silly man! It's witchcraft." She turned in a slow circle, as though to catch sight of the perpetrator. "We must have a very powerful enemy somewhere, and you"—she turned back to her husband—"ought not to provoke her with your threats."

"Be still, woman! It is you who is doing the provoking." He raised his great callused hand as though to clout her. "Someone will pay for this, and if you wish it to be you, continue to defy me!"

Daniel ran forward. In my innocence, I believed he was about to confess after all. Instead, he shouted in his most proper voice, "Please, sir, show us the miracle—show us all the birds!"

"You . . . you only wish to see how I have been made the fool," said the birdseller, his dark eyes glinting with fury. "All of you are against me!"

"Show us what St. John has accomplished," Daniel begged. "Please, sir, don't let your pride deny us a look at a miracle."

Others in the crowd seconded this noble request until the birdseller, indignant, found himself trumped by Daniel's acting. Making the best of the situation, the poor man unloaded the rest of the cages containing our carvings from his wagon, slamming down each one of them onto the cobbles. A dwarf woman draped in a black shawl shouted to him, "You have been chosen by St. John himself."

The birdseller could contain his rage no longer and kicked one of the wire-mesh cages at her. It hit the ankle of a stout merchant in a high-collared blue dress coat, who threatened to clock the careless wretch with his cane for such an affront.

By now, a hundred onlookers were pointing, gawking, and even praying on their knees, moved by this union of heaven and earth, the possibility of witchcraft abandoned in favor of saintly intervention.

"John, come with me," Daniel said, tugging me away.

We crouched down behind a gig thirty paces from the chattering crowd. "Wait underneath," Daniel said.

"What for?"

"So you're hidden."

"But why do I want to be hidden?"

"There's no time, John," he snorted. "Just do as I say."

God forgive me, I squatted down under the gig. He raced away, only to return, moments later, out of breath.

"Do a *melro* thrush."

"What?"

"You heard me, keep hidden and imitate a thrush. The birdseller's wife just picked one up. Do it loud, but only once."

Half-wit that I was, I cleared my throat, curled my lips, and warbled.

"Louder!" Daniel urged.

Under his watchful eye, I succeeded better the second time.

I now spied the same skinny lass who'd first called our hoax a miracle. She squatted nearby and was staring at me intently.

"Again," Daniel said. "But do it louder this time."

The lass had such large and pretty eyes that they seemed to stop time. Looking at her, I recalled one of the wee wrens we'd freed. So terrified it had been of me that it flapped wildly around its cage. After I'd cloistered it in my hand, however, it calmed, seeming to understand my motives. For a long moment, we'd been alone in the world.

The girl grinned now, but she was not judging me badly. I smiled my thanks to her and executed my imitation once again.

"Now come out," Daniel said.

He reached down for me and we raced back to the crowd, where we found the birdseller's wife sprawled on the ground, a hand over her brow, having fainted. But her husband was having none of it. He stood over her, shaking his head with exasperation, while two women dressed in widow's black attended to her.

"What happened?" Daniel asked a soldier.

"The wooden bird sang," he replied reverently.

The lad laughed from his belly while I prayed for a second and very personal miracle: to be swallowed by the earth and tugged all the way to Spain.

Daniel led me away. When I hesitated to get under the gig again, he pushed me down and told me to pretend to be a lark; the tall man with the mangled ear was holding one in his hand.

The lass was still watching, and her jade-colored eyes seemed to be looking deep into my doubts. "We're being watched," I whispered to Daniel, pointing at her.

He waved her over. She came to us without hesitation, her hands behind her back.

"What's your name?" he said, glowering.

"Violeta." She breathed deeply and pulled her waist-length auburn hair around to cover her front. Licking her lips, she added, "I might ask your name, young man, but your rudeness makes you unworthy of my question."

"Violeta, go away!" he shouted, plainly of the belief that he could banish her with an order.

The lass gave him a challenging look. "I saw what you were doing." She crossed her hands over her chest and stood her ground.

Sensing that only I could make peace between them, I stepped forward. "What we did was wrong. I shall do no more imitations."

At that very moment, I found myself rising skyward, impelled by a force tightening around my neck.

"Got you!"

A rush of cold terror gripped me; I believed I was in the clutches of the necromancer. I fought and kicked for freedom, dangling a foot and a half above the ground.

"Let him go!" Daniel shouted.

The birdseller had both his meaty hands coiled around my neck. He was not squeezing hard enough to choke the life from me, but it was evident that he could twist my head off at any moment.

Disregarding Daniel, he shook me violently and said, "You're the little bastard who wanted the dead woodpecker! You two are the ones who've done all this."

"Let the lad go!" Violeta ordered.

I was struggling with all my might to pry the villain's hands loose from me. Daniel kicked him in his shin, but that accomplished nothing. The lass then did something clever: She spit into the villain's face. And she kept on spitting.

Dropping me to the ground, the birdseller kept a firm hold on my collar while he wiped his face with his sleeve.

Struggling for breath and coughing, I felt sick to my stomach.

"Help! Please help us!" Violeta wailed.

The stout merchant whose ankle was hit by the cage slashed his cane over the birdseller's shoulders.

"I've had quite enough of you," said the merchant. "Unhand the lad."

But the birdseller was not about to release me without more of a struggle. Hence, the merchant brought his cane down against his back again with a cruel *thwap* that promised broken bones.

The birdseller fell forward and avoided a kiss to the cobbles by thrusting out both his hands. I was free. And the first thing I did was stumble forward, bend over, and vomit.

"Return to your wagon and leave the lad be," the merchant advised the birdseller.

"But this little bastard was the one who imitated a thrush so we would think there'd been a miracle," he pleaded in reply. "I saw him myself. Very likely he's the one who stole all my beauties."

"Is this true?" the merchant asked me.

As the birdseller got to his feet, Violeta rushed to testify on my behalf. "Sir, I have been with him for an hour or more, and he uttered not a single call."

With those words, she earned my eternal allegiance.

"She is lying to protect me," I confessed, wiping my mouth with my sleeve. "I am guilty as charged." I took a mighty breath into my lungs and imitated a thrush.

"Extraordinary," the merchant said. "Sing it again, lad."

And so I did.

"More!" a woman exclaimed.

Over the next few minutes I created warbling and whirring renditions of goldfinches, jays, canaries, sparrow hawks, and gulls, culminating in an animated rendition of two kingfishers in friendly conversation.

"Astounding!" The merchant smiled.

At the risk of blowing my own trumpet, he did, in fact, seem to speak for everyone in the crowd. It occurs to me now that given more encouragement in this direction, I might have ended up as a performer at circuses or touring monster shows, the kind that feature bearded women and two-headed goats.

After I was finished, the birdseller said, "That is all very clever, son, but you have hoodwinked me out of my stock."

"Hold out your hand," the merchant commanded the birdseller.

But he feared a caning and would do no such thing.

"Please, I shall not hit you again, my good man. And I believe that these"—he reached into his waistcoat pocket to take out two large silver coins of one hundred *reis* apiece—"will compensate you for your loss. I ask only that you give me the wooden birds as a fair trade."

He tossed the shining disks of silver to the birdseller, who, with his newfound wealth firmly clenched in his fist, walked off to complete the transaction. The merchant then inhaled a pinch of snuff and suggested, between sneezes, that I imitate a nightingale. A greater crowd gathered as I displayed my talents—more than two hundred souls, according to the counting done by Violeta, who was to become our greatest friend. Today, when I picture her as she was that day, standing right up front, alternately biting her lip out of concern that I might fail and giggling in wonderment, I cannot help but laugh along with her. Daniel was standing next to her, of course, his raised fist punctuating the cadences of my calls, watching me with such wild and generous enjoyment that I felt in some way that my imitations were truly only for him and Violeta. As for the wooden birds, all but one were given to the merchant; the jay that the birdseller's wife claimed to have been transformed to wood in her hands she insisted on keeping, as proof of St. John's intervention in our earthly affairs.

It is to her more than anyone else that we owe the continuing belief that a miracle took place that particular morning, June Twenty-Third, 1800. Indeed, the entire affair was later recorded in the chronicles of Joaquim Rodrigues, a city alderman, under the title "The Transfiguration of the Birds of Porto." In this account, I am erroneously referred to as João Stewart Zarco, my two family names reversed. Daniel's name is not given, but he is nicely described as *a lithe older accomplice to young Zarco*. It is also noted that *a pious and pretty lass by the name of Violeta was the first to broach the subject of saintly dominion over the birds*.

Belief in the miracle persists in Porto to this day, and I have learned to keep my lips sealed when it occasionally comes up in conversation. That the destinies of Daniel, Violeta, and me were forever linked in the space of a single morn seems to me the true and far greater miracle.

IF SOMETHING OF symbolic and lasting value was accomplished that day, as I like occasionally to think, then my debt is to Daniel, of course. Even today, decades later, when I dream of him, he is often holding one of our painted birds in his hand, and I can tell from his gleeful eyes that he is plotting some new exploit that is sure to lead us toward both trouble and grace. Sometimes, too, I find the two of us sitting on the stoop of my home in Porto, side by side, and there is a warmth all around me, radiating from the street, the houses, the day itself. . . .

ONE PERSON WHO makes no appearance in Joaquim Rodrigues's retelling of the incident is Grandmother Rosa. Yet she, too, played her part, since I continued my avian theatrics until I spotted her waddling forward through the crowd, an expression of abject horror on her face.

When she stood in front of me, glaring like an incensed queen, it was only too clear that all was lost.

I took her hand and stepped like a miniature Moses through a parting sea of congratulations and pats on the head. A number of coins were offered to me, all of which my grandmother sternly obliged me to refuse.

On returning to my house, I discovered Mother beside herself with worry. "John!" she exclaimed, pulling me into her arms. "Thank God, you're safe."

Grandmother ordered me to go to my room, telling Mama, "Wait till I tell you what mischief he's been making while you've been sleeping."

Mama gripped my shoulders hard. "Nothing bad happened to you?" I shook my head. "Thank God for that. Don't ever do that to me again, John." She wiped her eyes. "I shall be up shortly to see you. Go and change those filthy clothes."

I climbed up the stairs while Grandmother Rosa recited a list of my indiscretions over the past months, ending with what she referred to as a "circus show for all the early-morning riffraff." I undressed and sat on my bed, then fell into a sound sleep.

I awakened to find Mama seated at the foot of my bed. She greeted me with a wistful smile. She'd been crying again. "John, I've been thinking of what I ought to say to you."

I sat up and started to make excuses, but she hushed me with a hand laid gently to my chest. "Just hear me out. I want you to know that you had me frantic with worry. John, you are a bit like fireworks—volatile and bright and scattered. I cannot control you. Not even Papa can. I know that. So we must strike a bargain. Otherwise, I shall die of agitation. You must never leave the house before either your father or I have given you permission—not until you are much older. The streets are not as friendly as you think. You are never to leave the house without me knowing where you are—*never!*"

"But I was going to—"

"No *but*'s, John. We must strike this bargain or I shall have to tie you down at night, just as Grandmother would like. Have we a deal?"

I nodded.

"John, this is serious. You promise me."

"I promise."

Mama took a deep breath and walked over to my window.

"Did you quarrel with Grandmother?" I asked.

"Indeed."

Mama then told me of her mother's diatribe and how she'd ended by saying, "I've no idea how my grandson came to be giving such a shameful concert in the street—indeed, I do not wish to know. I only expect that it will never be repeated."

To which Mama had offered a surprising reply: "On the contrary, my John will make use of all of his gifts and explore them to their limits."

Her voice was taut with determination when she repeated this to me. Apparently, she and her mother had then fought as only a parent and child can. But the outcome was favorable—Grandmother Rosa had fled. In fact, she was punishing us by refusing to join us for supper!

After our special St. John's supper of grilled sardines, boiled potatoes, and roasted peppers, Mama listened patiently to all my excuses for having perpetrated what could only be rightly described as a theft. "Involving yourself in such a ludicrous escapade was foolish. And stealing another man's property . . ." she remarked.

"But birds are living things. They were in cages. They were suffering."

"I am aware of that, which is why I shall not punish you. What I don't understand, John, is why you and Daniel painted the birds with such care, all the while knowing that you would give them away."

"Daniel has odd ideas sometimes. I suppose he hoped that the birdsellers might see in our wooden substitutes the evil in their trade."

Mama smiled at me then, the way she had when she'd come to my tarn for the first time, greatly moved by my permitting her an intimate knowledge of my world. Taking my hand, she touched my fingertips to her lips. "You know, John, I think Daniel wished to show the birdsellers how their cages rob dignity from everyone concerned—not simply from the birds."

"That's it—that's it exactly, Mama!" I cried.

But a moment later I understood the depth of my failure. For the bird market would be up and flourishing next Tuesday as though nothing had happened.

"What's wrong, son?" she asked.

When I explained, she said, "Nothing so evil can be brought to so swift an end. But you will have your victories." She wagged her finger. "And without robbery, John—with words."

"With what words?"

"You will convince them of their moral duty to free the birds—and not only that, but other things besides."

"How do you know that, Mama?"

She squeezed my hand. "I know you. And I know what you can accomplish when you set your mind to it."

AFTER OUR DESSERT, Mama and I strolled through the city till after midnight. The evening was cool, and she draped her shawl over my shoulders. Several times strangers pointed to me and whispered, "There he is, there's the child who is part bird...."

Pride shone in Mama's eyes when she looked at me.

An elderly man with a crooked hand even patted my head and whispered to his wife, "They say this lad created a miracle today."

At that, Mama led me away and fell into a brooding silence. When we reached home that night, she knelt beside me outside our front door and whispered, "You must never make a show of yourself. It is dangerous. You must be careful to whom you show your gifts." She gripped me hard. "Remember to keep something for yourself. You have no need to always be so trusting. When in doubt, wait."

Without giving me the chance to respond, she told me not to worry myself with her foolish chatter; she was simply missing my father. "I must be mad to talk to you like this," she said, laughing. Turning the key in the lock, she sighed happily at finding our house just as we had left it.

Upstairs, Mama sat on my bed, and I laid my head in her lap. She combed my hair with her soft fingers and sang me "Barbara Allen": *In Scarlet town, where I was born . . .*

At the tolling of one o'clock, she tucked me under the covers. I fell asleep with her playing me into the arms of Mozart on her pianoforte. Indeed, she must have played for many hours, for when I woke after dawn, I found her with her head resting on the piano lid, still in her clothes from the night before. A folded piece of paper had fallen on the floor. I picked it up and found two lines from Robert Burns's "The Farewell" in my father's handwriting:

With melting heart, and brimful eye,
I'll mind you still, tho' far away.

VII

MY YOUTHFUL AFFECTION FOR THE UNITED States was provided by Violeta, whose late clockmaker father had been born to Portuguese parents in Boston. She was the third-born of five children and the only daughter in the family. Now thirteen, she was the first in her family to wake and often the last to find sleep. She ate quicker than anyone I'd ever met, ran faster than all her brothers, and talked in rapid bursts. Her mother said that simply listening to her was enough to make her lose her wits.

Losing her father three years earlier had faded her already fragile appetite, paled her olive skin, and left her helpless to cope with persistent nightmares of falling into fire. It was feared that she would burn herself out like a candle and never see the sunrise of her twentieth year.

The goal on which she centered her hopes was to reach America. Her father had told her that the night sky there was a radiant blanket of stars spreading out across a darkness so black that it hurt the eyes and frightened the mind. Violeta loved the stars and the darkness.

It was Daniel who first embarked upon friendship with her. In fact, as I was being hustled away by my grandmother, he convinced the lass to allow him to accompany her to her cousin's house on Rua do Almada, where she was to get some onions. Daniel told me that she squatted down and dug in the garden soil, unconcerned for the fate of her pretty shoes. Her lack of airs impressed him, and he found himself wholly charmed. As for her jade eyes, though he was unable to put his feelings into words and I am translating for him, their depth provoked in him speculations into who she was and who *he* might be now that they had met.

So enchanted was Daniel by the sight of Violeta digging in the dirt that he grew restless with pent-up energy. When he began jumping around, she turned to ask what silliness he was up to. "Shooing away flies," he replied solemnly.

"Are you saying, young man, that flies are attracted to me?"

"No, no—they were attracted to . . . to . . . to . . ." he stammered.

He never added the word *me* to his sentence because Violeta touched her fingertip to his lips to silence him.

WHILE DANIEL WAS courting Violeta, Father returned from upriver. On his first afternoon at home, while I sat shivering with fear at the top of the stairs, Mother explained my activities at the bird market to him, softening the more morally dubious aspects of my conduct. Instead of *stealing* the birds, I had *allowed them to choose a home for themselves.* I cheered her ingenuity, though I knew Papa would see things differently.

To my astonishment, however, she concentrated her account of the past fortnight on the appearance of the necromancer. She became so emotional that Father begged her to sit and sip slowly at a glass of brandy. I was surprised by the fuss, because Mama and I had both heard that the villain had left Porto for Lisbon. I had all but forgotten his threats against me and my family.

Later that day, Papa gave me only a mild reprimand. He hoped that I had learned my lesson, which I dutifully said I had, though I secretly knew I would do it all over again if given half the chance.

THAT EVENING, AFTER a visit from Luna and Graça Olive Tree, my parents—to my great delight—granted permission for me to take art lessons from them on Friday afternoons. On my request, Daniel was welcomed as well.

After one of our first lessons, Father accompanied Daniel and me to the lad's home, where he poked his nose into every corner. The next day, a sturdy washerwomen arrived to scrub it free of mildew and filth. While she was working away, two painters came and gave all the walls, inside and out, a fresh coat of whitewash. A splendid mattress was delivered for Daniel's bed that evening, and Mother bought him a new shirt and a pair of breeches.

My friend went pale with embarrassment on entering our home in his new clothes. Papa tousled his black hair, which was lice-free and growing back nicely, and hugged him to his chest. He bid me with his glance to say nothing about the lad's sniffles of gratitude.

I CAN VOUCHSAFE that Daniel and Violeta fell in love that summer of 1800, not that this pleased me at the time—quite the contrary. I was jealous of the silly faces they made at each other when they believed no one was looking. I hated their easy complicity, their kinship of secret purpose that excluded me. After all, I had only just met Daniel myself. And I already wished to be Violeta's knightly protector, since I thought she was the most beautiful lass I had ever seen. Before resigning myself to my secondary role, I occasionally spoke cruelly to her and made her cry. She seemed unaware of how awed I was by her, how unsettled by her very presence.

At the end of July, a month after we had begun to meet every few days for our adventures, she came to my window one morning long before dawn and stood on the street tossing pebbles up at it. Bleary-eyed, I opened my mosquito screens and shutters. "Come down here, John," she called plaintively.

In the years since, I have often laughed at my ludicrous nine-year-old Romeo to her Juliet on the street below. I cannot deny, however, that having her come to see me pleased me enormously. I wondered if Daniel knew where she was or if he would regard our tryst as a betrayal. A small evil part of me hoped he would.

"Please, John, come with me," Violeta said softly when I opened the front door. "Let's go away from the houses, so we can talk."

It is amusing, I know, but I truly believed that she would seek to beg my forgiveness for coming between me and Daniel. I even thought she might confess that she suffered his companionship only for the opportunity to be near me.

We soon reached the end of the street and stood at the top of the

Synagogue Stairs, which wind down toward the riverside district. "Look up," she said.

A scarf of lights unfurled across the heavens, high above the cathedral perched on a hill to the east.

"It's the Milky Way," she explained. "Thousands of stars huddling together. And look there," she added, pointing toward a bright one. "That's the North Star. It's the center of the sky."

She told me how this celestial body is so perfectly nestled in the heavens that it remains in the same spot as the earth turns on its axis. Then she explained to me something of the constellations and planets. Stars, I discovered, were serious business to Violeta. She didn't mention Daniel until we walked back to my house. "I want to tell you a secret," she said. "But you must not reveal it to anyone—even Daniel."

As I swore to keep silent forever, I felt as though we were about to cross a bridge together. I knew I would do anything for her.

"I want to follow the stars to America," she declared. "I shall live in the land of George Washington and Thomas Jefferson."

"But why is it that Daniel cannot know that?"

"Because I shall really go. And no one, not even he, will stop me."

"We would be heartbroken if you were to leave without us, you know."

She stared into the sky and took a long breath. We sat together on the stoop of my house and she asked me to scratch her head. I hesitated, suspecting that Daniel would clout me if I agreed.

The softness of her hair in my hands made me tremble. We said nothing to each other for a long while and instead let the night noises speak to us of our newfound intimacy. Then she kissed my cheek. "For being my friend," she said.

"When you go to America, I shall come too," I promised. And though I wholeheartedly meant it at the time, I was to forget my pledge in the years to come. Like most children, I lived with both feet firmly planted in the present tense and tended to let even the most important conversations fade into the past. Perhaps that was a blessing.

ON THE FIRST Saturday in October, Daniel disappeared. Violeta and I grew frantic because he had never been late for one of our weekend walks to the tarn before. We ran to his home, but found it empty and so decided to wait at my house.

After about half an hour, Daniel knocked at our door, out of breath. "Where have you been?" Mama exclaimed. "We've been worried." "With Senhora Beatriz."

The lad was bouncing with joy, so electric that he could not stand being touched. We tried in vain to sit him down and have him explain calmly what had transpired. Apparently, Senhora Beatriz had come to his house the day before and told him that there was a bedroom waiting for him at her house.

He beamed with joy as he told us that his new bed had been made with clean sheets. "Smooth as moss," he declared while performing a jig of delight all around the kitchen.

"Oh, Daniel, I am so pleased for you," Mama said. "I am sure you will both be very happy."

I remember thinking, *Let's not rush into things.* . . . For I could easily imagine his wildness causing havoc in his new home.

That evening, my mother confided in me that she had helped wear down Senhora Beatriz's resistance, and though I should like to say that she was proved immediately right, and that Daniel's new household became a refuge of calm and contentment, the truth is that he found living under his grandmother's roof rather too confining. He passed their first couple of months together inventing ever new ways to provoke her. I particularly recall him once setting alight a pushcart of dried flowers in New Square.

Then one day in December, about two and a half months after moving in with her, having come home filthy from an adventure with me down by the river, he tracked dirt all over the house. On purpose, I am quite sure. Senhora Beatriz was equally certain of this, and she raised her hand to strike him for the very first time. But she found herself unable to do so. She collapsed onto her bed and sobbed instead.

Daniel had never seen a woman cry as though her lifeblood were flowing out of her. He vowed aloud to be kind to her, caressing her hair as she wept. And to his credit, he kept his word. He still had his mad adventures, of course, but never again did he do anything on purpose to embarrass or hurt her.

Indeed, he only made her cry once again. And then it was beyond his powers to avoid.

VIII

FANNY, MY BORDER COLLIE, ARRIVED ONE DAY in December of 1800 on a ship from Glasgow. I soon discovered that she was a kind and noble beast, except when engaged in the serious matter of eating. If disturbed from her bowl, Fanny barked. If further pestered, she would curl back her lip and bare her lethal incisors with a low growl. Upon a third inconvenience, she bit.

By the end of April of 1801, Fanny, Daniel, Violeta, and I were the best of friends. The dog was especially fond of Violeta and would, I think, have had a difficult time choosing whom to cast her lot with, me or her, if ever such an unhappy decision were necessary.

On our outings to the tarn, Violeta hardly ever walked with Daniel and me anymore, instead joining us there at midday, since her mother had an unparalleled knack for inventing endless morning errands. The lass always completed her tasks as quickly as possible and never once failed to join us, until the second Saturday of June, 1801, when we had been friends for nearly a year. By three in the afternoon, she still had not arrived. Daniel and I began our walk home in a dejected mood, pounding the pathway in worried silence. When we were about a third of the way to the city, at the edge of a thick woods, Fanny lifted up her ears and came to a halt, sniffing at the air, her black nostrils flaring. Creeping off into a scruffy copse of trees, she went nosing along through ferns and weeds.

"Good girl," I called as I followed her. "Keep going."

On reaching her, I spied an elderly hunter about fifty yards away. "Sorry to disturb you, sir," I said as we approached him. "But we are looking for a friend—a young lass."

"I've seen no one."

Fanny sniffed happily at the man's shoes. He petted her head, then pointed his weapon toward a clearing far in the distance. "It may be of no help, but I did see a slipper over that way. By a large pine, just past an old stone wall."

We thanked him and raced off. Sure enough, we found one of Violeta's ribboned shoes by some rocks fallen from an ancient enclosure.

"Might he have hurt her?" I asked.

Daniel bit his lip and would not answer.

Near the road, I found Violeta's beige linen dress lying crumpled on the ground, mottled with sunlight filtering through the canopy of a tall tree. A chill descended over me, like a great shadow. *No,* I whispered to myself. *Please, no . . .*

Fanny ran off and began whining at the base of a gentle slope. We found the girl there, lost to consciousness, lying on her side, her legs hidden by ferns. She was wearing only her petticoat, which was ripped at the side seam. Her beautiful hair was a tangled mess. Soil and leaves were smeared on her brow, cheeks, elbows, and legs, and blood covered her mouth.

I was trembling. I believed her death would kill me too. Tears flooded my eyes as I fell to my knees. "Violeta, please get up, you're scaring me."

Kneeling beside her, Daniel lifted her head carefully and called her name, but she would not wake up. Tears were streaming down his cheeks. "What do we do, John? What do we do?" he cried.

Perhaps it was Daniel's pleading, or even Fanny's mad huffing at her face, but the lass started to awaken. Daniel leaned over her with an expression of gratitude so full and deep that I would remember it all my life. The gentleness of his smile in that moment—intended to show Violeta that all would be well because they were together—has always symbolized to me the great truth of love. Caressing the nape of her neck, he said, "Violeta, what happened—what's happened to you?"

She made no reply. "Don't go back to sleep—please say something, we're worried," I said.

But she would not—or could not—speak.

I retrieved Violeta's dress and covered her. So fragile and lovely was she to me in that moment that I made a solemn pact with myself: If she recovered, I would never again protest my secondary role in their lives.

She opened her hand to me now. In it she held a bloody molar.

I accepted her offering.

"What happened?" Daniel asked.

She rubbed her hand over her cheek and winced.

"We've got to get a physician," Daniel observed in a rush, as though our need for assistance had only now occurred to him. "Violeta, you'll have to see someone."

"I'll run to Porto," I said.

"No, be still," the girl begged.

She turned and hugged her arms around Fanny, seeming to sleep the slumber of fever for a time. Then, without warning, she breathed in sharply and held out her hand. "John, give me my tooth back."

When I handed it to her, she gripped it in her fist.

"Who did this?" Daniel demanded, his face tight with anger. "Was it a hunter with a tattered jacket? We saw him. We know. And we know what he did."

"No, two young bandits came after me to rob my jewelry," she answered matter-of-factly. "I started running and fell. That's all that happened."

"Bandits who wouldn't take your bracelet or rings are either blind or dimwitted," I stated for the record.

"Nevertheless, John, that is exactly what took place," she answered, plainly irritated.

"We don't believe you!" Daniel shouted. "Violeta, who . . . who violated you?"

Frowning, she shook the tooth in the hollow of her hand to hear it rattle against her rings. Opening her palm, she mumbled a prayer and then threw it away.

"Hey!" Daniel hollered. "What did you do that for?"

"Let the mice have it. They cannot practice witchcraft on me." She shivered. "Now, step away. I want to put on my dress."

"Come, Fanny," I said to the dog, who looked up doubtfully at me.

"No, leave her with me," Violeta pleaded.

Daniel and I skulked off. The lad was kicking the ground and mumbling curses to himself. "I'll kill whoever did this to her!"

"Did they . . . did they truly violate her?" I whispered.

He sneered at me, plainly considering my question an affront to his intelligence. "We did nothing to prevent it. Nothing!"

His pain and rage made me feel immensely useless, and I could not fathom how he could have known for certain what had come to pass. Likely he had discovered a telltale sign in her eyes that I had not detected. Or a mark of hidden significance on her body. I knew not what to look for, since I had no clear idea of what it meant to be violated. All I knew was that it was something abominable that happened to women and girls and an evil that could be broached in conversation only at the level of a shameful whisper.

After she had dressed, Violeta allowed us to approach her once again. Avoiding Daniel's eyes, she begged me to sneak her back into my house, for she could not be seen by her mother in such a state. There would be far too many questions asked.

"Look at me—I'm standing here too!" Daniel snarled, shaking a fist at her.

The lass gazed at the ground, her brow furrowed with worry.

With a renewed gentleness, he asked quietly, "Do you hate me now?"

Tears glazed her eyes as she forced herself to witness the hurt in his face. "No, Daniel, but I'm frightened. I cannot bear both your emotions and my own. I am not so strong. Not now. Have no expectations of me."

She would explain no further, and Daniel stopped questioning her after she allowed him to take her hand, which he brought to his lips only to have her snatch it away. We walked one on each side of her all the way home. I had taken a linen cape along with me and we covered her with it so no one along the city streets would notice her disheveled state.

I entered my house alone at first. Thankfully, Mama and Papa were out. Behind the closed door of my room, the lass cleaned herself with my towel and brushed her hair. Her face went pale when she saw her reflection in my looking glass. In the cold dark depths of Daniel's watchful gaze I sensed him plotting vengeance.

"Now I must go," she said.

Daniel begged to be permitted to accompany her, but she refused, although she did wish to keep Fanny for a few days.

Outside, I squatted to Fanny's level. Kissing her on her snout, I told her that Violeta needed only gentleness from those around her. There was to be no snarling, lunatic pawing, mad licking, or suicidal crashing into furniture. I felt compelled to say these things not so much for the dog but to communicate my love for Violeta. She showed no particular interest in my concern for her, however. Calling Fanny to her side, she rushed away down the street as though fleeing a storm. Next to me, Daniel tossed a large stone in the air and caught it in his fist.

VIOLETA'S MOTHER REFUSED to open her door to Daniel and me over the next several days. I only saw our friend again five days later, when she returned Fanny. Mama was busy cutting bread, so it was I who opened our door to her knocks. Fanny immediately leapt into my arms, her tail wagging furiously. Violeta stood frozen in our doorway. I gasped when I finally looked at her, because her auburn tresses had been cut in a scraggly line just above her shoulders.

"But, Violeta, what have they done to—"

She turned her back on me in mid-sentence and rushed away.

I saw nothing more of her until over a week later, when I woke in the middle of the night to the sound of her pebbles against my window. There was a moon out, and I could see she wore a frilly bonnet, which was alarming because she had always refused to hide her hair.

Sneaking out of the house, I ran to her.

"I'm sorry to wake you," she said, sobbing. "So sorry for everything. I have been very wicked. Forgive me, John."

"For what? I don't understand. Violeta, what has happened?"

She removed her bonnet. Someone must have again taken a rough shears to her, as her hair was now clipped just below her ears into a ragged mess. Nicks and scratches covered her neck.

"Violeta, who is cutting your hair?"

She shook her head and walked away without answering. I let her go thirty or so paces, then started to race after her, calling her name. When she started running, she proved herself too swift for me, but she stumbled near the jailhouse at the end of the street. When I caught hold of her, she shrieked and threw out a hand, catching me a fierce blow on the mouth and drawing blood.

We were both so stunned that we simply stared at each other. Tasting salt in my mouth, I spit on the ground. She embraced me as she apologized, and I could feel the fragility of her thin bones. We sat down in the street together, not caring about the filth. "He used to come to me sometimes," she told me, "and . . . and touch me—just touch me. But he did more to me that day in the woods. He'd followed me. He was drunk. And since then . . . He said if I told anyone he would kill me. I promised that I would not speak of it. But I did. I was wicked."

"Who was it—who hurt you?"

"I cannot say."

"Violeta, you must come with me to my parents. You must tell them."

"No."

I stood up and tried in vain to pull her to her feet.

"Do you not trust me?" I asked.

"Oh, John, I cannot trust anyone."

"You are lying. You *do* trust me or you would not have come to me."

"You don't understand. You're too young. Life . . . my life has become a locked room. I only wanted you to listen to me." She sprang to her feet. "I'm sorry to have hurt you," she said. She began to walk away, her head down.

"There must be a way out," I called after her.

Though she made no reply, I believed those words of mine; I had yet to learn that we do not always receive keys to the rooms we inherit.

WHILE SEARCHING FOR sleep that night, I foolishly decided to take matters into my own hands.

The following Friday afternoon, after lessons with the Olive Tree Sisters, I went to Violeta's home and called up to her window. Finally, to get rid of me, she agreed to meet me at the tarn the next day. I informed her that Daniel would not be able to join us. She was glad of that, she said, as she could not face him now that she was so ugly. She made me promise not to tell him anything of what she'd confided in me during our nighttime conversation. "It would only lead to trouble," she said. "For him, for me, for everyone."

To ensure his absence, I walked to Senhora Beatriz's house and told him that neither Violeta nor I would be able to go to the tarn the next day. I had decided, you see, to follow her alone and in secret. My expectation was that whoever had hurt her would try again. My very presence—and my eagerness to reveal his identity to the entire world—would be enough to frighten off the evil man for good.

Yes, I was indeed that reckless with her well-being.

As to why Violeta had agreed to join me, she undoubtedly wished our lives could go back to the way they'd been before. As I have had ample opportunity to learn in my life, a desire to return to a happier past can give us blind courage.

VIOLETA LIVED ON the Rua das Ventainhas, a bumpy road on the far eastern edge of the city that sloped down toward the river. The next morning, Fanny and I hid behind the stone wall of a nearby barn. At just past the stroke of ten, she stepped out her door and rushed off along a route I had not anticipated. She was behaving with foresight, hoping to elude any pursuer through this change to her usual route.

Fanny and I followed her from two hundred paces behind. I was quite sure that no one else was. But what neither of us had anticipated was that her enemy had left the city before her. There was but one possible route over the last mile to our destination, and it was there that he was waiting for us.

IX

A RAMSHACKLE OLD MILL, OVERGROWN WITH blackberry vines, used to stand alongside the country lane we walked on Saturdays. When this landmark came into sight, a man in a long dark coat emerged and stood in the road for a moment, then crossed to the other side and disappeared into a pine grove.

I recognized him as her uncle, Tomás Gonçalves. He was bald and barrel-chested, and he walked with a stoop, as though an invisible weight were tied around his neck.

It will sound preposterous now, but I believed then that we shared the intention of watching over Violeta from afar. I was infinitely gratified that an adult, and a large and powerful one at that, had had the exact same idea as me.

Violeta, hidden from me around a curve in the road, was now approaching the place where she had been attacked two weeks earlier. I rushed on, and when I saw her next, she was walking as though on tiptoe into a thicket of gorse. She must have heard a noise, for she knelt by a bush to conceal herself.

Then she jumped up and ran ahead. Tomás Gonçalves charged at her from the side, grabbing her arms just below her shoulders and shaking her violently.

When she shrieked, Fanny raced off, barking. I followed, screaming Violeta's name.

By now the villain had ripped her bonnet off and gripped what was left of her hair, tugging her head back with such force that I feared her neck might break. To silence her, for she was now screaming Daniel's name, he raised his other hand and struck her across the face.

On seeing Fanny heading straight for him, he threw Violeta to the ground. When the dog reached them, she stood behind the lass, about ten feet from Tomás, making a furious racket. Violeta, her mouth bleeding, had managed to sit up. We looked at each other, stunned. Everything had gone wrong and we both knew it.

"Run, John! Run!" she screamed suddenly, realizing that her uncle was about to try to throttle me, despite the threat of my border collie's fangs.

The last thing I remember was him charging toward me and wrapping a handkerchief around his fist. And a very loud noise.

I WOKE TO my mother's moist eyes. I had no idea where I was. My head was throbbing and my mouth was dry, as though I had swallowed sand.

"Water," I croaked. Mama lifted a cup to my lips.

I am told that I fell back to sleep immediately, my last sip dribbling down my cheek to my pillow. When I woke again, I recalled having been in the forest, but the reason escaped me. Mama, who kept vigil in my room, explained that Violeta's uncle had walloped me on the back of my head. I had fallen and lost consciousness. All this had happened the day before. My previous awakening had been twelve hours earlier.

She had little faith in men of medicine, but Mama had allowed Dr. Silva to bleed me twice at my temples with leeches to prevent the accumulation of toxic fluids on my brain.

"And Violeta?" I asked.

"She's safe, John. Do not worry."

Mama took my hand. She held it to her lips and kissed it, then folded it into a fist and gave it back to me, saying, "Keep that with you always."

Father stepped into the room and smiled down at me. "How is my wee man?"

"My head feels all broken."

He sat down on my bed, leaned over, and kissed me on the lips. Then he took an amethyst stone he had brought back for me from upriver the week before and placed it on my chest.

"You are a brave tyke. A *kelpie* of merit. But you disobeyed me again. You were to come and fetch me if you encountered trouble."

"Violeta made me promise not to tell anyone," I explained.

He touched his fingers to my lips to quiet me and said, "I am not cross with you, but this might have ended tragically for all concerned. We have been very lucky."

"What happened to her uncle?"

Papa said that the loud noise I had heard was a gunshot. The same hunter Daniel and I spoke to on the day Violeta was first attacked had heard Fanny's barks and come running. When Tomás grabbed me and hit me, the hunter fired a shot above our heads. Then, while Tomás looked around to find the source of the gunfire, Fanny leapt at him. Her teeth ripped clean through his breeches and tore a chunk of flesh from his thigh.

The hunter was still a long way off. He fired another shot aimed to do permanent damage this time, which came within inches of Tomás's head. In fear for his life, he cursed Violeta and lumbered off.

"The hunter carried you home," Papa told me. "We are greatly indebted to him."

He added that if it had not been for the good stranger, I might have been awaiting burial at this moment. I could not comprehend that. I tried to imagine being dead. I stopped breathing and made my face go blank.

"What are you doing, John?" Papa asked.

"Just thinking about things. Where's Violeta now?"

"She is with her mother, resting."

"And does Daniel know what happened?"

"Indeed he does. I went to his house to tell him."

"And where is Tomás Gonçalves?"

"He is no longer a problem," Papa replied, and would say no more.

VIOLETA VISITED ME the next afternoon, her wan face framed by a hideous black bonnet, which she refused to remove despite my entreaties. Mama gasped on seeing her, then fell into a disquieting silence, clearly afraid of all that might spill from her if she were to begin to express her feelings. She served us tea and sat with us, gripping Violeta's hand. After a time, Mama got up, kissed the lass on the cheek, and left us to ourselves. When I asked Violeta what punishment had been given her uncle Tomás, she informed me that she did not know. He had vanished from their home. Her mother refused to talk of him.

Daniel must have been hiding on our street, waiting for Violeta to visit, for he knocked on our front door a few minutes later and was led to my room by Mama. It was the first time he had seen the lass since the day of her attack. His eyes were red with sleeplessness, his voice brittle. Lacking a vocabulary equal to his emotions, he grew impatient with himself and short-tempered with Violeta. Too troubled and fragile to understand that his harshness was only the result of frustration, she in turn withdrew into her own sadness. Mama joined us after a while, and her presence prevented them from attempting to voice their feelings.

While serving Violeta tea, Mama asked if she might try to cut her hair in a pleasing shape. "I have been my husband's barber since our wedding," she said, smiling.

Violeta unfastened her bonnet. Her hair had been shorn down to her scalp, which was covered with scabs, making her eyes appear to bulge. "Not even the most skillful barber would be of help to me now," she said sorrowfully.

I was so overwhelmed that I could not speak, and I looked at Mama to make things right. She had set her teacup on our table and reached a trembling hand to her chest. Fighting for breath, she said, "I shall still be able to help you, dear child."

Daniel, unable to restrain himself, demanded to know who had done this to her. In a clipped monotone, the lass explained that her mother refused to believe that her uncle had attacked her. She had ordered her eldest sons to bind Violeta's arms behind her back and hold her down on her bed while she herself did the cutting.

"I kicked and fought, but it was of no use. It never is." Gazing down, she whispered that if her mother caught her in one additional "lie," then her head would be shaved every week and she would be denied a bonnet. Everyone in Porto would see that she was an incurable liar. "My mother said next time she would cut off something that would never grow back."

"I'd like to kill your mother!" Daniel shouted.

"What would she cut off?" I asked.

"Hush, John!" Mama snapped. "Not another word from you." There was fire in her eyes. "Listen to me, Violeta, you must never think for one moment they are right. You must remember that you are innocent." She crouched by the lass and kissed her brow. "And you are still beautiful. They can never take that from you. Never!"

"I am coming home with you today," Daniel declared. "And I shall sleep at the foot of your bed."

"We shall leave for America as soon as we can!" I exclaimed.

"Hush, both of you!" Mama ordered. "If your mother is not of a mind to believe you, Violeta, then how, in God's name, does she think you were hurt on these two occasions?"

"She says I am always falling because I'm so clumsy—that my evil disposition has left me unbalanced. And that my uncle would marry me were I not so awkward."

"You would marry a villain who has . . . who has done these things to you?" Daniel snarled. He took a step toward her and shook his fist. "Listen to me, you will marry no one!"

"There is a great deal you do not understand," said Violeta imploringly.

"Dearest child . . ." said Mama, caressing her cheek.

Violeta stilled her hand. "I must go. I've already stayed too long." She stood up.

"You cannot go!" I shouted. "I shall not let you go back to your home. Mama, tell her she can stay here with us. Tell her! Tell her now."

My mother did her best to calm me, saying that she would discuss these matters with Papa that very night, but it was all too much for me. I shouted like a banshee and cursed her as she led my friends away. Then I stumbled to the window and threw my shutters open, mortified by my powerlessness. I called after Violeta and Daniel, but that only made her race off, leaving the lad far behind.

LATER THAT DAY my father told me what he had done to Violeta's uncle Tomás. Two evenings previous, after I had been carried home by the good hunter, he commissioned two petty criminals to destroy each and every clock in Tomás's shop. The next night, Papa hunted him down to the Willow Tavern, a foul establishment behind the San Francisco Church. He discovered the villain seated at a table fashioned from a barrel, trying to drink away his ruin with a half-empty bottle of gin and gabbling with two cronies guffawing like mules.

Father marched up to the group and introduced himself as a Mr. Burns. "Sir, I have learned of your misfortune and I should like to interest you in a proposition," he said.

He explained to the men that he had acquired a watchmaking shop in Lisbon and was hoping to find a man of proper training to take charge. He suggested that a stroll outside might allow Gonçalves and himself to carry on their conversation in a more private manner. As there was no point in letting a bottle of gin go half empty, he purchased it for them.

Violeta's uncle limped along the streets, owing to the hunk of flesh that Fanny had happily ripped from his thigh. Papa strolled arm in arm with him, encouraging him to keep his lips moistened with drink. With the gin thus emptied, he steered the man off into a darkened alley, where he brought the glass bottle down squarely onto his head.

Gonçalves collapsed to the cobbles but did not lose consciousness. He moaned piteously, "Everything is gone, all gone," and began to weep.

Papa now informed the man of his true identity, explaining that he had had his shop smashed to pieces for hurting me and Violeta. "And I will have you reduced to kindling as well, unless you leave for Lisbon now and never return. That is your only choice!"

Gonçalves was nursing his bleeding head in his hands and struggling to stand back up.

Papa squatted next to the limp wretch and held the glass spikes of the broken bottle to his face. "I shall put you on the next coach to Lisbon and even pay your way. But should you ever return to Porto, I shall take a bottle just like this one and twist it round your nose until you have neither nostrils nor mouth nor eyes."

At precisely twenty-one minutes past seven by my father's watch, Tomás Gonçalves was gone forever from our city.

WITHOUT GONÇALVES AND the income provided by his shop, Violeta's family was rendered destitute in a matter of weeks, and all of the children were forced to go to work. Violeta became a wick-cutter at a workshop just off the Rua dos Ingleses. Inside that cavernous factory she worked from dawn to dusk, and all her wages were given directly to her mother, so she had nary a farthing to her name.

Saturdays and Sundays ought to have been her days of freedom and light, but as punishment for the "lies" that had lost her family its champion, her mother kept her imprisoned in their home. At times her ankle was even chained to her bed, I was told by Mama, who had witnessed this indignity herself. On these occasions she was made to embroider prayers on towels, for sale in the marketplace.

Perhaps owing to my father's partial responsibility for their poverty, Mama never failed during those first difficult weeks to carry carrots, potatoes, and other vegetables to Violeta's home on Saturdays. In this way, she said, they might at least partake of a warm and wholesome soup. She was the one who kept Papa and me informed about the lass. And it was she who told me as well that Daniel and I were forever forbidden from paying a visit to her house, for her mother maintained that we'd been a ruinous influence on Violeta's life. Even so, I later discovered that he stood below her window all night on several occasions, trying in vain to get her to appear at her shutters. He ended this practice when he was told by Violeta's younger brother that their mother beat her every time he was spotted in their street.

About ten weeks after her uncle's disappearance, in September of 1801, Violeta's mother even went so far as to call us curs who had spoiled her daughter's innocence. The quarrel provoked by this assertion was to mark the end of Mama's visits.

Upon informing me of this conversation, Mama added that she had been told prior to her outburst that Violeta would soon be starting additional work. Every Saturday she would be selling—at a stall in New Square—the embroidered goods she and her mother were sewing.

Mama gave thanks to heaven for this, since she saw it as our chance to help the lass. She encouraged Daniel and me to visit her there and offer her comfort. If anyone from her family was present, however, we were—under no circumstances—to allow ourselves to be seen by them. "If you take another risk with Violeta's well-being, I shall never ever forgive either of you," she warned us.

DANIEL AND I endeavored on numerous occasions over the next weeks to speak with Violeta at her stall, but whenever she saw us approaching, she seemed to choke as though she had swallowed poison. She would reveal nothing of her heart to us and would obviously have preferred to burrow down into the cobbles and bury herself rather than have to speak of her life.

As time went on, she grew more pale and drawn. Lice crawled freely over her bonnet, and I once spotted a red boil oozing pus on her wrist. Another time I saw what looked to be a burn on the palm of her hand.

The specific effects of her brutalized state on Daniel came as a surprise to me, likely owing to my youth; instead of conceiving a plan to kidnap her or blackmail her mother, as I might have expected, he began to inflict injury upon himself and others, frequently ending up in bloody fisticuffs with other boys and even with me. He hit me so hard once—as I was trying to drag him away from a young priest with whom he'd started a quarrel—that I awoke to find him sobbing over me and begging my forgiveness. "Look what I've done to you," he wept.

He carried me all the way home. Cradled in his arms, I felt his strength enveloping me, as it had before our troubles began. I never told my parents what he'd done. I explained to Mama that I'd fallen off the cathedral wall while imitating a goose.

Soon, Daniel began to go to the taverns in the Ribeira district to beg gin, rum, and *cachaça,* a liquor made in Brazil from cane. When drunk he often called himself unworthy of Violeta. He cursed her at times as well, as damnable and selfish. This perplexed me, but I can see now that his behavior, born of despair, was aimed at confirming his vileness in his own eyes and those of others. Yet his actions only bound me to him closer than ever.

Then, one moonless night, just before dawn, the lass slipped out of her house and tossed her pebbles at my window. She welcomed me outside with an embrace that was more solid than I had any right to hope for. When she laughed at my fear for her, I knew she had returned to me.

She removed her bonnet and let me scratch her hair, which was stiff with new growth. We spoke little on that first visit. Sitting on our stoop, she pointed into the sky and had me identify constellations as though she were tutoring me for an exam.

She began to visit me once a fortnight. I often suggested that we sneak off to visit Daniel, but she would not hear of it. "He would just ask me to flee with him. And I cannot."

"But why can't you go?" I dared to ask once.

She shook her head. "You are too young to understand, John. I cannot just run away. My family needs my wages. It's my fault that my uncle is no longer supporting us."

When I said that wasn't true, she replied, "John, I'm afraid there are people whose fate it is to remain unhappy. Perhaps wickedness makes some of us undeserving of a better life."

"But what of America?" I asked. "You told me you would really go there and that no one could stop you. Why not now?"

Hushing me, she told me we might remain friends only if I never spoke of her misfortune. I didn't understand why she wished this, but on her insistence I swore to it.

VIOLETA, DANIEL, AND I continued to live our lives largely independent of one another throughout that autumn of 1801. The lad was hardly ever at home, and I grew tired of trying to coax him from the taverns. Even on Saturdays he would often get drunk rather than come with me to Violeta's stall. He abandoned our art lessons as well, though I still loved my studies with the Olive Tree Sisters every Friday afternoon.

This wretched time reached its zenith shortly after the return of Daniel's adoptive father, in February of 1802, a bitterly cold and rainy month. I was now almost eleven years of age, fearful of Daniel's wild mood swings, and disenchanted with bird calls and most everything else.

As for Violeta's occasional nighttime visits, they served only to agitate me, for she refused to discuss her plight.

Daniel's father had returned to Porto because his relations in Newfoundland with a woman of French and Ottawa Indian blood had borne one too many fruits. The solution for him had been easy—he simply signed on for the next vessel back to Portugal and left without a farewell. He was of the opinion that unwanted children make all explanations useless.

Daniel already knew this, of course.

Senhor Carlos—for that was the man's name—insisted that Daniel move back to their house. And despite all of Senhora Beatriz's pleas and bribes, he refused to sign over the parental rights that had been given him when he and his wife adopted the baby given up by Senhora Beatriz's daughter. He even threatened to appeal to a judge if she continued to keep the lad from him, insinuating that her Jewish background would hardly weigh in her favor. Furthermore, he was determined to take Daniel away with him the next time he set out to sea.

I remember Senhora Beatriz coming to our house, carrying her small painting of her daughter, on the day Daniel left her home for good. When Mama left me alone with her to make some strong tea, she touched her crooked finger to her beloved daughter's image and whispered, "We've lost him again, Teresa, we've lost our Daniel...." She looked up at me as though to beg forgiveness and shuddered. "What a fool I am, John. I thought I'd changed destiny—redeemed our betrayal of that boy. But women are powerless against cruelty once it has claimed a child's life."

ONCE, JUST AFTER Daniel had moved his belongings to his old house, I saw him feign throwing a knife at his father's back.

"I'd do it, but not even his death would set me free," he told me.

Rather than attack him at that moment, he took up a wooden plate he'd been carving with the faces of wolves, foxes, and other forest creatures. After working away for a time, he showed it to me. None of the animals had eyes. It was chilling. When I asked for a closer look, he marched outside and hurled it in the river. Lifting his eyebrows like a rogue, he feigned a grin. He wished me to think it was just a game, but I knew better. I said, "You ought to have finished it at least—now they will never be able to see."

He shook his head. "There's nothing for me to finish. All that I have known is over now."

DANIEL'S FATHER DIDN'T want to maintain their house during what might be an absence of years, so two months after his arrival it was sold to a blacksmith from Vila do Conde, who was to move in on May the First. With the proceeds from the sale, Senhor Carlos bought Daniel a leather travel case, a knife of English steel, sheepskin gloves, a pair of fur-lined boots, and a woolen cape with a hood.

"Newfoundland freezes over as early as October," he explained.

This was hardly an enticing prospect to a young man who had never in his short life even worn a thick coat, though Daniel claimed to be overjoyed at finally being able to earn a wage worthy of a man. He scoffed at the very idea of remaining in Porto after his father's departure. He spoke of his grandmother as a burden and of Violeta as a waste of his time. Anyone unfamiliar with his theatrical gifts might have been convinced that he was grateful for this opportunity to travel.

I believe now that his acting was meant to keep us from discovering that there was nothing left in his well of spirit. So many times in years since have I wished that I had tossed a rope down to him, because I could have; I was good with words and might very well have convinced him to defy his adoptive father. But I was blind to my own gifts and to many things around me—not unlike those creatures he had carved.

Daniel's last day in Porto approached quickly. On April the Twenty-Seventh, four days before he was to depart, he and I took a somber walk to the marketplace in New Square to ask Violeta for a final meeting. We found her in a skeletal state, her once-beautiful eyes full of sorrow.

"I must...I must say good-bye soon," Daniel said. His eyes were so heavy with unspoken emotion that I thought he might faint.

"Say it now, then," she replied harshly, wiping her nose on her sleeve.

"Come to my house tonight after midnight, please, Violeta," I said. "We shall have some cake I saved for you from my birthday celebration. Please, we miss you so much."

She glanced at me witheringly and said, "Go home to your parents. I do not wish to see either of you ever again."

We were speechless with despair. "Can the world really weigh so much, Violeta?" asked Daniel solemnly. "I ask myself that sometimes. And can we not help each other—you and I? Is that not what we are meant to do?" He smiled sweetly, as though to apologize for the seriousness of his words.

Violeta pressed her hand to her forehead, exhausted, stricken by his pain. "Go, Daniel. You have your life. Do not wait for me."

"Are you sending me away?" He reached for her, but she turned away.

"Do not touch me," she ordered. Then her voice softened. "Please, I could not bear it."

She stared down at the ground. I felt time and the last vestiges of our innocence ending for the three of us. Daniel was pale with shock. He and I waited a moment, hoping she would look up. When she didn't, we left. The lad's face was hollow and despondent as we rushed away. Likely he was haunting his own barren life, imagining what would never be. Through my lonely tears, I begged him to talk to me, pleaded that we must not abandon Violeta. On hearing that, he proceeded to provoke a bitter quarrel with me, challenging me to come with him to the suggestively named Cucumber Tavern, a vile public house at the riverside that was a haunt for sailors, bandits, and scoundrels.

When we entered the tavern, several rough-looking men called out greetings to him and burst into laughter after asking my name and age, threatening to tell my mother on me. We sat at a table in the corner.

Daniel produced a coin from his pocket and ordered himself a rum and myself a glass of cheap wine. Bent on destruction, he downed his dram in two gulps and bid me do the same with my wine.

Even though I took modest sips, I could fairly hear my down pillow calling my name. Daniel was busy gabbling on about setting out to sea with his father. His false enthusiasm irritated me. I was confused by all that had happened and enraged at everyone—at Daniel, Violeta, and myself, and all the adults in my life, so powerless to help us. To end his absurd chatter, I did the unforgivable—I told him that Violeta had secretly visited me late at night on occasion and that she had even told me she wished to go off to America without him.

"It's only a fantasy," he scoffed. "She told me all about how her father loved the night sky there."

"No, she means it," I insisted. "She made me promise not to tell you. But when you are gone at sea, she will leave Porto forever."

His eyes filled with tears. I immediately regretted my rash confession and hurried to make amends. "Daniel," I said, "Violeta is too troubled at the moment to know what she wants. I don't think she'd ever leave without us. A lass so young could never go away alone, could she?"

His face went blank with hopelessness and too much rum. We ought to have simply left for my house and spoken to my parents. I was about to propose that we go there—and apologize, too, for pretending that I knew Violeta had always planned to go away without him—but a burly merchant with shiny black hair sauntered up to our table and challenged Daniel to walk on his hands all the way from one end of the room to the other. The gentleman then offered the lad a silver ten-*tostão* coin for his troubles, which Daniel snatched with a grunt. Soon the men had gathered round and had placed their bets. A healthy sum was at play—too much for even the youthful arms of my nimble friend. I knew that trouble had found us in this hidden place. I ought to have spoken up, but I said nothing.

Daniel was a gifted acrobat and could do all sorts of tumbles, flips, and flurries, but the rum had dulled his sense of balance. He started out well enough, stepping like a crab, his legs arching back over his head, his face reddening as though sunburned. I walked along beside him, urging him forward. The men were shouting and laughing.

But the lad's left hand soon slipped and his right leg dangled too far over his back. Down he came with a dry thud. Men who had lost their bets jeered at him, calling him a donkey. The merchant who had paid for

Daniel's effort leaned over him, cleared his throat noisily, and spit a huge gob into his face. My friend wiped it away and rolled onto his belly, the crook of his arm over his eyes. I squatted next to him and begged him to leave. I felt his hot shame as my own and wished we had never come.

It was the proprietor who succeeded in rousing Daniel, giving him a kick on his bottom and then hoisting him up by his arm. He shoved the lad toward the door. Once outside, Daniel raced away from me. He ran with a curious lumbering gait, like a wounded animal. Before passing through the gate to reach the wharf, he turned back to me. Shaking his head, he smiled wistfully before running through the stone threshold.

I dashed after him and found him standing at the water's edge on the mossy granite blocks, peering into the water, shading his eyes with the back of his hand.

My friend held up his hand and said, "No closer, John."

I might have expected to see defeat or hopelessness in his eyes, even rage. Yet what was there was love. For me, I used to think. But if so, I now know it was only because I represented all he had ever done and wished for—all, too, he might have carved with his hands. Had a boy ever loved the hidden possibilities in our world as much as he?

He swept his hand straight down now, as though drawing a line between us. Then he recited his favorite rhyme: *"Raptado, embrulhado, e entregado*...kidnapped, wrapped, and delivered."

He reached deep into his pocket and tossed me the coin that the raven-haired lout in the tavern had offered him to walk on his hands. "You are the owner of all that is mine, including my masks," he said.

I assumed he meant that I would inherit his things when he went to sea with his father. I wanted to beg him to come home with me. My parents and I would find a way to help him. But without warning he reached to his chest as though pierced by a bullet. "I've been shot," he said.

At first I was stunned, my senses dulled by wine. Then I understood that he was acting, pretending to have been wounded in battle.

Daniel limped along the edge of the slick stones, his hands clutched over his heart. Then he teetered, tilting away from land. Squeezing his eyes tight, as though resigned to the inevitable, he fell into the muddy water.

What was he thinking as he tumbled down? I cannot say for sure. I only know that when I imagine myself in his place, I sometimes feel the seamless wash of relief flowing through me as I enter the water.

I waited, expecting him to surface wearing an exuberant smile. I recalled the kingfisher we'd seen on our first day at the tarn, who had disappeared under the water only to emerge with wings flapping, a tiny fish caught in its beak. I shouted his name, then ran to where he had toppled off the edge. I thought I saw his hands reaching toward me, then receding and disappearing altogether, like a dream withdrawing beyond the recall of memory. Two sailors were standing nearby, pointing toward the water where he had fallen.

"Help me!" I shouted to them. "Please help me."

They didn't move or call back to me, so I slipped out of my shoes and dived in after him.

I was a strong swimmer. My father had made sure of that. I pierced the water with the arrow of my hands and swam down. The water was freezing, and fish jostled around me, battering against my face. Yet all I could think of was finding Daniel and getting him to the surface. I had to apologize—to tell him that the only thing I knew with certainty about Violeta was that she loved him.

The water was surprisingly shallow—no more than ten feet. When I came close to the bottom, I twisted in a circle. I could make out what looked like an iron wheel planted in the riverbed, but the water was thick with mud from upriver and the current was fierce. It was tugging me away. It must have already carried Daniel a good ways downriver.

I surfaced for breath and heard a man shout, "What do you think you're doing?" but I paid him no heed. Other people called out to me, but since none of them had Daniel's voice, I swam twenty strokes to the west, then flipped my legs up and dived down, reaching forward with my hands and pulling the water behind me with the most powerful strokes I had ever managed. Then I saw him, his hair swirling above his head like seaweed, his arms floating limply. I darted down for him and grabbed an arm. I tugged once, but he seemed to pull back. I tugged again and felt the weight of his resistance. He was alive! Yet his eyes, open, were staring neither at me nor at anything else. I was fully empty of air by now and was forced to surface. I took two quick breaths, then gulped a third deep down into my lungs, positive that I could rescue him. This time I threw my arms around his waist and locked my hands behind his back. *Help me, goddamn it!* I wanted to shout. I kicked and tugged for all I was worth. But he would not—or could not—help me.

I have no idea how long I stayed underwater trying to pull Daniel up, but I vowed not to surface until I got his head above the waterline. I closed my eyes and kicked madly with my feet, but may Daniel, Senhora Beatriz, and Violeta forgive me, I soon grew dizzy. About three feet from the surface, my arms gave out. He fell away from me, swallowed whole by the greedy river. Now I was forced to struggle for my own life. The water was very dark and I could no longer tell which way was up and which was down.

Then I heard my father's voice shouting my name. I closed my eyes again so that I might hear him better. But he spoke no more. I felt myself being pulled down.

After a few moments of complete blackness, I felt something brush against my hand. An instant later, light flooded my eyes. I was above the water. I heard jangling voices like scattered coins. "Good lad!" a man shouted.

There was a rope in my hands and I was gulping down air. A man reached for me and lifted me out of the water.

I was unable to catch my breath. My chest felt as though it had been scraped with rusty metal. "He's down there," I said between gasps. "My friend, Daniel. Please help him. It may not be too late."

A sailor took a rope in his hands and dived off the landing. He was under a short while, then surfaced. "Pull!" he shouted.

Daniel, the rope tied around his waist, was soon tugged to the surface.

"Help him!" I begged.

The men lay him on his back. The sailor who had rescued Daniel and whose dark, alarmed face I will always remember pressed his hands into my friend's chest at short intervals. Then he leaned his ear down to hear the lad's heartbeat. After a few more attempts, the sailor shook his head. He reached for me in kindness, to take my hand, but by then I was unable to feel the touch of anything in this world. Though I was shivering, I was not cold. I was listening to the throbbing in my ears, and it was telling me that the impossible had happened and that I was partly to blame. That now I would have to grope forward into a future that was never meant to be.

LATER THAT AFTERNOON, before news of Daniel's death had reached her, Violeta trudged home from the marketplace and discovered—leaning against her house, directly below her window—the table-top he had carved with the faces of children. Though I was placed at the center, peeking out from behind a small sweeping frond of fern, it was the lass herself who had the only face executed in exacting detail. Indeed, her eyes were so accurately rendered that, as she knelt to touch his gift for the first time, it occurred to her that Daniel had seen further into her than even she had imagined. He had understood her loneliness as no one else ever would.

X

IMAGINE THE NAÏVETÉ OF A LAD BORN INSIDE the soot-blackened warren of Porto's crumbling streets, who still believed that he would walk a straight path toward happiness. But after the events of the Twenty-Seventh of April, 1802, the knowledge that life would never be fair blossomed black inside me.

That first day, I refused to leave my room, too exhausted and bewildered to cry anymore. Sometimes I would close my eyes and try to find solace in sleep. When I was able to talk about what had happened to Daniel, Papa held me in his powerful arms. I told him the story from the beginning, even the part about my gulping down wine in the Cucumber Tavern, so I would never have to tell the story to anyone else ever again.

When I had finished, he said, "Goodness, John, you are only a young lad. Do not take the responsibility of the world on yourself."

Sound advice, but those first few days I stayed in the dark of my room with the curtains drawn, for I could not risk seeing either the lad's father or Senhora Beatriz—not to mention Violeta.

I believed that I would see accusations of my weakness in

everyone's eyes. We all knew that Daniel could not keep himself away from danger. I had been on watch that day, and I had not fulfilled my duty. Even worse, by telling him about Violeta, had I not pushed him to his death?

More than two decades later, I no longer think every day of the unfairness of his death and my guilt. Even so, it is nearly impossible for me to accept that I am now thirty-three years of age and he will forever be only fourteen.

It comforts me to think sometimes that, more than his masks, I inherited something of his daring and courage. I would guess that I imitated these qualities at first and, by so doing, succeeded in incorporating a small portion of them into my being.

The funeral was held three days after his death. My parents attended the brief ceremony, but I screamed and flailed when they suggested I go. In the end, Grandmother Rosa stayed with me. While I lay in bed, she said something to me I shall never forget: "It may be a good thing, you know, this lad's death. His adoptive mother was nothing but a cheap prostitute. That's why he never saw her. That stray dog was having a deplorable influence over you, my child."

Her words so infuriated me that I grew feverish. By the time my parents came home, my forehead was burning and my pulse racing.

When we were alone, I told Mama what her mother had said. She never left me alone with Grandmother Rosa again.

THE HALLUCINATIONS BEGAN a few days later, when I was lying on my stomach in bed and clearly heard Daniel call my name from the street below. I rushed to the window and thought I saw him running down our street, near the jailhouse. I called out, but he had disappeared.

THE FOLLOWING SATURDAY, I mustered what was left of my courage and approached Violeta in the marketplace.

"I am sorry," I began. "So sorry. I did not mean to let him die. I tried...I tried very hard. But I was...I was too weak. I apologize, Violeta—"

She reached out for my hand. My heart leapt as I sobbed in gratitude. But I was still too ashamed to confess that I had told Daniel she would go to America without him. Instead, I spoke again of the weakness of my arms.

"John, please, do not blame yourself."

"So you do not despise me?" I croaked, my voice nothing but a whimper.

"Of course, not," she said, kissing my brow.

"I cannot believe that he is really dead," I said.

Tears slid down her cheeks. She was so very fragile.

When she had calmed, I said, "Will you still come to me sometimes at night? I am very worried about you."

"Yes—yes, I'd like that."

"You swear?"

"You have my word."

DESPITE HER PROMISE, Violeta never again came to throw pebbles at my window. I would pass her stall from time to time and wave at her, but she would turn away from me as though I were filth. Eventually, I stopped looking for her, believing she had reconsidered her opinion and now found me contemptible.

I had murdered Daniel and there could be no reprieve.

VIOLETA DISAPPEARED NEARLY a year later. No one knew where she had gone. Once, Senhor Solomão the butcher told me that her uncle had returned secretly one night and killed her. But I knew a wee bit more about the world by now and was sure that she had escaped her fate in the only way that a lass without a farthing to her name might—by walking out of the city, never looking back, and earning a wage in whatever way she could. Just as I was certain that we would never meet again.

XI

EXHAUSTION LAID CLAIM TO BOTH MY BODY and spirit, as I had suffered insomnia every night since Daniel's death.

One morning Mama discovered I had a high fever. Over the next several days, I suffered throbbing headaches that made it too painful for me to even open my eyes. I was crawling with body lice as well and plagued by intermittent chills.

I still believed I heard Daniel calling to me occasionally. From my window I twice caught glimpses of him scrambling over the rooftops across our street.

My mother grabbed my arm when I told her this. "I don't want to hear another word about that lad again!" she screamed. "You hear me, John? Never!" While Papa led her away, she burst into tears.

Mama's theory was that Daniel's soul had been unable to leave our earthly realm due to the violent nature of his death and his attachment to me.

"More likely a bewitchment" was the differing opinion of Senhora Beatriz, who tied a sprig of rosemary to the back of my hair. She also placed around my neck the talisman that had belonged to Daniel. I kept it hidden under my nightshirt.

When she had gone, Father came to my bedside and flicked my tail of rosemary. "All this superstition is rubbish," he sighed, puffing at his pipe. "But it cannot hurt you, and if it makes Senhora Beatriz happy . . . All you need," he declared, blowing out a snootful of sweet-smelling smoke, "is a few weeks of absolute quiet and Mama's care to feel yourself again."

A PHYSICIAN NAMED Dr. Manuel came to see me the next afternoon. Papa explained that he had studied something called *phrenology* in the far-off city of Vienna—which meant, Mama told me, that he was able to diagnose illness and prescribe curatives based on his study of the skull.

When he took hold of my sore head with his meaty hands, I almost jumped, as they gripped me like a vise. He massaged my skull with his fingertips, then said, "You are a clever lad but reckless."

"That he is," Mother confirmed.

After several minutes of squeezing, tapping, and knocking, he located a telling curiosity at the back of my head. "Ah, yes," he said in his odd Portuguese. "Most swollen and *fluidaceous.*"

"What in God's name is he saying?" Father demanded of Mama.

"Mr. and Mrs. Stewart, your son has a much-translocated visual cortex—caused by his *plethoric* condition. He has a dangerous excess of blood in his head, making him far too attached to visual memories."

"Yes, that sounds right," Mother agreed again.

"I recommend application of *sanguessugas,*" the phrenologist declared, tapping my skull in the spot to be sucked dry by the little gargoyles. "Then we shall see."

"Leeches," he repeated in English, for my father's benefit.

He took a beige-colored ceramic vase from his leather medical case, from which he lifted a small perforated tube. I was so nervous that when I saw the first leech dangling in his gloved hand, I shrieked for help. I have little recollection of what occurred next, save for the unpleasant feeling of being rendered wholly immobile. I have every reason to believe that my hands were bound with a ligature, since that is what I suffered during my later treatments.

I awoke at dawn to discover Mother and Father asleep in my room, fully clothed except for their bare feet, entangled together on a settee they had moved in from their bedroom. Papa was snoring a comical *rat-tat-tat* with his mouth open, his right arm resting on Mama's shoulder, and she was curled like a cat, her head on his lap. Fanny had been let inside by them, and she was sprawled on her back at the foot of my bed, her feet in the air, her moist nostrils flexing in and out, as though she were dreaming of floating.

When I think of my parents and Fanny today, I like to remember that moment; I could not have felt more protected. I presumed that the worst of my treatment was over.

SUCCESS IN A medical case is determined by the physician, however, and never the patient, who is much too subjectively minded to be trusted. In the case at hand, which unfortunately was my own, Dr. Manuel's initial treatment was considered a stupendous victory over the putrid accumulation of my bile, which he discovered to be responsible for what he called my "plethoric skull transmigrations." Many years later a far simpler explanation was given me by an English physician: typhus. It frequently causes the delirium, hallucinations, headaches, and high fever I suffered intermittently for weeks, and it is caused by lice.

Though I have thankfully forgotten most of the details, I know that over the next three days more bloodsuckers were applied to the back of my head, and I was also purged twice daily by my mother. By the end of the third day of treatment, Dr. Manuel pronounced me cured, by which he must have meant that I had lost enough blood and absorbed enough poison to die slowly of my own accord. In any event, he'd not be back to torture me in the morning. I was delivered.

I slept soundly that night, stirring only in the wee hours, my belly growling from the mixture of metallic and mineral substances forced down my throat. I craved something substantial to eat and envisioned a banquet of sponge cakes, rice pudding, and *rabanadas*—bread soaked in egg, then fried and covered with sugar. I began to make my way on tiptoe to the kitchen to forage for sweets, but a quarrel in my parents' room distracted me.

"If you insist on leaving," Mother shouted, "then John and I will not be here when you return."

"May, try to understand that I am doing this for the three of us," Papa replied, calling Mama by his favorite name for her. "If you could just—"

"The three of us! How can you consider leaving with your son in the state that he is?"

"I have already put off leaving twice before. The ship sails the day after tomorrow. I must be on it."

"And how will you tell this to John?"

"I shall tell him the truth, as I always have."

"Shall the truth take care of him while you are gone? Shall the truth keep him from madness?"

My pulse began to race when I realized that Papa might be leaving out of disappointment with me. I turned the handle of their door.

"John?" Mama gasped. She was standing in her nightdress, holding in her hand a pewter candlestick with a lighted taper.

Father was naked except for the nightcap on his head and was sitting on their bed. Had I been feeling myself I surely would have had a good laugh.

"Come in, laddie," he said, beckoning me forward.

When he reached for me, I ran to him, crying. He picked me up and held me tight. I burrowed my head into his shoulder.

Mama came to us and kissed me where the leeches had sucked out my lifeblood. I shall never forget how she kept repeating, "Everything is going wrong—everything . . ."

Father informed me that he was leaving on a long voyage.

"Is it . . . is it because of me? Do you hate me, Papa?"

"Of course not, John. I could never hate you. It has to do with us—with the family. Give me a moment, and I shall tell you." He slipped on his dressing gown, then took his pipe from their dresser and began filling it with tobacco from his pouch.

"Are you leaving too?" I asked my mother.

"No, John, I shall be right here with you." She sat with me, left a kiss in the palm of my hand, and balled it into a fist for me to keep. "I shall always be with you."

After fiddling with his pipe and lighting it, Papa announced in a grand exhalation of smoke, "I am making a voyage to southern Africa, John. Please do not be upset, but I shall be gone for some time."

"What's in Africa?"

"Land for our vineyard."

"But we have land upriver."

Despite Mama's arm around my shoulder, I was still shivering. Papa clapped his hands. "Come, get under the covers. You're frozen."

"In you go," my mother said, lifting the sheet and blanket over me, smiling with renewed courage.

Papa sat down next to me and smoothed the red blanket of English wool over my chest and legs. Mama climbed in, put her arm under my head, and tickled my ear.

Tracing the stem of his pipe in the air, Father said, "I shall be taking a ship down the Gold Coast, past Angola to the very tip of Africa." He dotted his destination with a jab. "The British have taken the Cape. Soon there will be thousands of men farming that rich land."

"But we have seven acres upriver. You told me so."

"Aye, son, that's true enough. But at the Cape there are plots the size of Porto that the British government is selling for next to nothing. Imagine, John, within a few years, I shall have enough to purchase a hundred acres. Even two hundred, laddie. Here in Portugal, that will never be within my means."

"You mean . . . you mean we might move to Africa?" I asked.

"Aye, but not right away, son. In a few years—if I find the right place. That is why I'm leaving now. Do you understand?"

I said I did, but I was confused.

"All will be well. Now, go to sleep like a good wee *kelpie*," he said, kissing my cheek.

"But I'm hungry," I exclaimed. "I think there's a hole in my belly."

"At four in the morning?" Mama asked.

"I want something sweet. I'm all sore inside."

Papa laughed, then shook his head and said in his broadest Scots accent, "Dearest May, you cannot fight a lad who needs some porridge in his belly."

Mama made me *rabanadas*. They watched me eat with great pleasure, my father sneaking bits of crust with his fork and robbing what I would permit. Mama was so happy she played us the First Prelude from Bach's "Well-Tempered Clavier," a piece that has always meant joy to me. Afterward, I was invited back into their bed. I fell asleep between them, nestling into the side of my dearest father, who held my hand under the covers and whom I wished to beg to stay with us and never leave.

TWO DAYS LATER, at just past eight in the morning, he was saying his farewells to us on the wharf. Dressed in a blue serge traveling coat, bristling with excitement, he kissed first me and then my mother. After lifting me up for a final twirl in the air, he doffed his hat to us and told us again not to worry.

Boarding his tall-masted English vessel, he was off for Lisbon, then Africa. I should like to say that he offered some final words of counsel to me, but I remember that all he said to us both was, "Do not think too harshly of me. I mean to do only well. That is all I've ever desired."

AND SO MY mother and I were left alone for nearly two and a half months, until late August. I should like to say that we prospered together, but through an alchemical process known only to those left behind by their loved ones, we turned all that might have shimmered gold to the basest lead.

I cannot say whether I truly desired to kill myself, nor can I say why I chose our rooftop. I only know that a few days after Papa's departure, on a night of insomnia, I burned with fever once more. Daniel appeared at my bedside. Wearing a mask with a long snout and antlers, he said that my death would enable him to join God in heaven. I had no reason not to believe him.

It was nearly sunrise. I went up to the Lookout Tower, climbed through the dormer window in our roof, walked solemnly to the edge, closed my eyes, and jumped. I did not wake to find myself in heaven with my old friend as I'd expected. Instead, I was lying on the cold cobbles, and a man with a beard I'd never seen before was peering at me from an alarmingly close distance.

I had been discovered by a nearsighted vegetable peddler, who, after assuring himself that I was still breathing, banged on our front door till my mother was roused. On seeing me motionless, my eyes closed, she was certain her only child had been taken forever from her.

Dr. Silva, our neighborhood physician, later discovered that I had fractured my right leg just below the knee, bruised my left hip, and suffered lacerations to my forehead and hands. Once I had been stitched, salved, and bandaged, Mama explained to the physician, to Senhora Beatriz, and to anyone else who asked that I had momentarily fantasized I could fly.

I vehemently denied having seen Daniel when asked.

Over the next days, Mama kept vigil in my room while I recovered from my injuries. She grew so worried about me that she could not even play her pianoforte. Often, she would pick nervously at the pretty floral embroidery she sewed on the collars of her dresses.

We might have continued down this anxious road had my mother not discovered that by administering a half teaspoonful of a sweet-smelling liquid contained in a small amber vial marked *Tr. Opii* she could keep me calm and free of hallucinations all day. Who had recommended this admixture of opium to her, I never found out.

For me, the opium did indeed keep Daniel in his grave, but at the price of making me listless of mind, weak of body, and unbearably thirsty. I half-dreamed my life over the coming weeks, growing immeasurably frail, until I spoke in a whisper and desired only to lie in bed with the shutters closed. I felt like the center of me was now made of soft dark wool.

After a month of strict convalescence, my leg was strong enough to support my weight but, floating along in my drugged state, I refused to give up my crutches. Mama once said of this time that I was passing further each day through the Gate of Death. Yet she was too afraid to stop giving me opium. Panicked and alone, suffering from insomnia herself, she could not have been thinking clearly.

For years afterward, I considered that she had been exaggerating my nearness to death, as I was not aware of my own pitiful state in any conscious way. But when I spoke to Luna Oliveira about that time, she said that she, too, had been convinced that I would soon be joining Daniel. She said that losing him and Violeta had shattered my young heart.

WHILE I WAS struggling to remain in our world, Father sent us advance notice of his return. He had already reached Lisbon and had decided to spend three nights there in order to conduct some business for the Douro Wine Company, shave his beard, and rid himself of his seagoing odor. The letter was two days in arriving, however. It was on the very next day, the Twenty-Ninth of August, that he was to dock in Porto, around noon.

Mother and I feared that we would fail miserably in making a good first impression, so on the morning of the great day, at precisely eleven o'clock, she administered a dose and a half of her tincture of opium. I became so disoriented that, in order to appear healthy, I ran upstairs at the last minute, punctured my finger with a pin, and rubbed blood into my pale cheeks.

The ship was late, and it was not until well after one o'clock that we saw it sailing up the Douro. As the *Somerset* dropped anchor, Mama lifted herself on the tips of her toes to catch a glimpse of Papa. When he appeared on deck, she gripped my hand so tightly I winced in pain.

He had not come alone. With him was a wee dark-skinned man, no more than five feet tall. Months later, I found out his original name, which was Tsamma, the word in his language for a particular melon from the Kalahari Desert. This fruit was of special importance to his people and, indeed, to all the creatures of southern Africa, as its liquid-sweet flesh sustained one and all during periods of drought. But he was introduced to me as Midnight.

XII

THE FIRST THING I NOTICED ABOUT MID-
night on the wharf that afternoon was his coloring, which
was not pure black—as his name might imply—but bronze.
The second was his diminutive stature, for he was clearly
only a shade taller than my mother. This might have been
the expected size of a lad with some growing yet to do, but
he was surely a man of twenty-five or even thirty years
of age.

I was soon to discover that he, too, was uncertain of his
age, since his people dated their births by referring to natural events in the world. When we spoke of it, he offered a response that astounded me: "I might be the age of the
wildflowers that blossomed in the year of the hailstorm over
Gemsbok Valley. The whole of the valley was very, very
green, you see." He circled his hands in the air, then brought
them together and opened them in a swirl of blossoms. "As
bright and as colorful as a desert oasis of flowers."

More than that he could not say.

Midnight smiled broadly at me as he walked onto land,
his gait sprightly, as though he enjoyed the simple act of
walking as much as he might a rousing ball game. His
eyes—dark and slightly slanted in the Oriental manner—

seemed to harbor some secret amusement of which only he was aware. In my apprehension, I mistook this as an indication that he found me comical in some way, which irritated me. Though frail as a paper doll and drowsy, I kept my eyes wide open and my posture stiff. Midnight kept smiling at me as he and Papa approached, and I remember thinking, *He is frightfully ugly and I do not like him. I hope he will not try to touch me.*

I looked up at my mother, who wore an expression of dread.

Turning away from her, I noticed that Midnight's ears, tucked close to his head and tapering upward, were like those I'd seen at the Olive Tree Sisters' house in images of Pan. His black hair was wound into tight clusters, like small balls of wool.

Papa, after kissing my mother and me and saying that he had missed us enormously, introduced his African visitor. He said that he intended, if we agreed, for Midnight to stay with us for "a few short weeks." Dumbfounded, Mama ventured no reply.

Midnight lifted her hand to shake it, a bit more vigorously than might have been considered appropriate, and said, "Good day, Mrs. Stewart. We saw you from afar and we are dying of hunger."

There was no trace of humor in his voice; on the contrary, he spoke with veneration, as though in the presence of royalty. My father explained that it was the traditional greeting of Midnight's people.

My mother replied, "I am pleased to make your acquaintance, sir," mentioning nothing yet about his proposed stay with us.

I refused to shake his hand and said nothing at all when he told me that he was most happy to meet me after hearing so much about me from my father. I kept my arms locked behind my back and my mouth sealed tight in spiteful silence.

Papa looked at me crossly. That was when Midnight seemed to notice a stain or crumb on my face. Only later did I realize he had remarked on an L-shaped scar that I incurred in my tumble off our roof. With a worried look, he reached down to me. I flung my right hand up to prevent his fingers from touching me, but I wasn't quick enough. He held my chin in his hand and his fingers were cool. He stared at me. He had eyes like moons.

"The lad is indeed most ill," Midnight said, looking up at my father with concern.

Papa knelt in front of me and grimaced in fear. "How badly has it gone with John?" he asked my mother.

"I shall tell you at home."

"Tell me now."

She ignored him and asked if *Mr.* Midnight would be accompanying us to our house.

"Yes," Papa said, slapping his hat against his hip in anger, "I just told you that that was my intention."

"Then let us proceed," she said tersely.

It was a tense walk from the riverside to our house. Mama, who had been planning to fall into Father's arms and cede all her worries to him, swiftly abandoned that course of action. She spoke only when spoken to, and then only in monosyllables. Father held her hand as though afraid she would vanish if he let go. He stole worried glances at me and looked increasingly glum, undoubtedly convinced that our lives had grown more desperate than he had ever feared. I was painfully self-conscious and tried not to look at Midnight, who pranced along beside me.

Once at home, Mother ordered me to take our guest into the garden, in such a frigid tone that I dared not protest. As we stepped outside, Midnight said, "Your father tells me that you have been seeing a friend of yours who died."

Furious, I refused to answer, because I was not of the opinion that sharing this secret with strangers was within my father's rights.

Fanny waddled toward us, her tail wagging. Despite my stern look of warning, she took an immediate liking to our guest and was soon licking his hands and face. He giggled and spoke to her in bizarre clicking sounds.

"Leave her alone. She only understands my whistles."

He stood up. "Does she do many tricks perhaps?"

"Only one. She bites strangers!" I snapped.

He laughed at that, his broad shoulders jiggling. Drugged to a trance, perfumed like a princess, irate as a bull, and ornamented with a red ribbon at my collar, I must have been a truly wretched and risible sight. I naturally believed that this was why Midnight kept looking furtively at me as he stepped through the tangled mess that was then our garden, accompanied from behind by a very curious Fanny.

I stepped quietly back inside to eavesdrop on my parents. Mama was speaking in hushed tones of my fall from the roof. She delicately suggested that it might not have been an accident. She then went on to mention that, as a consequence, she had been administering a spoonful of tincture of opium to me every morning. At that, the trap sprung, and

Papa accused her of trying to poison me. "You have rendered him drug-damned, you foolish woman!"

"I am fighting for him in the only way I know how," Mama cried. "It's so easy for you to criticize me, but what would you suggest I ought to have done?"

Shortly afterward Papa apologized, and my parents went to their room. Hearing no further quarrel or conversation, I presumed my father unable to keep his travel-induced slumber at bay any longer. Grumbling to myself about their neglect of me, I returned to our garden, where I found the African sitting on his heels in the middle of a profusion of shoulder-high weeds, his eyes closed, breathing softly.

Loudly, so that he might hear and take offense, I said, "That must be the way Africans sleep. They don't even have sense enough to lie down."

His eyes remained closed, though I saw a smile cross his lips. Thoughts of murder entered my mind.

Dragging myself inside, I slumped down on the Persian rug in our sitting room, propped my head on one of the cushions my mother had recently embroidered with tulips, and dozed off. Doors opened and closed in my dreams. Mice scattered. The ceiling swelled and seemed to press against my chest.

I awoke a short time later with a dull ache in my belly. And my head . . . A devilish sprite was tightening a rusted winch in my neck.

Papa soon came bobbing down the stairs, too cheerful by half. "Hello there, John, how's my laddie?"

I sat up and stretched. "Fine, Papa. Tired."

I was not as overjoyed to see him as I imagined I would be, for he seemed greatly changed. His eyes seemed too blue, his long hair too tightly tied at the back. Being young, I didn't know that after a long absence a period of readjustment is often necessary. It seemed likely that I would never love him again as I had before.

"So what do you think of our Midnight?" he inquired.

"He is very dark," I answered.

My father laughed. "Why, yes, I suppose he is. Sable of color compared to a pale Scotsman like you."

Mama came down the stairs, pinning up her hair. She smiled at Papa, who winked at her. He took one of his pipes from a rack on our mantelpiece, a meerschaum beauty carved with the head of a bat that had been purchased in Glasgow many years earlier by his father. Removing his tobacco pouch from his waistcoat pocket, he sighed. "It is good to be home."

Mama announced that she would make us all some tea. "To give you two time alone," she beamed, whereupon she left us for the garden to pump water into her kettle.

Papa graciously invited me to sit next to him on the blue and green brocade armchair usually reserved for Mama.

"I expect Midnight is still in the garden," he said, leaning toward me and filling the bowl of his pipe with a pinch of tobacco. "I'm sorry you've been a sad *kelpie*. I shall try to make it up to you now that I am home."

"I have been just fine," I replied.

"Aye, I can see how *fine* you have been. And I know what medicine your mother has been giving you." He brushed some fallen tobacco off his breeches. "Don't think I don't know every hair on your head. I shall be counting them later to make sure none fell out while I was gone!" He smiled gently. I did my best to share his mirth, but the rusty winch was tightening at my neck. "I understand, too, you have lost your appetite. I'm not pleased by that, John. Now, what would you say if we stopped giving you your medicine? Do you think you might suffer again that . . . that particular problem of yours?"

The possibility that I would not have access to my spoonful of opium filled me with worry.

"Well?" he prompted.

"I shall try very hard not to see or hear Daniel," I told him, loath to spoil his homecoming.

"Midnight may be able to help, you know. What is your opinion of him so far?"

"I have no opinion, Papa."

"But surely you do." He pointed the stem of his pipe at me. "Out with it, lad."

Since being sent to bed was probably the worst that would happen, and since I should not have minded going to sleep, I said, "I do not like him. I think he's ugly."

"But why, lad?"

"I cannot think why he is here," I answered. "You must admit he is strange."

Papa puffed away thoughtfully, then said, "To one of your wee birdies he would surely seem not so different from you or me."

I was not so sure.

Mama returned to place her windmill-patterned teacups and saucers on our round wooden table. "Just waiting for the water to boil," she said. "Are you having a pleasant chat?"

I nodded and Papa kissed her hand. Then he turned to me and said, "Son, if he is a friend of mine, is that not good enough for you?"

Mama bit her lip while considering whether to voice her opinion. I was about to lie to avoid a crisis when she said, "James, please be reasonable. John and I have not come to know him yet."

"If he were a friend from London, May, would you be so reticent?"

"I do not know." She waved a dismissive hand in the air. "The point is moot, James, because John is right. He is too dark to be English, and the neighbors may not be so . . . so generous as you and I."

I sensed she had made a tactical error by mentioning the partiality of our neighbors. Father cared not a whit for their opinions on guests in our home or anything else.

He inhaled too sharply on his smoke, causing him to cough. After clearing his throat several times, he sought to trump her by saying, "I should like you to know, May, that Midnight was a subject of the British Crown in the Cape Colony."

Mama sat down on one of our Windsor chairs, moving it beside mine as though to present a common defense of hearth and home. "That, dear husband, does not make him British."

"Well, then, damn the British and damn the neighbors both! And damn you, May, for being so clever."

Papa puffed away demonically and came near to suffocating us in his angry cloud of smoke. But when he spoke, it was with renewed tenderness. "I have learned that he is a very good man. So I will enter into a contract with you both. If, after three weeks, you still find him disagreeable, I shall pay his way back to the Cape and you will never see him again."

"It is only that he could not have come to us at a worse time," my mother observed, sensing she had given more offense than she had intended. "Otherwise, I would happily welcome him into our home."

"On the contrary, May, a better time could hardly be found. As I was telling you."

"Yes." She clasped her hands tightly in her lap. "I only hope you are right."

"Three weeks is all I ask. Is that too much to give a husband who has been away for far too long and who has missed his wife and son terribly?"

These words weakened Mama's resolve, and my own as well. She and I agreed to his request.

Papa stroked my hair. "Do not fear, John," he said, patting my head, "for I am home now and you shall get better. I shall see to that if it is the last thing I do."

These words chilled me, since they implied that a long war might be necessary to win me back to health. Even so, I was pleased that he filled his pipe a second time and continued to caress my hair, for his soothing scent and touch brought him finally home to me. I gulped down my tea and held the warm cup to my temples to ease the throbbing. I prayed for Daniel to stay away.

AT ABOUT FIVE in the afternoon, my father left the house with Midnight in tow. He explained that he had an engagement at the Douro Wine Company that he could not miss.

No sooner had the front door closed than my mother turned to me and said, "I shall be back presently. Do not—I repeat!—do not venture off or do anything silly." Then she, too, left the house.

I sat in the garden, throwing Fanny's leather ball into the weeds for her to fetch, fighting the nausea in the pit of my gut. When my mother returned home half an hour later, I asked her if Midnight's stay had anything to do with me. She replied that the African was here to help Papa, though she admitted that she didn't have the vaguest idea what that meant. She also told me that she had been questioned by several women on our street about the strange, dark-complexioned "creature" they'd seen leaving our house.

"Over the next three weeks, John, we shall be hearing quite a bit of speculation," she added, raising a finger of warning. "And I do not intend to add any kindling at all to that fire."

WE SAW FATHER and our African guest again before supper. Midnight was not terribly fond of shoes, and he left his, along with his stockings, at our door. His feet were small and highly arched. Like those of an elf.

At the supper table I picked at my sardines and managed, through sheer will, to eat an entire one, as well as several boiled potatoes, though I had no appetite at all.

Prior to coming to the table, Midnight removed from his fob pocket a child's whistle and rattle, the very same one I had had as a toddler. It had a number of tiny metal balls chained to a central tube. He twirled it in his hands, making a tinkling sound that gave him great pleasure. He may have expected us to join him in appreciation of this trinket, but the only one who smiled at him was my father.

The African placed his toy down beside his plate and sat at our table in a most dignified and erect manner. After receiving permission from Papa, he started to eat. Mama and I watched him closely, hoping to find him wholly wanting for manners.

He had strong but delicate hands, like those of a weaver, I thought. Though he managed his knife and fork with a certain darting elegance, he used his fingertip to prompt a piece of potato onto the tines several times. Mother raised her eyebrows at these actions, storing each faux pas as ammunition. But what really bothered her was that he never said thank you—not when he was invited to sit, when butter was passed to him, or even when his wine cup was filled.

To each of these gestures, he simply smiled.

My mother was squinting, a sure sign that she would be engaging him in a prolonged interrogation in the near future. I was ready to back her sword-and-shield in any quarrel, since my parents had always insisted on my thank-yous at every opportunity.

"My husband tells me, sir, that you are from southern Africa," Mama announced.

"That is correct-correct, madam," Midnight said, smiling.

"It is *what*?"

Papa took Mama's hand in his and said, "Midnight often uses two words for emphasis, May."

"Is that so? Well, then, where exactly are you *from-from*?"

Papa laughed at her witticism but stifled his mirth when she frowned at him.

"I was born near the Hill of the Sky."

"The Hill of the Sky?" she repeated disdainfully, skewering a piece of potato with her fork. "And what might that place be?"

"That place might be a great-great mountain that glows blue in the sunset."

"Blue? How is it blue in the sunset, sir?"

"It is very, very blue." He nodded eagerly. "As blue as can be."

My mother narrowed her eyes again and licked her tongue over her lips as though preparing to dine on our guest. "'Very, very blue,'" she echoed sarcastically. "'As blue as can be.' Yes, it must have indeed been that."

I realized her tactic was to point out the peculiarity of his remarks by repeating them. It was a clever strategy that had the opposite effect on me, since hearing his expressions a second time only convinced me that he possessed an agile and creative mind.

"And how old might you be, sir?" she continued.

It was then that he told us he was the age of the wildflowers that blossomed in the year of the hailstorm over Gemsbok Valley. Unreceptive to his obvious flair for description, particularly given that English was not his native tongue, my mother insisted on a clearer answer. "But in years, how old?" she prompted, slamming down her fork in irritation.

Midnight smiled and shook his head apologetically.

Father gobbled down a steaming half-potato. Fanning the burning heat from his now open mouth, he replied, "It is hard to say, my dear. His people are Bushmen. They do not count their ages in years." He downed his wine in one gulp and sighed with relief.

"That's absurd," Mother replied.

Father wiped his mouth with his napkin. "Might I inquire how many steps it takes for you to get to your mother's house from here?"

"Naturally you may. And I have no idea."

"That is because you measure the distance in the minutes it takes you. A Bushman measures his age differently than we might like, but to him it makes all the sense in the world."

"What rubbish!" she exclaimed.

"Ridiculous it may be, May, but perfectly suited to his life."

They frowned at each other and said nothing more. "What is a Bushman?" I asked, for I had never heard that name.

Father poured himself more wine. "The Bushmen were the first people to inhabit southern Africa. They are nomads and hunters, and they wander for hundreds of miles to follow the great rains across the desert, savanna, and jungle. I assure you, having seen them in action, that no swifter and more accurate hunter lives anywhere on earth. But of late they have been killed by the hundreds and dispersed by the Dutch and the English and even other Africans."

He looked tenderly at our guest, who was gazing forlornly down at his plate. "Midnight was but a wee lad when he was stolen from his people. His parents were killed in a raid by a Dutch commander called Nel, a fearsome brute who killed thousands of Midnight's people. The lad was carried back to the farms of one of Nel's officers and made an errand boy. After that, he was abandoned and left to fend for himself. Through his own tracking skills, he found his way back to his people. Years later, in another raid, his new kin were all murdered. He was a young man by then and was sold again, this time to a Yorkshireman named Reynolds, who had a nearby vineyard. That is where I met him. So you see, there are good reasons why he does not know his age in ways we might understand."

"If they are all such great hunters, Papa, then how were his parents killed?" At the time I was pleased that I might be giving offense with this indiscreet question.

Father placed an imaginary arrow into an invisible bow, aimed it at our garden window, and let it fly. "The bow is of little use against a musket, John. Even you know that." He winked at me then, and I understood that he had used the word *even* to chastise me. "It is not an equal match. But I assure you, laddie," and here he emphasized the seriousness of his point by making a fist with his hand and holding it toward me, "that if the Bushmen were to meet the English on equal footing, Midnight and his kind would come away victorious every time. Just like the Scots." He said it proudly, leaning back in his chair. "I have recently seen one of his people fell a gazelle at a hundred yards, with an arrow straight to the heart. No, any man who values his life would not wish to upset Midnight or his kinfolk."

Our guest continued to hang his head, plainly troubled. Tiny wrinkles, like the spokes of a wheel, spread on his skin from his almond-shaped eyes.

"So what can you tell us of Africa, sir?" Mother said.

Midnight had never sailed beyond the borders of Africa, so asking him to speak of his continent was tantamount to asking him to speak of the world itself—which is why, I believe, he gestured up toward our ceiling and said, "In the heavens are the stars, who are the great and powerful hunters. They dance to bring back the sun, just as the Bushman dances to bring back the moon." Opening his hands to my mother and lifting them toward her as though presenting her with a precious gift, he added, "And then there is Mantis, who steps down from the sky to the desert."

My mother was clearly taken aback by his beautiful words, to the extent that I believed he had won her over. But she cleared her throat and replied curtly, "Yes, well, that was very pretty, I am sure, but I do not see what it has to do with Africa."

"Africa is where these things are known. Africa is memory."

It was as though a trumpet had sounded over the scene of a great battle, signaling all the soldiers to lay down their arms. None of us spoke. I believe each of us had a different reason for retreating into silence. To me, Midnight made no sense at all, but his words seemed magical—like those of a sorcerer. Mother had plainly concluded that this African was beyond salvation, a heathen who ought to have remained in his loathsome homeland.

As for my father, his eyes were gleaming with pride, as though he had welcomed Robert Burns himself into his home.

AFTER A DESSERT of pears poached in wine and ginger, Father's favorite sweet, he built a fire in our hearth and invited us all to sit with him.

Midnight declined and begged permission to climb the stairs to our Lookout Tower in order to view the city. Not to be rude, Papa withdrew with our guest for a few minutes. When he returned, he told us that the African was gazing through the yellow and red glass panels of the skylight as though they were a threshold to a future world. Earlier that day, on a tour of our house, he had been fascinated by their translucency and had said that we had managed to steal a piece of Mantis's son, who was Rainbow, and place him within our reach. Mantis, as we were to learn, was the chief god in the Bushmen pantheon.

Midnight's words had elicited a murmur of delight from Father and a *tut-tut-tut* of disapproval from Mother. "I think he may sit there all night long," Papa said now.

He then assembled his tobacco pouch, flint, and pipe, and reclined in his armchair. I fought to stay awake but was yawning shamefully. I smiled whenever Mama or Papa looked at me, as I did not wish to play Old Gooseberry and ruin their reunion by confessing how bad I was feeling.

And yet I soon succumbed to a paroxysm of sobbing, simultaneously bringing up my supper all over our Persian rug.

"It is all the excitement of having you home," Mama said to Papa, fetching me a glass of water.

Papa felt my pulse. It was weak and dangerously quick. "You have been ill all day," he said irritably. "You are brave, but foolish not to have told us." He led me straight up to my room.

While I lay in bed, Mama grabbed Papa's arm and turned her back to me. My hearing has always been first class, and I overheard her whisper, "God help me, I know he may be leaving us. It may even be what he wishes."

Midnight then joined them in the corridor. After receiving permission from Papa, he sat on my bed and placed a moistened towel over my forehead. Mama stood behind him, her hands clutching at her handkerchief, ready to pounce on him if he in any way tried to hurt me.

FOR THE NEXT three days, I was delirious with fever. While drifting over waves of light and dark, I once glimpsed a burning horse galloping up our street. I tasted opium on my tongue at times. It tasted of the moon, but I cannot say why.

It seemed to me as though Midnight stayed with me the entire time. During periods of lucidity, I reasoned that I must have been hallucinating. Yet I later found out that he did indeed spend three straight days by my side, sleeping on the settee that he and my father positioned at the foot of my bed. He spoke to me in a mixture of English and his own language, full of clicking noises not unlike bird calls, until I almost believed I could understand what he was saying.

On four separate occasions, according to Papa, when I was given to chills, Midnight curled up behind me to warm me with his body heat. I remember one of these times clearly, and I am firmly of the opinion that he gave me something of his own self, although I don't know how. I only know that something not easily explained was exchanged between us, because even now, decades later, there is a part of him that resides in me. If it had not been for his gift, I believe I would have succumbed then to the cold death wishing to claim me.

Several times I awoke from dreams of being buried alive to discover him placing his warm mouth directly over my nose. My mother later confessed that she was horrified to witness this the first time, but she realized that Midnight was simply sucking the noxious fluids out of me to clear my blocked breathing passages. Each time he completed such a treatment, she reported, I stopped wheezing and fell back to sleep.

Once, when I was still greatly congested, the Bushman puffed mightily at his tiny clay pipe and aimed the smoke into my ears, making them crackle like melting ice.

So impressed was Mother by his loyalty and care that she once brought his hand to her lips and kissed it, whereupon he smiled and said, "Hyena will not steal your son, Mrs. Stewart."

Mother was too panicked to ponder what he meant. She only cared that his intention to see me well was firm.

To know how iron-strong gratitude can be, ask any mother whose child has been saved by another person. Over the course of these three days of precious care, Mama was won to Midnight's favor forever.

On the third night Midnight sat me down on my bed, lit his small clay pipe, and blew sweet-scented smoke in my ears again. This made me feel as though iron gates were opening at my temples. Then he had me open my mouth. Puckering his lips, he directed a stream of smoke in there as well, then several more, each time instructing me to breathe in deeply.

This time the smoke was not tobacco—or not only tobacco. I do not know what weed, leaf, flower, resin, or combination thereof was in his glowing bowl. Years later, I spoke to a man in London who had lived for a decade in southern Africa and who told me that hashish is used in some of the Bushman rituals. I cannot vouch for the accuracy of this information, but I am certain that Midnight's smoke had the effect of deepening the beating of my heart at first, then lulling me into a soft slumber. As the bells of the St. Bento Church were tolling two in the morning, I woke to see an animal face peering at me from the darkness of the corridor. At first I thought it was Fanny, but when I took a step toward her, I realized it was Daniel, wearing one of his horned masks.

My heart swelled with fright. Daniel receded swiftly into the shadows, but the tips of his horns were visible as two glowing points of violet light.

"Is it Hyena?" Midnight whispered from his settee. He must have been watching me for some time. He approached me, naked. I could feel his heat radiating toward me.

"You there!" he called to Daniel. "We know who you are. We know your name and you are Hyena!"

The masked apparition ran away from us down the corridor and scurried up the stairs.

"Where is he now?" asked Midnight.

"I think he's gone up to the Lookout Tower."

The African took my hand and helped me to my feet. My body felt heavy and alien. Despite his having cared for me over the last few days, I wasn't sure if I ought to trust him. In the unsettling darkness, he seemed a creature of shadows.

"The Time of the Hyena is on you," he said. "He is a clever and powerful animal we have in Africa. He is fooling you. For Daniel is gone and you cannot win him back, no matter what you do. But Hyena is as good a mimic as you are. You are being tricked."

I made no reply; I was confused.

Patting my shoulder, Midnight said, "Mantis will help us." At that, he lifted the child's rattle he had been carrying with him and shook it.

"Who is Mantis?"

"Mantis is an insect, and he is very, very small, but with big-big power. I shall need his help to frighten Hyena away and make him never return."

Midnight went to the window and opened the shutters and mosquito screens. The moon was nearly full. Crescents of light fell across his back and legs. It was unsettling to see him naked, for the only man I had seen in this way was my father.

I noticed four lines of scars on Midnight's back. When I asked him about them, he told me he had once been attacked by a wild beast but had escaped with his life. "Do you know what a lion is?" he asked.

"Yes," I replied.

"Lions kill hyenas. They are very, very strong. Now, will *you* be strong and come up the stairs with me to fight Hyena?"

I offered him my hand. His grip was powerful; I could not have escaped him even if I'd wanted to. He lit his wee clay pipe again and blew his sweet smoke in my ears and my mouth, just as he had done earlier. It warmed me to the tips of my fingers and toes. I could feel my heartbeat swaying me. My breaths came like wind across stones.

Turning from me, he drew the fumes deep into his chest in a single continuous stream that vanished somewhere deep inside him. I imagined it forming a swirling mist in his gut.

"Now we shall hunt Hyena," he said, placing his pipe down on the table by the head of my bed.

"Do I have to?"

"I will not abandon you, John. Your friend Midnight will always fight alongside you." He smiled. "Come. We shall find Hyena and tell him that he must leave."

He led me through my doorway by the light of his candle and together we climbed the stairs. The door to the Lookout Tower was shut. I closed my eyes to try to calm myself. Time seemed to have come to a halt.

"Must we go in?" I asked.

"Yes. I came up here today to prepare the room for our hunt. It has to be now. We must face him like Bushmen and tell him that we know who he is and that he is an impostor. We must show him that we are lions and will devour him if he stays. And the time is now—that is why he appeared to you. When we go inside, all you are to say to him is, 'I know who you are; you are Hyena.' Nothing else. Nothing! He is a trickster. He is clever-clever. He will find your weakness if you say anything else. You understand, John?"

"I think so."

Midnight reached for the handle.

"Wait!" I cried, but it was too late.

The door swung open. Daniel stood before us in his horned mask.

"We saw you from afar and are dying of hunger," Midnight said to Daniel.

The African eased the door closed behind us. He placed his candle on the ground, then shook his rattle at the lad and said, "We know who you are; you are Hyena."

Midnight's eyes opened wide. A low rumbling commenced in his gut and increased in volume to a drumming sound so loud it shook the walls.

Daniel removed his mask. Pale and swollen, his skin looked as though it might drop off in clumps. He beseeched me to stop the Bushman from drumming. "Why have you betrayed me again?" he moaned.

I was tempted to plead for his forgiveness, but when Midnight squeezed my hand, I spoke as instructed: "I know who you are. You are Hyena."

Midnight handed me his rattle and told me to toss it at Daniel's chest, but I hesitated. When the lad took a step toward me, the African shouted, "Hit him with it! Throw it now, John!"

I tossed it at him. It hit against his shoulder and fell to the ground. But it changed its form as it fell to become a dark mantis, head proudly erect, arms raised in the air as though ready for attack.

Slowly, it began to crawl toward Midnight.

Daniel reached out to me in fright.

"Do not touch him!" Midnight warned me.

I repeated, "I know who you are. You are Hyena."

Daniel lunged, and I jumped back. Midnight moved in between us, his back to Daniel. I could no longer see the lad, but I could hear him pounding his fists against the African's back.

A great knot the size of my fist began to form at the midpoint of Midnight's gut—at his center, so to speak—bobbing in and out, the focal point of his inner drumming.

The Bushman raised both his arms in the air and began to stamp his feet. Whipping round to face Daniel, he ceased his drumming. The Lookout Tower was alone at the center of the world.

The African leaned back and inhaled quickly. A low growl emanated from his chest, growing in intensity until the air itself seemed to vibrate. The smoke that he had stored in his gut spiraled from his mouth and rose to the skylight in a swirling ribbon. "Growl," he ordered.

I did as he said. Our two voices rooted me to the spot. After a few seconds, Midnight roared with such animal ferocity and violence that he might have split the room in two.

It did not occur to me that Midnight must have woken the entire neighborhood until my father rushed into the room wearing a terrified expression.

Papa glanced between Midnight and myself with a startled expression, since we were both as naked as the day we emerged into this world. He demanded to know what in Robert the Bruce we were doing in the Lookout Tower at this ungodly hour and, additionally, without a single thread of clothing to cover our manhood. "I hope you two have a proper explanation," he warned, his voice threateningly deep.

"We are very, very much better now," the African declared. "We have chased Hyena away. Hyena is always afraid of Lion." He twirled the rattle. "And little Mantis told him that he was never to return to us. He will never bother your son again."

"THE *BOGLE* IS gone," I said to Papa. *Bogle* was a Scots word for ghost.

"You nearly frightened me to death!" he cried as Mama appeared in the doorway, clutching a poker.

She gasped at our nakedness, then looked me hard and long in the eyes. I was sure I'd be punished, but instead she laughed as though Midnight and I were the funniest thing she'd ever seen. Then, through a process of transformation known only to the heart, she wept.

"There, there, May," Papa said, kissing her brow. "Everything is fine now."

Finally, she dried her eyes. "I am so sorry. You must all think me such a fool."

We all assured her of the contrary, Papa adding rather charmingly that he would be eternally wed to such a fool with the greatest of happiness. Though her hair was a mess and her eyes red, I found Mama incomparably beautiful at that moment.

When she'd calmed down, she begged me to put on some clothing. "You can come back to bed with us tonight if you like," she added.

"No, Mama, I should like to return to my room, if you don't mind."

"You would prefer that?" Papa asked, plainly surprised.

"Yes, if Midnight may be allowed to stay with me."

"Of course," Mama said, smiling at our guest, who was grinning infectiously from ear to ear.

She then surprised me by grasping Midnight's hand and saying, "I sincerely hope that you will stay with us for quite some time. If you still desire a place in our home, we shall fix the Lookout Tower for you to use as your own apartment. That is, should you forgive my previous rudeness."

Tears filled Midnight's eyes. "Yes, that would be very, very good indeed."

Clasping his hand to her cheek, she added, "Thank you for returning John to me. I shall never forget your kindness. You will always be able to depend on me as though I were one of your people."

Papa thanked Midnight as well and kissed Mama many times. Then he hoisted me up over his shoulder and carried me downstairs, tickling me, pretending he'd caught a young monster of the loch, a *kelpie.* I was howling for him to stop, but he was merciless in his affection. Behind us, Mama was talking in hushed tones to Midnight, as though they had been intimate friends for ages.

Once I had been swung into bed, Papa ruffled my hair and said, "Now sleep. Enough of this excitement." He raised his fists. "No more lions, hyenas, mantises, or anything else."

"No," I agreed.

"Good night, Midnight," Papa said to our guest. "And thank you."

"Good night, Mr. Stewart," the African replied with a wave.

When my parents had gone, and long after Midnight was asleep, I remained awake, staring at his dark head, believing I could hear an almost imperceptible drumming coming from a strange landscape deep inside him.

XIII

I AWOKE IN THE MORNING AND DISCOVERED—to my disappointment—that Midnight had already left with my father. After breakfast, I took Fanny for a walk, having neglected her for weeks. At the wharf that day, I discovered that Daniel's drowning had removed all desire on my part to swim in the river. I was completely petrified by the idea of being unable to see through the murky water, and though I presumed that I would soon overcome this fear, I was wrong; I would never again voluntarily enter the water. Not even Midnight could cure me of this.

The African and my father returned that evening, just before supper. On seeing me, Midnight gave me a hearty smile, which I returned in kind, but I was unsettled by everything that had happened to me in his presence. I began to feel the enormous power he had over me. One word of reproach from him would have dried my spirits to nothing.

We chatted for a while, mostly about Porto. He found the city most entertaining, particularly its residents. He held that the Portuguese spoke louder than any people he had ever known.

I stared at him all evening and barely spoke. I wondered

if, in the tales of King Arthur my father had told me, Merlin might have been bronze-skinned and tiny. I tried to imagine the Bushman in his African homeland, a sparkling wand in his hand.

While wolfing down a gargantuan helping of baked apples, I commented on Midnight's having again removed his shoes at our door. But instead of saying that I found this a primitive practice—as my parents expected—I declared that it was the height of civilized deportment, since in so doing he avoided tracking all manner of muck into the house. Father stared at me in bewilderment. Mother, however, knowing only too well my predilection for mimicry, replied, "John, you may not walk in the house barefoot. You shall wear your shoes."

"But the filth!"

"The filth stays! And your shoes as well. Midnight is Midnight and you are you."

"That is very, very true," the African agreed, laughing.

"Aye," Papa seconded, "she's trumped you, lad."

I looked up at Midnight for some show of support, but he showed me an expression of helplessness in the face of our family disagreement.

Despite my parents' firm disapproval, in the end I began removing my shoes at the door as well, and it is a practice I have kept to this day. I also request it of my family and all visitors, to the exasperation of many but to the great benefit of my home.

I remember adding that night, as my final protest against my parents' wishes, "But with our shoes on in the house we must look like barbarians to him!"

This seemingly innocent statement of mine is one I have often remembered, as I believe I hit the truth dead center. Midnight must have regarded us all—my family included—as people living in dollhouses, leading porcelain and silk lives. How could he have not felt this when, as I later learned, his own early life had been one of two- and three-day hunts for giant beasts called eland; of treks through the desert sands in search of food, his water carried in ostrich eggs; of narrow escapes from Dutch muskets, English bayonets, and Zulu spears? Our Portuguese stage in comparison must have seemed tiny indeed, an African Old Testament drama reduced to the size of a European puppet show.

Not that I should have desired the life he'd had. Nor did he ever indicate disdain for ours, nearly always showing an amused curiosity when faced with things he didn't understand. Not that he was perfect, but I believe that his unqualified acceptance of us speaks eloquently for his tolerant spirit and faith in everyone's good intentions. None of us, I am sure, could have adapted to his Africa so graciously and happily.

I trailed him like a newborn duckling over those first weeks, delighted by his prancing gait, elfin grin, and woolly peppercorns of hair. I adored filling his pipe, helping him buckle his shoes, and leading him through the city by the hand. I listened in awe to his stories of the African desert while seated at his feet. I felt as though I had found a living treasure. I'd not have traded knowing him for a king's ransom in gold.

DURING THOSE FIRST months with Midnight, Mother, Father, and I tested his near-boundless patience by embarking upon separate projects with him—to varying degrees of success.

My mother's project was to familiarize him with Portuguese social etiquette, though she made it clear that by virtue of saving me he had forever won the right to behave as he wished in our home. She was encouraging and open with him, in a way I had never seen her with anyone else, never once raising her voice at him in anger—something I wish I could say with regard to myself. These lessons in etiquette were only for those times when we went out with him in public. They were for both his benefit and ours, since Mama was of the opinion that the quicker he could mix on equal footing with Europeans the easier his life would become.

Midnight had learned much in the way of European manners while working as a servant in the Cape Colony, but there were still rules to be learned in order to prepare him for his new life in a city far larger than any in southern Africa. Among the most essential were learning to stroll with my mother on his arm, tying a cravat without cutting off the blood flow to his head, referring only in code to bodily functions, and bowing to ladies upon making their acquaintance.

These lessons were given in English, as Midnight was never able to learn Portuguese in any depth. Nevertheless, he did well with the few social phrases he needed for the drawing-room parties my parents occasionally asked him to attend. These stock phrases were ghastly, in my opinion, and his favorite was especially awful: *Madam, not even the full moon over a dark horizon could be more radiant than you are tonight....*

In the end, the Bushman mastered all of my mother's social graces with admirable aplomb save for two: wearing a cravat, which was torture for him and a practice that he gave up after a first year of effort, and saying his thank-yous. The very concept of this latter commonplace nicety baffled him, and he could never safely conclude when to express his thanks and when not to.

In the hopes of avoiding any unpleasantness that might result from this confusion, Mother wrote out guidelines that she read aloud to us one evening while Midnight and my father sat smoking by the hearth:

Part I: Midnight was never to be forced to express his gratitude at home. His thanks would be assumed by everyone.

Part II: When in public with one of us, a signal would be given to Midnight at the moment he was to thank a person outside the family.

Part III: When he was alone in public, Midnight was to say *thank you* whenever anyone spoke more than a few words to him or did anything in his presence, even if it seemed to him highly unlikely that such an action merited his gratitude.

This last instruction led, at times, to comic results, as when Midnight would forget the rules and thank Papa for simply locking the front door or Mama for avoiding a dog dropping in the street. Regrettably, this difficulty also provoked some disagreements as well. The one I would most prefer to forget happened only a month after he came to stay with us. Midnight and I had just purchased custard tarts with powdered cinnamon at our favorite pastry shop on the Rua de Cedofeita when, not four paces from us, a large woman in a ruffled dress of crimson tripped on a dislodged cobble. She fairly flew through the air, shrieking like Lilith, as my grandmother Rosa used to say, and would have fallen flat on her face had Midnight not—with his harelike reflexes—dashed forward and reached for her, serving as a human barrier. It was a triumph against all odds, since she outweighed the African by forty or fifty pounds. Unfortunately, in pressing against him, the wayward woman crushed Midnight's tart against his chest, leaving a yellow custard stain on the beautiful blue brocade waistcoat my father had bought for him.

Unperturbed, Midnight steadied the woman, who heaved a sigh of relief in the best operatic tradition and patted her brow with a white silk handkerchief pulled from her bosom. Before I could stop him, he exclaimed, "Thank you so much," in all sincerity, but our matron believed herself cruelly ridiculed.

"Unhand me, sir!" she exclaimed.

As she stared contemptuously at Midnight, I tried to make amends. "He is thanking you for the honor of being able to assist you to your feet and see you safely on your way."

She stared at us as though we had insulted her again. And I shall never forget what she said: "Keep your ugly black paws off me, you monkey!"

She spoke this sentence in Portuguese, of course. Hence, Midnight was blessedly ignorant of the precise meaning of her words.

Enraged she evidently was, but not nearly as cross as I. For though I had overheard neighbors gossiping about Midnight, no one had yet spoken of him rudely in my presence. Before I could squash the rest of my tart in *her* bosom, Midnight recited one of the flattering phrases he had learned from Mother: "That dress, though most lovely, is but a pale shadow of your own beauty."

Now we are fried for sure! I thought. I did not expect, however, for her to burst into hot tears, perhaps owing to Midnight's near-perfect Portuguese, which left her completely nonplussed. Her sobbing served to draw a crowd, since the people of my homeland—like the English— gather around misfortune like vultures to a dying lamb. Soon, Midnight and I found ourselves surrounded by gawking faces.

"I've seen that monkey before," one man said, pointing at the Bushman. "He belongs to Stewart the Scotsman."

"He ought to be caged!" another shouted.

This latter judgment brought out the Highlander in me, and I let loose a flurry of epithets that Daniel had taught me, the choicest of which was that the woman in question plainly had the mind of a camel, since even a simpleton knew that monkeys had hands and not paws. I elaborated on this by stating that it was obvious that she had crashed headlong into my friend like a driverless carriage and caused him to stain his waistcoat, as anyone who was not blinded by stupidity could see, since her offending forearm—the size of a stuffed capon—was smeared with telling yellow stains.

Comparing the sobbing woman to either a camel *or* a carriage *or* a capon might have been acceptable, but saying all three so forthrightly in one sentence served not to win me admiration as a child of advanced vocabulary, as it might have, but rather condemnation as a rude and impudent cur. A man wearing a shearer's apron stained black with grease even dared to grab my arm and shake me. "You little sod," he said. "I ought to beat your bottom here in the street!"

This affront roused Midnight from his anxious confusion. Advancing toward the man, he said, "Please, sir, let the lad go."

Blood shone in the moon-whiteness of the African's eyes. It was lucky for our shearer that the Bushman carried no knife; he might have killed the man that day as quickly as he would have a jackal coveting his child.

Midnight's few words quieted the crowd, probably because he spoke them in English, which tends to intimidate the Portuguese. Or possibly it was because no one expected him to be able to speak any language at all—or to dare to defy a Portuguese man.

The shearer let me go, but only so he might confront Midnight. Yet as he strode forward, the African—to my great surprise—hoisted me over his shoulder. I do not know if he intended this as the brilliant coup it was. Likely, he simply wished to protect me. Whatever the case, the shearer was not about to fight a man carrying a young lad.

Midnight walked with me through the parting crowd without saying a word. After he turned the corner, he put me down. "The gemsbok is not bothered by ants, tortoises, and hedgehogs," he told me.

"What's a gemsbok?"

"A noble animal, a kind of deer. He has a crescent horn on his head." He held my chin in his hand. "John, this may come as a surprise to you, but you are not a crocodile."

"Sorry?"

"You must not let yourself be provoked so very, very easily."

Midnight spread his hands like a fan atop his head and crouched into a posture of expectancy, as though he were an animal listening for a far-off call. His nostrils flared and his fingers wiggled. He sniffed at the air, scenting something upwind.

This, then, was a gemsbok. He was imitating it. Or, as he would tell me later, *inhabiting it.*

"This is how you must act," he said. "No more shouting at strangers."

His criticism shamed me. "But that woman was rude to you! She said horrible things."

He made no effort to answer or comfort me, which struck me as heartless. Frustration cast tears down my cheek. Still he would not move. Finally, I gave in and imitated him, placing my own fanned hands atop my head and making believe that I, too, was a gemsbok.

"Good," he said, smiling. He took my hand and held it to his heart. "No more crying. It is much more important that you teach me a song. I've been meaning to ask you for one."

Children's moods change so quickly. "Which?" I asked eagerly.

"One of your father's songs. Any of them. I should very, very much like to learn one."

Right there on the street, I sang the first verse of "The Foggy, Foggy Dew": *Oh, I am a bachelor, I live by myself, and I work at the weaver trade. . . .*

That was to be the first of many tunes that I would teach Midnight. In exchange, he helped me learn several songs belonging to his people. I even mastered a secret one about rain bringing life to a barren desert. I am still able to sing it. And I believe I am the only European who can.

I DISCOVERED MY project with Midnight while reading aloud to my parents, a practice in which they both took great delight and which was intended to perfect my diction. In addition to Robert Burns and certain minor Scottish poets whom no one south of Hadrian's Wall had ever heard of, Papa was a great aficionado of Latin and Greek classics. He read English translations, however, since he was not a scholar, borrowing them from the library at the British club near the riverside. One particular night, I began to read from Xenophon's "On Hunting," which Papa had brought home that evening, believing it would entertain our guest. I found it mostly tedious myself, and Mama thought it appalling. She held that "chasing God's poor little creatures through a forest and killing them most cruelly" was depraved.

"The first pursuit that a lad just emerging from boyhood ought to take up is hunting," I read. *"And afterward he may go on to the other branches of education, provided he has the means."*

"Rubbish!" Mama scoffed.

"Continue," Papa prompted sternly.

As a piece of writing it was one extended yawn, but when I glanced at Midnight I discovered his head tilted in eager expectancy, as though this essay were the answer to a riddle over which he'd long puzzled, so I invited him to read from the book himself.

"I cannot," he replied. When I inquired as to why, he said, "Because . . . because I cannot read or write."

"Just try," I said, holding the leather-bound text out to him.

"John, please do not nettle Midnight," said Mama quickly, laying her embroidery down in her lap. "You were doing splendidly and we should all be pleased to hear more. Is that not right, dear?"

"Aye, your voice has improved greatly of late," Papa agreed, moving the candlesticks on our tea table nearer to me so I might have more light.

"No, let Midnight," I replied sulkily.

"But it is impossible," the Bushman repeated. When he smiled apologetically, my heart tumbled, for I realized it was true; no one had ever taken the time to help him to learn to read and write, which seemed a monstrous injustice. I continued to read aloud, but my thoughts were already searching out where I had left my *Greenwood's English Grammar.* That night, I found it at the bottom of my chest.

In the morning I discovered Midnight standing naked in our Lookout Tower, staring at the rooftops of the city. "I shall teach you to read and write," I told him, showing him my primer.

He laughed at my forthright statement and then, realizing that I meant it, pressed his fingertips to his temples as though his head were throbbing at the very thought.

"No, it will be easy," I said. "You'll see."

After he'd dressed, I took his hand and brought him to our garden, so that he might learn to design letters in the sunshine.

Progress was slow. During this first lesson, I only got him to draw the letters *A, B, C, D,* and *E,* and even those rather poorly. He preferred turning his letters into animals, the *A* becoming the legs of a giraffe, for instance, and the *B* the eyes of a crocodile viewed from above.

Over the next few weeks I worked with Midnight every day after breakfast. Soon he was able to sketch each of the twenty-six letters without addition of muzzle, horns, hooves, or tail. I thereafter settled upon a process that guaranteed us slow but steady progress. Standing as though spotlit in a theater, gesticulating wildly, I would read aloud a paragraph to Midnight from a classical volume, which always pleased him greatly and sometimes provoked him to giggles. Then we would sit next to each other and read over this same excerpt, the Bushman pointing with his finger at the words and sounding them out.

In this way, we read key paragraphs of military drama from Herodotus, Ovid, and Josephus at least a dozen times each. Midnight's favorite was far and away Strabo's account of the Roman general Pompey's defeat at the hands of King Mithradates of Pontus. Estimating that we read this one at least once a week for two years, I would say that we relived this unusual battle more than one hundred times, to the point where we could recite it by heart. It never ceased to delight Midnight how Pompey's superior forces were defeated by nothing more than honey. For while encamped on the Black Sea coast of Turkey, at a place called Trabzon, his troops gorged themselves on combs made by bees that had collected the poisonous pollen of rhododendron blossoms. Those who ate only a little were given to the wobbly walk and slurred speech of men who have downed several drams too many. Those who ate their fill were rendered mad or insensible. In their debilitated condition, they were slaughtered by Mithradates's forces.

Midnight and I referred to it as the Battle of the Mad Honey.

This inspired such mirth in him because, to his people, honey was the single most delightful thing in the world, a harbinger of health, good luck, and joy. As a youth, he would smoke the bees out of their hives to steal their treasure. Honey was also Mantis's favorite food. It was wisdom—and sunlight—given form. To imagine that it might be able to change the course of history in a military battle... This was so unexpected that he never ceased to be astonished and delighted by the notion.

MY FATHER'S PLANS for Midnight were responsible for his long journey from Africa to Europe. Papa had made the acquaintance of the Bushman while on an extended visit to a newly established vineyard belonging to a stern Yorkshireman named Reynolds a day's ride from Cape Town. Midnight was referred to as a servant in the man's home, but there was not a drop of liberty to his terms of employment.

Just after Papa's arrival, a terribly ill Dutchman from a nearby property turned up at the vineyard, seeking medical help. Over the next three days, Father watched Midnight cure the man of advanced pleurisy by applying poultices of mashed herbs to his chest and administering sweet-smelling infusions. On the fourth day, the Dutchman was fit enough to return home.

Several days later, through a ritual of smoke and dance, Midnight then cured—in Papa's presence—a youthful Zulu woman who had been possessed by an evil spirit. My father would not have bet a farthing on her recovery, yet recover she did.

With little faith in the merits of European medicine, having recently witnessed its barbarous methods foisted upon me, Papa realized that this was the man to help his ailing son—if he could convince him to return to Portugal. It proved a surprisingly straightforward task; Midnight wished to seek out medical men in Europe who might help him discover which plants might be used to combat the illness of chills and blisters that had already killed thousands of his people, since nothing he or any other local healer had yet tried was of any use. Upon further inquiry, my father learned that this particular affliction was smallpox.

Midnight's rationale for seeking help in Europe was based on the notion that the disease had been brought to Africa by the Dutch and English. He reasoned that the plant extracts needed to combat it would be found in its place of origin. When and if he found the medicinal plants he was looking for in Portugal, he would return to Africa with them.

Papa proposed to Midnight that he grow in our back garden any specimens that might prove useful to his experiments. He let it be known as well that it would certainly be appreciated by Mama if Midnight could at the same time restore a part of our small rectangle of land to its glory days before my birth. Back then, my Grandfather João had coaxed all manner of colorful blossoms, including some rare Turkish roses, from its soil.

The last part of Papa's plan, which he had not yet mentioned to Midnight, was that he wished for the African to serve as a companion to my mother and myself during his periods of absence, there still being the necessity of his traveling upriver to survey lands every six to eight weeks.

Only one obstacle to Midnight's leaving Africa with my father remained: He was a slave belonging to Reynolds, and the Englishman would not let him go for any price. Not only did he treasure the Bushman's considerable medical skills, but he also greatly valued his talents as an interpreter. Mrs. Reynolds, a frail woman of Swiss extraction from Geneva, who feared all manner of local illnesses, would permit no talk of Midnight's possible sale. My father and the Bushman were therefore forced to plan an escape.

Having given Reynolds a false date for his return voyage to Europe, Father journeyed alone to Cape Town on horseback at the appointed time: precisely three days before Reynolds and Midnight were to make their monthly visit to the city for supplies.

My father registered under a false name at the Black Horse Tavern, where, growing more anxious and ill-tempered with each passing day, he awaited Midnight.

It was customary for the Bushman to be given one entire night to spend as he wished while his English employer relieved himself of his Calvinist wife's religious constraints at an infamous brothel. Except that this month—smelling a foul Scottish trap—Reynolds didn't go to Cape

Town and he forbade Midnight from leaving the homestead. And so the night that Papa and the Bushman had agreed upon for their rendezvous came and went. The following evening as well. At which point, my father, gravely disappointed, made plans to leave two days later on a Dutch vessel.

The next evening at sundown, however, while Father sat sipping a gin at the Black Horse, Midnight stepped inside, huffing and puffing, naked from the waist up and barefoot. He carried a small sack containing medicinal herbs, a quiver with arrows, a bow, and an ostrich egg recently emptied of its last drop of water. A ruckus followed, because no *kaffir,* as the expatriate Europeans referred to the indigenous peoples, was allowed inside such an establishment. Seeing that he was not about to reverse this absurd ruling, Papa led Midnight outside, where the Bushman promptly imbibed so much water from a civic well that his belly swelled to near bursting. He then explained calmly that he had come directly on foot all the way from his farm, twenty miles by Father's reckoning. That might have been extraordinary enough, but he had accomplished this feat in little more than three hours, judging by the angle of the sun at departure and arrival, running most of the way.

Papa realized that Reynolds might already be in furious pursuit of Midnight, so they set off immediately on the first available boat, a schooner that took them not to Europe but to a nearby outpost, where supplies of wheat, barley, and cloth were unloaded. They remained in the only inn there under false names, though Midnight, as an African, was obliged to sleep on the floor of the stables. A few days later they were able to book passage on another Dutch ship headed for Holland.

After my father told me all this, I asked if he had indeed found suitable land in Africa, since he had mentioned nothing about it since his return. "I'm afraid not, John," he replied. "The land is good, but there is no political stability at present, and there won't be for some time to come. If I were to purchase land there, two years from now those same acres might belong to a Zulu chief or Dutchman. But do not fear, we shall get our vineyard here, sooner or later. That I promise you."

Then I asked the more troubling question: If Midnight truly was Mr. Reynolds's property, then was it right for my father to have helped him escape? "Is that not a form of robbery?"

"Aye, I asked myself that more than once, laddie." He took my hand. "But before I answer, I want to put a question to you. Is it right for one man to own another?"

I wasn't sure how to reply.

"Does not the bird market of Porto enrage you, laddie?" he continued. "How much more of an infamy is it when men and women are bartered, when such miserable conditions are foisted upon reasoning beings?"

My hatred for the traffic in birds was such that it was unnecessary to say an additional word on the subject. From that moment on, I knew where I stood.

XIV

VIOLETA HAD NOT YET VANISHED FROM PORTO, and one Saturday afternoon Midnight and I hid around a corner to watch her selling her embroidered prayers in New Square. The Bushman was charmed to learn that such a young lass knew nearly all the constellations in the sky. When I told him of the terrible fate that had befallen her, he said, "Likely she is being haunted now by Hyena, just as you were, John."

I begged him not to try to visit her, explaining she'd be beaten if she was discovered talking to him. Seeing my agitation, he agreed and gazed up into the heavens, speaking for a few moments in the swift clicks of his own language.

"What are you saying?" I asked.

"It will be up to the hunters in the sky to defend Violeta, and I have asked for their help."

I took him next to the spot at the river where Daniel had drowned. I told him everything that happened on our last day together, confessing that I may have pushed the lad toward his death by telling him that Violeta would leave for America without him. Midnight cupped my chin but said nothing. Instead, he made me stare at my reflection in the water, his strong hands on my shoulders. "John, we are each small beings. And you are not nearly as powerful as you sometimes think you are. Mantis had abandoned Daniel. *That* was what caused him to drown."

Midnight sensed my doubts and held the back of my neck as we walked away, perhaps hoping to guide me toward certainty. That night he heard me crying and tiptoed to my room. Once again he blew smoke from his pipe into my mouth until my room darkened and I could see nothing. Then, lighting my candle, he closed my door and asked me to hold my palm over the flame for as long as I could stand it. Petrified, I replied that I did not believe I could do it. He held out his arms and fluttered them amid the swirling smoke, then brought them slowly together over his head, explaining that the burn would attract a very special butterfly to me and that she would apologize to Daniel for me. "It is she who makes amends in the other world," he said.

He took my right hand and began rubbing it between both of his, so briskly that the friction seemed to create a moist layer of heat inside my palm. I suspect now that he coated my skin with a protective glaze of some sort; at the time I was too scared to notice, but I can recall a sour scent on my fingers.

"You must not shout," Midnight warned me. "Or you will frighten away Butterfly."

Taking a last deep breath, I slipped my hand into the center of the flame. The pain was crippling and I stifled a shriek. I held out as long as I could, surely no more than a second, then whipped my scorched hand away. Midnight told me I had done well. "Like a Bushman warrior," he said, admiration flashing in his eyes. Blowing out the candle, he told me to hold out my hand, with the burn facing up.

When I did, all my breath and life centered on that throbbing pain. My spirit seemed to be opening and closing, like a fist flexing, searching for forgiveness. At length, Midnight crouched next to me and whispered, "There she is!"

"Who?"

"Butterfly. She has alighted on your hand and is healing the burn. She is licking."

"What color is she?"

"Sssshhh—whisper. She has the pink, blue, and black of her mother, the Desert Wind." He patted my back. I felt my heartbeat swaying me. "She is almost finished, John. When I tap you again, lift your hand gently-gently and say, 'I send Butterfly into the forest of night.'"

As I spoke, the flutter of air against my rising hand made me start. "I think I felt her," I whispered.

Midnight then coated my burn with herbs he fetched from the Lookout Tower and chewed into a paste. "This will seal Butterfly's healing inside you."

"Does Butterfly always know where to find the dead?" I asked.

"Always." He touched his nose and sniffed. "She can locate every flower that has ever been born."

PAPA SOUGHT TO make Midnight familiar with the techniques of topographical mapmaking, a practice for which he believed that the Bushman might have some aptitude. But when he discovered that behind his back his colleagues cackled like magpies at what they referred to as "Stewart's monkey," he never again asked Midnight to accompany him to his office. With Scottish stoicism, he got on with the business at hand, purchasing shovels, rakes, hoes, and picks of varying shapes and sizes for the horticultural laboratory and verdant paradise that was to be our garden.

Midnight, Fanny, and I were recruited for this restoration, but nearly all the valuable labor was provided by our sturdy African. To our happy surprise, we soon discovered that the petrified ropes of rosebushes that swirled into a mighty tangle over our property were not all dead. It took weeks of daily toil to clear a good-size area for Midnight's planting and to prompt the long-suffering rosebushes toward health, by which time it was already the end of October. It was a mild autumn, however, and one rosebush gave us three yellow blooms in early January. We presented them to my mother, who threaded their stems into her slender vase of blue and white porcelain. She still has a rough sketch I made of this arrangement to this very day.

Midnight then gathered ideas on what medicinal plants to grow from a visit we made to the Quinta dos Arcos, a botanical garden on the outskirts of the city. Benjamin Seixas, our local apothecary and a family friend, offered the African seeds for hyssop, arnica, foxglove, coltsfoot, and other species of benefit to Europeans, as well as cuttings of lavender, senna, sage, verbena, and other useful herbs.

OUR FONDNESS FOR Midnight did not prevent us from having second thoughts about his staying with us, and I occasionally overheard my parents discussing behind their closed door whether they ought to subject him to the ridicule of the townspeople. Then there were the times when he was churlish and even rude. A sensible reason for such behavior generally came to the fore, however. Sometimes our own misunderstanding of his motives worsened an already unpleasant situation, as when he took ill the first time, developing ticklish pimples all over his body. We worried for a day or two that it might be a grave disease of some sort, but it soon became clear to Mother that it was only chicken pox, which was rather extraordinary, since it was unheard of in adults in Portugal. What proved vexing, however, was that he locked himself in the Lookout Tower and would not emerge.

After a day and night of this behavior, my father had had enough. He stomped up the spiral staircase with my mother and me in tow and banged on the door, finally persuading the Bushman to open it a crack. As Papa entered, Midnight scurried to the back of the room.

"Now, sir, what is all this about?" Father asked.

"Please!" the African cried out. "I would like you to leave very, very immediately!" He waved his hands madly in front of his chest as though keeping a wild animal at bay.

"But you are ill."

"Do not fight me. Just go. I command you!"

Sensing the nature of Midnight's fears, Mama said, "Listen to me, Midnight. The three of us have already had chicken pox. We'll not fall prey to it again."

"You are too close to me, Mrs. Stewart. I beseech you to leave. Get out!"

"Your behavior is that of a child," Father snapped, which brought tears to Midnight's eyes.

None of us knew what to do about this stalemate. Finally, Mama said, "At least leave your door open and allow us to bring you some food."

When he reluctantly agreed, my mother prepared *caldo verde,* our local potato and kale soup, and had me bring it to him on a tray. I left the steaming bowl in the doorway, then stepped back so he would approach it, rather like feeding a wounded animal.

That night I tiptoed into Midnight's room long after he'd fallen asleep. I sat at the foot of his bed, wondering what to do. I was terribly tired, so when he rolled to his side, I simply crawled under the covers with him.

Awakening near dawn, I found him squatting in the corner, his teeth chattering.

"What are you doing over there?" I asked, sitting up and yawning.

"You disobeyed me," he said, scandalized. "You are wicked. Go!"

"I'll not go unless you speak to me about what's troubling you." When he refused to speak, I added, "I shall have wrinkles like Grandmother Rosa before I leave this room."

"You . . . you cannot be sure it is chicken pox. Your father told me that European physicians are very, very slow-witted."

I laughed. "Has anything at all we've said penetrated that stubborn skull of yours? My mother *knows* what is plaguing you. She makes no errors when it comes to these things, since she worries about them more than anyone else in the world."

He shook his head as he stood up. "But, John, she might be wrong. I might have something incurable that came with me from Africa. You might catch it by proximity. Mrs. Reynolds was always saying our illnesses would be the death of all Europeans. Mr. Reynolds shot several Bushmen with smallpox at the edge of our property rather than allow me to treat them." He rubbed his hand over his hair and moaned. "I did not help you frighten away Hyena only to kill you now."

His explanation was so moving that I considered myself cretinous for not having understood sooner the depth of his fear. "Midnight," I said gently, "I have been in bed with you much of the night and I am not ill. There is no danger."

He began to cry. "You must leave me be. Please . . ."

Looking at him in tears, his head in his hands, I was unable to restrain myself. I rushed headlong into him and hugged myself into his belly. He tried to push me away, but I hung on and breathed in the hot moist scent of him until he kissed the top of my head.

"Listen closely," I said, "my parents and I have faced this same beast and beaten him dead. He cannot hurt us again."

Then, on my absolute assurance that Mama and Papa would exercise care and not touch him directly, he allowed me to lead him down the stairs. Papa sat him before the fire and praised his courage. Mama heated some soup, then watched him closely to make sure he ate it all.

Over the next several days, he allowed my mother to dab his itchy pimples every few hours with a solution of zinc oxide, which gave him pinkish spots. When he looked at himself in the glass, he bared his teeth as though he were a leopard, then howled with glee.

*   *   *

MIDNIGHT WAS ILL many times that first year. We kept blaming the fog, which mixed with the smoke of fifteen thousand chimneys till one could barely see fifty paces ahead. In truth, however, the poor man took ill even when the sun was in full splendor. He suffered bouts of croup, boils, quinsy, dyspepsia, diarrhea, and a terrible dropsy of the extremities in which his wee feet swelled up to close to twice their natural size. Once, a reddish rash the shape of a three-clawed crab broke out across his right cheek and down his throat and was accompanied by chills. Then he began coughing up blood. It might have been scarlet fever, but as this was also a childhood disease, we could not be sure.

Though we were often desperate with worry, neither Midnight nor my parents were in any way inclined to permit a physician into our house. And so it was Senhor Benjamin, the apothecary who had supplied Midnight with seeds and cuttings, who saved us.

I'D ALWAYS REGARDED Senhor Benjamin as mildly threatening and generally undistinguished. This error in judgment was due, I believe, to his shortness of stature—which, before I met Midnight, implied insignificance to me—and his knowing brown eyes. Framed by oval spectacles, they were far more vigilant than any lad of my character might like.

Now, however, with Midnight ill with what was probably scarlet fever, he showed himself to be generous, meticulous, and indefatigable. I believe he would have weighed every grain of sand on the beach if it meant finding the one that might help our guest.

By the time the African's fever and rash had vanished and he had been declared fit again, Senhor Benjamin had become a trusted family friend. A widower of fifty-seven years of age, he began to sup with us every Friday night, and Father found in him the great friend he had been searching for all these years.

Midnight benefited greatly from this acquaintance; not only did he gain his own personal nursemaid and guardian, but he also earned himself an apprenticeship. Due to his worsening eyesight, Benjamin needed an assistant, so who better than Midnight?

No contract was ever signed; a simple handshake between the two men was considered quite sufficient. The African was to work for the apothecary for three years, four half-days a week, since he was not convinced that he would be able to bear being indoors longer than that. In return, he would be paid a small but fair salary. After three years, if he so desired and if both parties were willing, the Bushman would enter into a full partnership with Benjamin on payment of a sum to be decided later, which Father agreed to pay. If Midnight chose to return to Africa instead, no impediments of any kind would be put in his way.

The Bushman was overjoyed by this agreement, and I danced Fanny around the sitting room upon hearing the good news, since it meant that our friend would remain with us for three more years at the very least. Given my selfishness in matters of the heart, it ought to come as no surprise that I prayed for him to find a cure for smallpox that could be shipped to Africa without his having to leave us for even a day.

XV

AT THE VERY BEGINNING OF THE WORLD, A female bee rescued Mantis from the rising waters of the Great Flood by snatching him up and buzzing away. On the third day of their voyage over the endless sea, exhausted, flying with ever more difficulty, she espied a gigantic white flower. It was half-open and rising out of the water as though to summon the sun, which was still hidden behind the angry gray clouds of the diluvial rains. Before giving up her life, she deposited Mantis at the very heart of the blossom. And in him, she planted the seed of the first men and women.

THIS WAS HOW Midnight described the beginnings of the Bushmen and all the other tribes and nationalities of the world—even the Scots, though the image of a kilted Highlander sitting in the heart of a water lily might be considered preposterous by some.

I cannot describe with what delight I listened to this tale and many others besides. Midnight possessed a captivating voice and had a delicate and musical English pronunciation. Occasionally, he spoke whole sentences in the Bushman idiom, and it was as though I were listening to the first language of the world. I have always thought of Adam and Eve as being of Midnight's people.

He told me this particular tale while seated on a boulder upriver, a few miles east of Porto. He almost never spoke of such things inside the city's walls, for he said that it was practically impossible to give one's full attention to a story with so many people rushing about and making noise.

When I asked how a seed from a bee had become a man, he told me that all seeds were essentially one. Upon my request for a further explanation, all he would say was that these stories took place during the Age of the First People, when there was less differentiation between things. There was neither past nor future. It was always now.

SOME OF MIDNIGHT'S stories spoke of the need to follow the rains in the desert, and the first time he himself disappeared on such a journey was in early December of his first year with us, immediately prior to the start of his apprenticeship with Senhor Benjamin. It had been a hazy morning wholly without wind, and we expected the sun to shine by midday. Yet Midnight must have scented the violent swirling of faraway vapors; he ran up and down the stairs throughout breakfast, unable to eat or sit. Finally, he could remain inside no longer. He grabbed his eland-hide quiver and bow, together with the leather pack that had come in his trunk from Africa, and marched out of the house.

"Where in God's name do you think you're going?" Mama inquired.

"Quick—follow him, John!" Papa instructed me.

I leapt from the table, still dressed in my nightshirt, jumped into my boots at the door, took my coat from Mama, and raced after our guest. I found him just past the northern entrance to our street, near the municipal jailhouse. From this vantage point he could see over Porto's cragged landscape of tiled rooftops toward the faraway hills at the eastern horizon. He was singing a melody—the secret one he would later teach me.

On finishing his song, he pointed to the southeast, where I could see a funnel of bluish cloud releasing a gray ribbon of storm. He put his arm over my shoulder as we watched the distant heavens darken. At a first strike of lightning, a deep vibration started in his gut, and the subsequent ripple of thunder made him moan. Then a gust of frigid wind picked up some fallen leaves and carried them to our feet, whereupon he announced, "I shall be gone for a few days. But I shall be very, very well. You must not be concerned for me." And then he was off.

"Where are you going?" I called.

The urge to follow him gripped me, but I knew I'd be courting trouble if I didn't go home. On rushing there for permission to pursue him, I discovered Father leaving the house for his office.

"Where have you been, laddie? Did you find him?"

"He said he's leaving for a few days. He told me not to worry. But I *am* worried. I think he wants to find the storm. Can I go with him?"

"You saw the rains coming?"

"Yes."

Papa smiled. "It's like this, son: His people walk for days to follow the rains. In a desert, water is life. So if the storms fail to come, there is great hardship. He shall be gone for several days, I would guess, but he knows what he is doing."

"There was lightning, Papa. He might be hurt."

"No, he shall be fine. His people use lightning as a compass." Seeing I was not convinced, he patted my shoulder. "Fear not for Midnight."

"Fear not! But he's all alone. And he doesn't know Portugal. And . . . and—"

"John, Midnight said to me once that the desert waits for the lightning like a bride for her groom. And when it comes, laddie, the desert unites with the lightning. All that lives there—all the great and small animals, and all the men and women and children—they abandon what they have been doing and move off. For them, lightning is a summons from the heavens. They must follow it or lose their purpose. Now, John, listen closely. . . . Midnight told me he was prevented from following the rains at Mr. Reynolds's farm. He was ordered never to leave the property. But he is his own man here, and I shall never prevent him from doing as he wishes. You would not want him to live without purpose, would you, lad?"

I knew the answer Papa desired, but I was feeling too troubled to give it. He answered for me. "No, you would not. And he'll not be hurt. He'll come back to us."

"But Porto is not a desert."

"Nevertheless, Midnight will always follow the rain and lightning, just as we all follow the path life gives us. You can count on that, laddie."

* * *

DURING MIDNIGHT'S ABSENCE, the heavenly floodgates opened for four days and nights, creating rivers of muck that flowed through our streets. We expected Midnight to be covered head to foot with mud and sneezing like a Druid on arriving home, but expectations always counted for very little with regard to our Bushman friend. When he returned five days later, his fawn-colored woolen breeches, white shirt, and blue waist-coat were impeccably clean. True, his bare feet were streaked with soil, but that, together with the dank smell of wet worsted, was all that indicated nearly a week spent under the rain, clouds, and stars. "Good day," he said, his amused smile lighting up his face. "We saw you from afar and we are dying of hunger."

After our exclamations of joy, Mother was the first to notice an inch-long gash across his forehead. She darted to him and touched her finger-tip softly to the bruise, where blood had crusted. Midnight laughed and said it was nothing, then took her hand and brought it expertly to his lips, as he had been taught.

"I shall bandage it for you presently," she said.

"Yes, but first let me look at the Stewart family again."

Midnight was plainly overjoyed to be home. When he caught my look of happiness, he winked, as though he would have much to tell me in private. I rushed over to hug him and breathe in the comforting scent of him.

Papa helped Midnight put away his pack, quiver, and bow, then sat him down at our table, where Mother tended to his wound. I could no longer stifle the one question that I was desperate to ask and shouted, "But how did you keep your damned clothing so clean?!"

"John!" Mama cried. "A gentleman never speaks such words, even if vexed."

To which I naturally replied, "But I am not yet a gentleman." I was not jesting in the least, since I had decided that I ought not be required to conduct myself like a gentleman until I was at least sixteen.

"A truer word you have never spoken," Mama replied, not without humor. "But I shall turn you into one if it's the last thing I do."

"So how *did* you stay so smartly attired?" Papa inquired.

"As soon as I was safe in the countryside, with no houses nearby, I re-moved my clothes and folded them carefully in my pack, then tied them high up in an oak tree. They became very, very wet," he laughed. "But they dried out today on my way home. Except the breeches."

"How did you remember where the oak was?" I asked.

He looked bewildered. "John, don't be silly—I could never lose such an important tree."

"Enough of this," Mama ordered. "Put on something dry this instant. I'll not have you ill again before Christmas. My heart could not bear it. And as you are to start your apprenticeship soon, it would not do for you to arrive feverish at Senhor Benjamin's doorstep. If you cannot—"

Mama might have gone on like this until dawn had Papa not risked her wrath and interrupted, "You must do as she says, Midnight, or we shall have no peace. I beg you to go up with John to your room and change, then come down and take some supper with us."

Midnight and I raced up the stairs to his room. While changing his clothes, he began to speak of his adventures. I nearly always felt a glow of privilege warming me deep inside when I listened to him. When I once described this sensation to him, he replied that when I was delirious with fever he had fed me a lightning bug to keep my chills away. The bug was still inside me. He harbored one inside himself as well, and when the two met they flashed their light in recognition.

Buttoning his shirt, Midnight told me how, after leaving Porto, he had sought out the heart of the storm, threading his way across farmland and forest toward the ever-darkening sky. When I asked if he'd met other people along the way, he replied, "No one. I stayed out of sight. I am clever-clever at hiding when I want to."

He said the rains reached him as he climbed a hill crowned by pines. He had danced there for hours.

"To summon more rain?" I asked.

He shrugged, then made a clicking noise with his tongue. When I insisted that he reply in English, he simply grinned. This was hardly the first time Midnight had made me settle for a clicking in lieu of an explanation, but I learned that his silence signified neither a betrayal nor even a withholding of secrets, as I first presumed. It was simply that he could not give me an adequate answer.

Downstairs, Midnight recounted—for the benefit of my eager parents—what I thought were the mere beginnings of an epic story of perilous adventure. But he brought the proceedings to a swift close by explaining that after finishing his dance he spent the next four days hunting. Unaware of my expectation of at least an hour's enthrallment, he picked up his spoon and began ladling carrot soup into his hungry mouth.

"Did you . . . did you kill many things?" I asked.

Mama thought this an inappropriate subject for a lad my age and tut-tutted me, but Father said, "No, May, let us hear a little of the spoils of war."

Midnight said, "I killed a large gazelle. A beautiful creature." His eyes shone. "I sketched him on a great rock as well."

"How could you bear to take his life?" asked Mother, shaking her head. "I should be brokenhearted to see such a thing."

"I am a Bushman, just as he was a gazelle. I must eat or die."

"Why did you sketch him?" I asked.

"I must mark the spot where he has died. So that Mantis knows."

"And how did you get that cut on your forehead?" Papa asked.

"My arrow pierced the gazelle here," he answered, pointing to his ribs, "and he ran off swiftly. I pursued him through the forest. A branch came at me—" Here, he made a swiping motion with his hand and laughed at his own carelessness.

"What else did you eat?" I asked.

"Two hares. And a great deal of ants."

"Ants?" Mama made a gagging sound, then couldn't stop coughing.

With his mischief-making apparent only as a glimmer in his eyes, Midnight added with grave seriousness, "Your Portuguese ants are not nearly as good-tasting as ours in Africa."

"I shall make a note of that," said Father, and feigned writing this tidbit on a notecard.

Mama's mouth had fallen open. Rapping her fist on our table, she said, "I'll not hear any more of this talk of vermin! You!" she said, turning to Midnight. "Eat your soup before it gets cold. And you," she added, facing my father, "you are to refrain from further jests. And you," she said, staring at me, "you . . . you just sit there and listen!"

"That's what I was doing."

"And don't speak to me in that tone of voice!"

"As you wish, Mama." While Midnight ate his soup, I nudged his arm and said, "Will you take me hunting with you someday?"

Before he could reply, my mother snapped, "This conversation is absolutely impossible. John, I forbid you from hunting."

"You don't understand what I mean, Mama. Not for four days. Just for one." I held up a single finger, then turned to Midnight. "We could go for just a day, couldn't we? When the sun is out. I mean, we would not have to stay in the forest during a thunderstorm and hide our clothes in trees and eat ants. We could hunt in a less . . . a less—"

Fearing a quarrel, Papa interrupted my stammering and said, "John, I would greatly appreciate it if you would allow your mother and me to discuss this matter later, please."

Mama frowned and said, "James, there will be no discussion of hunting in this household."

I decided to sulk, but none of them seemed to notice, which only infuriated me more.

After supper, I wanted to stomp off to my room, but Papa gave me a meaningful look and said that I was not excused.

Midnight took pity on me and said, "You know, John, while I was gone, I did see an unusual bird."

"What kind might that have been?" I asked imperiously.

It is a testament to my family's true fondness for me that they were all able to resist a good laugh at my expense.

"One day," he began, "when I was a lad no older than you, I stopped at a little lake to drink. It was near Gemsbok Valley, where I was born. In the water, in the reflection, I saw a great-great bird." He spread his arms as far as he was able, his fingers fanning out. "She was all white—purest ivory carved into wings and a long tail. But when I turned to look at her, she vanished over the tops of the trees of the Forest of Night, and from that moment on I was consumed by a longing to get a proper look at her."

He drew in deeply on his pipe, but only tiny wisps came from his mouth when he next talked, which made me imagine that most of the smoke had been transformed inside him to words.

"It was like love, John, this feeling of mine. So I left my people for a time to find the bird. But I was unable to. And no one I met had ever set eyes on her." He tapped my leg with his foot. "I never did catch another glimpse of her until just two days ago."

He leaned back and sat there smoking as though he had said all he wished to say on the subject. Mother picked up some letters she'd recently received.

"So what happened two days ago? What did you see?" I exclaimed, already changed in mood and eager for more.

"It was very, very strange. You see, John, I was drinking at a lake, and I saw the white-white bird in the reflection of the water again—just like the first time." He leaned forward expectantly and pointed the stem of his pipe at me, which had the effect of pulling me up into a kneeling position.

"This time, John, I heard a screech when I turned." Here, Midnight made a sharp cackle.

My mother looked up, furrowed her brows as though she might rebuke Midnight, then sighed dramatically and said, "I can see it is useless to try keeping my mind on anything but your story."

Midnight grinned and said, "I followed the screeching to the top of a nearby hillside. But my beloved bird was nowhere to be seen, so I danced our Ostrich Dance."

The Bushman clamped his pipe in his mouth and, without getting up, flapped his hands and jerked his head forward until we could all envision the flightless bird racing before us.

"What happened then?"

"A voice spoke to me: 'Look there! Look there!' And when I turned I saw a great white feather floating down out of the golden sunset." Midnight reached as high as he could and closed his fist around the imaginary plume.

"After so many years, I had her feather. I could feel it beating inside my hand, as though it were alive. And do you know, I felt a peace greater than I had ever known before. All my hunger was gone. It was as if I had reached my kin after years in the desert."

I was trembling with curiosity by now. "So what did the bird look like? What kind was it?"

"The kind that never lets itself be seen by anyone. No one has ever gotten a good look at it. No one even knows its name. But one feather of hers is enough to make a man content for life. And one feather placed on the head of a chief can bring happiness to all."

"Midnight, you're making this up," I declared.

He winked. "You think so? Then get my pack, if you please."

I jumped up, ran to our garden door, took the pack down from its peg, and carried it to him. Reaching in, he produced a slender white feather, about a foot and a half in length. He rubbed it under his chin, then inhaled its fragrance as though it were perfume.

My mouth fell open. I had never seen a feather so long and lovely.

"Where did you get it?" I asked.

"Are you not listening to me? It fell from the sky."

"From the bird without a name?"

He nodded.

"From the great white bird without a name?"

"Yes." He grinned and handed it to me. "It is for you, John."

When I took it, I, too, felt it beating inside my hand.

"Why are you giving it to me?" I asked.

"But who else could appreciate it as much as you?"

I CHOSE STRATEGIC moments over the next several days to flatter my mother in order to win permission to join Midnight on a hunt. As my first bouquets of charm elicited only snorts of disbelief, I grew more poetic. One day I said she was lighter and more agile than all the stars in Pegasus. I thought this a winning observation, but Mama burst into laughter until the tears were rolling down her cheeks.

By way of explanation, she said, "Forgive me, John, but I am not often favorably compared to a horse."

Though all looked lost to me, my father had learned certain techniques over the previous decade for wearing down her opposition, and in the quiet of their bedroom he soon succeeded in winning her permission, as long as I refrained from eating ants or injuring a single creature myself. This was an easy promise for me to make, as I had no intention of eating anything with six legs and antennae and I had never even once held a weapon of any sort, let alone one as difficult to master as a bow and arrow.

As the following Saturday was blessed with sun, Midnight and I left at dawn. Within two hours we were striding through a thick, damp forest of fern, pine, and oak, several miles east of the city. We removed our shirts and tucked them into Midnight's pack, which we hung over a branch. He also took off his breeches, stockings, and shoes. I was too shamed by my skinny frame to make such a bold gesture.

I quickly learned that he tracked animals in three ways: through their scent, their footprints, and their droppings. So adroit was he that in examining a single print pressed lightly in the soil he could tell how long ago the creature had passed our way and what its general shape had been.

A single whiff was enough to set him stalking on silken tiptoe. He crept and crouched with the precise care of his beloved Mantis—silence given purpose and direction.

He was so agile with his bow and arrow that they might have been a part of his own body. That morning I saw him pierce the heart of a hare shrouded by thick grass fifty paces away. The arrow sliced through the air, flying to the unsuspecting creature as though guided by an electric force. With his weapon, our good-hearted Midnight was transformed into deadly fate.

Most amazingly, the Bushman could release an arrow while running, and in this way I saw him strike a deer from seventy paces as it bounded through the trees. The wounded creature did not fall but instead bounded off with the arrowhead buried in its hide.

"Run, John!" he called to me, gesturing me over.

I raced to him and we took off after the deer, Midnight loping at a moderate pace to allow me to remain within sight of him at all times.

We pursued the creature for nigh on a mile. It died at the base of a pine tree, its eyes open but no longer staring at anything in our world. I had never been so close to a deer. I would have preferred it to be alive, it is true, but even dead it was beautiful.

"Hello," I said to it.

I was panting and confused by all I had experienced. The African was covered in sweat, the muscular contours of his bronze skin glistening. He patted my head and said that we would make our apologies to the deer later.

As he pulled the arrowhead from the creature, he explained to me that he fashioned his arrows so that the head bore a poison he had concocted from nightshade, monkshood, and other dangerous plants he grew behind a wire fence in our garden. He also told me he fixed a tiny part of himself at the tip, so that he entered into the death of his prey.

From this experience, I understood that preventing Midnight from hunting—as Mr. Reynolds had done in Africa—was tantamount to exiling him from meaning. His need to reenact the central story of our existence as mortal creatures may even have been the most important reason why he chose to escape from servitude. He could not go on without remembering—in his feet, hands, bow, and heart—the root of his being. *Africa is memory,* Midnight once told us, and though I have never been there, I believe he must be right.

MIDNIGHT SLUNG THE handsome deer over his shoulder and carried it back through the forest toward the city. I was given responsibility for the three hares he had also killed.

On the way home, we stopped at a great granite boulder, nearly as high as our house, where he had drawn the animals he'd hunted on his last excursion. This was what he had meant by apologizing.

Using reddish stones that he gathered at the base of the boulder, the African sketched the deer he had felled, using deftly executed lines to capture its swift nature. I did my best to design our three hares, with less success.

Before leaving the forest that day, Midnight took me to gather honey, a skill I was never able to learn from him, though he tried on several occasions to teach me. He told me that day that it was easier in Africa, where there lived a clever bird called the Honeyguide, who led people to beehives. I didn't know whether he was teasing me or not, but he promised me he would take me to his homeland one day to see this bird myself.

XVI

VERY SHORTLY AFTER OUR DAY OF HUNTING, Midnight and my family settled into a pleasant daily routine. It generally ensured that he and I were alone from two until five in the afternoon, the one exception being on Friday, when, from three to five, I had my art lessons with the Olive Tree Sisters.

My friend and I filled our afternoons as we pleased— with reading lessons, weeding, or lazy walks in the country-side. And so it was that we reached the afternoon of St. John's Eve of 1804. I had just turned thirteen and was now four feet nine inches in height, still—unfortunately—a few inches shorter than Mama and Midnight. But growing...

Our African visitor had now lived with us for nearly two years. I knew little about his work with Senhor Benjamin, but he seemed generally pleased with his progress in learning European herbal medicine.

By then we'd discovered that Violeta had disappeared without a trace. It was Mama who confirmed this rumor by secretly questioning the girl's younger brother late one night. Distraught, she had come directly home and awakened me. "I hope to God that poor sweet lass is safe," she whispered, choking back tears.

In the darkness behind her I pictured Violeta's jade eyes flashing defiantly, as they had on the day we'd met. "Safe and hidden on a ship bound for America," I'd replied.

The event on everyone's lips was Napoleon's proclamation as Emperor of France on May the Eighteenth. The political tension in Europe set Portugal coursing through a sea of apprehension about its own independent future, for it was clear that the Emperor had designs on our quaint little outpost at the edge of Europe, particularly as our paramount trading partner was England, his great enemy. There was no city in Iberia whose fate was more bound to Britain's than Porto, since ninety percent of our exports—including a thousand man-size barrels of wine per week—headed toward London.

For this reason it was believed by many, including my father, that Napoleon might soon launch an all-out attack on our city. Lacking even storehouses for bread, which arrived in Porto each Tuesday, Thursday, and Saturday from neighboring towns, a French blockade and siege would reduce us to starvation in a matter of days.

Midnight and I were taking tea in the home of the Olive Tree Sisters when the trouble began. At just past three on their mantelpiece clock, we heard a crowd coming down our street. A sharp cry soon pierced the air: " 'Think not that I am come to send peace on earth. I come not to send peace, but rather a sword!' All foreigners must be excised from the Portuguese nation. If we are to have a City of God, then the heads of the Protestants, heathens, and Jews must all tumble down our streets."

I recognized the speaker and rushed to the window.

"No!" Graça shouted at me.

But it was too late, for I had already peeled back the curtain and peered outside.

The necromancer who had threatened me years earlier, Lourenço Reis, was standing outside Senhor Benjamin's shop, only thirty paces away. Thankfully, he didn't see me.

Undoubtedly, he had chosen today for his return to Porto because St. John's Eve was, at its heart, a pagan celebration of the summer solstice.

"If you added up all the Jews in Portugal, what would you have?" he demanded of his followers.

A man shouted "ten thousand beasts"; another, "a herd of swine."

"John, step away from there or I'll flatten you!" Luna ordered.

I was so entranced that I refused to move.

"If you added up all the Jews," replied the necromancer, "you would have lumber enough for a fire reaching all the way to God!"

Midnight touched my shoulder. "What does he say?" he asked.

"John, you wicked boy! Get away from there now!" Luna pleaded.

She and her sister were staring at me in fury. I let the curtain fall but remained by the window. "He once threatened me," I whispered to Midnight. "He does not like foreigners, especially—"

I was about to say "Jews," but the necromancer gave a great wail, as though he had been stabbed in the gut. "I call upon Benjamin Seixas—"

I pulled back the curtain again.

"—the Jewish demon residing in this accursed house, to come to me and confess. I accuse him of treason against the Portuguese nation, of trafficking with the devil. And his sentence is death!"

Luna dragged me away from the window. "You do as I say, John!"

I turned to Graça, the less excitable of the two, who had started to cry. She rushed to Luna and hugged her. After a hushed exchange between them, Luna took my hand gently. "This is very serious," she whispered. "Now, do as I say—we are all in danger. Be very quiet," she told me, and she had me repeat this order to Midnight.

When the noise outside died down, we thought the necromancer was leading the mob away. What fools we were!

"Graça and Luna Oliveira," he shrieked, "I call upon you to come to me and confess your sins! I accuse you of treason. You must die so that Christ may live. . . ."

Graça clasped her hand over her mouth so as not to let loose a cry of terror.

"I call upon the Jewish whores to come out and confess their sins. I call upon them to open their wombs to Christ and allow Him to enter before they die. I call upon them to stand ready for the burning stake. . . ."

His threats seemed to stab through the wood of our door, until I believed that his voice alone might unlock the latch and allow his mob to seize us.

Luna whispered, "What shall we do if he breaks in?" Graça was mumbling frantically to herself in a mixture of Portuguese and another language I did not understand. I caught the word *Adonai*.

Drumming started in Midnight's belly and grew in intensity. "John, tell me very, very precisely what that hyena outside is saying," he whispered.

His use of the word *hyena* revealed that without understanding his words, Midnight had perceived that Lourenço Reis was evil. Before I could reply, the villain banged on our door, then twisted the handle. Graça wet herself in fright.

"Keep praying, sister," Luna whispered to her.

Midnight stood up, slipped out of his shoes, and grabbed the poker from its place beside the hearth. Positioning it over his shoulder like a spear, he rushed to the door.

"Don't go out!" I begged.

He nodded to me and crouched, eyes fixed on the jiggling handle.

Lourenço Reis spoke through the door. "Graça and Luna Oliveira, you must learn of sin. You must die so that Christ may live. You must perish in the burning heart of the Son of Man."

Shouting rose from the crowd like screeching gulls. Then, after a time, we heard them move on. Midnight came to me and we helped the Olive Tree Sisters back to their chairs, prevailing upon them to sip their cold tea. Graça gagged, then rushed upstairs. I wished to go to her, but Luna said, "She will be embarrassed. Stay here."

Upon Midnight's request, I began to translate for him the necromancer's hateful words. He could not fathom their meaning, and I could think of no way of explaining what I only barely understood myself.

"John, listen closely," Luna said. "I know that this must all seem rather odd to you, but—" She stopped in mid-sentence when Reis began calling for Senhor Policarpo, the wheelwright, to come out and face his judgment, along with his wife and children. I was stunned that he knew them by name. He must have been watching us all for some time.

Midnight held Luna's hand as we listened to a litany of curses against Policarpo's family. Then we heard a single shriek rise up as though to pierce the sky.

The necromancer was now only a short ways from my home. I took my key from my pocket and held it in my fist. Though I was certain I had locked the door, my heart tumbled toward dread; Fanny was in the garden.

"We have to go home," I declared to Midnight.

"No, John, you must not let yourself be provoked."

"But Fanny. She is sure to start barking and they might hurt her."

"No, I forbid you to leave. Fanny will have to take care of herself."

From down the street, I could hear the preacher shouting, "Maria

Zarco Stewart, James Stewart, and John Zarco Stewart, I summon you out to the street for your crimes against the Portuguese nation. I call upon you to bring out the African heathen—"

I dashed for the door, but Midnight grabbed my arm roughly and ordered me to remain still.

Luna said, "I shall tell you now why you cannot leave, John. Sit."

"No."

"Sit now!"

I did so, but before she could speak, the necromancer's shouting began again: "John Zarco Stewart, you have not departed from Porto as I have asked you. So you will now learn what it is to die for love. You shall be cleansed through fire, and I shall return you to God as innocent as the day you were born."

He then called for the death of my mother and father. We waited in silence for the rest of his tirade but heard nothing more. He and the mob must have turned a corner.

"John, listen closely," Luna said. "Under normal circumstances I would let your mother tell you, or your father, but now that this has happened . . ." She stood up, took a sip of tea, and smoothed a lock of gray hair behind her ear. "Do you know what a Jew is?"

"Moses was a Jew."

"That's right."

"And he had a horn. And a tail." Guessing what was to come, I shouted, "And I don't have a horn or a tail, so I cannot possibly be a Jew!"

"Do not raise your voice, please."

"I cannot be a Jew!" I shouted again, louder.

"John, we let you think those things about Moses. I'm sorry. Perhaps it was wrong, but we had no choice. We would not have wished you to guess sooner. Now, listen: There is no physical difference save one between Jew and Christian. On those lads who have received the covenant, a small . . . a small . . . I don't know how to say it. What I mean to say is that—"

"What's the covenant?" I interrupted.

"You are making me lose my place."

"Good! I do not want to talk of these things."

I desperately wanted everything to be as it had been. I wanted Daniel to be alive and Violeta to be happy. I wanted to imitate birds at our pond. I wanted to run to Fanny.

"You must listen," Luna begged, taking my hands in hers. "On lads, there is a small piece of skin taken from their . . . from between their legs, at the tip . . ."

"What piece of skin?"

"A small hood. It is removed from Jewish infants when they are but eight days old."

"But I've had nothing removed. I never had a hood or anything else."

"Perhaps not, but that does not change what I am saying."

"Which is what? You're not making any sense at all!"

"John, if you raise your voice again . . ." She looked to Midnight and said in careful Portuguese, "I'm afraid this is difficult."

Midnight replied, "John is clever. But very, very"—he shook his fists and pulled an ugly face, an imitation of me when riled. It was quite accurate and I was not at all pleased—"very excitable," he concluded.

"I am not!" I shouted.

"Stop being so quarrelsome with us all!" Luna snapped. "And make no mistake, young man, I will knock you straight from today into next week if I have to!"

Her anger abated almost immediately, and I soon saw in her eyes that she, too, would have wished to return to the way everything had always been. But all hope for that faded completely when she said, "John, you are indeed Jewish."

"I don't believe you."

"Your mother is Jewish, and in Judaism, heritage passes through her alone and not through your father." When I accused her of lying, she added, "John, your grandmother is Jewish too. And Grandfather João as well—blessed be his memory. He was a Portuguese Jew, but from Constantinople. He returned here before you were born."

Graça came down the stairs now, pale, holding a handkerchief to her mouth. She apologized for leaving us.

"I was just telling John about his heritage," Luna told her sister.

Graça bowed her head and gave a sigh, as though she had always been expecting this truth to cast a shadow over our lives one day.

"I have to go," I said.

Graça knelt next to me. "You know, John, your grandfather was a lovely man. Intelligent and kind. With a gift for gardening, just like Midnight. Do you know how he and his family came to live in Constantinople? And why they spoke Portuguese there, unlike the Turks?"

I shook my head. She caressed my hair and smiled. "Back in the sixteenth century, your grandfather's ancestors lived in Lisbon. They had been converted against their will to Christianity. Even so, they and their friends were still persecuted because . . . well, the Church and the Crown feared that they would maintain their Jewish customs, which some of them did. Thousands were arrested and put in dungeons, and many were burnt in public ceremonies. So one day your ancestors took a ship from Lisbon to Constantinople. To escape. They wished to practice Judaism openly. And to live without fear. Do you follow me?"

"Yes," I said, but I didn't think I did.

"They wanted to live as they preferred and not worry that they might end up as ash. The Sultan of Turkey welcomed them. He welcomed thousands of Portuguese Jews. Then, later—"

"But this is madness, Senhora Graça. How did they become Jews in the first place? Tell me that if you're so clever!"

"They . . . they always were Jews, I suppose," she stammered.

"That's impossible," I declared. I believed I had found the fatal flaw in her logic. "They must have started out as Christians, so why did they first convert to Judaism and then need to be converted back? It makes no sense. It's . . . it's not true."

I had no clear understanding of what being Jewish meant, but I feared that it would change everything in my life—that it would distance my parents and Midnight from me, and that they would no longer be fond of me in any way.

Luna sighed. "This has been a wretched day."

I stood up. "I must go now."

"You sit back down, John Stewart," Graça said determinedly, "or I shall never give you instructions in art again!" She grabbed both my hands to hold me down. Hers were freezing cold. "However it came to pass, the truth is that your maternal grandparents were Jewish, and their ancestors were exiled from Portugal hundreds of years ago. They kept their language and they kept their customs, even though they lived in a Moslem land. Then, after the Inquisition ended its worst abuses—you know what the Inquisition was?"

"Yes," I replied, but I had only a vague notion.

"Then you probably also know that it lost its power twenty-five years ago, though it is not yet completely dismantled. Since then we have been able to practice our religion more . . . more fully."

"Though we would not wish to call attention to ourselves," Luna added.

"No, that would be foolish," Graça agreed. "It's much better for everyone that we remain hidden. Now, the important thing for you is this, John: Under sacred law, the child of a Jewish woman remains Jewish. That's why you are what you are. You see now?"

"So is my father a Jew?" I asked. They both shook their heads. "There, you see! It makes no sense. If I were Jewish, he would be too. I cannot be what my father is not."

"For better or for worse," Luna said, "that is not how these things are decided. That's precisely what we are trying to tell you."

"Then why wouldn't I know it? Why wouldn't my papa have told me?"

"Your parents were waiting until you were a little older. It is part of our tradition. The children are only told when we are absolutely certain they are old enough to keep such an important secret. Unless there are circumstances that . . . that complicate matters and make such knowledge essential, like what took place today."

"Why do we have to keep it a secret?"

"Look, John," Graça replied, "the Inquisition may return, which is why that preacher, Lourenço Reis, came here today. We have known of him for many years. He was formerly employed by the Holy Office, by the Church, as a prosecutor, you might say. He has jailed Jews and made them burn. You can be sure he greatly regrets that such power was taken from him and that we are no longer completely at his mercy. He would like to see a return to the old days."

"So you're Jewish too."

"Yes, John, many of us are Jewish. At least, in secret."

"Who?"

"I think it best for you to talk to your mother about that. She may be very unhappy with us for telling you this much."

"But what shall I do now?"

"What do you mean?"

"I am Jewish and my father is not. If you are so clever, then tell me what shall I do?"

I TRAIPSED DOWN the street toward home. Midnight tried to talk to me, but I was too angry to answer him. I was wondering who I was.

Then we saw Senhor Policarpo sprawled on the cobbles outside his home. His wife, Josefina, was leaning over him, sobbing and covered in his blood. The bones in his face had been smashed in. Flies were already feeding at his eyes and lips.

Senhora Josefina gazed up at us in horror and started to wail.

"John, go home," Midnight said. "Get in the house."

"What about you?"

"I shall be there presently. Go home and make certain you lock the door."

I rushed away. Before I closed the door behind me, I saw him reaching for Policarpo's pulse. He shook his head and reached for Josefina's hand.

To my relief, I found Fanny alive and well, nosing through the leaves of a verbena bush in our garden.

"Senhor Policarpo is dead and I am a Jew," I told her, which only made her run to get her leather ball and drop it in my hand. I threw it into the rosebushes, which was a cruel thing to do. While she tried to contort herself to get through their thorns unscathed, I went to my room and cried. Then I peered in my mirror for a mark on my scalp where my horns might have been, but again I could detect no such sign. I found nothing unusual on the tip of my penis either.

Mama arrived home an hour or so later. "John?" she called in a worried voice. "John, are you in your room?"

I dashed down the stairs and ran into her arms.

"Thank God, you're safe," she said. She embraced me for a long time, and I could feel her trembling.

I wished to ask her if she and I were Jewish but reasoned that this was sure to insult her either way. For if it were true, then I would be drawing attention to a family fault, and if it were not, as I still hoped, then she might be offended that I thought so badly of her.

"I believe that something worrisome happened to you today," she said as calmly as she could. "You weren't hurt at all?"

"No, Mama."

"No one touched you?"

"No."

"You're certain?"

"Yes."

"You must have been frightened." When I shook my head, she asked, "Is Midnight here?"

"He must be in the Lookout Tower or in the garden."

"Thank goodness." She glanced down, weighing her options, then added, "Would you pump some water into a pot for me, John? I'll prepare supper. Yes, that's just what I'll do. Hot food is what we need."

I took a deep breath and said, "Senhor Policarpo is dead."

"I know, John, I've seen Josefina. We shall speak of what it means for us later."

"Mama, if I . . . if I were Jewish, would I . . . would I . . ."

I did not know how to continue and so said no more.

Mother held up her hand to have me wait a moment, then removed her black shawl. She laid it on one of the armchairs and returned to me. She held my head in her hands and pressed her lips to my brow. "Yes, John, if you were Jewish . . . What is it you wish to know?"

She seemed strangely confident, and I realized that I had expected her to become hysterical. Instead, she smiled encouragingly.

"If I were Jewish, would I know it?"

"That is a very good question, John, and I will indeed answer it. But first, will you tell me precisely what happened to you today? I need to know."

"No, you answer my question first."

She sighed, resigned to my inquisitive nature. I had no inkling whatsoever of what an overwhelming relief it would be to her to finally tell me the truth.

I now believe that many of her idiosyncrasies—particularly her constant fretting over the opinions of others and stern insistence on decorum—were the direct result of the need for secrecy both inside and outside her home. That she saw herself obliged by circumstance to lie to her only child must have seemed a cruel fate at times, given her devotion to me.

"Come sit with me, John, and I shall answer all your questions," Mama said warmly. On her insistence I sat in Papa's chair. "You're so big now that if I tried to sit you on my lap I'd be crushed," she said, laughing.

She looked at me as though greatly relieved simply to see me alive. "John, we were . . . we were waiting to tell you. Until you were a bit older."

"Then I *am* Jewish?" I prayed there was still a more sensible explanation.

"It isn't that simple. There are—how shall I put it? There are people, who are neither one thing nor another."

"Neither Christian nor Jewish?"

"That's right. Perhaps . . . perhaps I'd better start with some history. A long time ago, before you were born—"

"Grandfather João came from Constantinople," I interrupted. "His ancestors were Jewish. They fled the Inquisition. People were being burnt. I know all that."

"Who told you?"

"Luna and Graça. I was with them when the necromancer came."

"Yes, I know. They came to find me at the market."

"If you knew what they said, why did you ask?"

"On the contrary, John, they only told me a little of what happened. They said that you had been very brave and that certain secrets had been revealed to you."

"Did they take something from me?" I asked impetuously.

"Who?"

"The Jews?"

"Which Jews?"

I shrugged. "I've no idea. But you know what I'm trying to say."

"I most certainly do not."

I wished to broach, in the most delicate manner possible, the possibility of my penis having been disfigured. I said, "I don't know what they took. A horn perhaps."

"A horn?"

"From somewhere . . . from my head. They removed it."

"Please, John, this is no time for one of Midnight's stories. You are not a goat. Though there have certainly been times when you have smelled like one." She smiled at her own joke, which irritated me enormously. "Forgive me, John," she said. "I know I'm being silly, but I wanted to put you at ease."

"Maybe they took something else?" I said.

"Such as?"

"Well, from my tip." I squirmed in embarrassment.

"Ah, I see now where this conversation is heading. Yes, when you were eight days old, a surgeon came and took a small and unimportant piece of skin from your . . . your tip, as you so nicely put it."

She said this as though it were a trifle, but I must have looked sick, since she added reassuringly, "A very small piece. Nothing essential, I assure you. You are perfectly intact in that area."

"Why was a piece of skin taken?"

"It is our tradition. A surgeon comes and the baby sits on his grand-father's lap while the surgeon cuts away a small piece of skin that serves to hide things. It's called the *prepúcio.*"

"Does it hurt?"

She shrugged. "It must have. You cried. We put some brandy on your gums to soothe the pain."

"Brandy in my mouth to slice off the tip of my penis?"

She slapped her hand in her lap. "It was just a very tiny and useless piece of skin."

"Does Father still have it?"

"Yes."

"But why didn't he have it cut off?"

"John, your father is a separate subject. Perhaps we ought to discuss one thing at a time."

"You said I could ask anything."

She sighed. "John, listen, I'm afraid the truth is that your father is not Jewish." She looked away, as though it saddened her to admit it.

Far from upsetting me, I felt relieved. "Then I must only be partially Jewish."

"In a sense."

"Half-Scottish and half-Jewish."

"I think it would be more correct to say half-Scottish and half-Portuguese. As well as half-Christian and half-Jewish, of course."

"Mama, I cannot be four halves. Then I would be two persons."

"Indeed, John, I have often believed you to be several children, and each one more difficult than the one before. Honestly, it is like trying to converse with a bumblebee." She shook her head. "Look, you are Portu-guese and Jewish at the same time. Like me. Just as you are Christian and Scottish at the same time. Like your father." She leaned toward me. "But here's where things get tricky—the Jews are of the belief that religion is inherited through the mother. So, by our laws, you are completely Jewish, and the Christians agree. One drop of Hebrew blood makes you utterly Jewish, they say."

"Hebrew?"

"That is what the Jews are called in the Bible."

"So what things did I inherit?"

"Jewishness, you might say."

Now I felt we were headed where I had been trying to go for some time. "But what is Jewishness?"

My mother sighed deeply. "My goodness, I wish my father were still with us. I am quite certain he could explain all this much better than I can. John, dear, the Jews believe certain things that Christians don't. That's what it means to be Jewish."

"For instance?"

"For instance, that Jesus was not the Messiah. You know who the Messiah is?" I shook my head. "Well, he is a kind of savior. Now, the Christians believe he was Jesus. But we say that the Messiah has not yet come."

"Papa does not believe that Jesus is the Messiah, yet you just said that he was a Christian."

"He was born a Christian, but he is an atheist by conviction. Jews and atheists do not believe that Jesus was the Messiah."

This last point seemed to improve my situation even further. "So people can change? I could decide I am not half-Jewish and become one-quarter Jewish . . . or . . . or even less?"

"I fear that is not the way it works. Father remains a Christian by tradition, if not by belief. Just as you will remain a Jew by tradition, but not by belief, if that's what you decide."

"What tradition?"

"Well, now, this is where things become difficult, John. I am ignorant of many things—too many. I only know what my father told me. You see, I was raised here in Portugal, where such things as Jewishness remain largely a secret. There is much I have not learned, but I shall tell you what I know. . . ."

My mother then went on to discuss at great length such mysterious subjects as God, the soul, afterlife, possession, demonic spheres, angels, and hell. She used such complicated clauses and was forced into so many tangled rephrasings that after forty-five minutes of labor, when she finally gave herself a welcome rest and inquired, "Do you understand now?" it was my turn to confess to being totally lost.

As far as I could determine, the Jews believed that a single God would revive them in body and soul when the Messiah came and that they would rise up from the Mount of Olives in Jerusalem and live in paradise.

As to why my mother attended Mass nearly every Sunday and had had me baptized, she explained that these were formalities meant to still the viperous tongues of those who were spying on us. "In Portugal, my

son, everyone is always watching with both eyes wide open. There are
people to whom you have never spoken a word—such as that murderous
preacher—who know when you were born and the names of your grandparents." She paused, then said, "I think I ought to have Senhor
Benjamin talk to you about all this."

"Why him?"

"He understands our beliefs and knows our ceremonies. All I know is
how to light the candles before supper on Friday evening."

"So Senhor Benjamin is Jewish?"

"Yes."

"Who else?"

My mother's face grew solemn. "John, this is important." She stood
up and began to pace. "There are many people in Porto whose ancestors
are Jewish. Most have forgotten everything but a few words of prayer, for
we have not been permitted to practice our religion openly for many
centuries. If I tell you the names of some people who share our faith,
then you must never speak of them to anyone." She fixed me with a dark
look. "John, these people could be killed. You must swear to me that you
will never reveal any of their names—not even should the Church throw
you in the darkest dungeon. Otherwise I cannot tell you."

I was thrilled by the need to keep a dangerous secret. Perhaps being
Jewish was not such a curse, after all. "I swear," I said.

"Very well. It may even be a good thing that you know. In case...in
case anything bad should happen to Papa or myself, these are the people
to whom you must go for assistance. Never forget that." Lowering her
voice conspiratorially, she said, "I have already mentioned Senhor
Benjamin. Then there is Senhora Beatriz. And..."

She proceeded to name a score of individuals that I knew either as
family friends, neighbors, local artisans, or shopkeepers. It would be rash
of me to name them even now, since Portugal is a land of shifting political fortunes. Indeed, I have taken the liberty of changing the names of
Senhor Benjamin, Senhora Beatriz, and several others in my story, to
protect them and their children.

As Mama entrusted me with this information, I recognized that I was
being granted entry into a secret and ancient clan. What's more, Daniel,
too, had been a member, as Senhora Beatriz, his grandmother, had been
named.

It was only later that I realized that the thrashing Senhora Beatriz suffered years earlier was inspired by the hateful preachings of Lourenço Reis.

Once Mama had finished her list, she said, "John, if you have more questions, ask Senhor Benjamin. You may visit him tonight with your father."

After she hugged me again, I rushed to my room to consider my being half-Jewish. The more I reflected upon these halves and wholes, the less sense they made. Aside from a few rather confused religious beliefs expressed to me by Mother and a piece of skin evidently robbed from me at knifepoint when I was too young to defend myself, it was not at all clear wherein Jewishness resided or if even there was such a thing.

I decided to do my utmost to proceed through logic. I made a list of my mother's traits that were wholly absent in neighbor women who had not been mentioned and who were therefore, most likely, fully Christian. These, I presumed, would be the core attributes of Jewishness.

Knowing so few women well, I could come up with only seven characteristics: an uncompromising abhorrence of dirt in our home and on her person; a delight in hearing books read aloud; musical interest and aptitude; contempt for all forms of hunting; marked tendency to agitation in the presence of her own mother; timidity in public; and an overwhelming fear of standing apart. I had a wholly laissez-faire attitude toward dirt, so I reasoned that this was probably due to my being only half-Jewish. The same explanation held true for my lack of interest in playing the pianoforte; my joy in watching Midnight hunt; my occasional bursts of mischievous boldness; and my general ease in her presence. Subtracting these from my original list of traits, I concluded that my Jewishness resided in my delight in reading and my nervous nature. I concluded that I might therefore make every effort to keep these characteristics out of general view.

I then analyzed my father's Scottishness. Comparing him with Portuguese men, I decided it was centered in his outstanding height; his industriousness; his hotheaded sense of honor; his gallantry; his willingness to poke fun at himself; his dislike of the English; his partiality for whiskey and tea; his stories of elves, witches, and monsters of the lochs; and his odd Portuguese pronunciation.

Being only half-Scottish, I could not be expected to be tall, enjoy poking fun at myself, dislike the English, or appreciate whiskey, which I had sipped several times and already disliked. I was born in Porto, so it was wholly illogical to suppose that I might have a faulty pronunciation

of my native tongue. I deduced that my Scottish half resided in my industriousness, my aggressive sense of honor, and my love of frightening
stories.

This reasoning seemed sound to me. Yet I soon began to see that my
conclusions were lopsided. For my father played the fiddle with great
skill and had an even deeper love of poetry than my mother. And my
mother was nothing if not industrious, utilizing all her free time to embroider towels, curtains, and sheets for any person who might pay her a
fair wage.

And so my reflections reached a dead end, and I went bounding off
to discuss my confusion with Midnight, who I found weeding in our
garden and looking extremely troubled.

"What's the matter?" I asked. He ignored me and continued digging
with his trowel. "Will you not answer me?"

"John, I am not sure that you and I ought to be friends," he replied.
My heart stopped. "What do you mean?"

"There is so much I do not understand. So much that I cannot help
you with. I sometimes think I ought not to have come here."

The thought of him leaving was unbearable to me. "You cannot go!"

He wiped the dirt from his hands on his breeches. "Then if you wish
for me to stay you must help me. You must tell me the meaning of what
took place today."

I realized then that I had been neglectful of his concern for the safety
of my family. That he had seen preachers like Lourenço Reis in his native
country—inciting Europeans to murder *his* kin—had never occurred
to me.

We sat together and I repeated what Mother had told me about being
a Jew, adding that I'd love for him to come with us when Father and I
sought more satisfactory answers from Senhor Benjamin.

He was greatly relieved by my invitation. I'd have liked to ask him
where he thought Senhor Policarpo's *spirit of life* now resided. And to
show him my intimate parts and ask for an assessment of what had been
clipped from them. Courage failed me each time I sought to broach either of these subjects, however.

XVII

PAPA CAME HOME FROM WORK LOOKING AN-
gry and haggard. He had already been informed of Senhor
Policarpo's murder, so he asked no questions of me or
Mother. Instead, he lifted me up and embraced me, then
went straight to Midnight and hugged him as well. Then he
and Mama retreated to their bedroom.

When he returned downstairs, he asked us to sit with
him. "Worry not, dear May," he told Mama, kissing her
cheek. "The world is steadily advancing toward a better age,
and that hateful preacher will never succeed in tugging us
back into the past." Turning to me, he said, "If the truth be
told, laddie, I should have liked to tell you about this Jewish
heritage of yours when you were but a wee thing. And I say
this to you with no hesitation whatsoever—I think you are
all the more fortunate to be an alloy of different metals.
Would that I had your inheritance, my son."

This cheered me greatly, but I still wanted to ask a few
questions of Senhor Benjamin. When I said so, Papa gulped
down the rest of his wine and gestured toward the door.
"Then let's not dawdle, laddie. It is still St. John's Eve and
we've too much merriment planned to let conversations
wait. I shall not let any preacher ruin our celebrations!"

Father led Midnight and myself down the street to the home of the apothecary, who ushered us inside with much formality. Papa was about to broach the subject at hand when Benjamin jumped up, exclaiming, "Where's my manners?" and went off to fetch brandy for his guests. He seemed much more animated than usual, an indication of his different nature inside his home. Behind his closed door, he took off his mask.

I was offered a cup of wine as a special treat. It tasted sweet, and I was greatly flattered that Senhor Benjamin thought me man enough to appreciate it. To my great surprise, the three of them then toasted my health, which made me wonder if my mother had not already visited the apothecary to explain the reason for our visit.

"So, sir," Benjamin began, addressing my father and placing his glass on the table, "it seems clear now that Reis has returned to Porto with more than just slander on his mind."

"Aye," my father replied. "Tell me, Benjamin, is now the time?"

"Indeed, it is, James. His supporters have decided that their campaign must begin now in earnest."

"What campaign?" I asked.

"To reestablish the Inquisition," Papa replied.

"It was too soon when he first came, John," the apothecary added. "Even the Church needs some time to gather its forces." He stared at me pointedly over his oval spectacles, then whisked them off. Dangling them before me, he jerked his hand as though to throw them at me. I started, but instead of heading for me, they vanished without a trace. "The Church made Lourenço Reis disappear for a time," he continued. Benjamin stood up now and reached behind my head. The spectacles appeared in his hand, and he put them back on. "And just like that, the Church has summoned him back again."

"How did you do that?" I asked.

"I had you look where the spectacles would not be. It's easy to learn a few magic tricks, John. Anyone can do it. Even a man who likes nothing so much as to frighten young boys."

"And who summoned the necromancer back?" I asked.

"The what?" asked Benjamin.

"That's what John calls Lourenço Reis," Papa replied.

Benjamin laughed. "It's a good name for him. Though he has no special powers, I assure you. And you've asked a good question, dear boy. Alas, I cannot say for certain who is choreographing this spectacle."

"Whoever it is, they surely wish to have their apparatus of terror in place before Napoleon decides to advance on Portugal," Papa observed.

"Indeed so, James. I believe they will happily place the country in the Emperor's hands if he will permit them their indulgences." He turned to me again. "Now, I understand, young man, that you have been told that you are half-Jewish."

His directness cowed me. Noticing my discomfort, he said, "Forgive me, dear boy. I tend to speak plainly in my own home." Smiling, he leaned across and patted my shoulder, which only served to make my nerves plummet toward panic.

"We have much to talk about, John," Benjamin said gently, "and I would like to be able to speak to you about these things at our leisure. What I propose is that you come to see me once a week for a time. Would that meet with your approval?" Glancing over at Midnight and smiling, he added, "You might join us, too, if you like, my friend."

"I would like that very, very much," he replied. "If John agrees, that is."

"Yes, that would be perfect," I said.

"I assure you, John, that I mean no harm and that I am a true friend. Now, I have been given to believe that there may be some things you want to ask me."

I felt so shy that—to my shame—I began to hiccup.

"This happens," my father apologized.

While I held my breath to make the hiccups go away, Midnight said, "I may be wrong, for my Portuguese is very, very poor, but I believe the Oliveira Sisters mentioned a difference in the lad's intimate parts?"

At hearing this, my scalp began crawling as though riddled with a thousand lice. I was furious with him.

"Yes, I see," Benjamin said, and he emptied his glass. "It is rather simple." And here, this gentleman of unimpeachable respectability stood up and began to unbutton his breeches. "If you don't mind, James, I think that showing him will make things plain."

Papa simply downed his brandy and said, "If you really think that it will do the trick, Benjamin."

Midnight's eyes shone with amusement.

The apothecary held his manhood in his hand and gave me a brief anatomy lesson, but even his meticulous explanation and my previous familiarity with my father's nakedness were insufficient to answer my most embarrassing question. So Papa then stood up and showed us all the precise form of the hood that had been excised from me and Benjamin. I should have liked to have kept it, but he assured me it was mostly a nuisance and decidedly offensive to the nose when unwashed.

Papa took advantage of his now-inebriated state to explain to me the ABCs of procreation. It all seemed to make good sense except for the part about the process being enjoyable, since his description was very complex. Indeed, I imagined it more like an intricate operation in which the patient—the woman—might very well come to pay with her life, since, as he was careful to note, death was always a possibility in the event of pregnancy.

Once my tongue was loosened by my wine and by our conviviality, I decided to make further inquiries of Senhor Benjamin. "Will my father and Midnight be allowed to live with my mother and me in . . . in heaven, or will they be banished? And Senhor Policarpo, is he there now?"

"We are all made in God's image, and, among other things, John, that means that your parents and Midnight will indeed be with you on the Mount of Olives. As for Policarpo, he is safe now. He has rejoined the Lord. And"—he smiled—"if I have not ruined my own chances with all my meddling here in the Lower Realms, then I may very well be permitted to join him and the rest of you when my time comes."

"Have I a soul?" I asked him.

"We all do, dear boy." When I asked what it looked like, he replied, "I couldn't possibly say. I've never seen one."

"Then how do you know we all have one?"

"How do you know there is a China? And an Italy?"

"Because other people have been to those places. And they have written about their travels. I've read a bit of Marco Polo."

"Precisely."

Our host left us then and returned momentarily, clutching a thick, leather-bound book. Handing it to me, he said, "A man who saw God wrote this book. With your father's permission, I recommend you read it. We can talk about it together."

"What is it?" I asked.

"The Torah," he said. "That's the Jewish name of the Old Testament. A sage once said that there are two places where we may always find the truth—in the Torah and in our heart." Smiling mischievously at Papa, Benjamin added, "If you should like to join us in reading it, James, I would be most pleased."

"I am afraid I should make as bad a Jew as I do a Christian. All of religion I need know is that I shall be with my wife, my son, you, and Midnight on the Mount of Olives."

MAMA'S SUPPER WAS glorious that evening, but I picked over my potatoes and sardines because I couldn't stop picturing Senhor Policarpo's bloodied face. While she was serving stewed prunes, the Olive Tree Sisters brought over the two sheets that Graça had been sewing together that afternoon. She had cut—per my specific instructions—a hole one foot in diameter at the center of the seam. I had completely forgotten about this costume, which I was planning to wear on our St. John's Eve promenade. I took it from them with eager thanks.

"I sincerely hope," Mama said, "that you are not planning on walking around the city with those tattered old sheets draped over you. Honestly, John, the things you make the Olive Tree Sisters do for you. It's criminal!"

"Mama, please wait until you've had a chance to see us."

"Us? Which us? I shall not wear that foul sheet for all the—"

"May, dearest," Papa interrupted, "I'm fairly certain that John means Midnight."

I told him that he was indeed correct, whereupon he let the two of us leave the table.

One of the tricks I had taught Fanny was to brace her hind paws on my shoulders and forepaws on my head, so that her head rose far above my own. In this way, she resembled a goddess on the prow of a sailing ship, except for her wagging tail thumping on my back. She could stand this way for five minutes or more without the least discomfort.

I had also discovered Midnight was strong enough to walk with me on his shoulders.

In our garden, combining these two tricks produced a most spectacular effect; by covering ourselves in the sheets, we appeared to be a sphinx more than seven feet in height, with the feet of a man and the head of a Border collie. I had practiced with Fanny so that if we ever lost our balance she would be able to spring to her side and land safely.

We called the others out to see us. Mama gaped from the doorway while Papa shook his head and laughed.

"You are insane, John Zarco Stewart!" Mama declared. "You are going to fall. And you will break your neck!"

"Let them have their merriment," said Papa, drawing her close. "He will be young only once. And we must not let today's misery ruin our evening."

"This is madness," she moaned. "Utter madness, I tell you."

"Indeed it is," Papa agreed, but his eyes were radiant with glee.

MIDNIGHT AND I could see only directly ahead through our eye-holes, so Papa steered us around the stray filth on the street. Praise shouted by neighbors lifted our spirits, and children ran after us screeching with glee. After a hundred or so paces, Midnight grew tired and let me down. Senhora Beatriz kissed me and whispered that Daniel would have been overjoyed to see such a clever performance. Unfallen tears turned her hazel eyes to liquid, and I saw in her unsteady movements how she had weakened over the last year, shrinking under the weight of her grief. Likely we were both thinking how much better my trick would have been with Daniel walking on his hands down the street to herald our arrival.

Mama insisted on holding my hand now so that I would create no more "wayward miracles," as she referred to my mischief. And so, as a family, we headed toward the Rua de Cedofeita, where the street musicians had assembled for the festivities. We soon discovered that Lourenço Reis was standing there on a wooden platform, preaching to a crowd.

"There he is," Papa said to Benjamin.

Mama gripped my hand tighter. "Come, let us keep going."

"Why hasn't he been arrested?" I asked.

"We shall do better than that," Papa told me. "Just give us a few days, son."

We hurried away. But before we had gone another fifty paces, he appeared before us. Blocking our path just a few feet ahead of Benjamin, he declared, " 'I come not to send peace, but a sword!' "

Benjamin, God bless him, replied, "You, sir, are no Jesus of Nazareth, and you may sheath your sword up your arse, where it belongs."

"Devilish *Marrano*!" he spat in fury.

Papa grabbed Benjamin's arm and glared at Reis. "Sir, I know who you are and what you have done this day, and I tell you now to let us continue on our way with no further trouble or you shall forever regret it."

"We shall chase you foreigners from Portugal!" the hateful preacher bellowed. "You shall not have this city—not while I draw breath."

Given Mama's anxious nature, I'd not have expected her to speak, but in her tense, quavering voice, she said, "You may scream all you want, sir, but we are longtime residents of this city, all of us. And you shall not win this battle. Not while *I* draw breath."

Reis pointed his staff at her. "Sinful Jewess. Your very presence is offensive. You must die so that Christ may live!"

She gasped at his effrontery. Father steadied her and shouted, "You cowardly bastard! I have half a mind to strike you here and now."

"Let it go, James," said Benjamin. "Please, let us return home. Midnight, come here and help me."

"Make no mistake, we shall burn you all!" the necromancer cried. "We shall burn them for Christ, shall we not? And we shall send their smoke to Him on this holy night."

With my heart beating so loud that I could hear little except my own fear, I screamed, "You are the foreigner here! And you are the one who will die!"

Pointing a damning finger at me, he exclaimed, "You are the devil. You shall not tempt me. You shall not win a victory in this City of God. I shall see you burned at the cross!"

This was too much for Papa to bear. He raised his cane above his head and was about to charge at him. More powerful by half than Lourenço Reis, I believe he would have beaten him senseless had he not been restrained by Benjamin and Midnight.

"I shall kill you!" Papa was shouting.

"No, James," Benjamin said firmly. "Not now. I shall deal with him at the right moment. And when I get him, I shall send him straight back to hell. I promise you that."

But Papa would not be dissuaded. "I shall murder you, you coward!" he swore.

The necromancer smiled, then raised his staff over his head and shouted, "Let us burn them now! Let us send their smoke to God."

WITH MIDNIGHT'S HELP, Benjamin steered Papa back to our street. Something shattering had happened and no one could find the words to put the encounter into perspective. Mama had gone completely pale and stopped speaking altogether. We considered it best to return home.

There, with all the worry over Mama, Papa and Benjamin did not seem to notice Midnight slipping out of our house with his quiver and a basket, but I did. He held up a finger to his lips as he crept outside.

Mother leaned on Father as he walked her up to their room, where he put her to bed. Benjamin started a fire in our hearth, and he told me that when he was close to my age, he had witnessed an Act of Faith in Lisbon in which more than fifty shackled *Marranos* had been marched around a square and jeered at by the crowds. Three of them had been burned at the stake. "I never plan to smell burning Jewish flesh again," he said, almost to himself.

That night, I heard Papa and Benjamin whispering about having Lourenço Reis expelled from Porto by the civil authorities. It was fairly clear that this was not their first such conversation. This was when I first began to believe that Midnight might not have been acting on his own in slipping out of our home and that he and Papa might have been involved in a conspiracy that Benjamin had started weaving days—or even weeks—earlier.

MIDNIGHT TOLD ME of his clandestine activities the next day when, at dawn, I heard him creeping up to the Lookout Tower. Yawning in his doorway, my eyes still heavy with slumber, I asked him where he had been. He took me back to bed. Sitting by my side, he said, "Mantis spoke to me a few weeks ago in a dream. He told me that a beast would drink up all the water in Porto and create a terrible drought. Many of us would die. When I saw the preacher, I understood. So I took my quiver and arrows and hid them in a basket."

The Bushman told me that he had watched Lourenço Reis ranting to ever larger crowds until, at the stroke of twelve, the evil man climbed down from his stage and strode off toward New Square.

Midnight tracked him through the lantern-lit night. At each of three successive festive sites around the city, Reis succeeded in raising furious cries against the *Marranos*. A short time past three in the morning, he ceased his rabble-rousing and strode off alone toward the river. After rapping on the door of a large stone mansion, he was hastily admitted. From Midnight's description, I was able to identify this building as the Dominican monastery.

"Presumably, he is still there now," Midnight told me.

"So what will you do?"

"I have a favor to ask you, John. You must tell Benjamin that I shall not come to work today. Tell him that Mantis has asked me to do an errand for him."

"Will you follow the necromancer?"

Midnight nodded.

I asked, "Will you kill him?"

He lifted my blanket up over my mouth to keep me quiet, then patted my chest. "Return to sleep, my little gemsbok. You need not worry. I shall be safe."

I sat up. "But you might need my help."

"No, Mantis told me that you are to stay here. We Bushmen coat ourselves with a scent that Hyena cannot abide. We are perfectly safe. But a gemsbok"—here he growled and bared his teeth—"a gemsbok would be eaten." Then he gave me his wide, infectious smile.

MIDNIGHT LEFT THE house fifteen minutes later. Anxious, I dressed quickly and went to the garden to play with Fanny. After a little while, my father questioned me about Midnight's whereabouts. I lied, saying that he had gone off in search of rain.

Over breakfast, while handing me my second plate of eggs, Papa cleared his throat and said, "John, your mother and I intend to send you to school in England. We believe you will be happier there."

"In England?"

"Yes, to a boarding school. It is a grand place that will greatly benefit your education." He struggled to smile. "The lads stroll around the grounds giving Latin names to birds and reading Shakespeare. It will be just the place for you."

"No," I replied.

Mother handed me another cup of tea. "Many a lad would envy your chance to study at such a place."

"Good, then let them go instead of me."

Papa glared. "I'll thank you not to use that tone of voice with your mother."

"I shan't, if she will stop telling me how lucky I am to leave behind everything I know."

Papa had only struck me once in my life, but I could almost feel my backside burning again. "Even you ought to be able to see that this is not your choice. This is a decision we have reached. You shall travel to my sister in England, with a letter from me, and she will enroll you in a proper school. I already have some excellent suggestions from the English consul here in Porto, and he knows all the best schools."

Though I knew Papa would explode, I was adamant that I would never leave Portugal. "We shall see," I said, and reached across the table for the salt shaker, to signal that the conversation was at an end.

Mother grabbed my wrist and said, "You are not safe here. You know I would not send you away otherwise. That I should be separated from you—" Unable to finish her sentence, she withdrew her hand and looked down to hide her tears.

"Will Fanny be allowed to come with me?" I asked.

"No," Father replied. "But she will be fine. We shall treat her like a queen, and you can see her on holidays."

"Then I can come back?"

Father's resolve yielded now to sorrow, which was precisely as I'd hoped. I wanted to punish him for even conceiving of such a plot against me.

"Dear God, lad, do you think we are monsters?"

"And Midnight—I shall have to leave him too?" I asked, purposely ignoring his question.

"Yes," Papa replied.

"How much time do I have before this sentence begins?" I asked.

"Three weeks, I'd say," he replied. "Six weeks at the most."

Mama, sobbing, fled to her pianoforte. Father looked at me glumly and said, "John, you might try sometimes to make the unpleasant matters of life a trifle easier." Then he went to her.

I listened to their subdued voices from the table, unrepentant, furious at my father's criticism.

"I cannot," Mama whispered to Papa.

"You must. At least for a time."

"For a year, no longer. Any longer, James, and I shall die."

MIDNIGHT FAILED TO come home over the next two days, and I was greatly concerned for his safety. When I asked Papa if he'd seen him, all he would say was "Worry not, laddie. Midnight can take care of himself. I'm sure he's well."

Benjamin came to see us the following evening. From the top of the stairs I heard him explain that he had not been granted an audience with the Bishop but had spoken at great length to one of his staff. He had been told in no uncertain terms that nothing would—or indeed could— be done to silence the necromancer, since his activities were outside the jurisdiction of the diocese of Porto, which was a flimsy excuse at best. He suspected that the Bishop had decided to look the other way.

Benjamin believed that rousing the residents of Porto against the *Marranos* was of great use to the Church right now, for its power was waning. The ecclesiastical hierarchy wanted a strong hand to play at Napoleon's table should he become ruler of Portugal.

"Then we are on our own," Father said quietly.

MIDNIGHT RETURNED THE next day at dawn. He came to my room and knelt down next to my bed. His shirt sleeve was torn and he was dripping with sweat.

"Did you track the necromancer? Did you kill him?"

He smiled. "If I am taken away, my little gemsbok, do not be too upset. The important thing is that you are safe now."

My father must have heard him come up the stairs, because he appeared now in my doorway, clearly surprised. "Midnight! We were worried." Noticing the quill on the end of my bed, he said, "Have you been hunting?"

The African stood up and faced him. "I am sorry to have caused you concern, Mr. Stewart. Yes, I've been hunting. We must talk."

Mother then appeared. "What has happened?"

"One moment, Mrs. Stewart," the African replied. He went to my window and peered out, then closed the shutters. "I may have been followed here," he explained.

I saw that his hair was matted with wee twigs and that there were soil stains on the back of his breeches. "Who would want to follow you?" I asked.

"The men who were with Lourenço Reis."

XVIII

MIDNIGHT REMEMBERED MUSKET AND CAN-non fire exploding around him the first time he was cap-tured by Europeans. But most of all he remembered the horses. "Swiftness and power given life," he told me. "Even Mantis watched them with awe."

Dark heavy balls of metal launched from cannons ex-ploded in storms of fire. Blood spilled from his wounded tribesmen; all save three young children were left to rot in the African sun. Midnight never knew what happened to his two surviving kin.

The howls of hyenas gorging themselves could be heard from his new home, a farm owned by a round-faced Dutch-man, whose servant he became for a few short months. But although he could carry water, feed the chickens and cattle, and kill snakes with only a stick, Midnight had an enormous appetite and ate more than he could earn.

Rather than slit his throat, as the Dutchman ordered, a Zulu servant, under cover of darkness, walked Midnight an hour into the countryside, offering him to the will of the desert. The land and sky proved generous that night; he found his way by moonlight to a family of Bushmen follow-ing the rains to the Shaggy Hills, thirty miles east. They offered him water from a hollowed ostrich shell and some dried meat. They became his new kin.

Fourteen years later by Papa's estimation, Boer soldiers returned, different ones to a different place but mounted on horses just the same. By now they knew that even Bushmen adults could be "domesticated" with a regime of punishment and reward. So when Midnight was wounded by a bullet in the arm, he was allowed to be seen by a physician. His life was spared and he was sold by a soldier to Reynolds, the Yorkshireman from whom my father would later steal him.

When asked his name, he replied that it was Midnight, for this was the name Mantis had instructed him to assume when among Europeans. "It will help you to remain at your own center," the insect-god had told him.

It was an itinerant Welsh minister named Dee, with burning coals for eyes, who informed Midnight that his parents had been killed not by men but by God. Furthermore, he said, the Lord was no longer willing to permit heathens in the civilized Africa that Europe was forging out of the primitive, pestilent, and dark chaos that it had once been. Having had the misfortune to be born a Bushman, Midnight, too, would be barred from heaven unless—here the minister withdrew a New Testament from his small leather satchel—he received Christ into his heart.

Dee visited all the English farms on the Cape. Clad in a hat lined with purple velvet and a mantle of rabbit pelts, he told all the servants that their dancing and—in the case of the Bushmen—their nomadic way of life were affronts to God. The sole cure for both illness and ignorance was Baptism.

Unlike the other African servants on the farm, Midnight refused the minister's cure. Whipped until his skin was shredded, he was carried to the servants' quarters. There, Jackal appeared to him in a dream, peeing on Mantis. But the insect remained unperturbed. In fact, he was laughing.

The next day, Mrs. Reynolds took her carriage to town for some cordage that her husband needed. The next candidate for Baptism was a Xhosa lad called John, who was generally regarded as lazy and expendable. He was not as fortunate as Midnight. Though he had agreed to the ceremony, he was to be made an example.

With all the slaves in attendance, John was tied to the porch rail and whipped until the skin on his back had peeled off and he would never cry again. With his bright eyes still wide open, but with his life gone, Minister Dee untied him and pronounced him saved.

This was why Midnight allowed water to be sprinkled on his head. But the Time of the Hyena was on him, and he was unable to laugh like Mantis. In fact, he did not talk for many months.

FATHER, MOTHER, AND I listened in rapt silence while Midnight told us of these times in Africa. At first we didn't understand the connection of his past to what he might or might not have done to Lourenço Reis—until he said that after seeing the preacher on St. John's Eve he had remembered Minister Dee and the Xhosa young man named John who had been lashed to death. Midnight believed that the correspondence of names was not accidental. "I understood that Mantis was telling me that *our* John would die if Reis were to live."

"Just because he has the same name as that Xhosa lad?" Papa asked.

"I believe that such coincidences point to connections between destinies that we cannot always see. But Mantis can see them." Midnight told us that over the previous nights he had tracked Reis from one city square to another, where growing crowds welcomed his words with great cheers.

"Just after eleven o'clock last night," the African said, "Reis walked very, very briskly to the wharf. As he conversed with a ferryman, I ran up the hill and hid in the bushes."

"What happened after that?" Papa asked.

"Then . . . then I shot him . . . I shot Reis."

"Your arrow reached him from the hillside?" Papa asked.

"Yes, I could see him distinctly in the lantern light. My first arrow pierced his shoulder blade. It had a tip of strong-strong poison. There was no need for another. He is dead by now."

Before he could say any more, Mama rushed to Midnight, weeping.

"I care not for myself, but you have delivered my John from Pharaoh," she said solemnly. "You have saved him again. Thank you for your sacrifice. I shall always be grateful."

Kissing the African's hands, she rested her head against his chest. I was dumbfounded, and so, too, was my father. Neither of us had realized the extent of her fear these past days and the supreme effort she had made to conceal her emotions.

Mama later told me that she knew in her heart that the Inquisition would have started afresh had not the Bushman murdered Lourenço Reis. "There was no question in my mind. One man would have turned us all to smoke and ash. Do you understand? It takes only one."

"He was mad," I replied.

"No, no. He was quite sane. He knew precisely what he was doing. They always do."

I MUST CONFESS the story Midnight told us may not have been entirely true. I learned from the Olive Tree Sisters that Reis had been seen entering Senhor Benjamin's home on the night of his death—a fact later confirmed by the apothecary. Benjamin would also admit that a note from him requesting a meeting with the necromancer had been delivered to Reis, though he would never divulge the identity of the messenger.

With the benefit of hindsight, I suspect that Reis was lured to Benjamin's home by Midnight, who had been following him and who would have had ample opportunity to hand him a note. Once there, the preacher might have been given a clever poison in a glass of wine or water, one that would only take effect several hours later. Or the poison might even have been placed secretly in his snuff.

The ferryman who rowed Reis back to land told me that the preacher had not been wounded by any arrow. Instead, *after placing two pinches of snuff in his nose and inhaling,* he complained of deep chest pains and then fell almost immediately into a rigid paralysis. He was dead within minutes.

I did not discern the discrepancies in the African's story at the time because we did not discuss the situation with anyone outside our family—for obvious reasons.

I have come to believe that Reis's death was planned by Benjamin, who prevailed upon Midnight to lie to us so that we might only reveal a false version of events if ever questioned by ecclesiastical or civil authorities. In this way, we could neither implicate the apothecary nor be regarded as coconspirators. I have often wondered if Papa, too, might have been one of the originators of the plan.

I am quite sure that Midnight could have been convinced to lie to us, if he was sure that it would protect my family.

It might be considered that Benjamin endangered Midnight by compelling him to lie to us about having murdered Reis. But the Bushman would not have been in any true peril, since his story, even if recounted to representatives of the Crown or the Church, could easily have been refuted. Reis's body bore no arrow wound, as the ferryman and others could testify.

IN THE TWENTY years that have elapsed, I have read what I could find about Reis, who is mentioned twice in Artur Moura Carneiro's chronicle of Porto in the years prior to the Napoleonic Wars. It is written there that he had returned to Porto from Goa, where he had endeavored to reestablish the stranglehold of the Inquisition on Portuguese India. Why he chose our city for the revivification of his career in continental Portugal remains a mystery, but he probably thought that the greater part of commerce in our city was controlled by the British and the Christianized Jews. This was hardly true, but his hatred of us blinded him to the reality of our situation.

Another very intriguing possibility is that his true target may not have been the *Marranos* at all, but rather the Freemasons, a nearly invisible clan I knew nothing about at the time, but who were apparently well-placed in the city's hierarchy. Perhaps he wanted to take advantage of the traditional Christian distrust of the Jews as a way of reestablishing the Inquisition, intending to turn its persecutory power against these Masons at a later date.

WHATEVER THE TRUTH of this episode, we thought it prudent that Midnight leave Porto for a time. My father, who was due to travel upriver to survey lands, decided to take all of us with him.

We spent a peaceful fortnight in a stone manor house on the north bank of the Douro River. Papa, who had visited it often, dubbed it Macbeth's Castle, where *dark night strangles the traveling lamp*. But as we were all together as a family, we could not have been happier.

XIX

*A*S THE PRESENT DANGER TO OUR SECRET COM-munity had passed, my father, mother, and I never talked again of boarding school in England, and Midnight and I be-gan our weekly discussions of the Torah with Senhor Benjamin. The Bushman was enthralled from the very be-ginning, greatly pleased that the Lord of the Hebrews could be wrathful and even scheming, as well as occasionally inde-cisive.

And so our lives again returned to a happy routine, and we continued along this path largely without incident till October of 1806.

I WAS NOW fifteen and a half, and to my great joy, my upper lip bristled with a faint mustache. I was also nearly a hand taller than Midnight and Mama, fully five feet four inches, though I was still a year away from the growth spurt that would elevate me to nearly six feet in height. Unsur-prisingly, young women figured most prominently in my thoughts at this time.

Midnight was more preoccupied than ever with his work and studies with Benjamin. Indeed, the apothecary's basement had been turned into an alchemical laboratory of sorts, home to a dizzying combination of odd smells that often filtered out into the street.

Father had acquired seven more acres of land upriver, giving us a grand total of fourteen. He estimated that in just two more years he could begin planting vines for our very own vintage. Although my father had taken me upriver several times for lessons on wine growing and I had proved totally useless, we all agreed that the name Stewart & Son had a certain ring to it.

Mother had forsworn her allegiance to Mozart for the time being and been captured body and soul by Beethoven. She learned everything by him that she could order from London. New manuscripts were slow in arriving, however, due to disruptions in postal service caused by Napoleon's war, currently raging across most of Europe, though not yet in Portugal.

As for Fanny, she had given birth to four unplanned chubby puppies. While she was in heat, she had escaped from under my vigilant eye by launching herself like Pegasus out of the parlor window. Dashing up our street, she surrendered her maidenhood to the first passing suitor—a fawn-colored mutt raised in the sewers of Porto, judging from his matted hair and foul smell.

Of the four puppies, we succeeded in finding proper owners for three of them and kept the runt of the litter for ourselves. Midnight named her Zebra, owing to the white stripe that started at her nose and stretched across her black and brown back. She was the puppy my dearest Fanny loved the most. So much so that I feared her heart would break if we were to give her away.

IN THE WORLD beyond the confines of our home, Napoleon had won his greatest victory at Austerlitz, leaving fifteen thousand Russians and Austrians to rot in the Moravian sun. On land he had proved himself supreme, and there were many who believed that he would soon be the master of all Europe. Except for the British. And not if the Emperor were foolish enough to attack at sea again: Off the coast of Cape Trafalgar, in southwest Spain, Lord Nelson and his fleet had won a decisive victory precisely one year earlier, on October the Twenty-First, 1805. British forces had multiplied in strength since, and Napoleon hadn't dared to send his navy off again to battle.

Although we were nervous about Portugal getting involved in the war, we weren't lacking in optimism. It was firmly believed that the British—our main trading partners—would never allow Porto to fall to the French.

IN MATTERS OF the heart, I had become absolutely fascinated by a lass living on the Rua das Taipas. Maria Angelica was her name, and she was seventeen. I tend to hold Violeta responsible for instilling in me a liking for older girls with knowing eyes, and this young lady had the most stunning green eyes I had ever seen.

She was fair of complexion, and yet her hair was so thick and black that in one of my secret love poems I rhapsodized that it was *made of starless night.* Her breasts were also of great interest to me, and I simply could not drag my covetous eyes away from them.

In those days, we were expected to behave as proper gentlemen and ladies, so I dared not even speak to Maria Angelica, although I watched her from afar, utterly charmed by her delicate movements. To catch glimpses of her, I walked by her sitting-room window up to a dozen times a day. I would invent endless excuses for pausing a moment, such as fastening the buckles on my shoes or doing up the buttons on my breeches, until her neighbors, giggling with mirth, began to make loud kissing noises every time I approached.

One afternoon I had the good fortune to pass beneath her window just as she was opening it. "Good day, sir," she said, leaning out.

Before we could expand upon this promising start to our relationship, however, her mother yanked her inside and slammed the shutters closed. Yet I remained undaunted in my passion. Which was why, when I first learned of my father's impending trip with Midnight to London, on the night of our commemoration of Lord Nelson's victory, I failed to insist on being invited along. They were to be gone for six weeks.

"Am I to come?" I asked my father, desperately hoping that he would say no.

"No, son, I am afraid not."

"Why are you going?"

"Well, John, you may recall that one of Midnight's reasons for coming with me to Europe was to try to find a cure for smallpox. A few years ago, I learned of a physician named Jenner, who has been working in London, and of his theories on the inoculative effect of cowpox. And so . . ."

I must have looked confused, because he went on to explain, "John, all I know is that thousands of people have now been successfully inoculated against the disease. The good man provides this service to the poor free of charge—up to three hundred patients per day. So I wrote to the Royal Jennerian Society, requesting permission to witness the procedure, and they have graciously agreed."

"If this cure is a good one, then will Midnight return to Africa?"

"Aye, he may, son. We shall only know after England."

The possibility of him leaving us filled me with dread. "In that case," I said, "I should like to come with you."

"No, not this time, lad. You and I shall go to London one day soon, but not now."

"But it would be good for me to—"

"No," he interrupted. "I'm sorry, but it's completely impossible."

I DIDN'T BRING up the subject again until the following afternoon, when I was walking with Midnight by the dry docks along the river.

"Papa says that you will soon leave for England to find a cure for smallpox."

He patted my back. "Yes, John, I am very, very pleased. You cannot know what this means to me. So many of my people have died. So many Zulu and Xhosa too."

"If you find a proper medicine, will you leave for your homeland immediately?"

"No, I shall return to carry out experiments with Benjamin. I must be able to repeat the procedure or it will be of no help at all. If all goes well, then I shall indeed return to Africa."

Seeing my sadness, he added, "I have an interesting proposition for you, however."

I frowned at him, because I wished him to feel terrible about leaving me alone.

"Will you not even ask me what my proposition might be?" He winked. "I shall be cross with you if you don't."

"No," I barked, which made him laugh.

"May you always ride between the toes of Eland," he said.

"And just what does that mean?"

"May you always be you. And may you always go slowly."

"Why slowly?"

"Because in the African desert one must always proceed with caution or risk stepping on something that might bite or sting."

He linked his arm in mine, which he had started to do ever since I had grown taller than him. "John, when I return to Africa, I should like you to come with me. That is my proposition."

"Me—in Africa?" I asked incredulously.

"Yes. I'd very much like you to stay with me for a time. We have birds there that are beautiful-beautiful, and they have been waiting for you to imitate them for many years. I should not like them to wait forever."

"Have you suggested this to Mama and Papa?" I asked excitedly.

"Not yet. First we must see about England, then we shall talk to your parents."

"My mother will not let me stay long. She probably won't even let me go."

"You will come for a few months every year or two. And I shall visit Porto every other year as well."

"But it is very far to southern Africa."

"No, not so far," he laughed. "Just halfway around the world!"

"And dangerous."

"Less dangerous than Europe. The French will shortly cross the mountains into Portugal."

"Do you think so?"

"Napoleon is a hyena who thinks he is a lion. He will try to devour Portugal. I, for one, would prefer to be elsewhere when he comes. There will be much suffering and death. Perhaps I shall propose that your parents come to Africa as well. Your father might make a vineyard there, after all."

He motioned for me to sit with him on a great log by the river. Once we were settled, he said, "There was a year, John, when a drought fell over all the land. It was a very, very bad time." He took out his wee clay pipe. "Mantis was away in a distant desert, for he grew ill from his life among men and women from time to time, and he needed the sweet nectar of the white flowers that grew there to replenish his spirit. But when Bee flew to him to tell him of the good people dying everywhere in his homeland, he risked his own life and didn't hesitate to climb onto his friend's wings.

"Discovering many already dead from hunger, Mantis prevailed upon Ostrich to give them some of her honey or at least lead them to her hives. But the great bird refused to do so. Mantis chided her, of course, but she just ruffled her tail feathers at him. And then that silly bird tucked all her honey under her wing and flew away. So Mantis began to consider how he might steal it so the First People might survive. But without his nectar he was growing weaker every day."

Midnight leaned toward me and patted my leg. "One day he crawled slowly to Ostrich and said in his frail voice, 'I have found a tree with the most scrumptious plums on it. You would like them very, very much.'

"The gullible bird asked to be taken to the fruit tree quickly-quickly. So Mantis led her to a tree heavy with yellow plums. Ostrich picked joyously at the bottom branches, for the fruit was delicious.

"But Mantis said, 'The ones up higher are even better. If you coat them in your honey, no delicacy will ever be able to equal them.' And so the bird strained its neck to reach further up.

" 'You silly thing,' the insect told her. 'Not there—right at the top!' " Midnight pointed with his pipe into the sky and squinted. " 'That big one there, on the crown, it's the sweetest of all.' "

My friend stood now, shaping his thumb and forefingers into a greedy beak. "The bird stretched her neck as far as she could. And just as she snared the topmost plum"—here, Midnight snapped his fingers shut—"Mantis used the last of his strength and reached under her wing, stealing all but one of her honeycombs.

"Since that day, John, Ostrich has never flown again for fear of losing her very last comb. As for men and women, as you know, we have the wisdom of honey to sustain us through all manner of misfortune."

"But what happened to Mantis when he used up the last of his strength. Did he die?"

The African's eyes shone with delight. "No, John, he did not die. For the moon, crying over him, shed her tears of softened light upon him, and when he licked them from his lips, he recovered. Having some of the moon's eternity in him, he was never ill again."

Midnight winked at me to signal the end of his tale and puffed contentedly on his pipe.

"But what does it mean?" I asked.

He kissed my brow. "There is nothing that Mantis and I might ever be doing in the distant desert that will prevent us from coming to you and stealing you a treasure if you ever need it."

THREE DAYS BEFORE Father and Midnight were due to leave for England, I was awakened at dawn by a strange noise. At first, I thought it was Fanny whimpering. Wrapping my blanket around my shoulders, I followed the noise down to our sitting room. There, by the cold hearth, I found my father doubled over in his armchair, sobbing convulsively. I was just retracing my steps to spare his embarrassment when he called my name.

A candle flame illuminated his eyes. They were so full of misery that I thought he must have received some terrible news. Perhaps Aunt Fiona had died.

Starving for my touch, he held out his trembling hand to me and I rushed into his arms. His distress was overpowering. "Papa, what's happened?" I asked.

"A dream," he whispered. "I was all alone in an empty house. No heat. No light. Your mother was dead and you were gone—I had no idea where. I was all alone in the dark. And I would remain alone forever."

"I am here," I said, gripping his shoulders, "and I shall not leave you."

Wiping his eyes with his hand, he said, "You are kind. And I shall be well now. It was just a silly dream. Go back to sleep. I'm sorry to have frightened you."

"I shall take you to your room. Come, let me lead you. As you used to do when I was a wee lad."

"No, no. Let me stay here. I don't want to wake your mother."

"Then I'll stay with you."

"Yes, sit with me. It will do me good to feel you next to me."

His eyes fluttered closed, and he began to breathe more easily. For a time, he caressed my hair and began to whisper a story to me, about an elf who fell in love with a mermaid, but he never finished it, for he soon fell asleep. Shivering in the cold air, I waited until I was certain he would not wake, then climbed back upstairs, each footfall seeming a step into a strange world where my father was forever alone and weeping.

We never spoke again of his nightmare.

ON THE DAY of departure, I accompanied Father and Midnight to the wharf. Mama stayed in her room, too distraught to join us.

The sun was resplendent in the blue sky, casting light over the new bridge that had been built over the river, linking Porto on the north bank with Vila Nova da Gaia on the south.

"The city is growing," Papa said. "Just like my son."

He smiled affectionately at me and we embraced, for the last time in complete and true friendship, I think. He told me to obey my mother in all things, since even though I was several inches her senior, I was not yet her match in good sense and intuition.

He promised me he'd be home for Christmas.

I then hugged Midnight fiercely, which made him grin. He told me that upon his return he would tell me the story of how Gemsbok was wed by Mantis to Honeyguide, which I believe was his way of letting me know that he had noticed my newfound interest in lassies.

"Go slow," he warned me, and we kissed each other on both cheeks.

"You go slow too," I replied.

We continued to wave to one another even as they reached the deck. Midnight and I shouted sillinesses about Fanny for some time, simply to keep greater emotions at bay. Then, as the ship pulled anchor, we sang our favorite song: "The Foggy, Foggy Dew":

Oh, I am a bachelor, I live by myself,
and I work at the weaver trade.
And the only, only thing
I ever did wrong
was to woo a fair young maid.
I wooed her in the summertime,
and in the winter, too-oo.
And many, many times,
I held her in my arms
Just to keep her from the foggy, foggy dew.

Singing this tune with Midnight at the wharf... I never sang it again until my daughters were born. Even then, I would always hear the African's voice accompanying my own.

DURING THEIR STAY in England, I tried to steer my friendship with Maria Angelica into more intimate territories, but I was continually thwarted by the vigilance of her satanically sharp-sighted mother. Once, spotting me below her balcony, she called down to me, "Do not ever think that I should permit my daughter to be escorted by filth like you."

I was shocked speechless. Thoroughly disheartened, I thought it best not to risk another approach until Father's return, so that I could ask his advice on how best to proceed.

We received two letters from him during his trip. After first reading them alone, my mother shared them with me. The first one recounted some of the wonders of London, most particularly a walk through the gardens of the Royal Palace at Kensington, which, since the removal of the court to Richmond, had been opened to the public on Sundays. To Father's great joy, his elder sister Fiona had come up from Maidenhead to London for a week to stay in the same inn as Father and Midnight and was doing very well indeed.

In the second letter, Papa wrote that they had been received at St. Thomas's Hospital by Dr. Jenner, whom he had found kind and quick-witted. There, they were given a demonstration of the inoculation procedure. Papa was so impressed that he paid to have himself and Midnight inoculated. Dr. Jenner gave Father and Midnight an hour of his valuable time and answered all of the African's questions amiably, though his Gloucestershire vowels caused them both some ear strain.

Father told us that he had already booked passage from Portsmouth to Porto on a ship leaving on the Fourteenth of December. Depending on the winds, we were to expect him from the morning of the Nineteenth onward.

In a separate postscript on the back of the final sheet, he wrote to me: *I hope that you are being kind to your mother, for she is the only person in the world who loves you as much as I do. Your Affectionate Father, James Stewart.*

Midnight had also added a few sentences, letting me know that his meeting with Jenner had proved very, very fruitful, and although London was a magnificent place, it was too crowded for his liking.

I long to be with you both in our beloved Porto, he wrote, signing *Midnight* with an elegant flourish on the *M.*

I was very impressed with the way his penmanship had improved since those first weeks of study when he had insisted on adding wings, snouts, and antlers to his letters.

UNABLE TO SLEEP past dawn on the Nineteenth, I played outside with Fanny and Zebra until my mother opened her shutters and threatened to throttle me if they barked one more time.

Father's boat was sighted at approximately ten o'clock. To my great fury, Mother refused to let me miss my Friday morning lesson with my tutor, Professor Raimundo, and accompany her to the port. And so it was that I suffered another of his lectures on the glory of trigonometric functions. I could not understand what was keeping my parents, and I soon began to worry that Father and Midnight had missed their ship.

Professor Raimundo left at noon. Slipping on my woolen coat, I stepped outside into the freezing cold. I considered calling on Senhor Benjamin and asking him to come with me to the wharf, as I was convinced that something had happened. But then I saw them coming up the street, my father's arm around Mother's waist.

My heart leapt with relief, and I ran to them.

As I got closer, however, I could see that Mama had been crying. When I reached her, she looked up at me with eyes so bruised from pain that I feared she'd been physically battered.

"Papa, what's happened—what's wrong with Mama?"

"John, let me get her home. Then we shall talk."

"Where has Midnight gone? Shall I fetch him?"

Neither of them replied. Father's jaw was clenched tight.

"Is something wrong with him? Did he stay in England?"

Papa didn't reply.

"What happened in England?" I cried. "Is he still there? He's not hurt or . . . or—"

"Calm down, John, please."

I turned the handle on our door and let Papa lead Mama inside. As he escorted her to the staircase, he told me to wait in the sitting room for him. I paced around and around, consumed by terrifying thoughts.

Father came down and poured himself a brandy, then prepared a shorter glass for me.

"Drink," he said.

"Just tell me what's happened."

"Do as I say, son." Realizing that he had spoken too roughly, he added gently, "Please, John, just do as I say."

I sipped at the brandy, which burned my throat.

"Sit," Papa said, gesturing to Mama's armchair.

I continued to stand. "Tell me where Midnight has gone."

He put his glass down on the mantelpiece.

"Midnight . . . Midnight is dead, son. I'm sorry."

"No, no . . . it's . . . it's not possible. Papa, it's—"

He reached for me, but I took a step back from him.

"You're lying! Where is he?"

"Midnight is gone from us forever."

I shook my head. "No, I shall not hear this. No . . . No . . ."

I felt dizzy, as though I were falling into pure darkness. I could no longer remember where Father and Midnight had gone or even why. Papa's mouth was moving, but I could hear nothing. . . .

I AWOKE ON the Persian rug in front of our sofa with a blanket covering me. Luna Oliveira was staring at me, which seemed most odd.

"You fainted, John," she said. "You are in your home. Your mother is upstairs."

Graça joined her now and smiled at me. I felt as though I were in a glass jar. And then everything came flooding back. "Is Midnight dead?" I asked.

"Wait, John," she replied, and stepped away.

From somewhere behind me, Father said he would join us presently. After a short while, he knelt down and helped me to sit up. Lifting a cup of tea to my lips, he begged me to drink. I did as he asked. It was too hot and sweet. "Is Midnight dead?" I asked again.

Father sipped from the cup himself. "I buried him myself before returning to Porto," he said somberly. "I'm so sorry, son."

Luna and Graça told me that they would visit me again later. After seeing them out, Papa helped me to a chair and sat down opposite me. Leaning back and inhaling deeply to gather his courage, he began the story of what had come to pass:

"Following our visit with Dr. Jenner, we decided that Midnight ought to see something of the countryside. You see, he found the hurly-burly of London so . . . so very disorienting. We took a carriage to a small inn in the seaside town of Swanage—a quiet place I'd visited once."

There was a nervous, twisted expression on Father's lips I'd never quite seen before.

"On our third and final afternoon there, the moist air began to tingle with electricity, and that evening there was a fanfare of thunder and lightning. The rains came, falling in sheets from a leaden sky so low . . . so very low, John, that it seemed ready to collapse upon the earth. It was a frightful sight. But Midnight was beside himself with excitement. In the morning, I discovered that he had already left to follow the rains."

I listened to all this without comment, feeling separated from all things.

"Now, the next morn," Father continued, "the sun came out after breakfast. At about ten o'clock, a young man in rude clothing accosted me and told me that he had been sent by his master to take me to the scene of an unfortunate accident. The victim of this accident had been found with a piece of stationery from our inn in his pocket. The youth had described this unfortunate man to the innkeeper and had been told that I'd been staying with him."

Papa reached for his pipe from the side table. "I hurried into the youth's carriage, of course. After half an hour we arrived at a great iron gate, behind which stood a palatial home."

Wiping his eyes, he said, "After the gatekeeper let us in, we were met by an old periwigged man. In a puckered voice, he introduced himself as Lord Lewis Pakenham. He begged my pardon for dragging me away from my inn without warning, then took me to the small stone chapel standing next to the main house. There... and there..." Papa hung his head and cleared his throat. "There, John," he continued, "I discovered a blood-spattered blanket covering a body lying on a straw mattress."

He wiped his mouth with the back of his hand. "Once the blanket was removed, I saw the gaping hole in Midnight's chest that had been made by a musket ball. His color had grayed and the expression on his face was none that he had ever worn in life."

Father turned to the wall and continued speaking, his voice desolate: "Pakenham told me that his gamekeeper had discovered the 'black boy'—that's what he called Midnight—poaching on his land, and he fired three shots at him. It was the very last one that killed him... the last one." Papa faced me, enraged. "That periwigged English wretch offered me a pinch of snuff from his silver box as though it might make up for my loss.

"Not wishing for what he called 'this mishap' to disoblige me in any way," Father continued, "Pakenham then offered me a servant for the rest of my stay in England. I declined, of course. There's little more to tell you, son. Just that the Bushman's shirt and coat had been found nearby, hanging from an upper tree branch that no one save a cat could have reached. In his waistcoat pocket, among other trifles such as seeds and burrs, had been discovered a single sheet of stationery from the Swanage Inn."

Papa produced the piece of paper in question and unfolded it. "Read this, John," he said, handing it to me.

As I took it, Papa rubbed my cheek affectionately. I began to read Midnight's last words.

It was not a lightning bug *you swallowed, but a lightning* bolt. *I know that now. And I will tell you a secret. Only very, very rarely does Mantis choose someone who is not a Bushman to carry him. Know that he rides now between your toes. And always remember that you carry him with you wherever you go.*

Upon reading this, vague, cold thoughts filtered through my head like mist. I seemed miles and years away, and I did not understand who Midnight had intended these words for.

When I expressed my bewilderment, Father patted my leg and said, "They were for you, of course."

XX

THE FIRST WEEK AFTER LEARNING OF MID-
night's death, I neither dressed nor left our house. Papa took
breakfast with me in my room. We scarcely talked or even
ate, but his presence was comforting. I was unaware of what
my mother was doing at the time, for she remained behind
her locked bedroom door most of the day. Very occasionally,
in the late afternoon, I would come downstairs to find her
embroidering. She refused to speak of Midnight.

Sitting with her, staring into her lost red eyes, I slowly
came to understand that we now lived in a house of silence.
Midnight was dead and I was alive—this seemed a great
mystery to me.

By the time Papa returned home from his office in the
early evening, Mama had already locked herself back in their
bedroom. He and I would eat cheese and bread by the
hearth, or sometimes in my room. My bed became a sea of
crumbs. He sometimes made fennel soup as well—his one
specialty.

Father got into the habit of leaving Mother's supper
outside their bedroom door, then returning downstairs, at
which time we'd hear the door click open and the food
being carried inside. Two or three times I placed some

late-blooming yellow dahlias from Midnight's garden onto her tray, hoping this would, in some way, console her, but she never mentioned them to me.

Father said many times, "We must have patience, lad. Your mother... she is not a woman to be rushed. She lives by her own rhythms."

PAPA KEPT TELLING me that time would heal my suffering, but I did not believe him. He quoted Robert Burns whenever his own words failed him, and I remember these lines in particular, because they reminded me that I'd someday meet Midnight again on the Mount of Olives:

> *Hope springs exulting on triumphant wing,*
> *That thus they all shall meet in future days...*

At times, he tried to inspire hope in me, telling me that I was such a likable lad that I would soon find more loyal companions. We both knew this was a lie, since it was obvious by now that I had not a whisker of aptitude for befriending boys my age, but we pretended we believed it.

AFTER A TIME, I moved many of Midnight's belongings into my room. I slept in one of his nightshirts because its weave had captured his smell—or at least, I imagined that it had. I even took his quiver, bow, and arrows with me into the woods one day, but I never managed to hit so much as a hare.

In truth, I did not want to harm anything but myself.

I NEVER DID ask my father how I might win Maria Angelica's hand.

WHEN I FELT stronger, he and I took Fanny and Zebra on walks together outside the city. He told me of Dr. Jenner's keen interest in my ornithological gifts and suggested that I might even consider a period of study with him. He proposed that in another year or two I stay for at least a few months in London, adding that such an experience would surely help me decide what I wished to do with my life.

He also promised that we would travel together that summer to Amsterdam, a city I had often longed to visit because of its thriving Portuguese-Jewish community. I remember bursting into tears for no reason when he told me. I often cried now with no good cause. Or for reasons that were hidden deep inside Midnight's grave.

LOCKED OUT OF their bedroom by Mother, Father was forced to sleep on the sofa in our sitting room. We stopped inviting guests over and even intimated to Benjamin that it would be better if he stopped joining us for our Friday night meal for the time being.

Mama would often watch me from her window as I romped with the dogs in the garden. If I waved or called up to her, however, she would draw her curtains.

Then, one Tuesday morning in the middle of January, she walked into the kitchen dressed in the elegant blue silk dress she normally wore to dinner parties. Gripping her pearl necklace, she announced she was off to market. I expected Father to be as curious as I was as to this change in her disposition, not to mention her odd choice of attire, but he was too relieved to ask any questions. Jumping up, he rushed to her and pressed his lips to her cheek as though welcoming her home from a dangerous journey.

That night she admitted my father back into their bedroom.

I hoped that she had recovered from her initial shock and grief, but over the next week or so she seemed like a frail creature preparing for a long winter. She scurried about the house from task to task as though a pause to rest might prove her undoing. Once, she mistakenly prepared tea with oregano and another time left jagged pieces of shell in our supper of eggs, codfish, and potatoes. This indicated to me that her mind was on a great voyage elsewhere. Perhaps she was off to England to lay roses from our garden on Midnight's grave. I know that I often daydreamed of doing precisely that, and I cannot believe that our thoughts were so different. We were always alike in so many ways.

One afternoon in late January, I returned from fetching our ironed linens from Senhora Beatriz to find Mother sobbing at her pianoforte. She clung to its top as though in peril of falling into so deep an inner darkness that she might never return.

I pried her fingers from the piano and held her to me. She leaned into my chest and wailed, shaking violently. She was so small and delicate; it was as though I had become her parent.

Kissing the top of her head and breathing in the warm scent of her hair made me cry. It was a terrible moment, yet strangely comforting as an expression of our solidarity.

"I must apologize for so many things," she told me afterward, wiping her eyes. "Can you forgive me?"

"Forgive you for what, Mama?"

I expected her to say, *for neglecting you these past weeks,* since she had not offered me any comfort at all.

Instead, she replied, "For Midnight's death."

"But you had nothing to do with it."

"No, no, sadly, that is not true. I ought never to have allowed your father and Midnight to receive that cowpox vaccine. I ought to have made that expressly clear before their departure."

"What are you talking about?"

"Don't you see? They must have been feverish. It must have done something to them, after all. Why else would Midnight have run off during the storm? And how else could your father have failed to protect him? No, John, they must have both not been in their right mind."

This seemed perfectly ridiculous to me, as Father had never mentioned delirium or even mild discomfort. And Mama knew as well that Midnight often followed storms. Alarmed by her logic, I suggested that she rest.

Later, I was standing at our back doorway, watching Fanny and Zebra gnawing on the same branch, when Mama shrieked. She had poured nearly a quart of boiling water down the front of her dress. Steam was rising from her bosom. When I yanked the kettle from her hand, I discovered it was nearly empty, which could not have been accidental.

Mother looked at me in terror, realizing now that she had scalded herself badly. Her eyes rolled back in her head and she fainted. With a lunge, I managed to prevent her from crashing onto the floor.

I laid her on the sofa in our sitting room, placed a cushion under her head, then ran to fetch the Olive Tree Sisters, who roused Mother with a vial of salts. As I listened to them whispering to her, I understood that her rage had revealed itself in the only ways it could—first in small mad acts of hostility toward my father and me, such as cracking eggshells into our supper, and now by abusing herself.

When Mama was awake, she suggested that I leave the room. It was at that precise moment that I began to believe she had stopped loving me.

Over the next week, she locked herself once again in her bedroom, forbidding my father and me from entering.

MOTHER DID STOP loving me for several years, I think, though that is a damning thing to even suggest. Perhaps I should rather say that her fondness for me was placed in a box containing both her marriage and Midnight's body and that the lid was firmly shut.

I suppose it is possible that she was too fond of me and knew that I was the only one capable of penetrating her armor. If she let herself show her love for me, if she sought and welcomed my affection, she would have shrieked for days on end at the loss of all she had once held dear— her marriage, most of all. Anyone gazing at her pale gaunt face knew that suicide was a true possibility for her.

It is ironic to think, of course, that she still could have loved me had she been willing to risk losing her sanity. Perhaps that is not something one can ask of another person.

HAVING HEARD MY mother voice previously unspoken doubts about my father, I soon dared to accuse him of failing in his duty to protect Midnight. He begged my forgiveness, but I continued to rail at him even as he sought to reason with me. Finally, shamed by his tears, I allowed him to explain that he would never forgive himself for having let Midnight out of his sight.

Father's admission of regret did little to quell my emotions, unfortunately, and I was rude to him on a number of occasions, once even telling him that I wished never again for him to accompany me on my walks with Fanny and Zebra. I knew I was behaving abominably but simply could not control myself. The hurt etched on his face seemed a worthy counterpart to my own frustration and grief. But he never punished me or gave me anything more than a mild reprimand, telling me that time would heal all. "Aye, even your fury at me, lad."

I began to hide in my room during the worst of my depression, emerging only when he had left the house. I spent my days in solitude, reading and sketching. I never went to see the Olive Tree Sisters, Senhor Benjamin, or anyone else.

One afternoon in mid-February, Papa tiptoed into my room while I lay nearly napping and sat at the foot of my bed. I didn't open my eyes; even though I could hear him crying softly, I still refused to forgive him.

Eventually he shuffled away.

The terrible thing is that Father never came to me for help again. I missed my chance that day. And the regret I feel for withholding my love for him crowns me even today as a miser and a fool.

SEVEN YEARS LATER, before I was married, I told my bride, Maria Francisca, everything about this time in order to warn her that she was taking damaged goods for a husband. To my great surprise, she surmised that I had denied my father solace at that key moment, not so much to punish him, but out of a fear of losing him to death.

I thought then that she was simply trying to ease my guilt, but I can see now that she was right; I did secretly fear that death was taking everything from me. I may have even reasoned that Daniel and Midnight had died because of my great affection for them, which meant that I—in some way—had caused their doom. Death avenged itself on me through them. For what, I could not be sure. Perhaps simply for my having been happy—but more likely for my wounding Daniel when he most needed my help.

IN LATE FEBRUARY, Mother took sick with terrible stomach pains and went to stay with Grandmother Rosa for four days. During her absence, Father finally refused to tolerate my attitude any longer.

"This has gone quite far enough," he told me one morning, throwing open my door and striding into my room, his eyes flashing. "I had expected sadness and even rage, but not this stubborn refusal to return to the world."

Holding his nose, he said, "My God, John, it stinks like a hound's rump in here! Can't you smell it?"

He threw open my shutters and mosquito screens. "This is shocking!" he shouted, lifting my brimming chamber pot from beside my bed. Carrying it carefully to my window, he hurled away its foul contents while crying *sujidade*—filth—in his Scottish accent. "John, I am wholly disgusted with you."

"Close the door on your way out," I sneered, pulling the covers over my head.

This infuriated him so viciously that he came to me, threw off my blankets, and grabbed me by my shirt with his fists, as though to pummel me. I desperately wanted him to do just that, so that I could hit him back. And yet I knew the only act that would have truly satisfied my rage would have been for him to descend like Orpheus into the underworld and bring Midnight home.

"I hate you!" I shouted.

He loosened his hold on me in defeat. "I'm sorry. I know this is hard for you. You are still so young. You will recover one day, just as you did after Daniel's death."

"I do not wish to recover," I replied, for at the time I imagined that surrendering my grief would mean giving up my last intimate hold on Midnight; my tears were all that bound us across the barrier between life and death. "As for Daniel, I have never forgotten him. And I never shall."

"No, and you will never forget Midnight. That is not what I am trying to— Oh, John. Do you think Midnight would have wished for you to lie here day after day as though there were no sun in the sky? He should have liked you to dance—to dance his death if you must, but to get up and get on your way just the same."

I knew then that I had underestimated Papa; he understood more about my kinship with Midnight than I had expected. I felt a single seed of affection for him growing anew in me.

"Papa, do you not miss him?"

"I miss him every day, John. But life... it is not what we might wish. We lose those we love, one after another. I have lost my parents and now I have lost Midnight. And your sadness, lad... It's hard for your old father to bear. I do not appear downhearted to you now because I cannot indulge my emotions. I have a family to support. I have work to do, John. I must trudge on without allowing myself the luxury of despair."

I wept at how badly I had misunderstood his actions. "I am sorry about saying I hate you... and blaming you too. I could never hate you."

He rubbed his eyes. "John, I have grown to despise myself too. More deeply than I might ever have imagined. Perhaps more deeply even than you."

I promised then to carry out my duties once again, but I cannot recall what he said; so unexpected was his admission of self-loathing, so uncharacteristic was it, that I could think of little else all afternoon.

*　　*　　*

SO MANY THINGS about my parents' marriage throughout that winter and spring were to prove so disconcerting that I began to suspect Father and Mother might not have told me everything about Midnight's death.

Unwilling to risk Mama's fragile state of mind, I only questioned Papa. On several occasions I was reassured that my suspicions were totally unfounded.

It is a testament to human resilience that I was soon able to peel potatoes, pump water, build a fire, make purchases at the market, and perform all the other tasks expected of me. Mother, too, emerged again, this time for good. That she was able to take on all the duties expected of a wife and mother speaks greatly for her strength of spirit.

But I am fairly certain that she only imitated the spirited woman she once had been—*that* person had ceased to exist.

"It is our fate in this life to keep walking no matter what," she told me.

NOT EVEN MY renewed strength could bridge the gulf between the three of us. Papa never told me another Scottish story, nor crept up behind Mama to surprise her with a kiss, and his trips upriver were no longer regarded as hindrances to our happiness. Mama never tried to make Papa laugh or reprimanded me for taking the stairs two at a time, and I never asked either of their advice on choosing a profession.

It is now plain to me that once Father returned home alone, our destruction was inevitable. We had opportunities to alter the course of our destiny, but only if we had acted much earlier—if, for instance, I had made that fateful voyage to England with Father and Midnight. Had I gone, I am certain that I would have been able to prevent this tragedy. That is my most punishing regret. I can see the blood on my fingers even today.

IN DEFERENCE TO Father's request, Professor Raimundo and I recommended lessons three months after Midnight's death. I soon discovered, however, that I no longer had any patience for his pomposity.

In mid-April, I found the courage to broach the subject with my mother over supper. "I cannot bear Professor Raimundo any longer, Mama. I should like to give studying on my own a try."

Having adopted a strategy of changing the subject whenever a decision needed to be reached, she replied, "Eat your soup."

"I find him so tedious that I could cry at times. I'm sure he is impeding my progress."

"John, you are nearly a man and you may do as you please," she said matter-of-factly.

That's when I said for the first time in many weeks, "I miss Midnight. I miss him every day."

Mother would not look at me.

"Don't you miss him greatly?" I inquired, leaning toward her in my eagerness. "Remember that first supper we had with him? When he told us that Africa was memory. Do you recall how mad you and I thought he was?"

Without a word, she put down her spoon, stood up, and glided to the stairs. I called after her to apologize, but she refused to turn around.

I WOULD NOT speak again of Midnight to either my mother or my father for another year.

I admit that I couldn't understand why she would not talk to me of him, if even for a few secret minutes. I could not fathom how we had come to this.

It will seem absurd, but whenever we referred to that time of night when the minute and hour hands of a clock point straight up toward the heavens, we never again spoke of *midnight,* but only of twelve o'clock.

XXI

I WAS TO BE SIXTEEN YEARS OF AGE AT THE end of April and, having dismissed my tutor, I soon settled into a new and solitary pattern of study. I did little else requiring concentrated effort, the only exceptions being my lessons with the Olive Tree Sisters on Fridays, and my study of the Torah with Benjamin on Sunday afternoons.

Outside events soon dramatically altered our lives, however. It was Napoleon who impinged on the quiet independence of our city, just as he would on that of every town in Europe.

Britain's only remaining allies on the Continent were Russia and Portugal, and so it was to our unfortunate outpost that the French Emperor now turned his attention.

Prince João, our Regent, was the head of our monarchy. In August of 1807 the French and Spanish ambassadors demanded that he declare war on England, give use of his fleet to French forces, confiscate goods from English vessels, and imprison all British subjects in his kingdom. While negotiations dragged on, the British citizens of Portugal were given valuable time to prepare for departure.

Father told Mother and me that we would not be fleeing Portugal. As subjects of the Portuguese crown, she and I would be safe under French occupation, and he had never maintained any direct commercial connection to His Majesty's government or any British firm. He believed that his employment in the Douro Wine Company, the single most important mercantile enterprise in Porto, guaranteed him a measure of safety.

We argued with his logic, but he would not give in.

In truth, there seemed nothing for him to return to in Britain. He had obviously decided that he would live or die, suffer a broken marriage or rebuild it, in Portugal.

Then, on October the Twentieth, the guillotine fell on the oldest of European alliances: Prince João declared war on Britain. But the surprise was to be on him—Napoleon and his Spanish lackeys had made plans to betray their treaty with Portugal and divide the country between them. A mixed French and Spanish army comprising eighteen thousand troops commanded by General Junot crossed our border at the end of October.

A convoy of ships was sent from England to collect the British wishing to flee Porto, where many of their families had lived for generations. William Warre, as British Consul, was the last to embark. As the ship set sail, he raised his fist to those of us left on shore, but Mama only frowned when I told her of his defiant gesture. "It's easy for a man to preach courage when he runs no risk," she said. She then told Father and me that we were to bury all of our valuables in the garden.

Having never experienced occupation before and having heard Professor Raimundo praise the French as honorable people, this seemed a laughable precaution. Unwilling to risk rankling her, however, I did as she asked. She and I wrapped her few rings and necklaces in linen towels, along with our silver, including her beloved menorah. We deposited them into tunnels that Father and I dug underneath the rosebushes.

Then we dug other pits more haphazardly, burying knickknacks of little or no value. Our reasoning was that the French would discover these swiftly and remove their nearly worthless contents, leaving undisturbed the more important hiding places.

"And the pianoforte," I said, "how shall we hide it?"

Mama moaned.

"Don't you worry, May, I shall take care of it." Papa reached out to reassure her, but she yanked her arm free. In the end, we carried it up to his study, turned it over on its back, and buried it beneath books and papers.

Late that afternoon, when neither of my parents was at home, I also took the precaution of burying Midnight's belongings, along with

Daniel's masks, his talisman, the jay we had carved and given to Mother, and the tile of a triton that the Olive Tree Sisters had given me when I was only nine. I did this in secret, as I feared that my parents would say that these keepsakes were not of sufficient value for such precautions.

ON THE TWENTY–NINTH of November, when French and Spanish troops were only a day's ride from Lisbon, Prince João and the rest of the royal family, together with our ministers and much of our aristocracy, left for Brazil.

The news reached Porto that the royal family carried aboard their ships more than half of the coinage of Portugal. The miracle that day was that none of their vessels, thus loaded, plunged directly to the bottom of Lisbon Harbor.

WE OUGHT TO have at least been able to bless the dreadful roads of the Portuguese countryside for slowing the progress of the enemy marching toward Lisbon. And yet we could not. The French officers and their mixed army were made so miserable by their torturous advance that they compensated for it with pillaging and murder.

Once the soldiers reached their final destination and passed through the gates of the Portuguese capital on the Thirtieth of November, ecstatic crowds of Jacobins and Francophiles mobbed them, the women even tossing roses from balconies. After being toasted in the taverns and streets, they snoozed in the plazas and gardens, dreaming most likely of their loved ones back home. Asleep or not, these homesick, harassed, and murderous invaders were our new rulers.

XXII

THROUGHOUT THE NEXT SEVEN MONTHS OF occupation, all was reasonably calm in Porto. Our wine trade with England, though prohibited, continued unabated and guaranteed the city a small measure of financial security. Our ships made their way first to northern ports such as Rotterdam, where their cargo was loaded onto other vessels headed for Portsmouth and Southampton. Post failed to reach us from Britain, however, and so we received no direct news of our compatriots who had left months before.

My parents were too absorbed in their silent warfare to care. They hardly ever saw each other, since Papa spent most of his time at work. Of the two, he had changed the most since Midnight's death. His hair was now closely cropped, gray at the sides and thinning on top. His cheeks were gaunt and his blue eyes, so radiant when I was young, were distinctly cold and distant.

I only once talked seriously with either of them about what had happened to our family. It was on my seventeenth birthday, and I woke up in a foul mood, intent on making life difficult for everyone. Father had told me three weeks earlier that the moment he was given permission to travel upriver again, I would be learning to survey lands, test soils, and plant vines. He had decided that I would earn my keep in the wine trade. Even though I planned to fight him, I recognized that I had better choose a profession swiftly. But I had no idea how I could put my love of art and books to profitable use.

As a special birthday treat, Mama made *rabanadas* for breakfast. Papa gave me a blue silk cravat that had belonged to his father. Then, as always, he escaped to his office.

As soon as he was out the door, I asked Mama, "Tell me the truth—do you hate Papa?"

She frowned in distaste. "Hate your father? Such odd ideas you have sometimes, John."

"Mama, you never talk to him anymore. You used to play music for him. You used to smile at him secretly, when you thought no one was looking. Have you forgotten?"

"John, people change. We are not as young as we once were."

"That has nothing to do with it."

"Listen, we've all made mistakes. I have . . . your father has. But I do not hate him."

"What mistakes have you made?"

She looked at me as though I'd spoken a foreign language. "John, it may be your birthday, but you are still very young and I'll not have you talk to me like that."

"How was I talking to you?"

"Like a prosecutor. I am not on trial here, as far as I know."

"Perhaps you ought to be. Perhaps a trial would be fitting for both of you."

"That is quite enough."

She was trembling, and though I was dreadfully ashamed of myself, I could not control my anger. I pictured Mother's pianoforte, which at that moment seemed an extension of her most private self. I wanted to wound her there, where it hurt most. I picked up a plate. I imagined going upstairs and smashing it into the ebony wood, making deep gouges that could never be repaired.

I secretly wished for her hatred to scar me as well, which is probably why I lifted the plate over my head and brought it down over my skull. As I have had ample opportunity to learn, despondent people do desperate things.

Luckily, the plate didn't do any serious damage. I felt for blood and looked at my hand—nothing. Mother turned and saw the shattered pieces of porcelain scattered over the floor. Agitation made her astonishingly unobservant, and she didn't notice the pieces of pottery still in my hair, which is why she started to lecture me on my carelessness.

I interrupted her. "Damn it, Mother, can you not forgive him?"

"Do not raise your voice at me, John Zarco Stewart!"

"Can you not forgive Father? Answer me now or I shall break all the pottery in our house! Every damned windmill on every last plate. I promise you that."

"You . . . you're confusing me—like always. I don't know what you mean."

"Mama, we both know that he ought to have protected Midnight. But he didn't. And Midnight is dead. Father is alive. Can we not forgive him? I'll try if you will."

"John"—she frowned, shaking her head—"there is so much that you do not know. . . ." She closed her eyes.

"Mama, tell me what you are thinking. I promise not to interrupt."

She asked for my hand. "You always had beautiful fingers. Even as a baby." She smiled wistfully. "When you were very tiny your hand was no bigger than a plum. And your fingers . . ." She looked at me tenderly and caressed my cheek, which she had not done for months. "Each of them was so delicate, so finely made . . . all perfectly formed."

"Is there nothing you can say to me about Papa? Can you not forgive him?" I asked again.

She sighed with exhaustion. "It's not a question of forgiveness. People grow older. You cannot expect us to feel about each other as we did when you were little." She dropped my hand and stared ahead sadly. "No, he is not the same man I married, and I am surely not the same woman he courted. People change."

"What you are saying, Mama, is that you do not love him anymore."

She looked shocked. "John, what do you know about love?"

"As much as you do."

She pursed her lips as though I were being absurd, which infuriated me. I pounded the table and shouted, "I loved Midnight and you loved Midnight. I loved Father and you loved Father. Not in the same way, I know, but are we so different from each other?"

"John, must we speak of these things?" she pleaded in exasperation.

"Yes. I have not spoken of Midnight for far too long. It is as though he never existed."

"Perhaps it would be better if he never had. Or if he had remained in Africa."

"You don't mean that."

"Well, it surely would have been better for him, don't you think?"

I was left speechless. It was the last time I would talk of him with either of my parents for many years.

THE MONTH OF May arrived with a series of proclamations from the French general Junot, informing us what a loyal friend of Portugal he was and how delightful his reign would be. Then Napoleon made a fatal error. He took the Spanish royal family captive, handing their crown to his brother Joseph. The courageous people of Madrid rose up in revolt and sent the occupying army fleeing for the hills. News of this tremendous victory soon reached other cities and towns, provoking uprisings across Spain that soon decimated the French and had them wondering if a hasty retreat to Paris might not be in order for all their battalions.

This proved most fortunate for us, since a provisional government in the Galician city of Corunha soon ordered all Spanish troops to leave Porto. Not only that, but in a glorious show of solidarity, they also made all the French soldiers leave as well.

A PROVISIONAL GOVERNMENT headed by our elderly bishop, Dom António de Castro, was soon established in Porto. The British, who had been waiting for an opportunity to approach a friendly local authority, sent seventy ships to us, manned by ten thousand troops, including a thousand Portuguese soldiers previously regimented in England. Led by Sir Arthur Wellesley, who was later made Duke of Wellington, the first of these vessels cleared the sandbar guarding our river mouth on the morning of the Twenty-Fourth of July. Wellesley himself arrived on the H.M.S. *Crocodile,* a name that made me think of Midnight and his stories. How excited he would have been to see a flotilla of tall-masted ships flying the Union Jack and sailing upriver to our wharf!

The British and Portuguese troops disembarked to great applause. I glimpsed Wellesley myself that day, seated atop a great white charger in Ribeira Square.

By the next day, however, most of these British soldiers were on their way to Figueira da Foz, halfway to Lisbon, where they planned to begin chasing the Gallic plague from Portugal.

Guarding Porto at this time was a militia of amateur soldiers outfitted with arms by the British. I trained with this reserve force and learned how to fire a musket and, to my surprise, found being a soldier quite to my liking. Through much practice, I became as good a shot as any of the other recruits, and I was praised by our sergeant for my swiftness in loading and firing. Happily for all concerned, however, I was not called upon to fight.

IN HIS CAMPAIGN to oust the French, Wellesley's fleet reached Figueira da Foz on August the First, then marched toward Lisbon along the Atlantic coast. His troops quickly defeated the enemy at Roliça and Vimeiro—with such swiftness, in fact, and with so many hundreds of casualties, that rather than be further humiliated, the French rushed to sign the Convention of Sintra, by which they agreed to leave Portugal.

Thereafter, the fighting moved to Spain, where the combined British and Spanish forces hoped to push the French into their own territory and corral them there. The only problem was a numerical one: Napoleon himself crossed into Spain that November, leading no less than two hundred thousand troops. His objective was to throw all his power at these Iberian upstarts and subdue them once and for all. Though we in Portugal were free of fighting for the moment, we understood that the worst was yet to come.

XXIII

FROM AUGUST TO DECEMBER OF 1808, I WENT upriver with my father every month for at least a week at a time in order to learn his trade. After a time, however, Father began concentrating his instructions on surveying and map-making. It was now his solemn intention that I ought to put my drawing lessons to good use by becoming a draftsman.

Throughout October and November I made good progress, and in early December Papa told me he was satisfied that I would now be able to find employment either as a junior draftsman or even surveyor's assistant for the Douro Wine Company. When we were not involved in our lessons, Father remained withdrawn. I sometimes heard him leave Macbeth's Castle at two or three in the morning in our carriage, to visit a nearby brothel, I guessed. This bothered me, but not nearly as much as I thought it would. Though his adultery put to rest my hopes of a reconciliation with my mother, I reasoned that if he no longer loved her, then he might as well find some small consolation elsewhere.

When we were not at our work, Papa was generally morose. I should have liked to beg him to simply play cards with me or tell me a story set in the Scotland of his youth. I yearned to build a bridge to him, to prevent him from

plunging deeper into his own misery. Indeed, I fooled myself for months
that this bridge would be provided by our new relation as master and apprentice. I tried to shine as his student, so that he might remember I was
his son.

FATHER DID REACH out to me once, however, just prior to Christmas week, our last night in Macbeth's Castle.

"I shall give you your presents now, if you don't mind," he said, patting my thigh. "Rather than in Porto." After retrieving a small wooden
case and a fabric pouch from his room, he handed them to me. "For all
your hard work."

Inside the box I found a glistening razor with a bone handle and
handsome badger-bristle brush. Father had often said that teaching a lad
to shave was a necessity, so he would never have to submit his face to the
dirty fingers of a barber nor risk disfigurement through a drunken slip of
the hand.

Winking, he added, "You will appear more handsome to the lasses
once you have shaved yourself properly. You know, John, I am heartily
proud of you. I do not believe I say that enough." His voice caught in his
throat. "I am not even sure you wish to hear it. But I am very proud indeed."

I was greatly moved and told him I was forever grateful he was my
father.

In the fabric pouch were my first pair of proper trousers, which had
only recently come into fashion in Portugal. "Papa, they're wonderful," I
assured him, and he smiled in a way I had not seen for ages.

"Life moves fast, son. I see that now. Tomorrow is here before we
have taken a good look at today. So the important thing is to think out
the consequences of what you do. Think them out in advance. That's
why we have been working so hard at this new trade of yours. To make
sure you are prepared for your future."

He had begun to fill his pipe, and I asked if I might prepare it for
him. It had been years since I had asked to do this. He was taken aback
but nevertheless handed me his tobacco good-humoredly. I did my work
with renewed affection and respect for him, then clamped the stem of his
pipe in my jaws in imitation of his technique, cupped the bowl in my
hand, and lit it with kindling from the fire. I had never before taken a serious puff, and I almost choked.

Instead of thanking me, or even laughing at my incompetence, Father looked upset. Trying to hide his unhappiness, he said I needed practice at smoking but it was not a habit I ought to take up for another year or two.

I was at a loss to understand what I had done wrong until, lying in bed that night, I recalled how Midnight would often share a pipe with him at the fireside.

THAT NIGHT MY father came into my room and woke me.

"What's wrong?" I said, sitting up.

He sat by my side. His candle created stark hollows of light and dark on his face. I imagined he had again suffered his nightmare of being alone in our house, with the rest of us dead.

"I almost forgot, John," he said.

I held his arm. "Forgot what, Papa?"

As he leaned toward me, I smelled brandy on him. Panic seized me and I rushed to speak, but he interrupted me. "Expect nothing from anyone, son. Then you will never be disappointed."

"Papa? Papa, what's wrong?"

"Just listen to me, lad. Expect nothing. For though you may, if you are lucky, get some assistance in your life, it will not come from the people from whom you most expect it. They will nearly always disappoint you. I advise you to always remember that people are small beasties, son. In Britain and Portugal both." He gripped my foot through the blanket. "Listen to me now, lad! Always do what you need to do. Always work hard. Be selfish if you have to be. And count on no one. No one!"

With that, he stood up and shuffled, barefoot, out of my room.

IN THE MORNING, Papa took me into his bedroom, stood me in front of his mirror, and taught me how to shave. He was calm and steady and made no reference to his speech the previous night.

When remembering him at this time in our lives, I sometimes think of Goya's "Colossus." Alone, seated under a crescent moon, his back to the viewer, the once-powerful giant turns around with a hopeful look, wanting to find a loved one waiting there to whom he can say a final farewell.

Our last trip upriver was at the end of the first week in January 1809. We were forced to stop going after that because the war against Napoleon in Spain was going poorly and the blue light of warning had been posted at all our borders.

Early March brought the arrival of General Soult's twenty-five thousand French soldiers into Portugal, at our northeast fringe of mountains. After he took the town of Chaves, refugees began making their way to Porto. The poor carried their entire lives in wooden barrows.

Benjamin and I gave out bread and honey to these downtrodden creatures now forced to sleep in our squares and on our beaches. Seeing them filled him with awe, as he said they were the Old Testament made present. When I asked what he meant, he said, "They are the Israelites in exile, and they were each and every one of them present at Mt. Sinai for the giving of the Ten Commandments. Don't you recall? You and I were there too!" Summoning me closer to him, he whispered in my ear, "Moses's teachings are for each and every minute of existence, John. Each time we see how the Torah is reflected in our lives, we stand again at the foot of Mount Sinai."

BY THE TWENTY–SECOND of March, we received confirmation that Braga, thirty miles to the northeast, had been taken. Late that morning, Father announced that he had made plans for us to leave the city. Three carriages belonging to the Douro Wine Company would be leaving secretly at three in the morning from a tiny wharf at the far eastern edge of the city, just below the Bishop's Seminary. Mother and I were to go, but Papa was to remain behind.

"It is time I fought," he said. "If Porto falls, I shall join you upriver as soon as I can. Don't worry, the French will not take me."

"Papa, this is sheer madness. You must come with us. I'll not allow you to stay."

"Look who's giving orders!" he joked.

Despite his sudden good humor, he looked exhausted and reeked of brandy. I didn't trust him to care for himself in the state he was in. "Papa," I said, "if you refuse to come with us, then I shall stay too and fight alongside you."

"John, this is not a request. You shall wait for me upriver with your mother. I have not raised you these eighteen years to see you felled by a French bullet."

Mama agreed as Papa embraced me. I tried to push him away, but he held me firm and kissed my cheek.

"Goodness, man, you might shave a little closer," he moaned. "It's still rough. The lassies will not like it."

Before he let me go, he took a hard look at me, perhaps imagining what I'd look like as a grown man. "Please be patient, son," he said apologetically. "We shall be apart for only a short while." He reached into his fob pocket and took out his gold watch with the mother-of-pearl face. The chain had been the one used by the witch to shackle him when he was a toad. "Hold on to this for me," he said, handing it to me. "I shall want it back soon."

Then, as though embarrassed by his gesture of affection, he stood with his hands behind his back and stared out our window.

I accepted his gift gratefully, but it troubled me. I looked to my mother for support in continuing to encourage him to leave with us, but she was so lost within herself that she said nothing.

I SPENT THE rest of the day in a state of gloom. After supper, I bid good-bye to the Olive Tree Sisters, who were remaining behind, as they refused to leave their art collection unguarded. "If you don't come back soon, John, we'll never let you look at another Goya!" Luna warned.

I also visited Benjamin with my father. His two sons had already left the city, but he had decided to stay put. "An apothecary is always needed after a battle," he said, "so I am quite sure that the French will do me no great harm."

Mother went to see Grandmother Rosa, to tell her that Father had reserved a place for her in our carriage, but the windows of her home were boarded up. Neighbors said that she had already left for Aveiro to stay with her sons.

Father, Mother, and I went to bed that night but scarcely slept, as we had to be awake at two o'clock. When Papa poked his head into my room to wake me, I said, "Are you sure you will not come with us? I'm so worried—I can't think of anything else."

"No, I can no longer let other men fight for me. Portugal is my home now. I'm too old to go back to England or Scotland."

"You aren't too old, Papa."

"I'm fifty years of age, John." He shook his head. "You have no idea how tired I am."

"We all get tired, Papa. You work too hard, and you worry all the time. We could go to England and stay with Aunt Fiona for a time. I can find work there and you will be able to sit by our hearth and read. I shall support us all."

"That is a generous offer, son, and if times were different I might even take you up on it, but I am too old to change. You will understand when you are my age."

"But do you promise you will join us upriver?"

"John, life is unpredictable. These are promises I cannot make, even if I wanted to."

"I'll not leave unless you swear to join us."

"Very well, I promise to join you and your mother upriver."

He spoke too matter-of-factly for me to believe him. But before I could say any more, he pressed his lips passionately to mine, as though we were departing lovers. Then he clapped his hands together and said, "Now, get up and get dressed! In fifteen minutes we leave. There will be food in the carriages, even tea. I said that if there were no tea my son would turn into a Scottish monster of the lochs—a wrathful *kelpie*!"

I said good-bye to Fanny and Zebra, who would stay behind with Father, as they weren't allowed in the carriages. I hugged them both and told them to take care of him. Fanny jumped up and stood on my shoulders just as she had on St. John's Eve so many years before. Through my tears, I told them not to bark even once if they heard soldiers. By way of reply, they simply licked me. I felt as though I were leaving my heart behind with them.

Mother, Father, and I bustled out of the house into the cold and windy darkness. I was carrying my musket and Father his pistol. He began to softly sing "Barbara Allen." I joined in, and we held hands as we walked.

Mother said nothing, though she glanced furtively at Papa—in grudging admiration, I think. She must have noticed that he and I had made an attempt toward reconciliation over the past weeks. I believed that she approved of this for me, but not for herself.

Then Papa hummed a tune I didn't know. Being good at melodies, I was able later to scribble it out in notation and send this transcription to Healy's Music Shop in London. I received a reply naming the song as "Now O Now I Needs Must," by the Elizabethan composer John Dowland. I would hazard a guess that Mama knew this tune equally well and that Papa hummed it for her benefit, as a last attempt to win her forgiveness. The lyrics must have closely mirrored his feelings and his hopes for the future on this occasion:

Now O now I needs must part,
Parting though I absent mourn.
Absence can no joy impart,
Joy once fled cannot return.

Dear when I am from thee gone,
Gone are all my joys at once,
I love thee and thee alone,
In whose love I joyed once.

And although your sight I leave,
Sight wherein my joys do lie,
Till that death do sense bereave,
Never shall affection die.

Mama kept her eyes fixed on the ground as he offered this tune to the night. Her cool distance plainly silenced any last hope in him, for when he finished the song he attempted no other.

After several miles we reached a cove guarded by mammoth oaks concealing three large carriages. Nine people were already on board. Father chatted with the driver while we acquainted ourselves with the other passengers.

When the bells of the city tolled three, Mother and Father kissed each other on the cheek and he helped her up into her seat. I held Papa for a long time. My heart was pounding a warning to me about never seeing him again in this life.

I inhaled the glorious scent of him and gave myself over to his warmth. At length, he held me away from him, smiled to hide his anguish, and handed me his pipe and pouch of tobacco.

"Take this, my beloved John," he said, kissing my brow.

"But, Papa—"

"Take it and climb aboard. And think often of your father, who feels nothing but love for you. Be well, my son."

My steps into the carriage were the heaviest I had ever taken.

"And, May," Father said to Mother through the carriage window, "I shall always carry the burden of guilt, so it is not necessary for you to do so. Only one of us need be condemned. I release you."

Papa retreated several paces and shouted to the driver that he could get on his way. We were off, and I could no longer hold back my sorrow. As my father waved to me, I could see his tears freely falling as well. Leaning out my window, I shouted, "We shall return to you and all will be well, Papa."

How I wish I could have said something more important—words that might have changed his mind. When I looked at Mother, she was gazing at the moonlight playing like silver fishes across the water, afraid to look at me.

TWO DAYS LATER we found ourselves lodging in a dank cottage on the north bank of the Douro River, seven miles from Regua. Mother was in a foul temper due to the dirt and soot, and the first thing she did upon arrival was embark on a cleaning frenzy.

We survived for four weeks on turnips, potatoes, and kale, doing our utmost to stay dry and healthy, as the weather had turned wet and windy. But we were safe, and that was all that mattered.

WHILE WE WERE upriver, the French descended on Porto, sounding their trumpets as though about to enjoy themselves. As far as I can determine, Father had spent his first days after we left preparing himself for battle, practicing with his pistol in the garden, hoarding bread, drinking whiskey, and tending to Fanny and Zebra, whom he allowed to sleep in his bed.

Senhor Benjamin had boarded up his apothecary shop and moved into his cellar. He had no idea how to use a firearm, but he kept an old rusty sword with him that had been in his family for many generations. It had a silver handle, of course—just right for a Jewish alchemist, since the goal of their work was not to create gold but to find the silver essence in all of God's creations.

The Olive Tree Sisters continued sketching and molding their fruit by day. At night, they shared the same bed, clinging tightly to each other. As Jews, they wondered if they would be burned alive, since the French officers were rumored to be viciously anti-Semitic. If this did come to pass, they resolved to ask to be bound together.

In response to a call to arms that fateful morning, Father joined a line of Portuguese troops already positioned at the Olival Gate, very near our home. Shortly after the fighting began, however, the cannonading of the French guns and superiority of their musket power proved too much for the city's defenders. The men fell in heaps, moist red roses blooming on their chests.

The battle at the Olival Gate was lost within minutes. Miraculously, Father had only taken a grazing shot to his leg. Peeling a musket free from the death grip of a lost comrade, he rushed with several other men to the eastern defenses, near the Bonfim Church, where fighting had now begun. A terrific battle was fought there for nigh on four hours, during which time perhaps ten thousand more of the city's residents were given time to flee through Porto's gates. Papa soon came to the conclusion that he would be of greater use as a diligent orderly than a poor marksman and served in this capacity for most of the struggle. By just after eleven o'clock, it was clear to one and all that their cause was lost. Some two hundred men, Father among them, retreated to the Bishop's Palace.

Hundreds of French cavalrymen then led the greater part of the infantry into Porto. A few brave residents continued firing pistols from their patios and windows, but they were soon silenced. Papa and the other soldiers who had reached the palace were well-aware that their cause was lost, but they hoped to hold off the French forces as long as they could, to give the people of Porto more time to escape.

Cannons were soon hauled by French troops onto the plaza in front of the palace, where they fired away mercilessly.

The pontoon bridge across the Douro River was the only way of escape, and thousands fled in that direction. To the deafening roar of Gallic drums, the French cavalry charged down from the upper town to the river, firing indiscriminately and slicing their way through the terrified crowds with their swords. At the sight of the enemy, Portuguese artillery stationed at the Serra do Pilar Convent on top of the cliff on the opposite bank opened fire. It was then that the bridge surrendered to the weight of the terrified people it had been made to carry. With a wicked groan, it split apart, tossing two or three hundred into the river. There was no hope for them, even for able swimmers. They met their end in the greedy arms of the river, just as Daniel had seven years earlier.

How many drowned that day, no one can say for sure. I only know that I have it on good authority that scores of corpses washed ashore downriver, attracting a cloud of gulls the likes of which had never been seen before. Among the dead were Senhor Tiago the roofer and Senhor Policarpo's wife, Josefina, along with her two children. Bloated, gray-eyed bodies were still being pulled from the river three days later, and for years afterward fishermen complained of lines constantly becoming tangled in boots, wigs, and even skulls.

SO HORRIFIC WERE the next three days of violence that I do not believe any inhabitant of Porto will ever be able to think of the French again and not wish for revenge. The Olive Tree Sisters, like many women, were viciously raped by gangs of soldiers. Graça hemorrhaged on the night of the Twenty-Ninth, fell into a coma, and died in her sister's arms the next day. Luna's spirit was broken—precisely in half, I'd say. I shall never forgive what was done to them.

As for Benjamin, just after the French broke through the city's defenses, he heard someone in his sitting room. Tricked by a cry for help shouted in Portuguese through his locked cellar door, he rushed upstairs carrying his rusty sword, where he was confronted by a young French soldier.

This young man's triumphant grin unleashed the warrior in Benjamin, and when the Frenchman squeezed the trigger of his gun only to have it misfire, the apothecary lashed out, fatally wounding his foe in the neck. Benjamin then raced to the riverside. As this took place before the collapse of the pontoon bridge, he was able to scurry across to the far bank. He continued to make his way south and hid in the woods along the road to Espinho, returning to the city only after five days of hiding. Twice during his escape, a regiment of Gallic soldiers came within a hundred yards of him, and twice he lay facedown in the soil, silently reciting Hebrew prayers for the soul of the youth he had killed.

MY BELOVED FANNY and Zebra were not so fortunate. I never saw either of them again.

I would wager that on the morn of the great battle, Papa let them out into our garden, as I found a plate of bones there, most probably some chicken he had scrounged. When French soldiers broke the hinge of our front door, both dogs would have breathed fire like Scottish dragons—and been summarily shot, I have no doubt.

But I found no blood. Possibly it had seeped into the garden soil. Their bodies must have been tossed onto dung heaps with the rest of the fallen and set ablaze.

I only hope they were not made to suffer.

MOTHER AND I left our rural refuge for Porto on the Third of April, when news reached us of the sacking of the city. As there were no barges to take us downriver, we set out on foot. I would never have believed Mama would be able to walk such a distance—sixty miles, at least—but she was driven onward by terror, as though a burning metronome were beating inside her. Every day we walked from cockcrow to midday, at which time, with the sun highest in the sky, we rested by the side of the road, in the spring shade afforded by pine trees. Then we continued on till sundown, finding shelter in farmhouses and barns.

The peasants we met were kind, displaying the generosity one often encounters by accident. One old woman sat in a field munching raw cabbage and watching the night sky with me. She told me that the stars were not hunters, as Midnight had said, but rather seeds scattered by God. The earth itself was one such seed.

Gazing at the Milky Way, I wondered where Violeta was. I dearly hoped that she had escaped Portugal to America.

Eleven days after we had started out, we spied the Clerics Tower from a clearing several miles outside the city. Mother and I burst into tears.

OUR HOUSE HAD been ransacked and all my mother's porcelain destroyed. The skylight in the Lookout Tower had been shattered, and rain had soaked through to the upper floor of the house.

We hadn't the heart to dig under the rosebushes, so we were unaware that our silver and jewelry were safe. The pianoforte was undamaged, still buried under books.

Grandmother Rosa's house remained safely boarded up, and Senhor Benjamin, who had returned home by now, told us that he had heard she was still in Aveiro and that all was well.

Father was missing. Mama and I searched frantically for anyone who might have seen or spoken to him, and we finally found a neighbor up the street who'd spotted him leaving our house at dawn on the morning of the Twenty-Ninth. No one saw him again after that.

Two days later, I learned of his fate from a young sergeant in the Loyal Lusitanians, one of the lucky few to survive the cannon fire at the Bishop's Palace. His name was Augusto Duarte Cunha, and I found him in one of the overcrowded wards at St. Anthony's Hospital, where he was recovering from a bullet wound in his chest.

With his foreign looks and accent, my father struck a memorable figure, and the sergeant knew exactly who I meant as soon as I started to describe him.

"I remember him well," Cunha said, inviting me to pull up a chair to his cot.

Holding tight to hope, I asked, "Sergeant, do you know if . . . if my father survived the French attack?"

"No, I'm afraid not, son," he replied solemnly. "I was with him when the end came."

"You . . . you saw him die?"

"Yes, I was right beside him."

I fought to keep from crying but in the end had to dash out to the corridor, where I hid my face against the wall. When I returned to the ward, the sergeant shook my hand and said, "I liked your father a great deal, John. He was a brave man. I'm sorry."

"Please . . . please tell me everything you can about his last hours."

"I will tell you what I know, but you have to understand, the French attacks came one after another, and we were far outnumbered. Time for conversation was scarce."

"Father fought beside you?"

"Yes, he had a pistol—an antique of sorts. Not much good, I'm afraid. Though that didn't stop him from trying. Your father proved himself a good shot, but he was out of practice."

The sergeant then described the battle at the Olival Gate and how my father had been grazed with a bullet in his leg. "A short time later," he said, "when the fighting moved to near the Bonfim Church, your father put down the musket he had taken from a dead soldier and helped nurse the wounded men. He proved himself an able orderly. For the young lads, having an older man attend to them was reassuring."

"This was all on the Twenty-Ninth?"

"That's right, John."

"And when you were able to speak to him, what did you talk about?"

"I remember that the first thing I asked him was what made him decide to live in Portugal."

"And what did he say?"

"Love and wine." The sergeant laughed. "I didn't believe him at first, but he said it was the absolute truth. Your father said his gods were Venus and Bacchus."

"He worked for the Douro Wine Company, but he wanted his own vineyard—and he wanted me to join him. He married my mother shortly after coming to Portugal. They were very much in love."

"He spoke of her, John."

"What . . . what did he tell you?" I asked fearfully.

"Your father said he had a good friend who was always trying to turn lead into silver. 'Sergeant,' he told me, 'I've done just the opposite with my marriage.' I asked what he meant, and he told me he'd made a mess of things with your mother. John, I think he confessed that to me because we all knew we might not live to see another day. He made me promise to value my wife and children above all else."

"What else did he say?"

"Later, after we'd retreated to the Bishop's Palace, we spoke once more. Your father said something odd: 'Perhaps I've passed the test after all.' "

"What test?"

Sergeant Cunha considered my question. "He wouldn't say, son. He just said that when you came back from upriver he would take you to Amsterdam as he'd promised. He was thinking of taking you to Constantinople too. He said you had a grandfather from there and ancestors going back for many centuries. He gave me to understand that he was planning a grand tour of Europe. 'When we're done, we'll all go to Scotland,' he said. He wanted to take you up to the ramparts of Edinburgh Castle and look out across the entire city. 'I want to stand with my family as high as we can and let my son see where we come from.' "

"Did he say anything else?"

"He repeated that he needed to take you from Portugal. You needed to get out of 'the cage' he'd made for you, as he put it, which I thought peculiar, but he explained that he wanted you to see something of the world, to know there was a life beyond Porto. He said he'd failed to show you that, but he would make it up to you now. He spoke with great determination and hope, I would say."

"And then?"

"A few minutes later he took a shot to his right temple. Be thankful that he didn't linger."

"He died instantly?"

"Yes."

The sergeant meant well in telling me this, I'm sure, but it was of no comfort. He told me then that the bodies of the men who had fought at the Bishop's Palace, including Papa's, were dumped by French soldiers in a pile in front of the cathedral and set ablaze.

"Think well of your father. He died a brave man."

"Yes, but in dying...in dying he failed the test."

"Failed? I think not, John. You've never been in a war, but let me tell you something: All experienced soldiers know it's largely a matter of luck. You don't pass or fail a test given you by luck, son. No, the test, if that's what it was, was doing what was expected of him—fighting. And I can tell you in that regard that he may not have been the best shot, or even the most skillful orderly, but he risked his life many times that day, sometimes recklessly, to give hundreds of people in Porto time to escape across the bridge—and to comfort his wounded and dying comrades. Would you really call *that* a failure?"

HOW TO EXPRESS my feelings at this time? Papa was dead and Mama in despair after learning of his fate. Fanny and Zebra were murdered. We had precious little money, and I had no way to earn a living. There was almost nothing to buy in the markets, and neighbors were eating boiled hide to keep from starving. I wasn't sure of anything anymore, not even my identity.

Since Papa's body had not been buried, Benjamin and I recited prayers to ensure that his soul would not wander the earth.

Once, I dreamed that he hadn't been killed but had fled our family's misery to a new life over the bridge. After that, I found I regretted having never seen him dead; I felt an urgent need to confirm with my own two eyes that he was gone—and would never again tell me a story of witches and monsters, or bring me stones from his trips upriver, or ask me to read to him....

For Mama, the scent of him in her bed drove her mad. On the rare occasion when she emerged from her room, it was plain that she had hardly slept at all. Once, after she'd wept in my arms, she said, "Now James is having his revenge."

* * *

I FOUND THAT what I most desired now was to forgive Mama and be forgiven. I didn't have the strength to continue living if it meant fighting with her. She must have felt the same, for she came to me one morning and promised to love me as she used to.

We never again raised our voices or said anything cruel. Our peace was a good thing; I felt as though I'd ransomed the little that was still left of my heart.

I TOLD HER what Papa had said about taking us away to Scotland. "I don't know, John," she replied. "I'm not sure that even standing at the very top of the world would have helped your father and me. It might have only allowed us to see the mistakes we made that much more clearly. Perspective can be dangerous."

"But we could have made a new start in Scotland," I insisted. "And you always said you wanted to live in Britain."

"That's true, John. It might even now be best for us. Though I admit it scares me when I think of it." Taking a long, slow look around the sitting room, she said, "At least here, everything is familiar to us." Seeing my disappointment, she added, "John, I can't claim to know how two people who've lost their way in life can find their way home again. Perhaps your father knew. Perhaps taking up arms taught him what he needed to do to fight for our marriage. He may have seen things more clearly than I could. I'm afraid I can't offer you certainties anymore, and I'm sorry for that. I know you deserve more from your mother. I wish things were different."

"But you *would* have gone if he'd asked you?" It was vital for me to know that we'd have done what he asked and, at the very least, tried to begin again in a new place.

"I don't know, John. I think it would have been better for just you and your father to go. I'd have just ruined everything between you." Her voice broke. "Like I . . . like I ruined so much else."

She hid her eyes from me for a time, then picked up her embroidery, but her hands were trembling. I took them in my own and sat with her. It was good to feel the closeness and warmth we could still have together—it was like an old dream I thought I'd never have again. Then a startling revelation pulled me to my feet. "Mama, don't you see? If Papa was making plans to take us to Scotland, then it meant he was willing to give up the idea of having his own vineyard."

"Yes, I suppose so, John."

She plainly didn't grasp the deeper meaning of this. "He was willing to give up even that to win back your love!" I declared. "He'd never go upriver again and leave you all alone. He was going to give up everything to be with us and have another chance."

Mama's face turned ashen. She moaned when I touched her, then leaned limply against me. "No more, John," she begged. "Please, I can't hear any more of what might have been."

WE SPENT THOSE first grief-stricken weeks repairing our home. Unable to beg more than a few turnips and beans and some rotten cabbage, we were now starving most of the time.

My mother appealed to colleagues who had worked with Father at the Douro Wine Company, where all our savings had long been invested, but we were informed that access to his accounts was impossible. We could not dig up our silver and sell it, even clandestinely, for we could not risk the French learning of our hoard.

THE FRENCH MARRIED us to misery and remained our unwanted guests until three weeks after my eighteenth birthday, May the Twelfth, 1809. On that date enshrined in the history of our city, British and Portuguese forces under Arthur Wellesley, the future Duke of Wellington, expelled them for a second and final time from Porto. Our city was free.

AS SOON AS she felt brave enough to leave the house, Mama met again with the directors of the Douro Wine Company to discuss Father's investments. We knew that selling the deeds to our land upriver could prove lucrative, and Papa's former employer was the obvious choice for a buyer. Mother offered them all our holdings, but their counteroffer was far less than my father had originally paid. This seemed to us a great betrayal, but the bitterest surprise was yet to come. When she asked under what capacity I might be contracted to work for the Douro Wine

Company, as had been her late husband's wish, she was told in no uncertain terms that I would never be hired, even if perfectly qualified! And so Mama came to learn the level of animosity Papa's colleagues had harbored against him for his wish to own a vineyard. They also had never forgiven him for bringing what they called a "giant monkey" to their offices.

Our humiliation reminded me of Father's warning about not counting on anyone for assistance. Surely he had known of the seething resentment felt by some of his colleagues. I finally understood why he'd wanted his own land and to be lord of his own destiny so badly.

IN EARLY JULY, Mother read me a letter from Aunt Fiona, inviting us to share the small house in London that she'd recently bought. When she finished, she folded up the correspondence. "Now, John," she said, "it's like this. You know I've always hoped for a chance to live in London. Now that the worst has happened, it has become a real possibility for us. Your aunt Fiona is a considerate woman and she would not invite us to England if she did not want us there. I wasn't sure at first, but now she and I are both convinced that it would be for the best."

"Mama, did you become convinced of this after hearing of Papa's last wishes?"

"I don't know, John. I'm not sure I know my own mind anymore."

The bitter irony of our being able to go to Britain now that my father was dead made me ache with longing to see him.

"John, please," she said imploringly, "I beg you not to think about what your father would want. Once, a long time ago, you were haunted by Daniel and what you thought he wanted. You ended up jumping from our rooftop. Please don't make that mistake again. You mustn't listen so closely to the dead. Don't think about what Papa would want. Or even what I want, for that matter. Think only about what would be best for you."

"I don't know what there is for me in England," I told her. "Whatever shall I do in London?"

"Continue your education, for one thing."

"How? We've no money for that."

"We shall find a way. *Trust me.*"

No sooner did she request *that* of me than I realized this was precisely what I could no longer do. It even occurred to me that Father had meant Mother, too, when he instructed me to trust no one.

My feelings came down to this: Not only had her marriage failed, but she had also withheld her love for me for years, for reasons I could not fathom. Until I learned the truth, I might forgive her and love her as I always had, but I could place no deep faith in her.

"I would prefer to stay," I declared, largely to spite her.

"We shall see," she said, standing up and walking to the stairs. "We shall both think about what we want and then talk again."

These were conciliatory words, but I understood from her tone that her mind was already made up.

XXIV

THE SERIES OF SEEMINGLY TRIFLING EVENTS that was to greatly influence my decision to remain in Portugal and my choice of profession began when Senhor Gilberto, a local potter, paid a visit to Luna Olive Tree in mid-July, some eight weeks after the French had been expelled from Porto. At the moment of his knock, she had just discovered some drawings of sphinxes and other mythological beasts I had made when I was eleven. In the right lower corner of the first, which depicted a griffin swooping down onto the Clerics Tower, her sister Graça had inscribed affectionately, *John—January 1802. Fulfilling the potential we recognized in him. But needs discipline.*

"Clever little illustrations," Gilberto told Luna, once he'd taken a closer look. "Who did them?"

"John Stewart. A lad on our street. The one we gave your tile of a triton to years ago."

Chuckling, Gilberto said, "He has good taste, this boy!"

"Indeed, except for admiring your work, he has always shown sound reasoning."

"Ouch!" He feigned an arrow in his heart and pulled it free, then laughed again. "Is he still here in Porto?"

"Yes, but his father was killed by the French. And he needs work, poor boy."

THE TWO OF them came to my house later that afternoon. I was relieved to see Luna again, as she had dressed in black and not taken a single step outside since Graça's funeral. We kissed tenderly, as an even greater bond of affection had developed between us since her sister's death.

After she introduced Gilberto to me, I complimented him on his work and told him that his tile was still buried under the weeds in our garden for safekeeping.

When we were all comfortably seated on our patio, Gilberto made his proposal: Having seen my drawings and recognized a certain talent, he was prepared to employ me as an apprentice for a period of three years. During this time I would earn a small salary and have the right to fire as much pottery as I liked for my own use. He would work me hard but he would teach me valuable skills, and I would never want for a line of life. If all went well, he would either take me on as his junior partner on my twenty-first birthday or provide a loan for the establishment of my own enterprise, as long as I agreed to do business at a distance no less than three miles by coach from his own shop.

"This is a most exciting prospect," said Mother, "but I have my doubts as to its practicality. Of late, we have been considering a move to England, to live with my late husband's elder sister."

I felt none of Mama's doubt; so strong was my desire to remain in Porto and learn a solid trade that I knew I would accept Gilberto's generous offer.

"Shall I be allowed to work on my own designs?" I asked.

"Codfish cakes!" Luna exclaimed. "Where are your manners, lad?"

Gilberto placed a calming hand on her arm. "Not at first, John. I would not think it wise for you to begin too hastily. But after six months or so, you might start to add your own touches—I don't see why not."

"Senhor Gilberto, before we enter into any agreement, I want to tell you some things about myself—to avoid later misunderstandings, you understand. I would not want dearest Luna's fondness for me to blind you to my defects. First and foremost, I am stubborn. And despite Mother's entreaties and her stellar example, my manners are far from perfect. Also, unlike many Portuguese, I do not dislike the Spanish. I am most partial to Velázquez, Ribera, and Goya. I hate narrow-mindedness, and I am half-Jewish."

Gilberto took my arm. "Goya, you say? I have seen his prints at Luna's house, and his gifts are so great that they frighten me on occasion." Then he announced, "I'd like to follow John's sensible speech and say a few words about myself." Here, the good potter declared himself surly in the morning, neglectful of his own personal cleanliness at times, and inordinately proud of the beautiful things he could make with his hands. He concluded by stating for the record, "I make a special effort to sing off-key when I am with people I do not like and who are wasting my time." Leaning to the side as though to fart, he added, "And I sometimes have piles that make me howl when I use my chamber pot."

I laughed for the first time in ages. Even Mama was won over by his effort to make us smile. I was so fond of him already that I would have started my apprenticeship the very next day, but my mother explained that we needed to discuss moving to England and would give him an answer in a week.

She and I did talk at length about his offer several times, and I believe that my decision to stay was in some ways a relief to her. Not that she wished to leave me behind, but she needed to start a new life in a home unburdened by memory and grief—and by my expectations. We were learning to love each other again, but we needed to follow our own paths. I see that plainly now. Our house was simply too full of memories of Father and Midnight for her to bear.

BY THE BEGINNING of November, Mama felt confident enough to book passage to England. She also had her pianoforte shipped off to Aunt Fiona's home. On the day before she left, she asked me to fetch her menorah, which I had recently dug up from our garden. Gripping it tightly, she twisted off the round, scallop-edged base.

"I didn't know it could do that," I said in astonishment.

"Your father and I were the only ones who did."

Reaching inside the hollow of the lamp's stem, she pulled out a vellum scroll, which, once unfurled, revealed itself to be a colorful illumination. At its center was a gold-leaf square containing four neatly scripted lines of Hebrew writing, surrounded by garlands of pink and carmine flowers. At the very top was a peacock whose exuberant tail fanned across the top of the page.

I had never seen any design so stunning.

Allowing me to hold it, Mama said, "It was made by an ancestor of ours. His name was Berekiah Zarco. He was an artist from a family of manuscript illuminators who was born in Lisbon centuries ago and later moved to Constantinople. Berekiah was a very learned man, but that is all my father was able to tell me about him. This has been handed down in our family for many generations. I believe it is the cover for a book of European geography. At least, that is what your grandfather had been told by his parents."

"Grandfather João gave it to you?"

"Yes, and now," she said, smiling, "I am giving it to you."

"To me, why?"

"It was always intended for you. I ought to have given it to you on your thirteenth birthday, but with all our problems... For better or for worse, I thought it best to wait. I was worried, too, that you were still upset at being half-Jewish and that this would only heighten your sense of exclusion. As I must leave you now, I wish to delay my gift no longer. I need not say how valuable it must be, nor that you must keep it a secret, since possessing Hebrew writing may still be a crime in Portugal, for all I know."

"May I show it to Benjamin? He is able to read Hebrew."

She considered that request. "You may, John, but only upon the condition that he never reveal its existence while a member of our family remains in Portugal.

"I feel I ought to give you some advice," she continued, "but I find I have none to give. So I'll only say that I am proud of you and love you. I am counting on you to do better in your life than I have. I'm sure Papa would wish the same thing if he were here."

I was so sad and nervous that I could hardly speak.

"John, I mean what I say," she said, almost threateningly. "I think most parents hope their children will grow up to copy their lives, but that's the very last thing I want. I would very much like you to forget about me."

"I could never forget you, Mama, so I'm not sure—"

"John, that's not what I was trying to say," she interrupted. "It's not that I want you to forget me—I just want you to disregard any expectations you think I might have."

"I'll try," I answered.

"Good."

"But what about you? Will you be all right alone in London?"

"The truth is, John, I'm of no use to anyone else right now. We both know I'm not the woman I was, so I think it's better—and right, in a way—for me to be alone for a time. If you give me a few years by myself, I think I may be able to come back much stronger than I am now. Please be patient with me. I think that's the only thing I have a right to ask anymore. Though perhaps, given my behavior, I've even forfeited that."

THE NEXT MORNING at eleven, I said good-bye to Mother on the wharf. The last thing she did was to kiss both my hands and make them into fists. "You have my fondest affection with you always, my son."

Her posture was stooped as she boarded, and I feared she might faint. We waved until she was far enough downriver that I was sure she could no longer see me—which was in truth not so great a distance, since she refused to wear her spectacles in public.

SEVERAL DAYS LATER, feeling powerfully sorry for myself, I took Berekiah Zarco's illustration to Benjamin. By the light of a single candle in his sitting room, he deciphered its lettering, which had been penned in what he termed Sephardic script—the box-style characteristic of Spain and Portugal. According to his translation, it read: *The Bleeding Mirror: On the Need for the Jews and their Converted Brethren to Cast Out Christian Europe from their Hearts and Flee to Moslem Lands.*

Apparently, it was not a geography book at all, but rather an argument in favor of an exodus of Jews from Europe to lands then under the control of Moslems. As for the term *Bleeding Mirror,* Benjamin reasoned that it might have been a metaphor for the Ten Commandments, which reflect God's will, or the silver eyes of Moses.

It was signed on the back by Berekiah Zarco. In minuscule letters, a date and place of authorship had been scripted as well: *The Seventh of Av, 5290—Constantinople.*

Benjamin told me that the month of Av was the sixth in the Hebrew lunar calendar and generally coincided with part of July and August. The year 5290 for Jews was equivalent to 1530 A.D. for Christians. Hence, this cover page was nearly three hundred years old.

That night I slept with the page under my pillow, next to *The Fox Fables.* The illustration did much to bolster my confidence in my decision to become an artist and apprentice to Gilberto, for I now envisioned myself continuing a centuries-old family tradition.

I SURVIVED ON my own over the next years by clinging to a routine of work with Gilberto. I found him a sterner taskmaster than I'd first imagined, yet also affectionate and unfailingly honest. During my apprenticeship with him, I'm quite sure he often considered strangling me, but in his critiques of my designs, he never sought to belittle me. Even after ten hours in each other's company, we often still took pleasure in walking by the river in the evening or in sipping brandy at a nearby tavern. He was—and is—a very good man.

Mother wrote to me assiduously over those first years of separation, sending news on a weekly basis. In the spring of 1810, she joined a small congregation of Jews whose ancestors had hailed from Spain and Portugal. Having never before attended a proper synagogue ceremony, she found it most confusing. Furthermore, she regarded herself as wholly inferior to the others, knowing next to nothing of Jewish ritual. She was particularly shocked to discover that she and the other women were required to sit separately from the men. In her own family, her mother had not only lit the Sabbath candles but also recited many of the prayers.

One very positive note was that she had easier access to music for her pianoforte and had been able to attract six young students, two of whom she considered gifted. Along with her embroidery skills, which were highly esteemed, these lessons afforded her a steady income.

I was less diligent in my letter-writing and would sometimes let a fortnight pass without sending word to her. Oddly enough, I believe we became closer through our correspondence than we had been since I was nine or ten years of age. Her renewed devotion to me emerged in her joy over the progress I was making in my apprenticeship and her keen interest in my silly stories of life in our quiet land. I even began to notice that the passion in her heart, dormant for many years, was blossoming again. Often she would scribble out the themes of a new musical work by Beethoven that she had just purchased, writing to me of the emotions it inspired in her.

It's a paradox, but I think I've reached home again in a foreign country, she once wrote to me. *I'm discovering what it is I want to do with my life— and learning who a little Jewish girl from Porto has grown up to be.*

*   *   *

ABOUT A YEAR after her arrival in London, she visited Swanage to place a pebble from the surrounding grounds on Midnight's gravestone, as was the Jewish custom. The minister of the parish church had been in the town for only two years and knew nothing of an African who had died in the vicinity, however. The body had probably been placed in an unmarked grave. This upset her greatly, but she realized in the end that Midnight was safe wherever he was and that he would not have cared, since all the earth to him was home. She wrote to me that we would surely both meet him again on the Mount of Olives and that he would be wearing an elegant scarlet waistcoat and breeches, but no shoes. Carrying his quill and hollowed ostrich egg shell, he would be *very, very* pleased to see us. That was what mattered now.

IN MY WORK, I devoured all that Master Gilberto could teach me about potting and tile-making. When he allowed me to begin making my own designs, my first project was a tile panel illustrating a comic sketch of Goya's—a monkey painting the portrait of a donkey. Over the next two years, I transferred many of his works to tile and even painted some of his figures on vases and teapots. Then I began to execute works of my own inspiration based on the stories Midnight had told me. Gilberto purchased my first tile panel—nine squares depicting a great white feather falling into the Bushman's outstretched hand.

OVER HER FIRST three years in England, Mother offered all manner of excuses for being unable to return home for an extended visit, until I realized what ought to have been obvious from the very beginning: Absence was not increasing her fondness for Porto one whisker and she would not be making the journey home anytime soon. I read between the lines that she was fearful of the emotions that seeing our house and Grandmother Rosa would stir in her.

So in October of 1812, I inquired if she would like me to visit, and she replied that she missed me each and every day and that my coming to London would be a solemn blessing. As the idea of passing a winter fighting my way through the frigid English rain was unacceptable to me, I begged permission from Gilberto to visit her for two months that spring. I was now less than half an inch shy of six feet in height and wore my hair long, tying it with a black velvet ribbon in back, which I regarded as terribly dashing.

IN THE WORLD beyond my immediate surroundings, Napoleon's dream of European conquest all but died in November of 1812, when, starving and frozen, his troops retreated from an ill-advised attack on Moscow. Within eighteen months his throne in Paris would be handed to Louis XVIII. In consequence, another French invasion of Porto was impossible—for the time being. Yet I refrained from unearthing the mementos of Midnight and Daniel I had buried. Like Mother, I had no wish to confront such vestiges of my past.

XXV

I SET SAIL FOR LONDON IN TIME FOR MY MOTHER and me to celebrate my twenty-second birthday together. I was filled with trepidation, principally owing to a glorious complication that had occurred just before I left.

I had been out strolling when I caught the eye of a lass standing on her second-story balcony. She had long black tresses and darkly glowing eyes. Playfully, she lifted the edge of her royal blue mantilla and held it over her mouth, as though it were a veil. I could easily have believed her a sorceress of the forest, born during Midnight's Age of the First People.

Before I could call out and ask her name, she crossed her arms over her chest, pirouetted round, and disappeared inside her house. I waited for two hours, but she failed to emerge.

The next evening at sundown, I found her seated on a stool on the street beneath her balcony, selling plants and flower bulbs. She didn't see me, as she was painting a pot a fiery orange. Her hair sat in a swirl atop her head, except for delicate ringlets by her ears.

"Good evening," I said gallantly.

Startled, she dropped her brush onto her skirt.

"Shit! Look what you made me do!"

I was charmed that she had uttered a curse word. "I heartily apologize, young lady," I said, offering my handkerchief to her with what I hoped was a winning smile.

"But I shall ruin it," she said, plainly considering me daft to even suggest it.

My next reply would provide Luna Olive Tree and Mama with mirthful shrieks of laughter for many years. I held out my offering to her with redoubled sincerity and said, "I should not mind you painting all of me orange, if it meant being touched by you everywhere."

How in God's name I could have said such a ridiculous thing, I do not know. Incensed, her dark eyes flashed ominously. She bluntly refused my handkerchief and wiped her fingers on her apron instead.

Humiliated and tempted to rush away, I tried my best to turn the conversation toward a safer topic. "It is a lovely sunset—all that pink and gold." Receiving only silence by way of a reply, I cleared my throat and shifted my weight to my other leg in what I hoped was a gentlemanly manner.

"You are standing in my light," she said, not even deigning to look at me.

As the sun was behind her and my shadow fell in the opposite direction, I presumed she was joking. Encouraged, I gave a small laugh and launched another inane volley her way. Looking at her plants, I said, "I wonder if one might eat a tulip bulb. Some people call them *batatinhas*, you know—little potatoes. Do you suppose they are poisonous? Perhaps if they were cooked."

"Sir," she declared, "if I knew they were poisonous, you may be assured I would offer one to you at this very moment."

My eyes filled with tears at her harsh words.

"Oh, sir, what have I done?" she exclaimed.

Burning with shame, I ran off.

I barricaded myself in my bedroom and cursed all women as daughters of Lilith, queen of the demons. Then I took off my clothes and scrutinized myself in Mama's old cheval mirror. I was far too tall and pale. I wondered if a mustache might improve matters.

I made myself stay at home the next evening, but the day after saw a return of my blind courage and I risked approaching her again. At sundown, I found myself carrying a red damask shawl to her that I had purchased for a small fortune on the Rua das Flores. When she appeared on her balcony, she stared at me, and this time it was her eyes that welled with tears.

I tied two knots in the shawl and tossed it up to her. She caught it eagerly, then dropped her black mantilla to me.

She wore my shawl about her shoulders and flapped it like wings. Then she rushed inside.

By the next morning, I could stand no more insomnia. Begging Gilberto to be patient with me, I walked to the house of my tormentor once again, waited till the tolling of nine o'clock, and knocked on the door. I had practiced an eloquent speech for her parents all through the night, including impressive references to philosophy and art, but when a short man with a grizzled beard and long gray hair falling about his shoulders came yawning to the door, I fumbled my greeting.

"Speak up, son!" the man said gruffly.

"There is a young lady . . . a young . . . girl who appears on your balcony in the evenings. She sells flowers in the street as well."

"My daughter Maria Francisca."

"Yes, yes, that must be her. But . . . but perhaps if I begin again . . . My name is John Stewart. I am sorry to inconvenience you with my coming so early to your door."

"No, no, I am pleased." He smiled. "And starting with your name is always a splendid idea. But before we proceed any further, I should like to know precisely what your interest in my daughter might be."

"Well, sir, I . . . I intend to marry her."

I cannot explain why I dared to make this reply, except that I truly meant it.

Francisca's father laughed. "You are not the first to suggest that," he said. "But it is much more important"—here he reached for my arm to lead me inside—"to be the last."

He introduced himself as Egídio Castro da Silva Martins. He had only three or four crooked teeth in his head, but large friendly eyes and a sweetly puckered mouth. He told me that he was a flower seller and that his shop was near St. Anthony's Hospital.

A painting of Francisca's mother hung above the mantelpiece. I saw that her daughter had inherited her thick black hair and mysterious eyes. They both looked like women who knew how to keep secrets—and create them too. Senhor Egídio told me she had left him ten years earlier when Francisca had been seven. He made a fist and shook it at her. "You done me wrong, you wicked woman!" he bellowed.

After I commented on her likeness to their daughter, he looked bemused and said, "As you can see, I well understand your dilemma, son."

About his daughter's future, he made it quite plain that he would allow her to make her own decision with regard to a husband. I then explained that I wished to invite her to stroll with me along the riverside.

"I shall put that proposition to her this afternoon, young man, and if you will return at eight this evening, you will have an answer."

I thanked him for his help and then confessed that I had to leave in four days for two months in England.

"Perhaps it is a good thing," he reassured me. "You will get to know each other over the next evenings, if Francisca agrees. And if a true bond of affection develops between you, one that is not severed by weeks of separation, then we all might be inclined to believe that a promising future awaits you."

"And one other thing, sir . . ."

"Don't be shy, son," he said, slapping my back.

"I should only like to add that my Father was Scottish and my mother, though Portuguese, is of New Christian origins. I am, in short, half-Jewish and half-Scottish. I wish to make that plain from the outset. I shall understand if you consider it an obstacle, but I can assure you that—"

Senhor Egídio held up his hands and smiled.

"Son, all that matters between the young is loyal affection. The rest is simply decoration."

TRUE TO HIS word, for the next three evenings, Francisca and I were permitted to stroll through the city. She wore a different mantilla every night, and I bought colored lanterns for her to carry.

I was astonished to discover how timid she was: She refused to look into my eyes for any length of time. Months later, she told me that I was the first man she had ever felt an attraction for and that it sent chills through her down to her toes.

On our second evening, as we stood by the river, I talked of Daniel.

"I shall never get over his death," I observed.

"But you would not want to. If you could, then what would his life have truly meant to you?" She brushed my arm as she spoke. She had beautiful slender hands.

"Aye," I replied, "he was a wild and handsome lad." Thinking of my betrayal, I added, "And most loyal to me."

Continuing my policy of revealing my personality flaws from the start, I then said, "The many deaths I have known have left me broken and lonely. If you come to feel a fondness for me, which is what I hope, Francisca, then you will be giving your heart to a man who has done many reckless things and who may be a wayward misfit. I recognize the truth of this now, and the worst part is that I am not at all sorry for it."

While we walked to her home through the impasse of silence I had created, I fell into despair, presuming I'd scared her off with my direct manner. At her door, I apologized for speaking inappropriately.

"John, please say no more, you have done nothing wrong," she said, placing her hand over my mouth for a moment. Her touch made me jump. "I understand you better than you think. My father and I, there isn't a day that passes that we do not miss my mother." She smiled sadly. "Please come inside and sit with us. There is no need to be reticent. We are people who understand loss." She took my hand and gazed deep into my eyes. "Please, I am your friend," she assured me.

Five small words, but the way she said them—with the care of a person setting delicate flowers in a simple vase—convinced me that she understood that it was not mere momentary diversion I sought from her. I brought her hand back to my lips. The possibility that my loneliness was at an end... I smiled and kissed her once more, closing my eyes to breathe in her scent.

We discovered Senhor Egídio stoking the fire. I was touched by the eager affection he displayed toward Francisca and impressed by the sense of ease he created around him. He offered me a glass of wine.

"I should like to show you something, John," he said. Scratching the whiskers on his chin, his eyes twinkled mischievously. "I shall return presently. And, Francisca, if you discuss me while I am gone I shall know!" With that, he disappeared upstairs.

"He never sits still. I was born to a weaver's shuttle," Francisca whispered.

Egídio came back into the room carrying a stack of mantillas. When Francisca saw them draped over his arm, she hid her head in her hands and groaned.

"What is it?" I asked her.

"The clever lass is embarrassed because she made them," her father said.

He held them in the cradle of his arm for me to study, as though each were an infant. He had large coarse hands, with flecks of dirt in his fingernails, but his extreme gentleness in all things involving his daughter moved me—and reassured me as well that I was right where I ought to be.

Francisca cringed while we discussed her handiwork and refused to come and join us. "No, no, no," she said, shooing us both away playfully.

In one mantilla of deep red she had incorporated a fire-colored pattern of autumn leaves. In another of chestnut, she had created a white and yellow blazing sun. I had never seen anything like them, as shawls in anything other than block colors were generally not worn in Porto. But what impressed me most was her imagination.

When I caught her eye and smiled, she sighed. "Papa lives to torture his children."

"It is called *pride,* child," he corrected with a wink.

Francisca continued to dismiss her work as I asked her questions about knitting techniques and methods. "With all that goes on in the world, who could possibly care what I make?" she told me.

I refused to give in to her modesty. "If," I said, adopting the pose of a fine British gentleman, "if, young lady, I were to commission you now to make a waistcoat for me with the sun—or any other design you choose—incorporated in its weave, would you finally believe my admiration is real?"

As she still thought that I was merely being polite, I gave her a hard look and tossed her a hundred-*reis* coin, which she caught in both her hands. She shook her head at such an absurdity, then grinned. I could tell that although I may not yet have won her heart, I *had* indeed gained her trust.

THE NEXT EVENING she wore the red shawl I had given her as a gift. We walked again by the river, and she suggested that we take the ferry to the far bank. Without warning she looked at me defiantly, hoisted up the fringe of her dress, and raced off toward the boat, laughing all the way. I didn't try to catch her; it was such an unladylike thing to do that I couldn't take my admiring eyes off her.

Once on the ferry, I could think of nothing but kissing her, and my conversation was patchy at best.

In great danger of fainting, I risked everything by pressing my lips to hers.

*　　*　　*

LATER THAT EVENING, defying all convention, we dared to enter my home unchaperoned. We were so nervous that we did not speak. My heart seemed to be beating outside my body.

After we'd kissed for a time once again, I slipped my fingers under the ruffles of her dress. She started when I did so, and I begged forgiveness for my impetuosity. But she clasped my hand and said, "Your fingers are cold, John, that's all."

Then she asked where my room was.

Hence, it was in my old bed that we first made love, creating a raft of our own entwined bodies and drifting off to sea.

Afterward, I was giddy. I pranced about the room stark naked, singing Robert Burns's "Rantin' Rovin' Robin" in an operatic voice.

The next night, I asked if she would be my wife, and she agreed.

As a parting gift, I gave Francisca the letter from Joaquim to Lúcia that had fluttered out of *The Fox Fables* when I was seven, which had taught me so much about the language of love. She sat with her legs crossed on my bed like a child and read it by candlelight. While she was reading, I went to my window and, gazing up at the stars, whispered a prayer for Violeta's safety. I think it was my way of saying good-bye to her forever.

After Francisca and I had slunk back to her home like criminals, she brought out my going-away present. It was a vest knitted of black wool, with the moon in different phases patterned into the weave. That seemed the most promising gift possible, as it was the moon, Midnight had said, who had told men and women of their eternal life.

SO IT WAS that I left for London already betrothed, and though my two months' sojourn with Mother and Aunt Fiona was heartwarming, and the majesty and madness of London made my mouth drop open in amazement on many an occasion, I wished to be home in Porto at every moment.

Mama was, of course, overjoyed to hear of my impending marriage. She had become as eager and open with me as when I was young, and nothing gave her more pleasure than simply sitting with me. She had me describe everything about my evenings with Francisca, and though I was careful to omit the more intimate details, she guessed the truth soon enough.

"You have always shown great patience for many things, John, most of all for me. But you have never wanted to wait for affection." She laughed. "Though I suppose that is a good thing. Why must so deep a love as you have found wait?"

Francisca and I exchanged letters twice weekly, which served to deepen our intimacy. She wrote to me once that she had woken in the night to hear me imitating birds.

Then you spoke to me, and you said, "Fly, Francisca, anywhere you wish. I shall try my best not be jealous." Isn't that odd?

Dream or not, I wrote back, *we shall endeavor to make it true. Though I beg you not to soar so high that I lose sight of you. And you must promise to always return to me.*

I give you my vow, she agreed.

She always signed her letters, *Your friend, Francisca.* That meant everything to me.

WE WERE MARRIED three months after my return, on September the Fourteenth of 1813, by which time Francisca had missed her time of the month on three successive occasions.

I was eager for my mother to attend the ceremony, particularly as we had rediscovered so much of our spontaneous affection during my stay in England, but she was hesitant to declare herself ready to return to Porto. In the end, we decided it best to proceed without her. I assured her that she would be with us in spirit, and that her blessing was all that mattered.

We were married in the São Bento Church, where I compromised with Francisca and agreed to take Christian vows—like thousands of Portuguese Jews before me. Luna, Benjamin, Gilberto, Senhora Beatriz, and Grandmother Rosa were all in attendance. Having sobbed throughout the proceedings, my grandmother told me afterward that I was a villain for failing to bring Francisca to her for her permission.

I played the gemsbok and would not be provoked.

Our first child was born on the Twenty-Eighth of February of 1814. It was a difficult birth, and Francisca was weak for weeks afterward. We named her Graça in honor of Graça Olive Tree.

Lying with my wife and our new baby in my parents' old bed, I discovered for the first time that I wished to disappear into my wife and child. This, I've found, is one of the great mysteries of our fear of death, for if passing away were to mean merging into a loved one—into one of my daughters, for instance—I should not mind it in the least. Yet ceasing to exist the way we do, without this union with another being to whom we are tied by affection, has always struck me as damnably unfair.

ESTHER WAS BORN just over a year later, on the Seventh of March of 1815. This birth proved even more troublesome and led to complications for Francisca, who became prey to fits of rage and melancholy. For nearly two months she didn't care whether Esther lived or died. Nor could I trust her with Graça, since she had on two occasions struck out in fury at her.

The lighthearted friend I'd married was replaced by a bedraggled Medea. Her silken hair grew tangled, as though burnt by the heat of madness raging inside her. I contracted a wet nurse to suckle Esther, and as I was loath to let a physician purge Francisca or apply his accursed leeches, she was tended to by Benjamin. At all hours that good man would come to our home to help with Francisca and the children.

In my wife's lucid moments, tears of fear and regret fell in an endless stream, and I spent much of my time trying to reassure her.

"Do not abandon me," she once begged, clawing at me in her panic. "Please, John, I could not bear it."

"I could never abandon you," I replied, but my fears for our future compromised that pledge. I placed her shawl over her shoulders and sang softly to her until she fell asleep.

Needless to say, this was a miserable time for us—a terrible test of our love. For a time, I am ashamed to admit, my affection for her was eclipsed by anxiety and resentment.

I am certain that Benjamin's calming curatives saved her life in the end and safeguarded her sanity in the process. For as quickly as she vanished, she returned to me. A change became apparent to me in the wee hours of one cool night in May, when she came to my old bedroom, where I was trying to calm Esther, who'd been crying so much that I was worried for her health.

When I opened the door, my wife kissed me on the cheek and held out her hands for the baby.

I hesitated, but Francisca assured me, "Your friend is back and all is well."

"It is truly you?"

She took my hand and brought it to her lips. It is strange to say so now, but when we embraced I could smell the change in her. I nuzzled my head into her neck, then burst into tears and placed Esther in her arms. After we discussed what had transpired over the past weeks—for she had little memory of much of what she'd said or done—I returned to our bed in my parents' old room, where I slept for a good twelve hours.

Having suffered this terrible time, we thought it best not to have any more children.

GRANDMOTHER ROSA WAS still furious about the wedding and made no attempt to see Graça after she was born, but she did visit our house after Francisca's difficulties had ended to get a first peek at Esther. She was now almost eighty years of age, yet she still insisted on dousing herself with her expensive French perfume.

After holding the wee infant in her arms, she started to cry. "John, is there no chance at all for me to start over with your children?" she whispered.

Convinced that her sentiments were genuine, I allowed her to visit whenever she wished, though I made Francisca swear she'd not leave her alone with either of the children until she'd proved her affection. The two of us would observe my grandmother at play with the girls on dozens of occasions over the coming years. And though she never displayed great patience or understanding, she did show them a certain brittle tenderness, which Esther in particular grew to adore.

When I asked my grandmother once why she had swallowed her pride and come to see Esther, she rolled her eyes as though I'd disappointed her with yet another silly question and said, "I'm old, John, and I've not much time left to me. You've got many more years than I do, so you hold the grudge for both of us if you want."

Heartened that she had not lost her biting wit, I smiled admiringly at her, but she just cleared her throat and went back to the children.

OUR MARRIAGE THROUGH those early years was a good one, I believe, though not without its difficulties. I was young and mule-headed, and it took me some time to respect Francisca's opinion as equal to my own. I also worked too hard with Gilberto at our shop and occasionally returned home long after the children and Francisca were asleep, causing her to suffer bouts of profound loneliness. When I would inevitably fail to read her mind, she would sit sullenly by herself, her hands moving over her knitting with frightening swiftness. I would have to beg her many times before she would put down the shawl or scarf she was fashioning and tell me what was troubling her.

The more we found the courage to overcome our frailties, the greater our friendship became.

As anyone who has been married for a long while can attest, it is essential to adjust to the changes in one's beloved every few years and, if you will, silently agree to marry them once again.

ONE RATHER STARTLING discovery I made not too long after our marriage was that Francisca's fondness for mantillas and vests of her own creation had led her to experiment—without my knowing—with boldly patterned fabrics for her own clothing. The second summer after Esther's birth, by which time she had long regained her trim and girlish figure, she expressed this previously restrained desire by making herself two dresses from textiles woven in Morocco and the Portuguese colony of Goa.

As I say, I was not privy to this. Indeed, Francisca—demonstrating that penchant for secrecy I had first seen in her eyes—cut and sewed like a demoness during her afternoons, her patterns spread on the floor before her, while I was busy at my pottery and tile. By the time I returned home to her and the children in the evenings, she had everything safely tidied away, perfect innocence in her welcoming eyes.

I only chanced upon her secret one Friday evening at sundown while searching through one of her clothing chests for the red shawl I had given her when we'd first met, since—on a whim—I wished her to wear it at our Sabbath dinner with Luna Olive Tree and Benjamin. I ought to have asked her permission to rummage through her things, but since she was already at Luna's house with the girls, I was in one of my typical frenzies.

Holding my lamp in one hand, rather like a tomb-robber, I lifted out the first dress and laid it on our bed. "What's this we have here?" I whispered to myself, delighted by the mystery.

It had bell sleeves and a low circular collar and was made of tightly woven wool—very soft to the touch—on which pink and crimson circles spun against a background of brown. The second, a long-sleeved empire gown, was bright canary yellow covered in black butterflies made from triangles trimmed in burgundy and orange. From a distance, their wings seemed to capture three different positions of a single flutter. It was miraculous.

I ran down our street to Luna's house and, panting like Fanny at the finish line of one of our obstacle courses, insisted Francisca return home with me.

"What's wrong?" my wife exclaimed, reaching for my arm in concern.

"Nothing."

"Then why must—"

"Just come. You will see when we get there."

When she continued to protest, I dragged her off, like a child leading a parent to a treasure chest. Casting a look back over her shoulder as she shuffled behind me, she told Luna, "We shall return shortly—at least, I earnestly hope so."

"Have no fear, I shall not sell the girls unless I get a good price," Luna giggled.

Once we'd reached our bedroom, Francisca was confronted with the evidence of her deviousness. "You've found me out," she gasped.

I kissed her hands and peeled them from her eyes, which were sealed tight. "As the spontaneous generation of gowns is an extremely rare phenomenon," I said, "I am guessing that you made them."

I laughed heartily, but she refused even to smile. Instead, she began to cry.

"But, Francisca, whatever could be wrong?"

Through her sniffles, it emerged that she believed I would regard her creations as hideous and would resent such an exuberant expression of her gifts.

"Oh, John," she moaned, "sewing these dresses is the greatest folly I have ever permitted myself. I cannot say what made me do it."

She misinterpreted my astonishment and pledged that she would never wear either of them if I objected. "Indeed, I shall throw them into the hearth."

"You'll do no such thing!" I growled.

Remembering our courtship, I took two hundred-*reis* coins from my fob pocket and placed them in her hands. "Listen to me, Francisca, I shall pay you for a waistcoat in any fabric you choose on the condition that it is sure to astonish everyone who sees it!" I caressed her cheek, which was my way of winning her over. "They're the most stunning things I've ever seen." I moved behind her and started to undo the laces on the simple dress she was wearing. "This will take just a minute," I observed.

She reached back over her shoulder to still my hand. "Not now—we haven't time for that. Later, I promise. But we've our Sabbath supper, and Benjamin will be at Luna's at any moment."

I slapped her bottom playfully. "I only wish for you to put on one of the dresses, you wicked-minded girl. The one with the butterflies. Please, it's beautiful."

"But I shall die of embarrassment, John."

"Nonsense. It is good for us to be embarrassed at least once a week."

She snorted. "John, I assure you that philosophy is of no help to me at this particular moment. I shall cringe when they set their shocked eyes on what I've made."

I squeezed her tight, then bit the lobe of her ear so that she yelped. "Do it for your husband," I whispered, "who feels nothing but tenderness for you."

"You do not feel particularly tender at this moment," she observed.

"That is just the tip of my emotions. I assure you the rest of me is as gentle as a rose." I squeezed her tighter, then growled.

When Francisca was dressed, I held the lamp up as she stood before our mirror, so we might both get a good look at her. I had never seen her look more captivating. The butterflies on her sleeves seemed ready to flutter away.

"Admit it," I ventured. "You chose that particular pattern for me."

Francisca bit her lip slyly, then grimaced. "The Sabbath is sacred to Benjamin and Luna. It may be considered an affront."

"Shush. Do you really think any God worth our while would take offense at a woman who has become a landscape of fluttering wings?"

I pushed her toward the door and, when she continued to stall, lifted her into my arms and ran with her down the stairs, crashing into the walls on purpose, so that she could not help laughing and hollering. By the time I had deposited her inside Luna's doorway, Benjamin had already arrived.

The old apothecary leaned forward, his spectacles at the tip of his nose. "Goodness gracious me, Francisca. You are the meeting of heaven and earth, dear girl."

Luna started, as though remembering something long lost.

"Francisca made it," I announced proudly.

Suddenly, Luna burst into tears and ran from the room.

"What have I said?" I asked.

"It's me," Francisca moaned, her shoulders slumping. "I'll go home to change. I've offended Luna."

"No, no, no," I said. I grabbed a candlestick and the three of us followed the sound of muffled sobs to the back of the house. We found Luna in the larder where she kept the wax for her sculpted fruit. She was sitting on the floor, sobbing, her knees pulled up to her chest. Benjamin squatted next to her and kissed the top of her head.

"What's wrong?" I asked.

"It's my sister," she said mournfully.

I lifted her hands to my lips. "I miss Graça too," I whispered. "Every day when I paint my tiles, I think of you and her both, and how you changed my life."

Luna fingered the hem of Francisca's dress. "My sister never had an opportunity to meet you, my child. She would have loved seeing you at this moment." She traced her fingers across the butterfly pattern. "It's so unfair that she never saw the two of you married. How relieved and happy she'd have been that you found such a clever girl, John. Youth is incomparably beautiful, is it not, Benjamin? And they have no notion of it."

Benjamin smiled knowingly.

THE NEXT MORNING, rising to the challenge I'd issued, Francisca summoned me from bed before I'd fully woken and measured me for my new waistcoat, whacking me on the head whenever I yawned.

The following Saturday, I woke to discover my present on her pillow, with a note that read, *For dearest John.*

It was fashioned from shimmering lavender damask. Across the front she had painstakingly sewn rows of tiny diamonds in yellow and pink.

Thanks to Luna, who cherished a good game of cards, this marvelous creation became known locally as my "King of Diamonds" waistcoat, and for many years I never failed to wear it on my birthday, feeling rather like a present myself when I had it on.

FROM THAT DAY forward, Francisca and I were constantly on the lookout for unusual fabrics. We soon discovered a tumbledown shop at the back of a shipping office on the Rua dos Ingleses from which we could purchase woolens, cottons, and silks from India, Turkey, Persia, and even the west coast of Africa.

I remember, in particular, the dress Francisca made for the Christmas ball at the Factory House, our British club, in 1816. I ought to add that she and I had refrained from attending such gatherings in previous years because of her pregnancies and the ceaseless labor involved in caring for infants. This was to be our debut, in a sense, as a couple—at least for the British community.

As she had no desire to offend the more conservative guests, she insisted on a fabric that would not be too garish. In the end, she chose a soft cotton from Morocco emblazoned with black, olive green, and yellow twelve-pointed stars set against a background of lapis-lazuli blue.

Francisca designed a low collar and long sleeves ending in ruffles for her gown, completing it with a long, extravagant train that I carried for her. The small buttons were also black and shaped into stars, carved from jet in the workshops of Bologna.

When she put this dress on for the first time—her black hair pinned up, a pearl necklace around her neck—she naturally asked my opinion. The children were in their room sleeping, and I was reading the *Edinburgh Review,* wearing only my linen nightshirt and lamb's wool sandals. When I swiveled in my seat to face her, my pipe dropped from my mouth, bounced off my leg, and tumbled to the floor. It wasn't terribly amusing on a number of fronts, for aside from burning my inner thigh, I felt completely unworthy of her. There I was—absurdly dressed, almost naked—and before me stood a sphinx with a woman's face and a peacock's incomparable plumage. She wrinkled her nose and laughed, placing her hands on her hips in a very girlish gesture of impatience, and I realized in a reassuring instant that this radiant creature would always be *my* Francisca—and my dearest friend.

I WORE MY King of Diamonds waistcoat to the Christmas ball, of course, under a wide-lapeled coat of charcoal gray that Mama had made for me years earlier. Perhaps the two of us did look "fit for a lily pond," as I overheard an elderly woman by the entrance remark to her gentleman companion, but I didn't care; the disdain shown to myself and my mother after Papa's death had freed me forever from worry over such spite. It is a glorious moment when we finally begin to enjoy our own individuality, and I now had the confidence to do so.

We stood by ourselves for quite some time, drinking punch and feeling like discarded fish, but I soon insisted on dancing nonetheless.
Thankfully, the few steps I knew were graceful and surefooted, owing to
Mama's patient instruction. Even though Francisca thought she might
faint—indeed might have wished to as a means of escaping the sea of
scrutinizing eyes—I led her through the dance without either of us putting a foot wrong.

The first of nearly a dozen gentlemen to ask her for a dance came
over and identified himself as the son of a visiting merchant from
Manchester. Despite her resolute refusals, he would not relent. I found
the enduring hope in his brown eyes so very touching that I agreed to in-
tercede on his behalf, placing a series of coaxing kisses on her cheek. As
much to prevent any further embarrassment for herself and me, she
stood up and walked off with the young man, seeming to draw the light
of the room in her wake. All of the other dancers seemed mere shadows
alongside her. Not a single man or woman in the room could take their
eyes off her, though it is also true to say that a good many of them held
fast to their scorn.

I cannot honestly say that Francisca was the most sought-after
woman that evening, for we continued to be shunned by the majority of
guests and we were never invited to the Factory House ball again. But I
have no doubt whatsoever that it was plain to everyone in attendance
that she had the most proud and admiring husband by far.

XXVI

BENJAMIN, WHEN PREPARING ME FOR MAR-
riage to Francisca, once told me that if affection is to last,
one must love the person one knows in the present as well as
the one he or she may become in the future. I was not sure of
his meaning until the early summer of 1819.

This was a most troubling time for me, for I'd begun to
think constantly about the unfairness of death. Nights were
the worst. Lying next to Francisca, the gratitude I felt at being with her led me to thoughts of dying before seeing her to
old age and the children to adulthood. Trembling in the
dark, afraid to embrace her lest I wake her, I was frequently
unable to sleep.

Perhaps due to the exhaustion caused by my insomnia,
my feelings soon changed, however, and I began to believe
that my obsession with death was a result of impositions being placed on me by my family: the need to earn a living, to
care for the children, to encourage Francisca during her moments of doubt. I came to regard these as a threat to my very
existence and the cause of my morbid state of mind. In my
troubled state, I could not conceive of any way forward for
the boy and man I used to be. They had vanished. Or so I

thought. At times, I seemed to be looking through a window at all the things I would never get to do and see.

I would frequently sit for hours in the Lookout Tower, watching the successive phases of the moon, allowing the glowing petals of red and yellow filtering through the restored colored glass of the skylight to fall across my body as though to camouflage me. Beneath all that beauty, however, I felt barren—that my life, just like the tinted moonlight, was nothing but a clever illusion. My shadow cast across the floor seemed that of a straw man.

I tried to hide my feelings from Francisca—after all, no woman could react well to being cast as her husband's jailer—which created distance between us. Despite the pain this caused her, she never mentioned my lack of enthusiasm. Pity the young husband who forgets that his wife may not be so different from him. . . .

One Sunday, after daydreaming all morning of a life with the Bushmen in the deserts of southern Africa, I decided we ought to journey to the beaches at the river mouth by donkey, as I had on occasion as a lad. By so doing, I hoped to compensate for my recent lack of attention to my wife and the girls.

Just as I predicted, Francisca was skeptical from the very beginning. Making a sour face, she said, "Are you sure a two-hour ride atop a smelly beast is how you want to spend a day of blessed rest? Would you not prefer to sit in the garden and read?"

"Your husband is game for adventure," I declared.

I can see now that a part of me wanted her to fail this test so as to have proof that she was holding me back. To my surprise, she agreed and slipped into the oldest dress she could find. Bedecked in black, she looked every inch the youthful widow, which did little to improve my disposition.

"Black will fail to show any stains," she explained to me with a cheeky grin.

I HIRED THE best beasts I could find, at a stables near Cordoaria Park. We started off without a hitch. The two girls rode on Lídia, a sable-colored donkey with large, almond-shaped eyes. Francisca gripped the reins of a brown one named Filipa.

"I suppose you were right all along," she told me. "It's going to be a pleasant journey."

So I am not mad, after all, I wanted to shout at her.

I would have considered it cruel at my weight to sit on one of the diminutive beasts, so instead I walked alongside Lídia, while Graça gripped the reins in her tiny hands. I also held the blue croquet ball of which the child had grown fond of late; she refused to go anywhere without it.

Unfortunately, the animal kingdom soon turned against us. Flies attracted to the infinitely patient donkeys began to swarm around the girls when we reached the riverside, where it was especially filthy. Despite all my attempts to swat them away, Esther began to fuss and cry. Desperate, Francisca covered the girl's face and chest with her mantilla. Graça, unwilling to ride alone, then voiced her disapproval with a volley of piercing shrieks that might have summoned hailstones and frogs had there been but a single cloud in the June sky.

While Francisca comforted Esther, I lifted Graça into her mother's saddle so the three of them could ride together. Poor Filipa began to labor under the strain. Lídia was staring intently ahead, afraid to turn round lest I change my mind and demand my rightful place on her back. On we journeyed, me swatting and cursing, Francisca growing angrier by the minute, a red-hot *I told you so* burning in her eyes.

After ninety minutes of this march toward doom, we reached my favorite cove by the river mouth, where Francisca and I decamped like weary soldiers recovering from a lost battle.

The girls were happy enough by now, as the ocean was magnificent and the breeze much cooler, but nothing I did could rouse a smile from Francisca. I built sand castles with Esther, whose chubby little hands poked and patted with glee, and even overcame my fear of the water for a few minutes to lead Graça giggling into the frigid foam at the edge of the surf. All this time, Francisca refused to talk to me. After we had eaten our picnic and had begun packing up our belongings, she finally said, "I refuse to ride those donkeys back. My bottom is black and blue."

"I can't abandon them here."

She took off her bonnet and shook her long black hair loose. "John, you will please explain yourself to me," she said impatiently.

"Whatever do you mean?" I asked, feigning ignorance.

My theatrical talents had apparently improved little since childhood. Frowning, she shoved me, so hard that I almost fell. "Tell me what is wrong with you!" she screamed.

I was shocked to speechlessness, then shouted, "Me?! Nothing is wrong with me. It's *you*—you've been acting as though your tongue were cut out. And now look at how you're behaving!"

I hated the way I was speaking to her, but I was powerless to stop myself.

"You can be sure there is much more to this than any silence of *mine*," she countered, a prosecutor's certainty in her voice.

"I thought we could have a pleasant day, an adventure, that is all. But apparently nothing is possible for us anymore. Nothing!"

I had hardly wished to speak so frankly, but I suppose the truth has a mind of its own.

"Nothing possible for us...?" Her great dark eyes flashed dangerously. "You, sir, have gone too far. I shall not move from this place until I know precisely what has caused your foul mood these past weeks."

I searched through my bag for my pipe to stall for time.

"Do not fear me, John. I may be angry, but I am still your friend," she said sharply. "And you will never find a more loyal friend—never. Of that, I can assure you."

"I am not questioning that," I replied, insincerity making my voice sound hollow.

"Then what is it?"

Seeing her dressed in the widow's black, I envisioned the future I most feared. I said, "It's the weight...the weight of being a father, of having a family for which I am responsible. There are moments when I simply cannot breathe. I'm sorry. It's terrible of me, but I imagine escaping—somewhere, anywhere..."

I felt as though I'd been walking in the African desert of my daydreams for months—crossing miles of sand and bushland simply to get here, to this wee cove with Francisca and the children. I was so confused. I seemed to be in two places at once.

When my wife finally looked back at me, her eyes were moist. "Is that all it is, John—the weight of having a family? Is that truly all that has been troubling you these past months?"

"That's enough, I should think—a father who doubts his capacity to care for his family, who does not know where he is or what he is doing, who fears that death may come for him at any moment. I feel as though I've lost my way."

"Nothing more, are you sure?"

"What more could there be, Francisca? Isn't that enough for you?"

She ran her fingers through her hair and sighed with relief, tears rolling down her cheeks. "There could be much more, John. You could have given your heart to someone else."

I realized with knife-edged clarity what a silent monster I'd been. I'd thought nothing of her welfare. "Oh, God, where have I been?" I kissed my apologies over her brow and cheeks. "Francisca, I'm sorry. It's just that I do not understand how a man can be both in love and still feel the things I feel. I never expected it. Can you forgive me for being such a fool? There are still so many things I do not understand—about myself most of all."

I wiped away her tears with my thumbs, a gesture that triggered a memory of Midnight doing the same for me. I felt his strength inside me, deep down, drumming in my gut.

Neither of us spoke for a time. Francisca studied me closely, then said, "We saw you from afar and we are dying of hunger."

"What ... what was that?" I stammered in astonishment.

"We saw you from afar, John, and we are dying of hunger."

"Why do you say that? How did you know I was thinking of him?"

"John," she explained, "there is a certain look you get when you are remembering Midnight, as if you are gazing far off toward a darkening horizon. When you spot him there, your eyes open wide, perhaps in response to the great light in him that you have always told me about. I thought that hearing his greeting now might reassure you that I mean you no harm. I wanted to remind you that I am not so different from him. Our affection for you makes us almost brother and sister, in a sense."

I saw that she and I were growing closer than ever before. It seemed to me now that it was precisely this closeness of spirit that I had been resisting of late, perhaps fearing it as a betrayal of Midnight, Daniel, and Violeta—of all my past.

"John," she said, "I understand you better than you think. You see, I share some of the same feelings. Can a woman's spirit not suffer from strain? Can a mother not wonder about the worth of how she passes her days? Am I so different from you, John Stewart?" She laughed at my surprise. "There are times when I cannot breathe either, you know, as though you and they"—she gestured toward the girls, who were drawing with sticks in the sand—"were a corset being pulled tighter and tighter around me."

"You feel such things?"

She sighed, plainly irritated that the thought had never occurred to

me. "John, I have two tiny children who need me all the time, and a husband of whom my fondness knows no bounds but who might have been
finding consolation in the arms of another. And I could say nothing, for
fear of driving him away from me. Think of the hunger in that."

I took her in my arms again and kissed her with a desperate intensity.
In our renewed ardor I recognized all I had been withholding from her,
all I had failed to do for her.

"Forgive me," I said. "I am not so strong as I thought, and I worry
that I may fail you when you most need me."

This fear was one I'd never contemplated before, but I now realized it
had existed in me ever since my father's death. I have reflected on this period of my life at length in recent years and have concluded that the
legacy of my parents' unhappiness had just caught up with me—and terrified me.

I explained everything to Francisca, searching desperately for the
right words, suggesting hesitantly that we might very well suffer the same
fate as my father and mother. They had loved each other once like playful children, after all, and had ended as strangers. They were surely no
different from Francisca and myself, and yet their friendship had shattered into recriminations and regrets. "What is to prevent us from becoming like them?" I asked her.

"John, I do not know if love will stay with us throughout our lives,
though I hope and pray it will. So all I can expect of you, and you of me,
is honesty. From what you told me of your dear parents, that seems to be
the one quality that was missing at times from their marriage. Forgive me
if it hurts you to hear that."

"Francisca," I sighed, "it's not as simple as that. Anything might happen to us, even if we are honest with each other. We cannot know what
plans the world has for us."

"Yes, that's true, John. But since we cannot know those plans, we
have only our faith in each other to rely on. John, what I think you need
to know is this. . . ." She scooped up some sand in her hand. "I shall go
with you wherever you wish. And I shall help you accomplish whatever
you choose. Or . . ." She paused. "Or stay behind." As she sprinkled the
warm sand on my toes, she repeated something I had once written to her
in a letter: "Just do not soar so high that I cannot catch sight of you. That
is not so much to ask, is it?"

"No, it is more than fair," I agreed, smiling as best I could to hide
how moved I was; by now, the children, sensing something was wrong,

were watching us suspiciously. When I saw Graça's worried face, I covered my eyes with my hands, so that neither of the girls would see my tears.

Francisca kissed me on the cheek, saying to Graça and Esther, "Everything is fine. Your father and mother are well. They are simply in love, and people who are very fond of each other occasionally go slightly mad."

With the girls now clamoring for our attention, we could not wrap the quilt around us and make love, as we wished. But perhaps that was not what we truly needed at that moment. It was, in fact, reassuring and comforting for the four of us to sit together and speak of the ocean and other things beyond our own lives.

We fetched water for Lídia and Filipa and hitched them to a lamp-post—I would pay their owner to retrieve them later. As we started home, I lifted Graça into my arms. She fell asleep immediately, her head on my shoulder, her croquet ball safely stowed in my bag. Francisca cradled Esther, who was carrying a white scallop shell, determined to ask as many questions about it as she could think of.

When we finally reached home, totally exhausted, Francisca said, "John, know this—should you wish to steal all the goldfinches, jays, and wrens still kept in Porto's bird market, I shall help you. Plan any escapade you wish—with or without me. I will love you whatever you become and whatever miracles you might make."

GILBERTO AND I were now full partners. I had long since given up hope of selling works based on Goya's drawings or my own fanciful imaginings. The good citizens of Porto wanted tilework in the old styles—depictions of saints and idyllic landscapes. The Portuguese will probably always be happy to place either St. Anthony or a cow on their walls—it makes little difference to them which.

For Francisca, I glazed wainscots of my own design and paneled the wall leading to our garden with scenes from Exodus. Animals played all the parts, including that of Moses, who was a lion with eyes glazed in silver and black. I believe Midnight would have admired my work, though most visitors considered it perfectly obscene.

I was always experimenting with colors and brushes, and I never tired of painting narratives for my family based on Torah stories and Midnight's animal tales.

In the children's room, I plastered tiles of chimeras, dragons, and sphinxes all over the walls. When they were tiny things, they would feign grabbing these creatures in their hands, shake them, then spring their fingers open and allow the winged beasts to fly free. It made them giddy with laughter.

The girls proved to have very different characters.

Esther, the youngest, was like Daniel: She always lived an arm's length from peril and would have it no other way. When she ran it was with perfect abandon, her thick auburn hair flying behind her. She was composed of sprightly things—of butterflies, tops, twigs, and bells. Her mind was a fugue. She could exhaust you by simply sitting on your lap and making requests. *No, I cannot read you the story a fifth time tonight. . . . No, it's already dark and we cannot walk to the river. . . .* One might have thought her capricious, but time proved that she kept many of her thoughts secret, like Francisca. And like Mama, she was gifted musically, which afforded her a creative outlet. I purchased a violin for her, and with some instruction from a local teacher, she was able to play simple melodies from the *Anna Magdalena Bach Songbook* by the age of six.

Graça was demure and thoughtful. Blessed with her mother's dark knowing eyes, she observed people carefully. She was frequently disappointed that life was not as she would have wished it—that the secret treasure she sought eluded her. Reading to her and consoling her were very serious matters indeed. As a consequence, one of my great joys was to make her laugh. Often, by the light of a single candle at her bedside she would study maps I found for her at Senhor David's bookshop, rather as though they held the key to the mysteries of life. I predicted that our provincial city at the edge of Europe would become too small for her when she reached adulthood.

At night I sometimes read to the girls from the Torah, which Graça always enjoyed very much but which put Esther immediately to sleep— not always an easy thing, so it served a useful double purpose.

After our talk on the beach, things between Francisca and me grew easy and calm. The four of us weeded our flower beds and pruned the roses, sat crosslegged on our bed playing cards, and went to the river to watch the coming and going of ships. We planted four fruit trees given us by Grandfather Egídio in each of the corners of our garden, where Midnight had previously had his medicinal plants: a peach, a lemon, an orange, and a quince.

Francisca continued to knit her astonishing creations, selling some of the more modest examples at a clothing shop on the Rua das Flores. She also made dresses and shawls for herself and the girls, and waistcoats and suits for me—which made us infamous in the neighborhood.

I always spoke to the children in English, as I wanted them to have that advantage in life. Like me, they understood both languages without difficulty by the time they were five or six.

Once, when the girls were six and seven, we took them to London for a fortnight, handed them over to Mother and Aunt Fiona, and escaped to Amsterdam, where Papa had hoped to take me and where I had long since wanted to see the synagogue. The harmony of its wood and glass, and its simple silence, were thrilling to us both, and I was astonished to find many men and women with whom we could speak Portuguese, though their families had not been back to our homeland in more than two centuries.

OUR FAMILY WAS a happy one, I would say, but more than that I began to perceive it as a metaphorical voyage made by the four of us, with additional travelers—like my mother, Benjamin, Luna, Senhora Beatriz, and even Grandmother Rosa—welcomed along whenever they wished. I still often thought of Daniel, Violeta, and Midnight, of course, at times with pain and guilt. Radiantly defiant of distance and death, they, too, stowed away on our journey—perhaps because so much of them continued to live inside me.

DURING THE FIRST years of my marriage, I learned nothing more of Midnight's death and the loss of affection between my parents. Curiously, an odd, persistent doubt remained with regard to my father, as I had never glimpsed his body after his death. In many a dream I discovered him in the midst of crowds—at the marketplace in Porto's New Square, at the Great Fair in London's Hyde Park, in the synagogue in Amsterdam. He was alive, and he had absented himself from our family, believing he had caused enough misery.

Upon waking, the pain of him not knowing Francisca or my daughters would sometimes constrict my chest so badly that I'd have to jump up simply to breathe.

I occasionally gave in to the mad belief that these dreams of him might be true—that he had not died in Porto, that Sergeant Cunha had identified him mistakenly. Or lied.

I never mentioned my doubts to anyone but Francisca.

"Where would he have gone?" she had asked, sitting up with me in bed one night.

I could not say. But I had a better question: "Will he ever return?"

XXVII

Fairly early on in our marriage, Francisca and I developed a strategy to fool fertility into glancing the other way when we were feeling amorous. Yet despite all our many precautions, in early April of 1822, a child-to-be made its presence keenly felt every morning to my wife.

Remembering how she had suffered after the birth of Esther, I was furious with myself for allowing this to happen. In the past, I had sneered at couples who forswore the pleasures of intimacy, preferring abstinence. But now I dearly wished that we had listened to reason.

"Very well, perhaps we ought to have two beds," she agreed when I told her that I thought it best that we abstain from now on.

"Absolutely right!" I declared, oblivious to her trap.

"But I am apt to become lonely at times," she said sadly. "Would you mind me occasionally sleeping beside you?"

"No, that would be acceptable—occasionally."

She knelt next to me. "And would you come to me if you grew lonely? We are friends, after all, and I should hate to think of you all alone and miserable."

"Yes, indeed, I should tiptoe to your bed."

"Now, in either of those cases," she added thoughtfully,

"I might then brush up against you. Accidentally, of course. The bed being so small, you understand. And if your flagstaff were to stand up—accidentally, I mean. What then?"

"Then you would have to fight me off."

"And if I should endeavor to lose too swiftly," she giggled, "would you be very cross with me?"

Wagging my finger like Mother, I told her, "Very well, you may be pleased, but I'll not again play Jason to your Medea. If that enraged harpy dares set foot in our house again, this time I shall chain her to our bed."

Smiling, she placed my hand over her belly. "We shall have ourselves another healthy child—now stop ranting and bring in more wood for the fire."

Over the coming weeks, despite my grave reservations, I grew resigned to another baby, particularly as our girls were greatly excited about having a little brother or sister. The two of them scribbled lists of names and howled with laughter over the worst possible choices—Adalberto for a boy and Urraca for a girl. Witnessing their delight, I came to the conclusion Francisca's pregnancy was a good thing, after all.

Then Francisca hemorrhaged. I was at my workshop, and Esther came running to fetch me. By the time we reached home, Benjamin, Senhora Beatriz, and a local midwife were already at Francisca's bedside. She had stopped bleeding, but we had lost the child.

"It's my fault," she moaned as I kissed her tears away.

"No one is to blame. The important thing is that you get better quickly."

That evening her condition took a turn for the worse and she lost consciousness. Neither I nor her father could rouse her. Esther again ran to fetch Benjamin. Thanks to his ministrations, Francisca awoke for a time, but she was so weak that she couldn't keep her eyes open.

"I'm here," I told her. "What may I get for you?"

She was very pale. "Sing," she said. "Let me hear your voice. I do not wish to lie here in the dark without your voice."

So I sang for her—all the Scottish, English, and Portuguese songs I had ever learned. I continued until daybreak, when she again lapsed into a deep slumber. When my voice failed, I spoke the poetry of Robert Burns, which is song to me even when recited.

Grandmother Rosa sat with Francisca for a time, gripping her hand between both of hers, as though to squeeze strength back into her. She and my father-in-law tried to lead me away from her so I might eat or sleep. They promised to stay, but I would not leave her. I asked only for hot tea so that I could continue to sing.

I was convinced that if I were to step away from her for even a moment, I would lose her forever. My father-in-law brought me my King of Diamonds waistcoat, which I put on, hoping to draw her toward life with all the beauty she had ever given me. Benjamin held my hand and whispered prayers over her for a time, writing secret inscriptions in Hebrew upon her forehead to protect her from harm. The girls took turns bringing me strong bitter tea made by Grandmother Rosa, their faces questioning and frightened. Esther scrambled up into bed and lay with her mother on occasion, whispering in her ear.

"You are my one true and good friend," I told Francisca, "and you cannot leave me." I was sure that I could pull her back to me with my devotion.

SOMETIME AFTER DAWN, I felt her hand twitch. She had stopped breathing. In trying to rouse her, I discovered more blood on the sheets. I shouted for Benjamin, but it was too late.

This, then, was the last lesson Francisca taught me: that I, John Zarco Stewart, had no magic at all. There were no songs of love powerful enough to defeat death. All of the most important things were beyond our control.

SHE MAY ALSO have taught me one other thing: If there was a God, then He was what Benjamin referred to in Hebrew as *Ein Sof*—a Lord of infinite vastness totally removed from our concerns, deaf to our prayers.

GRIEF...

My grief soon became a palace shrouded by perpetual night, where I had at my disposal a hundred rooms of despair, each crowded with visions of what was and what might have been. During the summer and autumn of 1822, and much of the next year as well, I paced its cold stone corridors, climbed its high staircases, and polished its statues of memory. During those first and most terrible weeks of loss, I blamed myself for never having loved her enough. In my madness, I ranted to the girls about their father's selfishness, though they had no idea what I meant.

I sat sometimes holding the love letter from Joaquim to Lúcia that had fluttered out of *The Fox Fables* when I was seven years old, wishing I had written to Francisca all that I had ever felt for her.

My hair grew wild and I refused to shave. I ached to be held by her again. I often stared in my mirror and wondered how such an empty man as I could proceed alone into the future.

I regretted having done so few drawings of her. At times, I could no longer remember the shape of her eyes and the contours of her slender hands. I thought I would go insane not being able to bury my nose in her hair at night.

Luna Olive Tree, Senhora Beatriz, and other neighbors made condolence calls, bringing us bread and soup. Grandmother Rosa and many other women whom I'd never even met sat with the lasses at our hearth and whispered to them of the pain and worry of motherhood, warning them about the obligations of marriage and the duplicity of men, lamenting having had their youthful forms stolen by birthing. Strangers cleaned our chimney and patched the Lookout Tower. Secret Jews came to my shop and talked to me about the Mount of Olives.

For nearly a year, I did what was expected of me. I created enough jars, vases, and ewers to hold the waters of the Douro. My glazes were mixed with spite for those who were happy.

I looked after our daughters as best I could and saw to it that they continued their lessons. Esther refused to play her violin for two months and stayed in her bed until I absolutely insisted she get up. Graça caused me endless worry with her terrible insomnia, an affliction she had doubtless inherited from me. Then there were times when she metamorphosed into a bolt of lightning, eager to lash out at her sister and me.

I tried my best to be understanding and to console them both. I passed the greater part of each and every day in their company, but sometimes I fear I was of precious little true help to them. I began to understand more of why Mother had distanced herself from me after the death of both Midnight and Father. We were alike in so many ways, she and I, and for too long I simply lost all desire for conversation, could think of no subject worth my full attention, not even—I am sorry to say—the misery of my children.

MAMA SENT ME long letters of encouragement thrice weekly for many months. She even overcame her fear of the memories hiding everywhere in our home to stay for an extended visit. Once, after putting the girls to bed, she took me aside and said, "I know it's of little use to tell you this now, but I shall say it anyway. You were the best of husbands to Francisca, and I feel certain that she died without any regrets—without anything left unsaid. I do not think you could have given her a greater parting gift than that. When you meet again, there will be nothing you need to apologize for. And that, John, is a priceless blessing."

MUCH HAD HAPPENED in the world beyond the borders of our provincial city since my marriage to Francisca, of course, including Napoleon's death. But the vicissitudes of politics caused us little concern until almost a year after my wife's burial, when the French army crossed the Pyrenees into Iberia to quash a Spanish rebellion in favor of liberal reform.

During a period of nightmares in which I imagined these troops continuing west to Porto and silencing our city again with their muskets and swords, I received a letter from New York. Holding it in my hands, I learned that the ink of the past had not dried so completely as I'd thought. Closing my eyes, I saw a lonely lass in a black bonnet tossing pebbles at my window.

Tears filled my eyes when I saw her handwriting. As though it were a triumph against all evil, I whispered to myself, *She made it to America!*

I actually received two letters from Violeta, the second arriving three days later, as it had been sent to me care of the Douro Wine Company and delivered by one of their couriers. Violeta explained that she had taken care to send two, as she didn't know whether I was still living at the same address. The letters were identical save for one sentence.

She explained almost nothing of how she had reached New York, saying only that she had lived many years in Lisbon and England, then had been snatched up by good fortune and carried to America. She was living in a house near the southern tip of Manhattan Island. She wished me to know that many colorful birds came to her small garden. One of the most beautiful was blue and white, with a crest.

I like to think of you, me, and Daniel seeing the same stars at the same moment, our hands touching inside their light, she wrote.

Her address was Number 73 John Street. She wrote that living on a street named after me always made her smile.

Toward the end of her letter, she said that many years earlier she had dreamed that Daniel had begged her to write to me. She apologized now for failing to heed his wishes, but she was at the time in no position to do so.

She hoped I was well, but as she had learned of my father's death, she feared that her dream had been a harbinger of that terrible event. She sent best wishes to my mother, whom she would never forget for her many kindnesses to her.

She gave no explanation as to how she had learned of Father's death, nor how she had discovered I was a tile-maker, nor even if she had learned of Francisca's death, but she concluded her letter with an astonishing proposal:

One day, if we should ever meet again, I would like you to execute a tile panel for my home in New York. Perhaps it could be of our lives when we were children. It would be lovely to have something of Porto and that time long gone. Always, Violeta

In the letter sent directly to my home, she added as a postscript: *I was overjoyed to learn that you have two daughters, and I should be honored to meet them someday.*

I DIDN'T KNOW what to make of it. New York? It was preposterous. I could scarcely imagine making the journey to Lisbon, two hundred miles south.

I was glad that she had made a good life for herself, of course—it seemed such a blessing after all our misfortunes. But receiving her letters proved too much for my tattered nerves. Behind my locked door, afraid to let my daughters see me, I sobbed alone until dawn.

BY MAY, THE struggle in Portugal between forces favoring our recent constitutional reforms and those hoping for a return to an absolute monarchy had nearly reached the point of civil war. Then we learned that both our parliament and our constitution had been nullified by King João VI and his son Miguel, commander-in-chief of the army, with hundreds of subsequent arrests of their opponents across the country. These unfortunate prisoners favored Miguel's older brother Pedro, a liberal reformer.

We knew not what agonies these men might be suffering, but the oldest among us sniffed at the air for the unforgettable scent of burning flesh that they remembered from their youths, when prisoners of the Inquisition were burnt alive in Lisbon and other cities.

Additionally, with the king and his supporters claiming absolute sovereignty, many of us believed that a French occupation was inevitable, as the great forces at play in that country would wish to ensure that our newly reinforced monarchy was friendly to their interests.

Quite literally overnight, we were all afraid to voice opinions in public on any subject, no matter how trifling. I never let an English word pass my lips in the street. Luna, Benjamin, and I no longer celebrated Sabbath supper together. Instead, Esther and Graça took turns lighting the candles and I spoke our prayers. We kept our shutters and curtains closed in the evenings.

I also obliged the girls to put away all the scarves, shawls, and dresses their mother had made for them and to wear only the most modest clothing, as the clergy preferred. As a further precaution, they carried rosaries and whispered an *Ave Maria* at every opportunity, even to acknowledge a sneeze.

After being warned by some secret Jews that my name had come up in gossip about *Marranos* being considered for arrest, I also began making weekly confession, and—with a mixture of spite and juvenile amusement—fashioned tales of adventure involving much intemperate whoring. One of the elderly priests to whom I unburdened my sins quizzed me about the details of my escapades with great eagerness, plainly astounded that I could service so many women. I assured him that it was unusual for me as well, but that I was feeling most inspired by our King's successes against the dastardly reformers and Jews threatening our moral foundations!

Two days after the nullification of our constitution, I witnessed a tumultuous gathering of hundreds in New Square, crosses and effigies of saints carried aloft like swords and shields. Both liberals and *Marranos* were denigrated as enemies of the Portuguese nation and Christ. These were slanders I had not heard since Lourenço Reis's death, almost nineteen years earlier. Owing to this climate of folly and persecution, Benjamin in particular lived in fear, as it was common knowledge that he gave Torah lessons to anyone desiring them. Indeed, on June the Eighth, he simply vanished, though neither soldiers nor bailiffs had come for him, as far as anyone knew. I tried to learn if he had been jailed, but my inquiries were mocked by both prison officials and clerks at City Hall. Along with other neighbors, I helped board up his shop and home.

On the night of his disappearance, I dreamed of becoming a flame, then fading to nothingness. All the next day I kept imagining that this nightmare had been a portent of things to come and that my daughters would soon be orphans.

Three evenings later, while I was rereading Violeta's letter for what must have been the dozenth time, there was a knock at the door.

"Who's there?" called Graça. She was sitting near me, studying a map of Europe.

As there was no answer, I jumped up and opened the door a crack. It was Benjamin, cloaked from head to foot in black.

XXVIII

THE GIRLS RUSHED FORWARD AND CLUNG TO Benjamin, kissing his cheeks. He feigned a groan at being attacked. His eyes were tired and his gray hair stuck out in a dozen directions. Several days' growth of white beard stubbled his chin.

"I'm sorry I was unable to get word to you," he said, removing his spectacle case from his waistcoat pocket.

"Where have you been?"

"A secret. The less you know the better." He scrutinized me over the rims of his spectacles. I must have been grinning, for he said, "What is it, lad?"

"Just that I shall always think of you that way—two eyes of glass and two of owl."

He laughed. Esther moved her chair next to his and held his hand. When Graça asked if he had been in prison, he replied, "Happily, no. I have been helping to ensure the victory of Cyrus. I must return shortly to my hiding place, however, and it is better that you do not know where I am or how I am to accomplish these things."

Cyrus was the ancient Persian ruler who, upon conquering Babylon, emancipated the Hebrew people, permitting them to return to Palestine and build their temple anew. Benjamin intended this as a reference to Dom Pedro, the King's elder son and a champion of democratic reforms. Benjamin believed if Pedro won the throne from his younger brother, Miguel, he would usher in a Golden Age for Portugal and the Jews. Tens of thousands of our brethren exiled by the Inquisition would find their way home from Constantinople, Amsterdam, and other cities in the diaspora.

For a time, Benjamin sat and talked of trifles with the girls, who prepared us *rabanadas*. When our stomachs were filled, they bid our guest good night, for I had matters to discuss with Benjamin that I preferred them not to hear.

Before sending them on their way, he asked them to sit very quietly, then pressed his fingertips to their closed eyes so they might see the inner colors always residing inside them and thereby gain courage from the secret universe to which they each had access. He had them do the same to him. "Now our inner landscapes are joined," he told them. "Neither you nor your father can ever escape me!" At that, he bared his teeth and growled, a trick he had learned from Midnight.

When they were safely ensconced upstairs, I told him that I had received a letter from an old friend.

"Who, dear boy?"

"Violeta, the lass whose uncle . . . whose uncle hurt her so badly."

"I remember well the prayers we said on her behalf. Where is she now?"

"In New York, of all places. She wrote that she'd been in London as well."

" 'Weep not for the dead nor brood over her loss. Weep rather for she who has gone away, for she shall never return, never again see the land of her birth.' "

I hazarded a guess: "Isaiah?"

"Jeremiah," he replied, shaking his head.

"In any event, there's no need for Jeremiah or anyone else to pity Violeta. She wrote that she has been fortunate, and she has invited me to execute a tile panel in her home. I think she has come into money."

"Will you go?"

I shrugged. "It's awfully far." I stood up to take my pipe and tobacco pouch from the mantelpiece. "And it's undoubtedly a bad idea to revisit my past."

"Virginia cannot be so very far from New York, can it?" he asked.

Inside a cloud of smoke, I laughed and said, "I fear I dismissed Professor Raimundo long before reaching American geography."

As though revisiting a faraway memory, he looked away and added, "My goodness . . . Midnight . . . after all these many years." He sighed and shook his head. "That would truly be something, finding him, wouldn't it, dear boy?"

Thinking Benjamin too tired to know what he was saying, I replied, "Dearest Midnight has been dead for seventeen years. The only place we shall find him now is in our dreams."

"Dead? Perhaps not, John. But . . . what have I said?" The apothecary jumped to his feet. "Dear boy, forgive this old man his wandering thoughts. It's my mind. . . . You will see when you are my age. You cannot trust your own thoughts. It's like living with an impostor."

His dramatic denial convinced me that he was concealing something. "It would seem your thoughts have not wandered anywhere but toward some hidden knowledge you may have. Tell me what you meant," I said hotly.

"No, no, I meant nothing." Relying on Ecclesiastes to save him, he said, "*A fool's tongue is his undoing.* Forgive me."

"Benjamin, this is not a time for quotations from the Torah. You obviously cannot stay long. Now, what's this about Virginia and Midnight? Tell me now!"

"John . . ." He sank down in his chair and held his head in his hands. "I have some letters at my house that I should like to place in your care, dear boy. Forgive me for keeping them from you, but it was your father's dying wish."

I sprang to my feet. "You were with my father when he died?!"

He looked up sadly. "We were all with James when he died."

"I don't understand. Please, Benjamin, speak plainly."

"We shall get the letters and then all will be clear. Come," he said solemnly.

"But we boarded up your house."

"Bring a hammer. And take a candle with you as well. This cannot wait."

As I knew the girls would still be awake, I rushed up the stairs and told them that Benjamin and I were going on a brief errand.

At his house, we ripped away the planks over one of his windows.

Once inside, we retrieved from a locked iron strongbox in his cellar eight letters, all addressed to James Stewart. They were tied with a white ribbon grown yellow with age.

"In giving you these, I am emptying my pockets of blood-splattered stones," he said. "They have weighed me down for years. Dear boy, the burden of spoken secrets is great, and of written ones even greater."

Holding letters that my beloved father had read, I felt his presence as a pang so sharp and deep that I feared losing myself if I ever stopped feeling it.

I told Benjamin that I had always felt as though my father's death, more than any other, had been an error of destiny. I confessed how much better a man I might have been had he been by my side all these years.

"James is gone," Benjamin replied, "but the best of him still resides in you. I only hope you will not hate me when you read these."

He linked his arm through mine as we walked back to my home. I read the letters in the sitting room, hoping that they might finally solve the riddle of the collapse of my parents' marriage.

THE FIRST LETTER was dated October the Sixth, 1806, one month prior to that fateful trip to London by Midnight and Father. It had been posted to Papa from Bristol, England, by a Captain A. J. Morgan:

Sir, thank you for your letter of the Fourth of September. I believe I do know of a place of work that will meet most, if not all, of the sensible conditions you summarized. There is, in short, a good and prosperous gentleman by the name of Miller living near the port of Alexandria, whom I have had the pleasure to meet on several occasions and who will, I believe, be only too happy to take on a careful and obedient assistant. If you might tell me in your next letter when we may expect delivery of your property here in Bristol or, if you should prefer, at our offices in London, then I should be most pleased to carry out our plan as previously agreed upon.

The next letter, from the same Captain Morgan, was dated January the Twenty-Seventh, 1807, two months after Midnight's death:

Per your instructions, I have successfully placed the property into the hands of Mr. Miller, who was most pleased to receive him. Though he is not speaking at present, the property will, I am sure, relent soon in this willful wickedness and prove most helpful. Mr. Miller is not too inconvenienced by his behavior, I should add, so do not worry yourself unduly. It is not uncommon for such transactions to render the primitive mind disoriented and unruly at first. Under the whip, however, all prove useful and manageable, you can be sure.

"Benjamin, what is this property that Captain Morgan speaks of?" I asked, afraid to hear what I knew now to be the truth.

"Please, John, just read on. Then we'll talk."

"But you *do* know what all this is about? You know?!" I shouted.

"Alas, I do," he replied.

APPARENTLY, FATHER HAD thought better of having sold his *property* to Mr. Miller, and on May the Eleventh of 1807, the Captain wrote:

I shall certainly endeavor to propose such a transaction to Mr. Miller upon my return to Alexandria, but I cannot guarantee that he will accept. Surely you were aware, sir, that once sold, you had no claim over the property in question?

Then, from July the Fourteenth:

The property is no longer with Mr. Miller, I am sorry to report. The apothecary was taken quite suddenly to God in late May, having been ill for a week with the yellow fever. His sons, having no use for your man, sold him to a local trader. I have made inquiries as to his present whereabouts, but I have been unsuccessful. I fear that we may have lost the trail for good. He may even have been sold further south. The United States is a very large nation and there are thousands of Negroes in every nook, I can assure you. Telling one from the other, even one as diminutive and yellow-hued as yours, will not prove easy, as most Americans are unused to the fine distinctions in primitives to which you so properly refer.

"Benjamin, my father ... my father ..." I was dizzy with panic, my thoughts spiraling toward a crime so monstrous that I could not believe it possible. "What in God's name did Papa do?" I cried.

"I promise to tell you all I know, dear boy. But you must finish what you've started and read all of them."

"My parents lied to me for years, didn't they? And Midnight—oh, God, Midnight, what has happened to him? Where is he? You must tell me exactly where he is. I need to know now, Benjamin. Where is he?!"

"I cannot say. But the last letters speak of where he may have gone. You'll see."

My hands were freezing. I felt as though all of me had been turned to ice. I took the next letter from the pile:

It is believed that he must be in one of the Carolinas, perhaps in the city of Charleston, as several score Negroes were marched there to be sold shortly after Mr. Miller's untimely demise, and your former property may have been among them.

Your offer of a reward is most generous, and should I discover more information as to his whereabouts, you may rest assured that I shall not hesitate to let you know.

"Sold? But how can that be? These letters," I said, holding them up, "these damned letters must be forgeries! That's the only possible explanation."

He shook his head. "There is slavery in America even now. People of Midnight's shade live in bondage inside Pharaoh's empire of rice and cotton. They have been left behind by Moses."

"But Midnight was no slave. He lived with us as a free man. Papa would never do . . . never do anything so . . . so—"

Drawing in a deep breath, Benjamin said, "I could never bring myself to find Alexandria on a map, but I think it is a port town near Washington. That was where he was taken."

"No, I cannot believe it. There must be some terrible mistake. Look, even I know that the slave trade in England has been outlawed for many years."

"For two decades only. In 1806, when your father completed this transaction, the slave trade was still guaranteeing riches. Any African living in Britain without papers attesting to his free status might find himself kidnapped, shackled, and dispatched to the markets of America."

"No, you are lying to me! Father could not have done this! Why are you hiding the truth from me? Was there an accident? Benjamin, did something terrible befall Midnight and Father in England?"

"John, please keep your voice down. The letters in your hands tell you all you need to know. They are . . . they are . . ." In his desperation, Benjamin closed his eyes and began reciting a prayer in Hebrew. After a time, he said, "I know I ought to have given them to you years ago, but I was so very frightened. You and Francisca and the girls were so happy. I said to myself, 'Why must I ruin their lives? Midnight is gone and I shall try to find him by myself.' I continued writing over the years to many men in England and America, but I had no better luck than James. It has been suggested to me that Midnight may even be dead. The African slaves . . . Dear boy, their lives are brief in America."

My head was throbbing, and a stern voice was telling me that my nine years of happiness with my wife and children had been beyond contemptible; all the while, Midnight had been caged.

"But what could have made my father do such a thing?" I demanded. "I don't think anything could make him do something so evil."

"John, this is difficult for me. It is not my place—"

"I shall not hold it against you. *Tell me.*"

"Your mother . . . your mother and Midnight—"

"Out with it, man!"

"John, forgive me, but it seems that May and Midnight . . . that they . . . that they had shared a bed together as man and wife."

Benjamin spoke some more, but I heard nothing. Time was ticking outside of me. I closed my eyes and could feel Father and Midnight by my side. Their presence bore down on my chest, suffocating me. Then I saw Francisca on her deathbed—pale and withered. I was singing to her: *In Scarlet town, where I was born* . . . Midnight had been in captivity all the while we had been raising our daughters—during every moment of happiness. I had betrayed him with my own good fortune.

Had my wife been taken by God to pay for my wickedness?

A wail rose from the depths of my being. I wanted it to shatter the roof and the Lookout Tower, to summon the dead from their graves—to shred my life into so many bloody strips that it could never be sewn together again.

XXIX

MY DAUGHTERS RUSHED DOWN THE STAIRS, summoned by my unholy cry. Benjamin calmed them, saying I'd had a spell of dizziness thinking of their late mother and had shouted in fright.

My usually dependable stomach heaved at that moment, obliging me to call for a basin—thrust at me by Graça just in time.

With his quick hands, Benjamin cleverly hid the letters under his cloak. I had a chance to reread them only after the girls were sent to bed again. When I'd finished, I took my father's watch from my waistcoat pocket. It was half past one in the morning. I had just passed through an invisible threshold. I was no longer the person I had been.

"Benjamin, I beg of you," I said quietly, "was the reason for Father's betrayal truly as you said?"

"John, your mother and Midnight—must I tell you again what your father told me?"

In vain I studied his face for a sign of treachery. I said, "But what you're saying is preposterous."

"Nevertheless, it is what James told me."

"I would have known. I would have been able to tell."

"John, you were only a lad. You could not see what they

hid from you." He shook his head. "No child understands the ways of the adult heart. These things were beyond you. And not just you. I had not guessed."

"For how long were they presumed to have been . . . to have been—"

"Your father and I did not discuss that."

"I cannot imagine Mother betraying Father in that way. And Midnight would never have been a traitor to him."

"Perhaps not—I do not know. I can only repeat what I was told. John, there is one other thing, for I must unburden myself of all my secrets before I go. And I pray again that you do not hate me. You will recall that your mother left your home for several days after your father's return from England. She was feeling sick. She went to stay with your grandmother."

"Indeed, I remember well."

He stood up and warmed his hands at our hearth for a time, plainly gathering his courage.

"It was then that she lost . . . she lost the child," he said to the flames.

"What child? Speak plainly."

"John, your father . . . he said your mother was with child by Midnight. A time came when she was having the sickness in the morning. She quit your home to be with your grandmother. It was then that she lost the child."

"What? How can this be? This is insanity, Benjamin!"

"I only know what I was told, dear boy."

"That she was with child—Midnight's child?"

"Yes."

"I cannot see how that is—did she lose it or was it killed?"

"I do not know."

I walked to the foot of the stairs. I looked up, thinking of my daughters safe in bed. What an inheritance I had given them! My thoughts carried me into the past—to just after Father's return from London. I stood outside the locked door to my parents' bedroom, where Mother had hidden herself away—to ensure that I would not notice her pregnancy.

I despised Benjamin at that moment, just as he had feared. "Mother was often given to agitation," I said crossly. "Her sickness was simply a loss of equilibrium brought on by—"

"John, say what you will. I am only repeating what James told me. He swore me to silence. I must tell you that. I am breaking my vow to tell you."

I wondered then if Grandmother Rosa had known about Mother. I doubted it, since she would certainly have used it as a weapon against us if she had.

Benjamin handed me a glass of wine.

"John, despite your anger at me, and despite any errors in judgment an old man may have made, do you think you might permit him to give you some advice?" When I agreed, he said, "If you ask your mother of these things, I'd tread lightly."

I shook a fist at him in a fresh burst of rage. "She will be the one who will have to tread lightly! I have been lied to all these years."

"Even so, she is apt to react badly to you knowing. She would not have wished that for anything. She will be terribly angry with me."

I threw my glass into the fire. "Damn her! You've done the right thing. Damn them all!"

"Calm yourself. The girls."

"My girls have been cheated out of their grandfather by his own selfish perfidy. Not only that, but they might have grown up with Midnight. Goddamn it, don't you see how Papa cheated us all—even himself!"

"John, I have been cheated as well, do not forget. Midnight and I . . ." Benjamin's voice faltered. "Well, let us just say that I lost a powerful partner for my true work. He . . . he was like a son to me."

Filled with remorse, I apologized for my disrespectful words. I saw now what had to be done. "Benjamin, I must go to London now to speak to my mother. Afterward, I'll take a ship to New York. Violeta will not mind putting me up there for a few days. And then I shall go to Alexandria and Charleston. If Midnight has been living in slavery these seventeen years . . ."

The world suddenly seemed to darken and I felt very weak. "I cannot understand any of this," I kept repeating. Yet I was beginning to see how each link of the past met its neighbor perfectly. I now had the explanation for the collapse of my family that I had so long sought. What a fool I had been to believe that the answer would bring me solace!

I wondered then if Mother had known of Father's betrayal of Midnight. If not, and if she had been in love with the African, then she probably believed that Father had murdered him.

"Benjamin, you are absolutely sure that my father knew that my mother and Midnight had . . . had been together?"

"Yes. It made him insane with anger and grief, and he fell into evil. Later, as these letters indicate, he was consumed by regret. John, your father could not live with what he had done. He was utterly lost, dear boy."

Benjamin looked wholly beaten. I poured some wine into his empty teacup. I swigged mine directly from the bottle, fully intending to get drunk.

"Your father loved no one so much as you," he said. "I think I ought to remind you of that."

I laughed bitterly. "That means nothing when compared to such a betrayal."

"You are wrong, John. You must remember that he was devoted to you."

"Not so devoted as to prevent his selling Midnight."

"That was his fatal error. But it did not prevent his wishing the best for you."

I laughed again and took another long swig. "When exactly was it that he confided in you?"

"Just before he was killed."

"He gave you the letters then?"

"Yes, just as he gave you his pipe and his watch. It is what men do before they end their own lives. They make gifts of what they possess."

"What are you saying?" I was suddenly trembling with rage again.

"John, your father... Lost men sometimes seek out the Angel of Death. He hoped, I think, that sacrificing himself would compensate for what he had done. And so he remained behind and fought in a hopeless battle. That, dear boy, is why he gave you his things."

This made unbearable sense. I recalled the moral of the fable "Mouse, Frog, and Eagle," the tale I had read in Senhor David's bookshop when I was seven: *He that pursueth evil pursueth it to his own death.*

After I'd taken several more healthy gulps of wine, Benjamin slapped my hand playfully and took the bottle from me, placing it on the mantelpiece. Seeing nothing but fond affection for me in him, I knew then that he had intended all along to tell me these things tonight, as he might need to stay far from Porto for a long time. He had feigned his accidental revelation on hearing that Violeta was now living in New York, then acted his befuddlement. He may even have regarded her being in America as a sign.

I didn't begrudge him his pretense. I was grateful that he told me in any way he could. "Thank you," I said.

"For what?"

"For everything. You have shown nothing but kindness to me these past years."

"I am the one to give thanks." He beckoned me to sit by him. It was then that he told me how Midnight had helped him rid the world of Lourenço Reis, the hateful preacher. My suspicions that Benjamin was responsible for the murder were finally confirmed, though he would give me no details. He didn't want me to ever be able to reveal the truth if I were taken prisoner by the Church or the Crown.

Thinking of both this secret and the ones related to my family, I said, "You wanted to tell me about my father and mother for many years, didn't you?"

"Yes, but I was stronger when I was younger and could carry these secrets alone. Now I am old, dear boy. I needed to rid myself of them to be able to move forward and help Cyrus. But listen, John, secrets are not like mortal men—they can remain dangerous twenty, fifty, even a hundred years after they are conceived. So be careful. And forgive me."

"I do, Benjamin. You can be sure of it. And I shall be careful. If nothing else, I have learned that these past years. You know, Father could have journeyed to the United States to find Midnight. He might have tried, at least."

"He was given to believe it was hopeless."

"And what do you believe?"

His shoulders sagged. "It's been so many years—nearly two decades."

"Midnight could not have been more than thirty or thirty-five when I knew him. He would be in his late forties or early fifties if alive." I tried in vain to picture him with gray hair. "Do you remember when he saved me from Hyena?"

"I know what you are thinking, dear boy—*Hesed.*" When I asked what that meant, he replied, "It's Hebrew, John. It is the idea that good deeds require compensation."

I spoke then of the dream I'd had in which I found myself reduced to a flame and then nothingness. I was now of the opinion that it was a reminder of how lost I'd become since Midnight's death.

Benjamin smiled. "On the contrary, John, unless I am greatly mistaken, you can at this very moment see your road ahead clearly. For the great mystery of your dream is this: You yourself will light the way. The heart of the Lord, which is your own, is where the very last flame resides, and it will illuminate your path."

His encouragement only served to irritate me, since I did not wish to talk in metaphors.

"The fall and rise of the sun, the phases of the moon—these are events that also occur inside ourselves," he continued.

I sighed impatiently.

"No, you must listen to this, John—it's important. The rise of the sun occurs inside each of us, or else we could not even dream of it. This, as I have told you many times, is the essential reciprocity of movement that marks the boundary between each person and the world. All that you do in your life affects all that is done here on earth and in all the other realms. This is one of the greatest mysteries of all. No, I cannot tell you whether you ought to go, but I will tell you this: If you succeed in freeing Midnight, then you will not only set an entire universe free, as the Torah tells us, but in so doing you will also be helping to repair all that has been broken since the very beginning of time."

"Benjamin, even if I find him, I might not be able to buy him back."

The apothecary laughed. "Tell me where in the Torah it says that Moses asked permission of Pharaoh before leading the Hebrews from slavery! Robbery, John, may be the holiest of acts in certain circumstances."

"If only Daniel were here to help me."

"Daniel? Have you not heard a single word I've said? Though he is long dead, he lives inside you, dear boy. You will summon him to the fore when he is needed. Of that I am certain."

"And my daughters—what shall I do with them in my absence?"

"Leave them with your mother and your aunt Fiona. They will flourish together. And they will love you all the more for trusting them."

I shook my head, for I considered myself unequal to the task. I was afraid that the girls would resent my absence. They were too young to be without at least one of their parents.

"John," he said, "it is only natural that you are unsure. You have just discovered these things now. You will go to England and speak with your mother. Only then will you decide. Do you remember what Midnight always said upon parting?"

"Go slow."

"Precisely. Scorpions may be hiding under every rock. There is no crime in waiting a few days to decide how you will proceed."

Quoting a proverb of Solomon, I said, "*A bird that falls from its nest is a man far from his home.* I know nothing of America."

"Ah," he laughed. "But that's where you have an advantage being a Jew. You shall bring bread with you on board your ship and make all the world into your *eruv*—your symbolic home."

"That's absurd, Benjamin."

"Indeed so. But a man who wishes to save a world makes recourse to absurd tricks."

"There may not be time to wait. What if Midnight is in danger?"

Benjamin's countenance turned grave. "Make no mistake, if Midnight is alive, then he is most definitely in danger. That is the nature of slavery. I shall tell you another thing: As long as one man or woman remains a slave, then the Messiah will not come. For we shall make our own paradise or not have it at all."

BENJAMIN MUST HAVE guessed that I would want to go to America after reading the letters, for he now took out of his cloak pocket the child's rattle that Midnight had used to fight Hyena. Father had apparently saved it and given it to him.

"You give this to Midnight, along with a blessing from me. Tell him that I have continued our work all these years—and that I searched for him. He has never left my thoughts for a single day."

A few minutes later, he threw on his cloak, hugged me, and started on his way. As I stood in my doorway, my heart was racing as though to impel me to beg him not to go. But I discounted my thoughts of death and eternal separation as a symptom of fear.

HOW DOES A good man do evil? Sometime after the tolling of two, I saw that I might ask the question not only with regard to Father but also in relation to Midnight and Mother—if they had been guilty of betrayal.

It seemed to me that the three of them had done me a great wrong. Their lies had pulled up my anchor and cast me out to sea; their secrecy had left me shipwrecked. They willingly sacrificed me so that they might continue their secret lives.

I resented them all, but it was at Father that I silently hurled all my curses. He was a blackguard and a poltroon. And I despised him.

*   *   *

I AWOKE TO the dawn, choking, seized by panic: I had never dug up all the keepsakes I'd buried before the first of the French invasions—including Midnight's feather. I had to make them mine again before leaving for London.

Dashing down the stairs, wearing only my blanket, I rushed out to the garden. Squatting among the prickly weeds, I started to dig frantically.

I dug three holes, each in error, then succeeded in finding the two shafts from so long ago. Soon, I had in my arms Daniel's amulet and masks; the jay we had carved; Midnight's quiver, arrows, and feather; and Gilberto's tile of a triton. All were caked with dirt but not much the worse for having been buried these many years. Clutching them to my naked chest, I danced a jig in my stocking feet. Then I dropped everything to the ground and fell to my knees.

LATER THAT MORNING, I felt curiously compelled to rebury Daniel's frog mask, our jay, Midnight's quiver, and all but one of his arrows, so as to leave something of myself and them in Porto during my trip. While doing so, I knew for certain that I would voyage to New York and hunt for Midnight—for as long as it took to find him. I was not frightened, for I had Mantis between my toes. And I had found what had been lost.

II

XXX

The Power of Silence

I'M NOT GOING TO SAY WHO DID IT JUST YET. Because if I were to so much as whisper it, then my friends at River Bend might pay for my carelessness. I've seen one good man die because of me, and I'm not about to put anyone else in harm's way. No, sir. It's not too late for Mistress Anne to tell her new man to tie a rope around any old neck that might strike her fancy and hang yet one more borrowed body from the nearest oak. I say *borrowed* because our ears and fingers and toes don't belong to us. I found that out for real sure when I was twelve, and I'm not likely to ever forget.

My papa once told me that the master even tries to own our dreams—*to get his chains round our wings*, as he put it. I'm damned sure he owned mine for a time, because I sure as hell never dreamed of flying or fluttering.

I remember the moment I knew my dreams had gotten clean away—a few years back, in December. What came to me in the soft dawn of my room was what I'd last been dreaming—a girl, me, strolling down an avenue bigger than any in Charleston, in a city of red brick, like a fortress built to last forever. I was singing, because there was no weeds or rice anywhere. The snow I'd only ever read about in books was covering lampposts and carriages and rooftops, and it was so white that tears stung my eyes. Then a tingling wetness began falling onto my face from above and made me go quiet. I looked up, and what did I see but a million flakes of that blessed snow filling all the sky, as unstoppable and as alive as butterflies carried by the powerful breath of God that Moses writes about in the Bible. I was shivering, but it was good, because I knew then there was a place protected by a cold so powerful that nothing from River Bend and South Carolina could ever survive there.

I thought about that girl and that city every day, and the possibility of them being real wore me down so much that I couldn't say no any longer. *"You might lose yourself if you say no to the night inside you too often"* was what my papa always told me. He knew about losing things, if anyone did.

THE WHITE FOLKS think the overseer committed the murders. Or, at least, that's what they said in their newspapers. Nobody knows what they truly think, least of all me. I'm not so clever as that. If I were, Weaver might still be alive.

So I'm not going to whisper a thing about *who* just yet. I hardly got any power to speak of, but I got my silence.

I'm not going to say why our masters were murdered either. You're going to have to discover that for yourself. And it'll make sense to you or it won't. Just like Mantis is either out there on the plantation or he ain't. No *perhaps* and no *maybes* about it.

So I can't help you with the *why* just yet. Even so, you're going to have to know a slip about Big Master Henry. Him first. Then the other masters who came along after him.

You're going to have to know about him alive if you're going to understand how important it was to have him dead and buried. Because it sure meant a good many things to us when we laid his casket in the ground on that glorious day of September sun. For one thing, it meant that Mantis might be out there in the wild grasses sprouting up along Christmas Creek. Inside us too, getting us ready. Waiting beyond our master's reach for a chance to lead us toward that everlasting fortress in our minds where snow is always falling.

SO THERE BIG Master Henry is, standing on the piazza with his hands on his hips like he done own the sky over all of Carolina. *Big,* because he's over six feet tall and wide too, like a wagon filled with horse manure. Some folks think he's handsome, but they haven't seen him with an empty bottle of whiskey clutched in his hand, his face all puffy and his eyes darting like spiders figuring out a way to get at you. *Ain't nobody look maw o'nery den dat man,* my mamma used to whisper. And if you ask me, she was right. Not that anybody's waiting in line to ask me much. Though I've got plenty to say, because I got fifteen years of keeping my mouth shut sitting behind me.

So now you know why there's a *Big* in Big Master Henry. We always call him *Master* because he may not own the sky, but he owns every weed, wattle, and Negro from Christmas Creek in the east, to the Cooper River in the north and west, on down to Marble Hill in the south.

Yes, Massa, I's do jus' what ya seh, Massa.... I talk like that sometimes in front of the white folks, since they don't much appreciate me speaking like I've got any education. But my papa won me the chance to read and write when I was barely done crawling. Not that I'm any different from the others. The scars on my back that are never going to come off, no matter how hard I scrub, remind me of that every day. That's why I sometimes reach around to feel them just before I go to sleep. Pain that makes you the same as people you love can be a good pain, I think.

Marble Hill used to be Marylebone Hill back when my mamma came over from Africa, but she and the others shortened the name because Marylebone didn't fit in their mouths too good. Papa still called it that though, because he liked the sound. He used to say the strangest and most beautiful things, though he hardly ever wrote anything down. He left writing things down for me.

Most folks call me Morri, but that's not my real name—it's Memoria. I tried to keep it secret, because at first I wasn't too happy with it. No, ma'am. But I don't mind telling everyone now. It means *memory* in Portuguese. My papa knew a bit of that language, owing to his having lived in Portugal for a few years.

Grandma Alice was called Blue because she was so Cabinda-black that folks said she shined blue in the moonlight. She used to call Big Master Henry by the name he had as a boy—Hennie. She'd been his wet nurse and was allowed a few liberties beyond the reach of the rest of us. "Ya must nevah feget yassef, chile," she used to tell me. "Ya feget yassef, Morri chile, ya like on die." Once, when we were stooped in the fields, I called Big Master Henry a fat old hyena for ruining the neat border of rice plants we'd just made. I spoke so loud that he nearly heard me.

Mamma lifted me up and shook me like a rag doll. She shrieked that I had to keep my lips as still as sleep because she was never ever going to see me tied to the whipping barrel. I had to sit her down right in the mud and comfort *her* because she was so upset at losing her temper. Later, that made us both laugh till the tears were falling down our cheeks and I had to beg her to stop making faces. My mamma laughed better than anyone, even my papa. She was much taller than him—tall as most any man. With high cheekbones and eyes so black they reflected things nobody could normally see—even the future, some folks thought. Looking at my parents together made me smile because they looked so different, but it was like they fit together.

Mamma carried herself high, and when she aimed those black eyes at you in anger she made your spirit just shrink away in shame. Or if she was feeling goodly toward you, she made you think you were better because she was watching.

Mamma died of the fevers seven years ago, in June of 1817. Papa was the next to go. He left me all alone three and a half years later. After that, I was the only one from my family still around. That's why I just had to write these things down. Otherwise, nobody'd know anything about us, and that would be like being swallowed up by the ground. Like we were never here.

IT WAS THE rough boots and the bunions. And the moonshine. That was why I thought Big Master Henry never had a kind word to say. He'd side-shuffle all 'round, always smirking—"Comin' up at ya sideways like a rattlesnake with its rattle hidden," Weaver used to say. Weaver used to be allowed to go hunting with Big Master Henry. He could spot a mole's nose poking pink out of the grass from half a mile away, Papa used to tell me. And know just what the mole was thinking too!

Weaver was a good friend of my parents. As I grew older he became a friend of mine too. I always liked older folks. I never had much luck with the ones my age. They used to say I was too yellow-skinned and skinny and that my eyes were peculiar. Likely some of them thought I used to act superior. Maybe I did think I was better than them because I could read and write. Till I got myself whipped. After that, we all knew that I was just the same as everybody else.

Weaver had two children and his wife, Martha, over in Comingtee

Plantation, which is just across the Cooper River to the north of River Bend. He'd get a pass to go there on Sundays. It was mighty hard on him not being with his family most of the week, but he didn't mind it all the time, if you want the truth. Because he liked teasing some of the young girls around here. He was a rogue, if you ask me, with them light-brown eyes always shining at the shapes of girls.

He's dead now, and mostly because of me. That sits heavy on me when I lie down at night and think of my life and what's gone right and what's gone wrong. Likely it always will. But I wouldn't want a man to die with a bullet in him and me not to think about how I helped put it there. It would be like claiming he was nothing and ain't never been anything but nothing.

BIG MASTER HENRY liked hurting each person differently, I think, in the way that would do the most damage. It was a Friday evening in July of 1820 when my turn came. The night was moist, the air clinging so tight at your face that you didn't really sleep, you just kind of fainted away. I was nearly twelve years old and was working in the Big House. I slept in a shed next to the kitchen, and one evening the Master sent his personal slave, Crow, to fetch me from bed, saying that he had some more silver for me to polish, which was one of my jobs.

Big Master Henry grabbed my arm as I stepped into his room. Maybe I hadn't polished something right, I thought. My heart began thumping something fierce. But then he kissed me on my forehead, like he was an old friend. "You're soft, Morri," he said. Then he offered me a glass of wine he'd already poured. "You've never had any, have you?" he asked. His eyes were kind and he didn't seem drunk.

When I shook my head, he lifted the glass to my lips. It tasted sweet and syrupy. He said my tongue was real pink. He wondered why nigger girls always had such pink tongues. Then he gave a laugh and said not to mind him, that he was just being curious in his own way, and he hoped he hadn't offended me.

He knelt on the ground, took my shoes off, and rubbed my feet.

"Morri, you just keep drinking and let me do the rest," he whispered.

When I had finished my glass, he stood up and took it from me. He licked the rim with his tongue, winking, then put it down on his night table. Seeing him unbuttoning his trousers, I knew the real reason I'd been asked to be a house slave, and it didn't have nothing to do with how well I did my polishing and ironing.

Maybe I only thought these things after he'd had his way with me. I can't recall so well what I thought at the time, because I was so afraid of how ashamed Papa was going to be when he found out.

"Please don't hurt me, Big Master Henry," I pleaded. I was worried he'd make bruises on me that everyone could see.

"It won't hurt unless you want it to," he said. "You've got your woman's blood by now. So you must have been expecting it sooner or later."

"I ain't ready," I said.

"You're plenty ready." He laughed. "I've been feeling how ready you are, and my hands don't lie." He took my hand and brought it up to just where he wanted it. "You see what I got for you?" he said, grinning because of how quick I pulled away. "It might frighten you now, but you're going to think it's real nice once it's all yours. Trust me, I know what you girls like."

Pretty soon he was on top of me, pushing and grunting, and I could smell the perfume on him, like he'd bathed in it. "Please, Big Master Henry, don't do this to me."

"In a few minutes you're gonna wonder why you fought me so hard. And you're going to know why God put you on this good green earth, nigger girl."

Him talking about God must have made me remember the leather-bound Old Testament I kept under my pillow. Papa said it had been printed all the way over in London, a hundred years before, so I figured it must be worth some money. I told the Master I'd give it to him.

He said, "Don't you know the only scripture I want is right up between your legs."

There comes a moment when you know that there's no use fighting, and I knew it then. So I shut my eyes and tried to make myself go dead. But it didn't work. It felt like he was pushing broken glass into me. No matter how much I begged, he just kept on going. I couldn't risk shouting for help. If I was going to die, then I was, and there was nothing to be done about it. I'd have chosen death any day of the week over having anyone find out.

I remember he whispered in my ear, "You're mine now, down to your little nigger soul."

No, I'm not, I thought. And I began whispering a line from Ezekiel as if it could protect me: *Nor shall wild beasts devour them . . .*

Strange, but that's mostly what I remember about that first time—whispering crazy things, anything I could remember, as if the sound of my voice could save me.

Afterward, he said, "You're just about the worst I ever had, Morri. You ain't got no crackle, no spark. You're dead inside, nigger girl."

He patted me on my behind and sent me back to my room, but I ran out of the house all the way to Porter's Woods. I wanted to slip out of my soiled skin so bad I couldn't stop trembling. I knew I had to put what had happened way behind me or I'd have to tell my papa. I had no control over time, but of distance I had a little, and it was the only thing I had to help me keep quiet. When I was far enough from the cabins and the Big House, I started hollering for Mamma, because I didn't want to give anyone alive the burden of my truth. I fell on my hands and knees like the ruined animal he'd made me into, and I pleaded with her for help. It was as if he'd cut out the best part of me and left only blood behind. I told her that. And I told her that the worst thing was that I didn't know who I was now.

I told her it frightened me too, not being myself, and him having my soul. She didn't answer. Though I know she would have if she could.

When I stopped crying, I cupped my hand in the river and brought the water to where he'd broken me. Then I stepped into the river itself and sat down in all my clothes. Maybe I was just trying to reassure myself I was still alive and could feel something like being cold. It'll sound right peculiar, but when I stepped onto the bank again I took some Spanish moss from a low branch of a cypress tree and held it there too. I held it there to me and whispered from Ezekiel that he'd not devour me, and tried to become the wind carrying away my voice and nothing else at all, so I wouldn't have to feel anything ever again.

A twelve-year-old girl isn't ready to have who she is taken from her. No one is.

So many times I wanted to tell my papa what the Master was doing, but I could never find the courage. That secret of mine was just about the worst part. It made me believe I was nothing.

The Master seemed to be cutting new things out of me each time he touched me. All I knew was that they were gone and that they must have made me who I was. I was moving further away from the person I'd been every day.

All that bloody moss I made down by the river... Maybe I wanted someone to find it, to leave some trace of what had been done to me out in the world in plain sight.

I read my Old Testament too, by the light of a single candle: *Deal kindly with us, O Lord, for we have suffered insult enough....*

I slept with that good book open to Psalm One Hundred and Twenty-Three right on top of where he was hurting me, spine up, like a shield, praying I wouldn't have his baby. I was thinking, too, that maybe if he cut enough of the deepest things out of me, I wouldn't be able to have a child and that would be a good thing. So sometimes when he was on me, I admit I was thinking, *Cut more, cut it all, leave nothing behind that can grow....*

AFTER THAT FIRST time, I saw my papa in the morning. I'd hardly slept, so I couldn't keep from crying in front of him. But I lied and said it was just me missing Mamma. He hugged me tight, and when I winced he said, "You're not ill, are you?"

I told him his touch reminded me of her even more, which was true, since love has always felt alike to me no matter who it comes from.

Once Crow heard me hollering in the woods. I told him I'd nearly been bit by a big old rattlesnake, and he nodded like he believed me. But he knew what was going on. He listened to everything that went on in the Big House. And he knew just as well as I did that we ought not to say anything to my papa, because he might try to kill Big Master Henry and end up getting lynched.

"The woods ain't safe, Morri girl," he said, taking my hand.

We walked most of the way home in silence, but near the Big House he held out his arms to me. "Let me hug ya, girl, 'fore we get so close that they can see," he said. "Don't be 'fraid a me. I ain't like him. I ain't gonna hurt ya evuh."

THE MASTER WAS getting pretty fed up with my lying still as death beneath him and might have stopped his wickedness all by himself, but one day he got one of his spells of weakness real bad and had to leave me alone. Then that ugly giant got so ill that he couldn't move. He just lay there and moaned.

Die, I thought, *because no one's going to regret it, not even your wife.*

After a few days of suffering like that, he got himself the kind of burning fever that brings demons. He was so misty-minded that he started asking questions that made no sense at all. *Who's inside the lantern? Where's the river riding to today?*

This is September of 1820 that we're talking about.

He'd always recovered before from his spells, so we weren't too concerned. Not that it was Dr. Lydell who ever once pulled him back from death. No, sir. It had always been my papa and his curing work. He knew just about everything about herbs and potions. He was famous for that—even among the Indians, because he once cured a deathly ill medicine man who came with a group of Creek braves to River Bend when I was only five or six. He began teaching me most of what he knew about that same time. Though I wasn't born to it, like him.

Papa told me years before that he'd studied curing in Portugal. He'd lived with a family there and worked with a Jewish magician who had his own apothecary shop. He learned all about which European plants could be used to cure most anything. He'd even been to England to see a man named Jenner who'd discovered a way of preventing smallpox.

Mistress Holly was counting on Papa to save her husband once again. Even though this time he was worse off than ever. I remember her saying in that breathy voice of hers, "Ahm a-cantin' on ya, Samuel, no wun aylse."

That was my father's name—Samuel. In Africa, they called him Tsamma, which is the name of a melon that grows there. His master in Virginia was the one who changed it.

With the Master out of the way in his sickroom, the air of the plantation had lost its bite. We almost believed we weren't being watched, but we were, since the overseer and the black foremen were always waiting for one little sign of tiredness to call us just plain nigger-lazy, then drag us off to the whipping barrel. Even so, I'd begun thinking nothing would bother me again if the Master would just let me be from now on.

On the night of the Twentieth of September, when the tea-room clock rang its nine o'clock bells, I knocked on Big Master Henry's door, just like I was supposed to, to bring him his glass of hot lemonade. Lily the cook had made it for him every day for the past decade, just as my papa had told her to. It was made with lemons grown right on the plantation down by Christmas Creek, with honey that my father collected from his hives in Porter's Woods and Wilson's Meadow. He had special permission to wander the plantation to collect his honey.

One time the Master told me that the Israelites lived on honey and lemon in the desert, so that was why he drank it. Big Master Henry supposedly knew these things because his papa had been a minister in Charleston. But I'd read the Old Testament from front to back by the time I was ten and never saw any such claim. It was then that I knew for sure that he made up the Bible as he went. Nearly all the white people do, even when they get their quotes right.

"You can remember the words and still not know anything about the meaning hidden underneath," Papa used to tell me.

So after I'd knocked on his door and been ordered in, I put his glass down on his table—not looking at him because I didn't want him to notice me ever again. I could hear him wheezing though. Then I slipped out of his room. An hour later, when his wife came to wish him sweet dreams, she found his door locked. She called to him, but there was no answer. He had one of the two keys to the room in his possession. The only other one was in her night-table drawer.

Frantic, she rushed off to get the key. She was powerful afraid to use it though. She didn't want to find him dead, with his ghost lingering over the body. Mistress Holly was mighty afraid of the dark—because her mother had seen a ghost once rise from her crib and float right out the window—so she shouted to my papa to come up from the larder and open the door. By that time, Mr. Johnson the overseer had been told by Lily the cook that something was wrong in the Big House.

Papa took a long time getting to Mistress Holly, because he couldn't walk so well. Not since after both his heel-strings were cut by Big Master Henry in the year before I was born. But she wasn't about to trust anyone else.

Just as he opened the Master's bedroom door, Mr. Johnson barged into the Big House and came bounding up the stairs. "Get your skinny nigger hands away from there, Samuel!" he shouted, and grabbed the key from Papa's hand.

My papa said thank you to him, because he was always thanking folks at the strangest times.

The house slaves, me included, were all standing at the bottom of the stairs listening to the hellish caterwauling of Mistress Holly. Lily and her grandson Backbend, who used to help serve supper, were praying that nothing had happened. But don't be fooled—if they prayed for the Master's heart to still be beating, it was only because they were worried they were going to be sold to someone even more mud-minded if he died.

As for me, I was hoping real hard that he was as dead as a headless catfish, and I was squeezing my eyelids so tight I might have drawn blood.

Whether my wishes had anything to do with it or not, Big Master Henry was gone as gone can be. Since his drinking glass was empty and had fallen on the floor from out of his big cold hand, I might have been suspected of poisoning him and would likely have been hanged that very night, but there was also a wood-handled knife buried in the side of his neck. That blade saved me from swinging from a tree, I'm happy to say. And Lily too, since she mixed the lemonade. Not that we poisoned him. Lily believed in God's retribution and wouldn't have risked His vengeance. As for me, I confess I wanted to. I'd thought of it every time he stuck his broken glass up inside me.

HOW THE KILLER had stabbed Big Master Henry and escaped through a locked door was the mystery everybody wanted to get to the bottom of. It was a twenty-four-foot drop to the ground from Big Master Henry's window, so nobody could climb up or jump down without using a ladder.

As for the two keys to the room, one was found by Mr. Johnson in a pocket of Big Master Henry's dress coat, which was folded on a chair in his bedroom. The other had been in Mistress Holly's night-table drawer. She'd been playing solitaire on her bed for two hours previous to finding her husband's body. If the killer had taken the key earlier, then how did he—or she—return it to the night table where Mistress Holly had found it?

The ladder was found safely locked away in the First Barn. There was no blood on it. And none of the field slaves had seen anyone climbing up the side of the house. So Mr. Johnson had the foremen tie Crow over the whipping barrel. Then he raised his cat and let it fall, because "that damn careless nigger" had been the Master's personal slave and ought to have protected him.

Crow wept like a baby under his ten lashes, since the skin that had been flayed from his back years earlier had grown over the bones with thick scars that were sensitive as burns. Mr. Johnson kept spitting out tobacco juice onto the black man's legs to humiliate him.

The next day Crow told me, "Ya know, Morri, I was so ashamed to let go like that, but it was like I was bein' cut open with a rusty saw."

I hugged him and said we were all proud of him. I promised myself I'd see them all pay one day. I just didn't know how yet.

We all kept our mouths shut during the whipping except to count the strokes and pray for Crow. The overseer then picked out Lily's grandson Backbend from our line. He was only eleven and his mamma was dead. He had big dark eyes and the softest lips of anyone at River Bend.

"I'm gonna whip this boy ten good strokes too," Mr. Johnson said, "unless you niggers tell me what happened last night. And I'm gonna keep pickin' out your children till one of you speaks the truth."

Lily shrieked and fell to her knees and begged him to be kind to her boy.

Most likely any one of us would have stopped his suffering by calling out the name of the culprit if we had truly seen him.

"Shame, shame, shame!" I yelled. "You is payin' yer toll to hell right here, right now, Mr. Johnson."

"You next, Morri!" he hollered back. "I ain't gonna suffer your big mouth. And you're getting twenty strokes!"

I was too angry to be scared. And too lightheaded with the truth of the Master being dead. I figured that the worst had happened to me already.

My papa then said he would not let anyone hurt me, but Mr. Johnson said, "Shut up, nigger, or I'll give her thirty!"

"Thank you, Mr. Johnson, sir," Papa replied real nice. "But if you whip my daughter, I can promise you some very, very serious consequences that you are not going to find agreeable," he added, smiling.

"You can, can you?"

"Indeed, I can. Mistress Holly will need me should either of her children take ill. And I shall need Morri with me. And healthy. Just as I need Backbend in one piece as well."

"Shut that big mouth of yours, nigger!"

Mr. Johnson turned to Backbend and raised the lash above his head.

After the third stripe across the boy's back, when his tears were rolling down his cheeks and he'd already filthied himself, Papa limped forward and said, "I did it. I killed Big Master Henry."

"Done it how?" Mr. Johnson demanded.

"I took the ladder and I climbed up quietly-quietly. Big Master Henry was asleep and I stabbed him."

"You, with that gimp of yours? Climbin' up the ladder would be near impossible."

"Yet that is just what I did, sir."

"Why would you?" said Mr. Johnson, squinting.

"He cut my heel-strings, sir."

"That was more than ten years ago."

"Still, that is the reason."

"So how d'you kill him without getting blood on you?"

"I wore gloves."

Mr. Johnson spit. "Where are the gloves now?"

"Christmas Creek."

"And how did you get the damned ladder out of the barn?"

Papa couldn't answer that, since everyone knew only Mr. Johnson had the key.

"Not another word from you, Samuel!" he warned.

He was about to start whipping Backbend again, and then it would be my turn, but Weaver stepped forward and said that he had done it.

"And how did *you* get the ladder out of the barn?" Johnson asked. He spit twice real quick, which meant he was at the end of his patience.

"Wid da key, Mistuh Johnson."

"My key?"

"Yessuh."

"But I had my key with me all evenin'. I'm sure of it."

"I duhn used mah root bayag," Weaver confessed.

"What bag was that, nigger?"

"De condrin' bayag."

"What in God's name are you talkin' 'bout now?"

"His conjuring bag," Papa repeated, because Mr. Johnson sometimes pretended that he was plain unable to understand Weaver and some of the other slaves.

"Weaver," the overseer spat, "get your ragged black hide back in line now!"

Papa stepped forward again and said, "Nobody knows who killed Big Master Henry, Mr. Johnson. So take me instead of my Morri or I promise I'll put an arrow in your heart."

His words made me shake. Papa was just over five feet tall, with tight peppercorns of gray hair growing a bit thin on top, but he was more than Mr. Johnson's equal, and we all knew it. Now that my papa had threatened him, the overseer was finally getting the idea that he was losing this wrestling match with us. Because if my father was willing to risk being lynched for speaking the way he did, then he could be pretty damned sure that we weren't lying and that no one knew the identity of the killer.

"You niggers get back to work. I've had enough of your lies for one day," he shouted.

After that, he cut Backbend free, and the boy ran off.

THE CRIME WAS never solved, though I was pretty sure I knew who'd done it—Little Master Henry. He'd been out at a party, but he could have walked the last few hundred yards of his way home and snuck back into the house without being seen. Or maybe he *had* been seen. And heard too. Likely no slave would have admitted to that, even if Backbend had been flayed down to his skeleton. Accusing the heir to the throne of River Bend would have been a death sentence.

Little Master Henry had everything to gain from his papa's death. With the blade of one small knife, he inherited half the plantation. The other half went to Mistress Holly, of course.

In any event, we were about to have ourselves a new Master.

TWO WEEKS AFTER Big Master Henry's death, on a bright Sunday afternoon, Papa asked me to sit on a stool with him inside a circle of fuchsia bushes he'd planted. Dozens of pink, purple, and red bell-shaped flowers were dangling all around us. Papa always said that fuchsias liked people knowing how pretty they were and grew offended if you looked away too quickly. I knew what he wanted me to tell him, but my heart was thundering. He said, "I'll not make you say a thing. You can tell me when you're ready." I leaned my head upon his shoulder. "Sleep," he said. "Sleep against me, Morri. I shall not let you fall."

XXXI

AFTER LEARNING OF MY FATHER'S BETRAYAL from Benjamin, I immediately posted a letter to Mother and Aunt Fiona asking that they be ready to receive us in their home in about two weeks.

Grandmother Rosa clearly wished for me to invite her too, if only so that she might be allowed the dignity of a refusal, but Mama would have had my head on a platter if she joined us.

Grandmother's last words to me were "John, you were always a clever child, but never kind. Much like your mother in that regard."

"I am genuinely sorry, Grandmother. I'd have preferred being a better grandson. I assure you that if I could stay in Portugal, I would. Cruelty is not my intention."

"It is never our intention, John."

LUNA OLIVE TREE had no living relatives, so I went to her home on St. John's Eve to ask her if she might consider joining us in England once we were settled in; Portugal's precarious political situation was making me think we'd all be better off there, at least for the foreseeable future.

"Oh, John, it's too late for an old goat like me to go anywhere," she sighed.

I argued with her, but she kept telling me that it was impossible. I thanked her for all that she and her sister had ever done for me, which was a great-great deal. "You saved my life by finding Senhor Gilberto to train me," I told her.

To make me cry, she said, "We never had children, but we had you, John, and both Graça and I were eternally grateful."

ABOARD OUR SHIP, a sense of death lodged itself in my gut. The mad thought that Papa might still be alive somewhere, hiding from us out of shame, kept me bound to silence. I knew it could not be true, but I could not fully accept his death, even after all these years. When my daughters came to my side, we held hands and watched our home disappear.

WE ARRIVED IN London on the afternoon of July the Third. We found Mother and Aunt Fiona in hearty spirits, so thrilled by our arrival that they hopped around like schoolgirls and asked endless questions without waiting for replies.

Our initial conversation set the slightly hysterical and comic tone for our first days with them, which pleased me greatly as it served to camouflage my worry.

Fiona's blue eyes were radiant. "I *canna* believe it!" she kept exclaiming. "They are *bonnie burdies* indeed. Why, their *doony* feathers are all gone!"

"What's *doony*?" Esther asked.

"Downy," replied Mother.

"And *burdies*?"

"Lassies."

"Let me get a good look at you all!" Fiona said, moving back to take us in as we sat on the sofa.

"You're frightening the children, staring like that," Mama joked.

Fiona patted her bun of gray hair. Her eyes filled with tears as she whispered *bonnie burdies* to herself. Then she said what Mother and I had been hoping she would not: "If only James were here to see you all."

*   *   *

MOTHER LOOKED WONDERFUL and had allowed her hair to shine with its natural silver. That first day she wore amethyst earrings and a pearl necklace I remembered from my childhood. She attributed her overall confidence to London, where she felt perfectly at home and could live openly as a Jewish woman.

Fiona agreed that the city's astonishing diversity had certainly helped my mother, but she ascribed more importance to her piano lessons. Highly regarded as a teacher, her fame had spread, and she currently had students from as far away as Camden Town. One of her former pupils, a twenty-two-year-old Londoner by the name of Ian Pitt, had accompanied the well-known tenor Renato Vecchia on his recent tour of France and Italy.

As for me, I attributed much of her change to Aunt Fiona herself, who was very little put out by what others—particularly men—thought of her. She dressed the way she wanted, spoke her mind, and anyone who didn't like it be damned!

One last reason for Mother's sense of peace may have been that, in moving to England, she had placed herself a thousand miles from her own mother's criticisms. She and I did speak of Grandmother Rosa upon my arrival, of course. When I suggested that she might consider inviting her for an extended stay, she retorted, "John, my mother only wanted your sympathy. She and my brothers have always been at war with me, so now let them delight in each other's company."

Mama finally told me what had caused the rift between them and how her deep affection for Violeta—and even Daniel—was connected to her own past.

When she was just fourteen, her piano teacher had touched her in inappropriate ways. "I was left scared and confused," she said. "I'd looked up to him like a god—he played so beautifully. And I'd always trusted him. To have him betray me like that . . . in that terrible way, it took away my faith in so many things."

"What did you do?"

"I thought it best to keep quiet, but during our next lesson, he did it again. So after he was gone, I told my mother, but she only accused me of being too flirtatious with adults. She said that if he had touched me inappropriately—which she wasn't willing to believe just because I said so—then it must have been because I'd been leading him on. To punish me, she forbade me from taking further piano lessons with anyone else ever again. John, you know how I adore playing the piano. I was broken-hearted—completely lost.

"As if that wasn't enough," Mama continued, placing a hand to her chest to steady her breathing, "my former teacher spread vicious gossip about me, claiming that I was a wicked *Marrana* girl and that I'd tried to seduce him."

She shuddered when she said that adults from her neighborhood had referred to her for years as "that lying Jewish whore."

"So you never took another lesson?"

Mama grinned slyly. "You know me better than that, John. I found a teacher on my own and for more than two years studied with him in secret. His name was João Vicente, God bless his memory. He didn't ask for any payment at all. He told me that when I was a rich and famous concert pianist I would pay him back. But then one of my *dear* elder brothers followed me in secret across the city and told my mother what I'd been up to. You know what your Grandmother Rosa did? She beat me on the palms with a paddle, shouting with each strike that I'd never play music or humiliate the family again. It took weeks before I could even sew a few stitches. I felt like an outcast for years after that. The worst part was that I was prevented from doing what I most loved. I only started to feel like myself again when I left home and could play anytime I wanted."

It was Father who saved her life in a sense, since he'd cared not a fig for the rumors about her character and believed only in the love they'd found together. "His first present to me after our marriage was a pianoforte he ordered from London—the one I still have." Mama's eyes radiated love for him.

"Then, when I gave birth to you, John," she said, tapping my nose playfully, "I knew that I had overcome all the evil done to me. You were my proof that all would be well in my new life."

To me, of course, this fierce and intuitive solidarity between my parents made the destruction of their marriage even more terrible.

We then discussed my life since Francisca's death, and she listened intently. I had been unaware of how strongly—and for how long—I yearned for this simple act of listening. She in turn spoke to me of her desire to open a music school, where, with Fiona's help, she might begin to accept scholarship students.

She burst into tears upon hearing that I'd received a letter from

Violeta, for whom she had prayed every night for many years. I refrained from telling her about my plans to see her in New York. I could not yet bring myself to speak of the troubling matters that concerned Mother directly.

OVER THE NEXT days, Esther and Graça enjoyed visits to St. Paul's and Kensington Gardens and were much taken with the perfumeries in Shire Lane and a Fantoccini performance on Oxford Street. Secretly, I posted a letter to Violeta saying that I would be arriving in New York as quickly as a ship might carry me. I added that I'd very much like to make a tile panel for her home, but that it might have to wait for a month or two while I attended to other business that I would explain to her upon my arrival.

I begged the others for a day alone to rest after the sea journey. From the sideways looks that Mother and Fiona gave me, I was sure they believed I had an afternoon of debauchery in mind. Not so. On Oxford Street I hired a hackney to a shipping agent's countinghouse in King William Street, where I booked a room aboard the *Saxony,* which only a few months later would sink famously in a storm. I would be departing from Portsmouth precisely eight days hence.

I was feeling very relieved to have the ticket in my hand, until I asked the booking agent how long we would be at sea. "Last year," he replied jovially, "at the very same time, her sails caught every gust of wind and she made the crossing in twenty-four days."

I ought to have kept my mouth shut, but I could not help asking, "And if she fails to catch just a few of the breezes?"

"In that case"—he grinned—"I'd say you were looking at a journey of three months at least."

XXXII

THAT EVENING, THE GIRLS WENT OUT WITH my aunt to the Covent Garden Theatre to attend a production of *Macbeth,* with Charles Kemble in the principal role. Though I had long hoped for a chance to attend one of his performances, this was the last play in the world that I wished to see. Mother, too, wanted no part of it, and so we remained at home together.

Knowing I could not delay discussing my travel plans any longer, I carried the letters addressed to Father from Captain Morgan into the sitting room, where Mother was embroidering.

"What do you have there, John?" she asked.

"Letters, Mama."

"From whom?"

Taking a deep breath, I replied, "I shall tell you presently."

"Aren't we secretive tonight," she said, smiling. Then she saw my distress and added, "But whatever is the matter, son?"

"Mother, you'll excuse me if I ask a difficult question, but what precisely do you know of Midnight's death?"

"I know just what you know."

"You're sure of that?"

She switched to Portuguese. "I'll thank you not to adopt that super-cilious tone with me." She put down her needlework and set it on the side table. "John, I am in no mood for whatever nonsense you are planning at my expense."

"Was Midnight truly killed poaching?"

She crossed her arms over her chest defensively. "That's what I was told."

"Did you not think it strange that there was no grave for him in Swanage?"

"Indeed. But the minister there explained— John, I told you all this in a letter years ago. Are you losing your memory or is it—"

"Did you never suspect Father?" I interrupted.

"Suspect him of what?"

"Of having killed Midnight?"

She sighed, rubbed her temples, and stood up. "John, I fear that sleep is upon me. You'll have to excuse me, but I—"

"Sit!" I shouted, surprised at the vehemence in my voice. "We're not finished."

"You are not to talk to me like that, young man."

"I'm thirty-two years old. I shall talk to you as I like."

"I see that not even Francisca's untimely death has improved your manners."

I regarded that as a very cruel thing to say. Yet I was also decidedly glad that she'd made a tactical error, if the truth be told, for wounding me in this way served to make us equals; she could no longer oblige me to proceed with delicate caution.

"John, forgive me," she said, shaking her head disapprovingly at her own behavior. "That was terrible of me. Please forgive me."

"I do, Mama."

She sat back down. "Yes, I suspected your father of having caused Midnight's death. Whether through his negligence or willful encourage-ment of his hunting on private lands, I knew not. James could be irre-sponsible at times."

"Encouragement?"

"*Permission* may be a better word. I still regard your father's behavior as criminal in allowing Midnight to venture off into the countryside in a land so unfamiliar to him. But it has been so long. Can we not let both of them rest in peace?"

Convinced that she knew nothing of Father's having sold Midnight to a slave-trader, I said, "Mama, what if I were to tell you that Midnight might still be alive?"

She snorted dismissively, so I added, "I'm deadly serious."

She leaned toward me. "Are you telling me you saw his ghost? What did you see?"

Picking up the letters and handing them to her, I replied, "I saw these. Please look at them. They're addressed to Father."

She opened the first one as though it were a curiosity. "I don't know a Captain Morgan. And I must say, reading letters addressed to your father makes me feel a bit like a thief. I think it better—"

"Read them, Mama, please. . . . Do it for me."

As she read, she complained about the illegibility of the handwriting, hoping, no doubt, that she would be able to dismiss the contents of the letters that easily as well.

After Mother had read the first of the letters, she said, "John, I'm not sure if this means . . . if this means what I think it does."

"Read them all, Mama. Then we'll talk. And after tonight, I shall not speak of them again, if that's what you prefer."

She nodded her agreement. To avoid the temptation to watch her while she read, I went to the window and pulled up a chair. I was picturing Mama preparing tea for Violeta and Daniel. How kind she had been to the three of us.

When I returned to her, her bottom lip was trembling and her cheeks were flushed. She removed her spectacles and said, "John, the English is beyond me. Tell me what this means."

"I think you know."

"I may. But your English is much better than mine. It is still a foreign language to me. I want to be sure I understand everything."

"It means that Father sold Midnight to a man in the American state of Virginia, through a ship's captain by the name of Morgan. After that, Midnight was sold again and was probably taken to South Carolina. That is a state still profiting by slavery. He could not be located—not, at least, in 1807. And not by Benjamin in years since. In short, it means that Midnight may still be alive—shackled as a slave in South Carolina. Or somewhere else in the United States."

"John, you cannot expect me to believe such a tale—to believe your father would do such a thing!"

"Nevertheless, he did."

"But why? Why would he—" As she spoke, her voice caught on the truth of her own role in this tragedy. "I simply ... simply cannot believe it," she stammered. "I refuse to believe any of it, John. It's completely impossible!" She held the letters out to me. "Take them, I do not want to read these lies—these damnable lies!" She threw them to the ground.

"Mother, for how long did you and Midnight ..." I could not complete my question.

She picked up her embroidery, but her hands were quivering and she could make no progress. "Damn my eyesight!" she snapped.

"How long did you and Midnight—"

"John," she interrupted, "I don't suppose you might bring me another candle." She looked up with a determined squint, defying me to continue my questioning. "This eyesight of mine ... Old age—it's positively unforgiving."

"I'll get you a candle, Mother, but there are old secrets I must now be told."

She returned to her needlework. "When you are an old man, John, I hope your daughters do not subject you to an interrogation like this."

"When I am old, I dearly hope they'll not have to."

I let the silence fester, hoping its weight would unsettle her and prompt her to speak, but she would not utter a word. "You are not going to tell me, are you?" I asked. "Mother, I do not wish to hurt you, but I need to know these things."

"I shall not speak of them."

"You might consider that I've a right to know."

"I might not."

"I've lived with lies for nearly twenty years. And Midnight may still be alive. Don't you think it would be best to speak the truth?"

"Truth!" she shouted. "It's so easy for you to say that word. If these letters sent to your father tell the truth, then I was lied to too, you know!"

"Mama, you stopped loving me."

"That's not fair," she replied more gently.

"You stopped loving me and only truly started again when you came here. Please admit it after all these years."

She clung to silence as her only defense.

"But I kept loving you, Mama, and I kept loving Midnight," I said desperately.

"So"—she glared—"it was only you? Is that what you think? We *all* kept loving Midnight, John."

At length I said, "I shall ask you again, Mother. And if you answer truthfully, I shall never mention these things again."

"I warn you. If you say another word, I shall ask you to leave and never allow you to come back to my home."

Time slowed as we locked eyes as enemies. I had nothing more to lose.

"Did you and Midnight lie together as man and woman?"

At that, Mother tried to leave the room, but I caught her arm as she passed me and gripped it hard.

"Take your hand off me!" she screamed.

"No! Not till you've told me the truth."

She tried to jerk free of my grasp, but I wouldn't let go.

"John, you're going too far this time!"

"I haven't gone far enough. Not yet, at least."

"You're hurting me. Let me go this instant!"

"Only if you finally speak the truth, Goddamn it! What happened between you and Midnight?"

She drew back her free hand to slap me, but I caught it just in time.

"What would your father say about the way you're treating your mother?" she demanded.

I shook her savagely, leaving her speechless with shock. "I don't care what he'd say!" I hissed. "He's dead, Mama—dead! And I'm not. I'm here with you and I need the truth. You owe it to me for not loving me all those years!"

When she burst into tears, I reluctantly let her go.

"I don't give a damn about your pride!" I shouted after her as she ran from the room. "It's Midnight's life we're talking about. If you ever loved him, then you must tell me the truth. You have to or—"

She slammed her door before I'd finished my plea.

I SMOKED IN the sitting room, gulping down whiskey to calm my nerves. I wished I could twirl the hands of Aunt Fiona's clock back to an hour earlier. Not to spare Mother. No, to speak even more harshly. This time, I'd force the truth out of her if I had to.

When I heard a carriage rattle to a halt by our door, I slunk away to my room, unable to face my daughters. To the sound of Fiona and the girls chattering about the play, I fell into a whiskey-induced slumber.

When I awoke, Mother was playing the first movement of the

"Moonlight Sonata." In my dressing gown, I crept into her room. I stood next to her and turned the pages. We didn't speak. She made no attempt to look at me.

Forgiveness entered my thoughts. Filtering into the soft arpeggios, it became the melody. Was that what Beethoven had composed—an homage to *forgiveness*?

My rage had been dissipated by sleep. I was grateful for that.

When she stopped playing, I said, "Midnight may be living as a slave, Mama. I cannot bear that. It's killing me. I shall not live again as the man I was until I find him. Mama, I shall try to find him whatever you tell me."

"Will you go to America?"

"Aye. My ship leaves in a week, on the Seventeenth, from Portsmouth. I must leave London the day before."

She reached for my hand and brought it to her lips, then rubbed it along her cheek.

"You still have the most beautiful hands of anyone I know."

"Mama, I am sorry for—"

"Sssshhh. You were right. What we did to you was terrible—terrible and unfair."

She led me to the sofa. She played with my fingers some more, then sniffed their scent of tobacco. I was quite sure this reminded her of the loving presence of my father, as it always did for me. She kissed both my hands, then made them into fists and handed them back to me.

"John, when you used to go to your tarn, I used to worry myself sick about you. I never told you that because I didn't want you to be thinking of me sitting at home, concerned for your safety. I wanted you to feel free, as I never did as a child. I felt watched. I may have failed as a mother, but I want you to know that I tried as best I could."

"You didn't fail. That's not why I need to discuss these things now. I shall always be grateful to you for the happiness of my childhood."

I stood up and went to the fireplace, stirring up the coals and ash. "Mama, if I do not come back," I said, "then you must...you must—"

" 'If I do not come back'?" she interrupted. "What is that supposed to mean?"

"I cannot foresee what will happen. I do not know under what circumstances Midnight is being held captive. If I cannot buy him, I shall steal him. One way or another, I will see him to freedom. I cannot resume my life otherwise."

"But you *will* be able to purchase him, will you not?"

"What if his master does not want to sell him?"

"Then you will offer more money. I shall give you however much it takes. I must have . . . I must have three or four hundred pounds that I can give you. They are all for Midnight. And if you need more, I shall sell my jewelry and everything I own to get more."

I sat down next to her. "Mama, if I am not able to return for any reason, you must take care of the girls. I cannot go otherwise."

"John, this is absurd."

"Tell me that you promise to care for the girls if I do not return."

"Very well," she said, her voice breaking, "I swear to raise and protect them."

I kissed her on the lips for the first time in many years. "Thank you."

We sat in silence for a time, then I gave in to my weariness and rested my head on her lap. She stroked my hair. When I was nearly asleep, she whispered, "I shall tell you my secret, but you must never tell the girls or Fiona. You can tell no one."

My eyes were closed. I was drifting away. "You have my word," I whispered.

"Your father went upriver quite often, you may recall." She rested her hand on my chest. "On one of those trips, Midnight and I . . . we . . . we—"

"You fell in love with each other," I said. I kept my eyes shut tight, sensing my blindness would help her reveal the truth.

"No, no. That's not it. I was enormously fond of him—that's true. And he was very fond of me. But we were not *in love* with each other— not like you mean. But not even that is the point. John, I was still hopelessly in love with your father. That had not changed. I assure you it had not. And yet, I needed to touch Midnight. I was foolish and young, and I could not bear to think I would die one day without knowing him in that way. It seemed vitally important. Does that make any sense?"

"Yes."

"After a week, we agreed to stop what we were doing and never speak of it again. It wasn't difficult. If anything, we became closer without our previous desires getting in the way. But James, he learned of what we had done."

I was tempted to ask about her pregnancy, but I could not bring myself to.

"James sensed that something had been altered between the two of us—between your father and myself, I mean. I admitted that it had, though without mentioning Midnight. Then, to your father's great surprise, I said that what had changed was that I was happier than ever to be married to him! Which was true, since lying with Midnight only proved to me how much I wanted to continue my life with your father. But he accused me of concealing a dalliance. He mentioned men from the neighborhood. Senhor Samuel the roofer—even Benjamin.

"Then I made my fatal error—I told James the truth. I assured him that it had ended and that it was unimportant in terms of our marriage. Isn't that odd, son—that the truth undid my life? If I'd lied believably, I'd still be in Porto now and your father would still be alive. Midnight would probably be living in our home and working with Benjamin on that strange magic of theirs. But I couldn't continue to lie to him. I adored him—as I adored you. But James was furious, and he threatened to kill me. I counted on his affection toward me to vanquish his hot sense of honor in due course. After a week or two, I believed that his higher nature had indeed won the day. By the time he went off to England with Midnight, he was still troubled but also reassured. He was kind and gentle to me and you, as you may recall."

I remembered how I had found him weeping on his last night in Porto.

"At no time during our quarrels did he accuse Midnight of having acted improperly," Mama added. "He held that I was responsible for what had happened—and he was probably right."

She suddenly gasped. I sat up.

"Oh, John, what a fool I was! Now I can plainly see that he must have been planning for weeks to betray Midnight. That was what returned a measure of calm to him. It wasn't his love for me. It was . . . it was—"

She held her cheeks in her hands and closed her eyes. After she'd regained her composure, she said, "When James returned without Midnight, I blamed him, it's true. And I saw that he still hadn't forgiven me. I discovered that almost immediately. We were never the same—as you, of all people, know. We lived a life of recrimination. He faded away from me. And I . . . I was selfish, so very selfish. I withheld the love I still felt for him. I regret it more than you can ever know. And until this very evening, when you showed me those letters, I believed that all our unhappiness could justifiably be attributed to Midnight and myself. But now...now I can see that it was what your father did that took away our last chance for happiness. How unbearable his life must have been after selling Midnight into slavery! Oh, James, all the mistakes we made...”

She began to sob.

“You cannot know the guilt I've felt all these years,” she moaned. “Forgive me. Forgive me, John. Please...I cannot go on without your forgiveness.”

I sat up and kissed the top of her head.

“Now it's my turn to beg,” she said. “I need to hear you say you forgive me. I need to hear those words.”

“I forgive you, Mama. And I love you. The bad times are gone now— all gone.”

“But they're not, John. Midnight is a prisoner! And as long as he remains so, it will never be finished. Not even for your father, though he's been nearly fifteen years in his grave.”

MOTHER'S CONFESSIONS MIGHT have been expected to give me a sense of completion about the past, of finally understanding why our family had come apart. Instead, they left me feeling desperately fragile. In consequence, I insisted on spending every waking minute of the following three days with my daughters. A grave error it was; living at such close proximity, we fought over nearly everything—over their desire to take tiny sips of my beer, whether the cold rain called for a warmer bonnet...

Three days before my carriage ride to Portsmouth, this fever of anxiety broke. I had ordered the lasses to the sofa and asked if there were any questions that they needed answered about their mother before my departure. I grew furious at their reticence to speak, which I took as an affront to Francisca's memory.

“Well, have neither of you anything to say?”

They groaned, plainly thinking me daft. *Calm down,* I could hear Francisca telling me. So I sat with my eyes closed. After a time they came and clung to me.

Thinking back to Graça in her mother's arms, her skin all wrinkled, then seeing this same child in front of me...I apologized for being so difficult with them over the previous few days. I kissed them all over their faces, which made them laugh. After a happy conversation about trifles, we all felt much better and I encouraged them to go off with Aunt Fiona, chasing them giggling out of the house with my growls.

Over the next days, we had no more quarrels. Each of the *kelpies* came to me separately to have her hair brushed, a task their mother had always done for them.

When I begged Mama's forgiveness for my sour mood, she said, "Don't you think I understand that it is worry that makes you so ill-tempered? John, I shall be here for you no matter what you find in America. You and your daughters will always have a home with me in London."

BEFORE I LEFT, Mother handed me a waistcoat of gold and black stripes that she had sewn in secret, asking me to put it on to show her the fit.

"I have sewn fifteen golden sovereigns into the lining," she said, giving me a wink. "Just rip it open when you need them."

I felt for them. "You are very kind, Mama, but I have enough money for my voyage."

"Not for that, son. I told you: I am counting on you to ransom Midnight—no matter what it costs."

I'M AFRAID I created quite a scene at the carriage taking me to Portsmouth. The possibility that this was the last time I would ever see any of my family again left me inconsolable.

"Come home soon, son," Mama told me, doing her best to smile. "And worry not for the girls." She pressed my hands into her cheeks, then kissed them. "I shall turn them into fine English ladies."

"Lord, I hope not," I replied, which made us all laugh.

"Give my love to Violeta. Tell her that my prayers have always been with her, poor girl!"

"I shall indeed. Thank you for all you have ever done for me." As I understood that she wished more than anything to participate in my effort to redeem our past, I said, "Your golden coins shall set Midnight free."

We looked into each other's eyes. I do not know what she saw, but I saw years of shared history—I saw Daniel and Violeta, Fanny and Zebra,

Francisca and the girls. I saw Midnight. Most of all, though, I saw my father.

"May I have your blessing?" I asked.

"You don't need that. You're a man now."

"But still—"

"John, of course you have my blessing," she said, kissing me. "You make me proud—you always have."

Aunt Fiona wrapped me in her arms and said, "Do not fear, your girls have fine characters and will not come undone in London."

I hugged her again, then approached my girls.

"Take good care of each other," I begged them.

"You take care, Papa," Graça whimpered.

I knelt and took one in each arm, wishing to remember their wonderful touch and scent for as long as I was gone. Esther started to cry.

"Listen," I told her, "I shall return as soon as I can. I promise."

"I know," she replied glumly.

"And I shall expect your violin-playing to be much improved when I return. You are to practice at least two hours a day while I am gone." I whispered in her ear, as though it were our secret, "Your grandmother will insist on Mr. Beethoven, but do not fail Mr. Bach.

"And, Graça," I said, facing the dark, somber eyes of my eldest, "please don't worry about me, I shall be fine."

The girl nodded forlornly.

"Now, both of you," I said cheerfully, "please heed what your grandmother and Aunt Fiona ask of you. I shall be home before you even have a chance to miss me, so do not be sad."

Then we were off and I was alone, gripping Midnight's arrow as though it might fly off of its own volition.

XXXIII

IDNIGHT ONCE TOLD ME THAT THE MOON, in full radiance, is female. But when it is cut by night into the form of a crescent, it is male. Then it is called *nui ma ze,* meaning small new moon. Also male are the ponderous clouds that speak to us with their thunder and that cast hail and lightning upon the earth. But the soft gray clouds that nourish the plants with their dancing rains are female.

As far as I can recall, we did not encounter a single female cloud at sea. We seesawed instead between battering storms and full sun. I began to think of the world as ruled only by male gods. Hence, by the time we arrived at the southern tip of Manhattan Island I knew this: that I had neither been meant to journey by sea nor live in a world where the natural forces were wholly male.

COMING IN FROM open ocean, under that great dome of blue American sky, New York Bay was a splendid site. In my mind, I made a list: *I shall walk on the earth. Smell flowers. Eat oranges. See the blue bird with a crest that Violeta wrote me about. And forget the indifference of waves.*

The city of New York spread out across the island's

southern tip, but a dense forest blanketed the north. Soon we could make out brick houses and even carriages. To our right, on a broad peninsula, was another waterfront called Brooklyn. A few dozen people were standing there on a tall bluff. I waved to them, and three or four hailed me back.

The *Saxony* eased into a wharf jutting out from a bustling thoroughfare. We passengers cheered heartily at our final lurch. The emotion was such that many of us laughed through our tears.

Soon, the walkway to land was in place. I felt for Daniel's talisman about my neck, then gripped Midnight's arrow, picked up my bags, and rushed ashore.

I have made it to America, and I am closer to Midnight! I kept repeating that exciting phrase to myself, picturing myself on one of Graça's beloved maps.

The coachman for my hackney cab gave me his arm to help me up, as the world was still pitching and rolling. I handed him a paper on which I'd written Violeta's address.

We passed leafy squares and many rows of fine trim houses as we rolled along in fits and starts, since there was much carriage traffic at this time of morning. Our route took us north into the interior of the island. After twenty minutes the driver called "Ho!" to the grays and tugged on their reins. We had arrived at Number 73 John Street. Violeta's house was of handsome dark red brick. Its three floors rose to a steeply slanted slate roof.

I sat my luggage down on the stoop and took a deep breath. Then, gripping the knocker—a brass ring in a lion's mouth—I rapped on the door twice. I glanced upward just in time to see the curtains closing in the second-story window.

XXXIV

Nigger Fate

T HE MEN THOUGHT THAT LITTLE MASTER
Henry was going to be a diamond of compassion compared
to his murdered papa. But the women and girls knew different, and we were proved right. As soon as he got his hands
on River Bend, the Little Master started drinking fierce as
fire and whipping everything in sight.

It was an open window that started him toward *his* grave,
the way I look at it. Mistress Holly was of the notion that the
icy wind that reached him that night must have come all the
way from Canada. I hardly ever found myself agreeing with
her, but this case was an exception. Up there in Canada was
where all the Negroes were free, and I reckoned they had
vengeful winds for taking the lives of the likes of Little
Master Henry. At least, I sure as hell hoped they did.

This one particular night, the Master's carriage came
across the Big Bridge at a couple hours past midnight. He'd
been at a party at Comingtee Plantation thrown by Mistress
Nancy Ball. We all called her Captain Nancy owing to how
she enjoyed lashing her slaves with her ivory-handled whip.

Little Henry was so drunk that he must have lifted open
his window to get some air into his whiskey-fogged chest.
He didn't remember a thing about opening it, but that didn't

mean much, since he didn't recall tripping on the stairs up to the piazza either, or vomiting into his washbasin. But Crow saw both of those things just as plain as day, and even emptied the basin into the lime pit, so we know they happened. Besides, none of the white folks wanted to consider who else might have lifted up his window, because that would have meant somebody had a plan.

I figured it didn't matter much who opened that window because, however it happened, the wind rushed inside as if it had been waiting for weeks. Then it curled its icy fingers down around his throat, so that by the next morning he had a bad cough and a burning fever. Over the next few days, the fever got worse and the Little Master grew crazy with it. It was a spell, just like one of his father's.

It was my father who watched after Little Master Henry. He lifted cups of brewed dogwood berries to his lips to ease his chills and made him breathe in the steam rising off boiled peach-tree leaves to cool his fever. After two weeks, he was able to stand on his own two legs. And as soon as he was able to walk down the stairs, he started giving orders again in that squeaky voice of his, just like he'd never been ill. And the very first order he gave was that he was sure as hell not granting any freedom to Samuel, his daughter, or any other uppity niggers with Yankee dreams in their heads, no matter whether they had brought him back to life or not.

You see, Papa had asked him for our freedom in exchange for keeping him out of the arms of death.

A week after Little Master Henry denied us our chance to be free, he took ill again real bad. Papa tried everything on that boy, all sorts of brews and potions that only he and I knew about. But nothing he worked up did any good.

Every evening I brought the Master his lemonade, just like I did his father. By now he couldn't keep down even a spoonful of Indian mush. He was all bogged up. If you ask me, his refusal to give us our freedom was the cause of that. And there was nothing in any curing book that was going to get that sort of mud-minded evil unstuck.

One night, I carried his lemonade to his door and found it locked. I was afraid to wake him up in case he'd dozed off. So instead of knocking, I stood there like a spider in its web for a time, just waiting and wondering. Then I shuffled off to Mistress Holly's room. When I told her about her son's door being locked, she took the key from her drawer and shouted for Crow to fetch my papa. This time, no one ran off for Mr. Johnson the overseer, since we couldn't believe that so young a man as

Little Master Henry might be dead. He was only twenty-four, after all. And he was a white man. By that I mean he had powers over life and death that we didn't have.

Papa said thank you for being given the key, then clicked the door open. And just like three months earlier, we discovered that our Master had a blade stuck in his neck, right above the collarbone.

The young man died on November the Twenty-Second of 1820—just in time for Thanksgiving, a few of the more evil among us said.

I guess you might say we aren't ever prepared for death to come looking for anyone we know. I learned that when Mamma was ill. Though she was feverish for three weeks, I never once let myself think she was about to leave us behind. The shock nearly chased my spirit clean out of my body. Papa's as well. He didn't say a word for four months.

You can say what you want about Mistress Holly, but she had a big fondness for her son. I think that he was the only person she really loved. So we reckoned she'd start wailing something awful. Not a one of us expected that terrible silence when she crept on over to her son and lay her head in his bloody lap. His eyes were still open, but she didn't reach up to close them. She didn't want him dead forever.

For the first time in my life, I felt bad for a white person. After Dr. Lydell had come and gone, I tiptoed in to Mistress Holly in her room and asked real nice if I might bring her some lemonade with a few of the almond biscuits that Lily had made. She looked up from her bed with eyes so red that I thought she'd rubbed her dead son's blood into them. I got a fright. She glared at me as if I had laughed at her. In the meanest voice I'd ever heard from her, she said, "You get your black feet out of my room, nigger girl, or I'll have you peeled, pickled, and quartered."

WHEN A PLANTER is murdered in South Carolina, all the white folks start shivering nearly all the time, even when they're sitting right up close to their hearths. Because they know the killing might have been the work of a Negro wanting freedom. Like Mr. Denmark Vesey. He was the preacher who was hanged for trying to start an uprising in Charleston back in 1822. He once even came to River Bend, and you could feel that big power in him. "Like black lightning," Papa described him, by which he meant a whole lot of things, I'd guess.

So with a few hundred thousand Negroes thinking about vengeance every night, it was no wonder that the white folks didn't sleep none too peacefully. They figured that once we got started it was only going to stop when the last of their race was lying in a Charleston street in a puddle of his own blood, being picked by vulture birds. And they were likely right.

This death meant something else besides. It was proof of a terrible curse having been put on River Bend. No one said that any louder than Mistress Holly herself. She hardly got dressed anymore. Most of her time she sat in her dressing gown in her room, losing at solitaire and consoling herself with rum.

Life gets stuck repeating itself from time to time, I guess. Mr. Johnson didn't bother measuring the distance from the window to the ground this time, since the Big House wasn't made of rubber and couldn't have gotten much higher or lower. As for the ladder, it was locked in the First Barn and only Mr. Johnson had the key.

Twenty-four feet from the window to the ground... Little Master Henry dead at twenty-four years old... Lily, Weaver, and some of the other slaves believed this coincidence was proof that we were finally getting some divine justice in South Carolina.

Mr. Johnson got powerful furious at us for not knowing who did it, but he didn't whip anybody. He was waiting to see who the new master would be before working himself up. Maybe he was frightened of the killer ghost that might be haunting River Bend, as well.

Whatever was in his mind, I guess he started making plans right about then to leave River Bend with Mistress Holly. Crow overheard him talking about that with her not two nights after her son's death.

This time, South Carolina justice found a culprit, though we only knew it three days after the fact. In the story we heard, a runaway slave named Hilton had been caught by a patrol while he was fording the East Branch of the Cooper River near where it meets French Quarter Creek.

The hounds might have lost his scent but his shoe had come off in the mud of the riverbank. You might say that his destiny got stuck with him right there. *Nigger fate,* my mamma used to call it—I mean, things like your shoe coming off at the worst moment. She was the one person I ever met who could spot that nigger fate the moment it targeted its falcon eyes on you.

We heard the report of what happened from Crow, who got it from Aunt Bessie. Hilton had been dragged nearly drowned out of the river by the patrol. Finding a silver watch in his pocket, they said it must have been Little Master Henry's. No nigger could get himself such a pretty thing without stealing it.

After they lynched him from a big old oak tree, they cut him down, tied the rope around his legs, and dragged him by horse all the way back to Cherry Hill. They rode across five or six miles of ugly roads gouged with stones, so that by the time they discarded him in front of his poor mamma's cabin, every last bone in his bloody face had been broken.

I guess you could say that motherhood has got to be the bravest thing of all, since she knelt by his body and tried to put him back together.

I can't think of anything more evil than to do that to a man and show him to his mamma.

Nobody in the patrol knew or cared that the silver watch had been a present from his father, Papa Lucius.

My papa told me that men like them only listened to Hyena and did his bidding. Papa talked like that sometimes. Most folks at River Bend didn't understand him, but I did.

A few days later it rained all night, and Papa danced out front of the Big House till dawn. He got so sopped and tired that I thought he'd just fall right down in the mud. He closed his eyes when I held him in my arms and whispered, "I've got to make sure they don't take the dances from us too."

We all knew there wasn't any justice in South Carolina, but I still kept thinking there ought to be. I guess thinking like that was the root of all my problems.

AFTER LITTLE MASTER Henry's funeral, Mistress Holly moved into her town house in Charleston and never once came back to River Bend. She didn't invite Mr. Johnson to join her either. I guess she was fond enough of him when there was no one else nearby. Folks said that she was playing cards every night with other widows and winning enough to buy all the rum she could drink.

Mistress Holly would die five months later, from the ague, the doctors said. But the rumors were that she just drank herself to death. I guess no one can live so very long with that much unhappiness in their heart.

Mr. Johnson took his frustration out on us. For three months afterward we were whipped for so much as sneezing at the wrong moment.

He cut stripes in me too. For the very first time. Papa was in Charleston doing marketing that day.

Mr. Johnson must have seen my father being in town as his chance to take out all the hate he'd been collecting against me in his old pockets over the years. What got him all in a fit was me telling him that the field slaves would likely work better if their chimneys were made out of brick instead of clay.

"What kind of nigger stupidity you spoutin' now?" he asked me.

"If they was made of brick, they wouldn't melt every time it rained, and the field hands could keep them cabins of theirs heated even when it was pourin'. Maybe then they'd get themselves a full night of sleep." My real mistake was glaring at him and asking: "You ever try workin' sun to sun after getting only two hours of sleep, Mr. Johnson?"

That was when he grabbed my arm and had the two black foremen drag me off to the whipping barrel.

I struggled, of course, and even caught one of the foremen on the chin with my fist. But that made him throw me down in the dirt, and I broke a tooth. I spit it out at him. The other foreman gave me a kick on my backside for that and told me to just be still or he'd kill me with his own two hands.

"For how long you gonna hurt your own people?" I asked him.

He kicked at me again. He aimed for my head but only got my shoulder. I flapped my hand at him and shouted up at Mr. Johnson, "You gonna pay for this!"

He just laughed and told the foremen to tie me down. I shouted for help as loud as I could. I wanted Lily, Weaver, Crow, and the others to see what they were doing to me.

"Bite down hard, Morri chile," Lily hollered to me as she came running.

"T'ink a somet'in' good," Weaver shouted from a long ways off. He must have been running in from the fields. "You's sittin' in a garden, Morri girl. You's surrounded by flow'rs."

I pictured what he told me, but the second stroke chased all the roses right out of me. I was nowhere but where I was. The stinging on my back felt like the skin was coming off.

"Help!" I shouted. "Help me. God help me!"

I squeezed my gut tight, but by the seventh stripe I'd peed on myself right good. And I was crying like a baby from the pain. Then I started whispering a verse from the Psalms over and over to myself. Just like I always do when I'm in big trouble: *Since I was young have men attacked me, but never have they prevailed.... Since I was young...*

The last stroke I remembered came across the back of my neck. That one was a special gift from Mr. Johnson, I reckon. But I like to think that that mean-spirited lash started my dreams looking for a way out of River Bend. Because it was right after that day that I started seeing that northern city where the snow was always falling.

I told my father right away about my being lashed when he got back from the city, because there was no way I could hide my wounds and the gap where my tooth was gone. But I told him I didn't mind. It made me more like the others and I was glad for that. He paced round and round my room while I spoke, then hollered so loud for Lily that she came running in.

"Take care of my child," he told her.

Lily held me back from following him outside, saying I'd only make things worse. Later, I heard from Crow that Papa stepped right up to Mr. Johnson on the piazza, shook his fist at him, and said that if he ever touched me again, his body would be feeding worms within the week.

"I'll neither strike you nor fire a shot," he said. "But you will die in such pain that they'll need to gag you so whoever the new master is will be able to sleep."

Mr. Johnson laughed and told Papa to shut his nigger mouth, but the truth is he never dared lash me again—at least not while my father remained with us at River Bend.

XXXV

Except for One Thing

I'M GOING TO HAVE TO TELL YOU NOW ABOUT how my father ended up coming to South Carolina, since the way I see it, that sent everything else rolling toward the future that's come to pass.

Back in December of 1806, Papa and the Portuguese man who'd brought him to Europe were visiting England. The man, Mr. James Stewart, had a meeting one morning he couldn't miss and asked to meet my papa at two o'clock that afternoon at a home near a large palace. When Papa arrived at the place, he was shown into a small, hot room by a crooked old lady. Three white men came barging in right away and tied his wrists and ankles, then stuffed a filthy rag in his mouth and covered his head with a sack.

When Mr. Stewart arrived, he must have been told that my father never reached there. Papa never saw him again.

The next morning he was driven to a stinking room and tied to a wooden column. The sack was removed from his head. Slivers of light shone in through a tiny window. The floor was tilting and the ceiling was real low. Men were walking above him.

He came to understand he was on a ship, below the main

deck. It was so cold that his teeth started chattering a whole conversation.

Two goats and a cow were put in there with him. The sailors fed him and the animals nothing but biscuits and hay. He begged to see the sun, since no one from southern Africa can stand a whole day in the dark, but they weren't about to let him go up on deck. He drank water from the same bowl as the animals till one of the sailors felt sorry for him and gave him a jug. He slept right up close to his companions so they could keep him warm.

It was then that Mantis appeared to my papa in a dream. Crawling to his ear and lifting up his heart-shaped head, he whispered, "Tsamma, they will want to learn the secrets of the Bushmen. Say nothing." He then crept off.

So it was that Papa decided to never talk to the Captain or the crew.

Why that insect-god left my father all alone is a question I can't answer. Maybe he didn't want to be trapped in the dark below deck, where the stars and moon couldn't be seen.

THIS FIRST VOYAGE lasted two or three weeks—my father lost track of time. During storms, his desire to follow the thunder and lightning was fierce. Papa tugged at his manacles and made his wrists and ankles bleed. One of the goats licked at his wounds.

Papa sang at night—songs he'd learned with his family in Portugal. But misery weighed him down during the day. He imagined the stars hunting his pain. And though they could find it, they had lost their aim. Their arrows missed him.

The weather grew powerful hot. The cow and the goats were killed and cut up so that the crew could have fresh meat.

When the ship reached shore, Papa was chained on deck to a mast. He saw a stone fort and many small houses. The Captain told him the ship was now on the west coast of Africa. If he was thinking about trying to escape, he ought to change his mind, *since they would cut off his nigger balls and stuff them up his rump when they caught him.*

Africans in chains carried boxes of rum, wine, gunpowder, and cotton cloth from the ship to the wharf. Papa learned that these were to be given to the local kings in return for slaves.

When my papa told that to me, I remembered my mamma saying that she had been traded for two yards of indigo-dyed cloth.

That evening, Papa was chained below deck once again. Maybe fifty or sixty slaves joined him. He could not understand their language. There was no room for any of them to move. Then they got on their way again. For many weeks this time.

Papa said what he remembered most was the thirst. It was worse than the three days he'd walked in the summer desert as a boy to escape the Dutch guns. Then he knew where to look for water, could feel it beneath his feet, resting cool in the heart of the earth.

But even on board the ship he knew that he wouldn't die. Because death did not ride the waves. And did not wear shackles. Any death that came for a Bushman would never ask him to stay inside a belly of wood while lightning was painting the sky the white of bone.

The Time of the Hyena was on my papa. He had visions of the great flood that almost cost Mantis his life, when he was saved by a bee. Sometimes he spoke to Noah, who told him that this time they would not reach dry land and that all the animals would vanish from the earth. Only the fish would remain. And they would not remember the Bushmen or even Africa. All the stories of the First People would be forgotten.

He never said so, but I think Papa must have decided at this time that if he ever had a child, he would call her Memory. Because every night he prayed that the footprints of his people would not be forgotten. He wished for a boulder where he could draw his misery so Mantis would know where he was.

WHEN PAPA'S SHIP anchored, he was taken by a man named Miller to a shop in a town of dusty streets. His ankles were still chained. He drank four jugfuls of water, and his belly grew so big that Miller and his three children laughed and said that he looked like he was having a baby. I've seen my father drink like that, after my mother died, so I know just what he must have looked like.

If I said my papa was like every man and like none, would that make sense? He was short and yellow-brown, with tight knots of black-gray hair and slender eyes—eyes like a man from China, some folks said. Yet there was something about his face and form that was not so very odd at all—as if he was the inner form all of us shared.

All I need to do is to stand in front of a mirror to see him clearly. Though I haven't inherited too much of his power. And surely not his talents at healing. If I'd have had those things, then Weaver might be alive today.

Mr. Miller noticed right away that my father wouldn't speak. Or couldn't. He was mighty vexed that the ship's captain who sold the little man had not told him he was a mute.

Papa had no idea what part of the world this Alexandria was in and what they wanted from him. He pretended not to be able to understand English. He was locked in a small room with no windows. But Mr. Miller didn't beat him. Maybe he even felt sorry for him.

One day my father made it understood with his hand signals that he wanted a pen and paper. In his careful handwriting, he wrote out the name of his family in Portugal and their address. For an hour he worked on a letter, explaining how he'd been captured and put on a ship. He handed what he wrote to Mr. Miller, giving all his hopes to him.

Mr. Miller was pleased that the little Negro was able to both write and understand English after all. But he must have burned the letter, because no one ever came from Portugal to find Papa.

When Mr. Miller's daughter Abigail got real ill, Papa wrote a note asking to be allowed in the workshop where the apothecary made his medicines. There, he mixed a tea to take away her fever. Mr. Miller made Papa drink it first to be sure it wasn't poison. After it helped Abigail get better, Papa began to spend all of his days and nights in the shop, sleeping on the floor in a back room, helping his new owner, learning what American herbs, barks, and roots could do. The power of doing useful work slowly freed him from Hyena.

After two months he was rewarded by being allowed to go out on his own on Sunday afternoons. He wrote again to the Stewart family and stole a stamp from his owner, but he never learned whether they got the letter. No one from Portugal ever wrote back to him.

On his outings, Papa used to stand at the port and gaze out to sea. He thought of escaping but knew he had to wait for word from Mantis, who would tell him when to go.

YELLOW FEVER STRUCK Alexandria a hard blow in the spring of 1807, and Mr. Miller got it real bad. Nothing Papa tried could cure him. He'd been a widower, so Papa was inherited by his young children. Their guardian, Mr. Miller's brother, sold him to a vicious slave-dealer by the name of Burton.

Along with other Africans, Papa was taken by ship to Charleston, where he was auctioned at market. His purchaser was Big Master Henry, of course, who always said he bid one hundred dollars for the little nigger because just looking at him made him laugh.

PAPA FINALLY SHOWED everybody he wasn't mute after he saw my mother for the first time. He told me that the moment he got a glimpse of the depth in her black eyes and that long ostrich neck of hers, he saw Mantis coming back to him. I guess she was the sign he'd been waiting for. So he courted Mamma with swamp lilies and other flowers that he'd pick for her on Sundays.

AS TIME WENT by, Papa earned Big Master Henry's trust and was allowed to go to Cordesville and Charleston with Wiggie the coachman or even all by himself. He'd collect salt and oyster shells from the beaches, buy medicines, and do marketing for the household. On these trips, he had lots of chances to meet freed blacks who might have helped him escape. But the reason he didn't even try to leave was me and my mother. Then when she died, just me.

Like I said, Big Master Henry never once let all three of us out of River Bend together. I sometimes thought that Papa ought to make a break for it just the same. Other times, I was so scared he'd leave me behind that I'd run as fast as I could after his coach as it rumbled toward the gate.

THEN, ON SUNDAY the Twenty-First of January, 1821, he did vanish. There wasn't anything strange about that day, and, except for one thing, nothing unusual happened that whole week.

That one thing was the visit a few days earlier of a tall brown man—a mulatto, we reckoned. He had short black hair, stiff as a porcupine, and a gold ring in his ear. I'd never seen a pirate before. I imagined that was what he was. Now, what a pirate would be doing visiting River Bend I couldn't say, but I hoped he was looking for some helpers. I knew my papa and I would have left with him if he'd asked.

Little Master Henry was two months in his grave by then, and Cousin Edward Roberson was running things for Miss Anne, who had inherited the plantation when Mistress Holly moved out.

We never liked Cousin Edward. We called him Edward the Cockerel, since he was all puffed up about himself, in the best family tradition.

To give you an idea about Edward's mud-mindedness, let me just tell you that when he first arrived he was convinced that "the sable savages" in his possession would work harder without their gardens. Not that he had the courage to tell us himself that he wanted us to destroy our gardens. No, ma'am. Instead, Mr. Johnson lined us up one morning at dawn and told us to dig up all the plants and bushes and herbs and cover them over with soil.

My father begged Mr. Johnson's leave and met with Master Edward alone in the tea room, putting a quick end to his cruel plans. Papa told me later that he didn't say much of anything to him. He simply told him of all the illnesses that had laid River Bend low in recent years, blaming the climate of the Low Country.

"You are at the mercy of a land whose limits go far beyond your own," he told Edward. "And your people do not know what it means to go slow." Then he spoke of the curse on River Bend and the early deaths of the previous masters. To end, he said, "Now, sir, I might agree with you that allowing us to grow our fruits and flowers is a great concession to ask. But I do believe that Mistress Kitty, Elisabeth, and Mary will be better off with well-fed Negroes who like to sniff roses and add beans to their rice.... Better off with them than with hungry slaves who never benefit from beauty. Though being an African myself, I would understand it if you disagreed with me and did not wish for me to have access to the plants and herbs I shall need to cure your family's ills."

After that conversation, we had less trouble with Edward the Cockerel, usually only when he was out to prove his manhood to Miss Anne, who we were now expected to call Mistress Anne. She was living year-round in Charleston since her marriage to John Wilson Poyas and visited us once a month. He was a physician from one of the wealthiest families around these parts. We hadn't worked out yet how she'd caught him. But the rumor was that she'd got herself in a woman's way, pointed her pistol at his head, and given him only one other option. Her papa had trained her to shoot about the same time she'd learned to embroider—in case of any uprising. We figured that while staring at the snout of her gun, Dr. Poyas took both the hint and his wedding vows.

Despite her marriage, Cousin Edward was sweet on Mistress Anne. She was still pretty, everyone said, with blue eyes that Cousin Edward described to Crow as "downright dazzling." His own big eyes rotated on antennas when she was anywhere nearby. But she didn't pay him much mind. She had two children of her own, a fair-haired girl, Elizabeth— just like Edward's daughter, but with a *Z* instead of an *S*—and a boy named Douglas. He was the image of Little Master Henry, flame-red hair and all. She came to River Bend only to inspect her land and visit her "darling niggers," as she called us.

We waved at her from wherever we were working when she rode up in her carriage. When we were made to stand in a line for her, we sang one of my father's old songs, "Barbara Allen." We acted like we were up to our hair in heartfelt joy at her arrival. A couple of times tears came to her eyes. Her head must have been nothing but night soil.

ANYWAY, ON THE day the mulatto pirate came to River Bend, my papa was away in Charleston. He was picking up some willow-green cotton cloth Mistress Kitty wanted Lily and me to make into a new ball gown. The visitor met with Master Edward in the drawing room. Crow overheard shouting, and some of it had to do with Papa. Best Crow could figure out, this man had met my father decades before and wished to see him again. Apparently, Edward the Cockerel hadn't taken kindly to that notion and had asked him to leave his property one, two, three.

I got all worked up because I figured it was John Stewart, the little boy who'd been my papa's friend in Portugal. By now he'd be all grown up. He had finally come to claim my father and set him free!

But later that day, when I described the man to Papa, he said that it couldn't have been him. Even so, he closed his eyes and took a big breath. Then his belly began to drum.

We never found out who the mulatto was, by the way. All Master Edward would tell us was the he was "some blasted troublemaker" from Georgia.

Papa gave me a letter in a sealed envelope the next morning. It was for John Stewart. He said he'd written most of it years before and had been waiting for a sign to give it to me. That sign, he told me, was the mulatto man coming to River Bend for him. I was to put the letter in a jar and bury it out in Porter's Woods.

I said, "But, Papa, you'll be able to give it to him yourself if he ever comes."

"No, Morri, in case I am away from the plantation, you must have the letter in your possession. We mustn't take a chance on his not understanding you are my daughter."

ON THE DAY my father disappeared, Mistress Anne had come up to River Bend for one of her monthly visits. I remember that because when Papa didn't return to the kitchen to help Lily with supper, she came to me in the parlor where I was polishing the silver. On her orders I looked for him everywhere in the house and in all the gardens too. I ran out to the fields, but no one had seen him. To win him time for escaping, if that's what he'd done, I then sat myself down on a log by Christmas Creek and watched the clumping commotion of the frogs. *I hope you can run after all, Papa,* I kept thinking. *'Cause them patrols are going to be hungry on your track.*

When I finally told Mistress Anne that Papa was nowhere in sight, she had Mr. Johnson get the dogs ready. She sent Crow with Wiggie the coachman to all the nearby towns to alert folks that River Bend had a runaway.

I counted those first hours as if a pistol were pointed toward my heart. I sat up on the piazza steps fending off the mosquitoes, praying hard for Mantis to help him. My hands were fidgeting something terrible, so I polished every infernal crevice in that scalloped punch bowl we only used on Christmas Eve. When the dawn rose in orange and red, no silver had ever shone like that before, and I was thinking maybe we had a chance.

Crow, who'd been up all night spreading the news that Papa had run away, told me there'd been no sign of him anywhere. With a dark look, he took my hand and apologized, because he had to take the carriage right away to Charleston to put an announcement in the newspaper.

The days passed with me thinking of nothing else. After a week of sunups and sundowns, I still didn't let myself think he'd made it, in case they brought him back half-dead and roped to a horse.

A month went by, then six weeks, then seven. Each day I thought it less likely they'd catch him. I wondered what I'd do if they brought him back to whip him to death. That's when I stole a knife from the kitchen and buried it below the piazza. They could lynch me if they wanted, but I wasn't going to hear Papa howl without making a ghost out of Master Edward.

But I never had to use that knife, because Papa never came back. Maybe he drowned, or was bit by a cottonmouth. Maybe he died all alone.

I let myself dream sometimes that he escaped from nigger fate and made it all the way up north to the city where snow was always falling.

Crow, Lily, and the others said he probably made himself invisible with some potions he'd fixed up. They pictured him walking like a British lord to Charleston, stepping right onto a boat bound for Europe, and sailing home to the Portuguese family he'd left behind. But I knew that if my papa meant to escape, he'd have taken me with him. Though it was possible he'd decided to get out first and then come back for me.

JUST SHORT OF three months after he was gone, that was precisely the conclusion that Master Edward came to. So one night he had some white men I'd never seen before rush into my room and bind me with ropes. They gagged me too. Then they carried me to a carriage. I thought he was going to *send me for a little sugar* in Charleston. They say that because the Workhouse used to be a sugar factory and they got special mechanical machines there for bruising and breaking a person. But that wasn't what he had in mind at all. No, he had something worse hiding behind his smile.

XXXVI

A TALL AND SLENDER WOMAN WAS STARING AT me, pale surprise turning to gaunt, hollow-cheeked fear. Her eyelids were puffy and red, and her lips were dry and cracked. Stiff of posture, she wore a high-collared lilac dress with bell sleeves tightly fastened at her wrists. A white bonnet hid her hair, and a beige lace fichu was draped over her shoulders, which were thin and hunched.

But her eyes were the same jade color they'd always been.

"Good morning," I said, taking off my hat and smiling.

"Yes . . . yes, good morning." Her voice was brittle. "May I be of some . . . of some help?"

"Violeta, it's me."

"Do I know you, sir? How . . . how is it that you know my name?"

Before I could reply, she took a step back and brought her hands to her mouth. Smiling again to soften the shock, I said, "Yes, it's me—it's John. All the way from Portugal." I found myself making Daniel's tortoise face, which he had always made when he was feeling awkward. I had not imitated this expression in fifteen years. "*Sou eu*—it's me," I repeated in Portuguese. I expected her to rush into my arms. I'd lift her up and dance her around her house. We would crash into furniture and fall together into the depths of our gratitude.

I advanced to the top step so I might reach out to her.

She confounded my plans by receding into the shadows inside her doorway. "John, I never expected... It has... It has been a lifetime." She spoke in English. "John, you are so... so very different."

I was so startled by her apprehension that I felt a nervous tingling all over my body. I might have been just ten years old. "It's just me—just me," I pleaded in a rush, as though she hadn't realized who I was. "Didn't you get my letter?"

"A letter, no, I'm sure I have not."

"I sent it... why, it must be six weeks ago now. It must still be at sea."

I began to suspect just then that I'd misinterpreted the words of her letter. What a fool I'd been! She had written of her desire for a tile panel in her home simply to be polite.

I turned to wipe the tears betraying me, coughing to conceal my emotion. "It is plain that I have come at a bad time. I shall return this evening, and then... and then we shall talk." So cool was her continued stare and so defensive her pose that I added, "Yes... yes, that's... that's what I'll do. It's been lovely to see you, Violeta. I shall... I..."

Unable to say a final good-bye, I put on my hat and gripped my luggage. I was careful not to retreat too quickly down her stairs, since that might have revealed the depth of my despair, and I wished to avoid making her feel badly about her own behavior.

I decided to find a room at a nearby inn and head off to Alexandria as soon as possible. I counted my steps, not caring which direction I went as long as I might get away from her. By the count of twenty, sure that I'd never see her again, I shuddered.

I heard my name called. Violeta was waving at me from her stoop. "Please, John, come back! John, do not move. Wait there...."

She disappeared inside her house. A few doors down, a woman held a small Persian rug out her window and shook it. Leaves fluttered to the ground and I picked one up, staring at its brittle veins.

Violeta returned holding a square of old, yellowing paper and handed it to me. It was one of my portraits of Fanny—sprawled on her belly, her paws wrapped around a bone, her head tilted so she might gnaw at it with greater ferocity.

If only I could have held Fanny in my arms once more... How strange the heart is—hope that Violeta would not reject me again was kindled by our shared fondness for the dog and by her having kept my simple drawing, without a single fold, over twenty years of separation.

"You remember her?" I asked.

Her eyes turned glassy. "Oh, John, she lived a long and contented life, I hope."

I spoke then of her disappearance during the French occupation. My voice was clipped by my desire to keep emotion at bay, and I spoke only of facts and dates. She bit her bottom lip and struggled against tears. Handing her back the sketch, our eyes met.

There are memories that are love itself: the touch of my mother's hands; the scent of Papa's pipe; Midnight's grin. And Violeta's eyes. I realized that she was both a stranger to me and the greatest of friends.

I whispered her name twice, and it seemed to me the most secret of incantations. I wanted to speak of our dead friend, but the tower of memories in me loomed too high right now to try to climb.

She looked down at her feet, and in her distraught expression I recognized the lass who'd been trapped in a room with neither windows nor doors. Yet I was an adult now and could break down walls too strong for the child I'd been. I held out my hand to her, but she would neither take it, nor gaze up at me.

"I shall never withdraw my hand," I declared. "I shall stand here waiting forever for you to take it if I have to."

I am not sure what made me say the peculiar words that followed. I can only think it was all the time I had passed in the company of Benjamin and Midnight—and my fear for the Bushman in his state of bondage. "Violeta, you may think the sun and moon have set forever upon the years we shared." I gazed out at the horizon and pointed east, toward Jerusalem. "But there they both are, sun and moon, at the very same time, over the Mount of Olives. It is impossible, yet it is true. We are both afraid to step inside the waters of the river Jordan and to touch their reflections. But what you do not know is that we are already inside. Though we are older, we have never left. To know that for sure, all you need to do is take my hand—to take it now."

She would say nothing. Her eyes closed as though never to open again.

"You may want me to repeat the past, but I'll not do it. I now have some small power to do as I please. And neither I, nor the Daniel that lives inside me, shall turn away from you now. If we are to part, then you must return to your home and lock your door. And even then you may expect me to keep knocking—all night long if need be. I am a man now, and I have suffered, and I can outwait even a woman who once had no choices in life."

When she snatched my hand, she gripped it as though she'd been in danger of falling. So filled with love and admiration was the look she gave me that I whispered, "May we begin again? May we try to make up for what was unfairly taken from us both—and from Daniel?"

Tears flooded her eyes. And mine. I took her in my arms and lifted her off the ground, turning her round and round.

"John, oh, my God, John . . ."

"I have known much death," I told her gently. "We've both been broken. But you have found me. And I have found you."

She clutched me tightly, shaking so violently that I feared for her. "I am holding you," I told her, "and in my arms you may finally rest."

She laid her head on my shoulder. We breathed together till our borders were all but erased.

"Remember the day we met—the Miracle of the Birds?" I asked.

"You were beautiful," she whispered.

"You saved my skin. If you had not spit at the birdseller he'd have yanked my head off!"

We laughed, giddy with excitement. "Just now, at my door, I was horribly rude," Violeta said. "I'm sorry."

I switched to Portuguese. "*Estava meramente supreendida*. You were just surprised. It was nothing. Everything is fine."

"John, I hardly ever speak Portuguese. I may make errors." She leaned down and reached for one of my bags. "Come on, let's go back to my house."

We had been through too much together to lie. "Aye, I'd like to stay with you, but only if you truly want me to. Violeta, I'm sure I shall be comfortable at any old inn nearby. I mean that. For the sake of all we have been through together, do not stand on ceremony with me. I confess I am far too weak from my journey and from all these emotions. I could not bear it."

"Oh, John, you know there is no other place for you in this city."

I've never lent much credence to the possibility of an afterlife, but I looked then into the sky and whispered to Father, who had chased her uncle from Porto, "She made it to New York, Papa. Your efforts have been rewarded."

Violeta said how sorry she had been to learn of my father's passing. I spoke of him as we walked to her door. I tried to put the events of his death into an understandable context for her but failed miserably.

"John," she said, squeezing my arm, "you are all I ever dared to dream you'd become. And more. Your dear mother must be so proud of you. And your daughters... Tell me, are you great friends with them?"

"I think they are very fond of me—despite my oddness. But their mother, Francisca, died a year ago. It has been very hard on them. And now with me here..."

"I'd have liked to have met her. Did she love you greatly?"

"Yes, I think she did. We were the best of friends for many years."

"That is a very good thing. And a relief to me, if you will forgive me. I always worried you'd never have your affection fully reciprocated." She gazed down, shamed. "Because of what happened with Daniel and me."

We studied each other. The heaviness in her eyes troubled me, and her lips were so very dry, as though she had withered through lack of love.

She covered my lips with her fingertips. "Please, John, say nothing yet." She linked her arm in mine, and together we walked up her steps.

From her stoop, she gazed up and down her street, her head swiveling like a pendulum.

"You almost expect him too," I observed.

She nodded and caressed my cheek. "I have lived alone for so long that I may not be a good hostess. I feel I ought to apologize beforehand."

She would have liked to continue speaking, I was sure. But after looking down the block once more, she bit her lip instead, hard, almost drawing blood.

VIOLETA LIVED IN a house nearly bare of furniture. I was given a room on the third floor overlooking the back garden, which was in a state of disarray. I had a bed and a washstand at my disposal, nothing more. Not even a chest or wardrobe. I suspected now that she had little money.

Violeta fetched me a pitcher of hot water so that I might wash my face. She inquired after my mother, and while she brought me towels and put new sheets on my bed, I told her about London.

"Would you consider slowing down a moment," I begged her.

"John, we'll talk later. You need time to rest. And I'm sure you must be famished. I'll make some breakfast."

"Do you still hate cooking?" I asked.

She shrugged. "A woman gets used to almost anything."

She was still wearing her bonnet. When I asked if she'd take it off so I might see the glory of her hair, she wagged her finger at me. "That can wait till later too, young man."

I would have liked to accompany her to the kitchen, but she wished to be alone. I had the impression all that first day that my presence had disoriented her so badly that she could simply not stand still for fear of toppling over.

Setting out my inkstand and paper on the floor, I sat on my haunches as Midnight had taught me and began a letter to my daughters, Mother, and Fiona, describing the more appalling and amusing aspects of the sea journey. Of Violeta, I said only that she was looking very well and that her house was comfortable.

As I wrote, I added tails, snouts, and paws to my letters, just as Midnight would have. I felt him staring over my shoulder and praising my penmanship as finally worthy of a Bushman.

When Violeta called me down, I found she had laid out her oval sitting-room table with pretty blue and white porcelain—like Mother's, with a windmill pattern.

"I shall never forget her many kindnesses to me," she told me. She took my hand and brought it to her lips. "That is for your mother when you next see her."

I gave her Mama's message of love, then made quick work of a chicken pie that she had been kind enough to purchase for me at a nearby pastry shop.

We were seated at opposite ends of her table, by the windows to her garden. Her yellow curtains were closed tight. She asked questions about my sea voyage in a voice of studied calm, endeavoring to keep her own nervous nature in check.

Standing, she lifted away a corner of the curtain to gaze outside. When she turned back to me, her face was drawn and sad.

Believing I must have offended her with something I'd mentioned about my trip, I said, "Violeta, I shall stop droning on about nothings. Please forgive me. It's just that I'm extremely agitated. I wish to know everything about you coming to America. I want to hear about your life."

She fiddled with the lace of her fichu. "No, no," she said with a frown, as though the very idea of talking about herself was distasteful. "I am certain it would only put you to sleep."

"*Ao contrário,*" I countered. "I would love to hear the story of your travels."

"John, why don't we go for a walk," she proposed in Portuguese.

"A walk? Now?"

"It sometimes helps me. Though you'd have every right to refuse me. You're probably too tired."

She used the formal tense of *you* in addressing me. It was upsetting and I was unable to read her intentions. "No, I'm fine," I assured her, "and a hearty walk might be just the thing. Yes, let's see a bit of the city!"

While she got ready, I took advantage of my time alone to caress open the drawers of a breakfront in her sitting room. I did not know what I hoped to find. At first, I came upon only thread, remnants, and other such nothings. Then, in one of the lower drawers, I discovered an ancient leather ball, the size of a man's fist. It was one of Fanny's—I could still see her jagged teeth marks, as though she had only just made them.

VIOLETA AND I ambled down John Street without speaking, under the shade of cottonwood and horse-chestnut trees. The warm sunlight danced on and off my shoulders.

"Are there many Africans in New York?" I asked Violeta.

"There must be several thousand."

"None are kept as slaves, I hope."

"I've been told that any Negro who was born in New York after 1799 is considered free by birth. Those who were born earlier are still in bondage. Though most, I think, have been sold elsewhere. I confess I'm not sure, but there can't be very many left in the city—a few hundred perhaps."

At Broadway we turned north. I watched the passersby under parasols and the carriages rushing here and there—admired the cleverly painted shop signs, as well.

"It's wonderful, isn't it?" I smiled.

Violeta had walked ahead. "Yes, indeed," she replied matter-of-factly, waiting on me.

Risking being run down by a wagon or trampled by a horse, I stood at the center of Broadway to gaze south at the stone fortress at the tip of the island and the masts of sailing ships beyond. Then I faced the other way and looked out toward a horizon of woods far to the north. *I am in New York now,* I whispered—not only to myself, but to Midnight as well. Making a fist in my pocket, I added, *And nothing can stop me from coming for you. Not even a chance for a new life.*

ON OUR WALK, Violeta asked me no questions at all, and I dared not make further inquiries of her. I grew glum and quiet. Onlookers must have presumed an unhappy marriage. When we reached Grand Street, a popular boulevard of shops perpendicular to Broadway, Violeta said, "I should like to continue on with you, but there are things I need to attend to at home. We'll meet in the afternoon for tea. Shall we say four o'clock?"

Before I could say anything, she rushed off. Cursing her inscrutability, I continued my walk. Curiously, I thought of Lourenço Reis, the necromancer. I suppose that in my childish mind I believed that Violeta had been placed under a wicked spell and that only I might free her.

AT THREE–THIRTY I started back toward home. Violeta had baked a dozen scones during my absence, and the smell was heavenly. Watching me with charmed eyes, she said, "You eat as you always did when your mother was out. Crumbs everywhere."

"Is that good or bad?"

She laughed; our time apart had plainly rekindled her affection for me. "Very good indeed, you evil thing!"

I again asked her to tell me how she had reached New York.

"Not now, it would just spoil our fun," she replied.

We talked instead of events in Portugal and Europe over the past two decades. On her insistence, we spoke in English. I sometimes framed my replies so as to try to learn whether she had maintained a correspondence with her mother and brothers. But she was too clever for me and wouldn't give anything away.

AFTER TEA, I headed upstairs to finish my letter to my family. To my surprise, I discovered a room full of new furniture: a chest of drawers with brass handles, a handsome case clock with lion's feet, two comfortable armchairs in willow-green brocade, and a dark mahogany writing desk on which Violeta had left a note:

John, you will always have a place in my home. And I shall make no claim upon your time while you remain here. It is enough to find you doing so well. After all I have lived through, after so much that I never wish to see again, to find that someone for whom I have nothing but fond affection has become so fine a person ... Well, let us just say that your presence is a gift I had no right ever to expect. Indeed, if you will excuse my emotion, it is the greatest gift I could ever have imagined. Be patient with me. Fondly, Violeta.

THAT NIGHT, I awoke at three in the morning. Venturing down the stairs, I discovered Violeta fast asleep in her chair. I considered waking her so that I could help her up the stairs. Instead, I tiptoed away like a thief to her bedroom door. I planned to hunt through her wardrobe and secretary, to search under her mattress and pillows, but I stayed only a moment; over her bed hung the round tabletop Daniel had carved and left her as his last gift. The likeness to her at its rim was still uncanny, but when I moved closer, I discovered that cuts had been made in her cheeks and eyes. None of the other children's faces had been damaged in the least.

THE NEXT MORN over breakfast, I summoned the courage to tell Violeta about Midnight.

"Was he the small man I sometimes saw you with in the months before I left Porto?"

"Aye, he befriended me after ... after Daniel's death. And after we had ceased being friends. If he hadn't helped me, I'm sure I'd never have lived to adulthood."

I told her then how he and I had watched her from afar in New Square. "He'd prayed for the Hunters in the Sky to help you reach America," I said.

"Then there were two of us praying for that," she replied quietly.

I naturally had to speak of my father's treachery and of the ruination of my parents' marriage. She listened attentively to everything I said, her chin on her fist. Her only movement was to give my hand a firm squeeze when I spoke of my certainty that Mama had ceased loving me for years.

SPEAKING OF MIDNIGHT left me in a state of anxious despair, and I knew I could wait no longer to make my travel plans to Alexandria. I told Violeta that I wished to book my passage immediately, to which she replied in a firm voice, "Yes, it would be wrong for you to let our renewed friendship delay you. We can talk at far greater length—and with greater ease—when you come back and start designing your tile panel."

At a shipping agency on Broadway, I learned that the journey to Alexandria would take only three days if we were blessed with good winds. I signed on to the *Exeter*, a frigate leaving the following day.

That evening, after supper, I told Violeta of my imminent departure. I should have liked to speak of many things before going—of Francisca and the girls most of all. I also wanted her to tell me about her life, but she went pale at the news of my leaving so soon. When I went to comfort her, she told me that the excitement of having me in her home had left her nearly sleepless and she needed to go to bed before she fainted from exhaustion. She pushed my hands away roughly, then apologized.

"Please speak to me," I pleaded. "Tell me what you are thinking."

"I cannot." She moved her hands into a position of prayer. "John, have mercy on me." She slipped out of my grasp and rushed up to her room.

I awoke near one in the morning, having dreamed of Midnight standing before my bed, speaking in sign language with whirling hand gestures. I could understand nothing of what he wanted to tell me.

After a moment, I heard Violeta stepping down the stairs. When I heard her open the back door, I went to my window. By the moonlight, I could see her threading her way through the weeds in her garden. I'd have sworn she was naked.

XXXVII

T HE NIGHT AIR IN VIOLETA'S GARDEN EM-
braced me with its damp warmth as soon as I slipped outside. It was as though I'd entered a liquid dream. I crept in
my bare feet, wearing only my dressing gown. After about
ten paces, I spotted her, sitting on a low wooden bench, gazing up at the sky. Scattered moonlight blanketed her in
leaves of darkness and light. She might have been a goddess
of night. Her long hair shimmered silver and black down her
back. I knew then that I'd been waiting for her to remove her
bonnet not just since the moment of our reunion but ever
since I was eleven. I stood very still, unwilling to compromise her modesty, but she must have heard my breathing,
because she started in fright.

"It's me," I rushed to say. I stepped forward and held my
hands up to apologize. "Just me."

"John, dear God, you nearly made me shriek." She
shook her head and patted the bench next to her. "Quick, sit
here where no one can see you."

She made no attempt to conceal her nakedness. I
dropped down next to her, careful not to brush against her.
She pointed up to the starry sky. "Right there is the Archer,"
she told me. "He can find things, John—even tiny beings

like you and me. So whenever I am feeling unsure of myself, I look for him."

She spoke to me in Portuguese using the informal *you,* as though we were once again intimate friends.

"Midnight said that *all* the stars are hunters," I told her.

With her fingertip, she reintroduced me to the constellations. Then, caressing my cheek with the back of her hand, she said sweetly, "If there is anything I can do to help find Midnight, then you must tell me—anything at all."

The suggestive smoothness of her skin made me shiver. So true to her youthful self was she in the starlight—so forthright and good of heart—that I was left speechless. I was confused: How could I ache with longing nearly every night for my wife and yet feel so fortunate at being near Violeta?

"It is quiet out here in the early morning," she whispered. "One would almost believe we were back at our tarn in Porto."

Facing me, she guessed the cause of my shame and grinned. "John," she said, slapping my thigh, "do not be such a baby. I am not inconvenienced by your desire. The only ally I have ever had among men has been their physical need for me. It is the only thing I've ever been able to trust in them."

"I don't seem to understand anything of what has come to pass in my life," I confessed. "Why Daniel died, how I got to this precise moment, why you and I have again met."

She looked at me gravely. "I have no answers for you. None."

Warm breezes swirled around us. Relief at being with Violeta's old self made me smile. "It's as though we are hiding from our parents."

"My mother will never find me here." She stole a look toward her house. "The weeds are too high for her to see me."

"And the house too dark."

"Night is good for me. I see less then. Let night have its dominion."

"Violeta, except for now, you seem to be wherever I am not."

She took my hands and stood up. "Sing," she pleaded. "Any of the old songs. Please, John, sing for me."

I sang the first verse of "Ae Fond Kiss," her favorite song by Robert Burns: *Ae fond kiss, and then we sever, ae farewell, and then forever. . . .* She gazed away forlornly toward wherever my melody was taking her. "John, you would like me to be the same, but I can never be," she said. "That is why I have been so silent and difficult at times."

"You mistake my wishes. I only want your happiness."

She looked down at me with a pained expression. "John, we come from different worlds. Happiness ceased being my purpose many years ago. Now I merely wish to have my own life. If that means that I must be lonely at times, then it isn't such a high price to pay. Maybe it's no price at all."

"Is that true? Is having your own life really enough?"

"If you were a woman, you would not need to ask that," she declared.

"I cannot believe men and women are so different."

She sighed. "John, if you were me, you would also wear a bonnet all the time—just to keep men's eyes from you. If I were to tell you that there are women my age who dream of their husbands dying young so they might be their own person, so they might have their own property and friends, would you think me mad?"

"Is that true, Violeta?"

Replying with a solemn nod, she said, "Come.... Come with me now and I'll tell you what you've wanted to hear. It's a story that no one but you will ever know."

She led me inside and took a crocheted blanket of green and gold stripes from her sofa, wrapping it tightly around herself. We sat next to each other at her oval table and, by the light of a single candle, she began to tell me of her life since we'd last been friends. She spoke first of working for a chandler in Lisbon and living in a tiny room above his workshop, where she had a view over Graça Square. "I was so happy to be free of my mother and brothers that even my loneliness was a blessing. I belonged only to myself. And my hair"—she gathered her tresses around to her front and breathed in their scent—"grew back. I would let no one cut it."

"Did you know how much I loved you back then?"

"I did. But you were just a small lad. And I was becoming a woman."

"How I wish Daniel had lived. He might have changed everything."

I'd have liked to say much more, but the subject of the past seemed too dangerous.

"Perhaps the dead can be generous," I observed hesitantly. "Daniel might be glad that we've found each other again."

"Perhaps. But others, John—others can be unforgiving.... Let me continue before I lose my courage.

"John, the chandler I worked for was a good man—very clever and kind. Then one day I saw my uncle Tomás in Graça Square. After that, I peeked out of my room and our shop only on rare occasions. He was looking for me, to take me back. He was probably sent by my mother." She shivered and clutched her blanket around her neck. "A few weeks later I was approached by an Englishman promising work at a woolen mill near London. I left with him. Uncle Herbert, I called him. He said that I would be working with other girls from Portugal and Spain. He was kind to me at first."

"But when you arrived in England, you discovered he had lied."

"Yes. I was given frilly new clothes and set to work as a prostitute in Hyde Park. I was sixteen by then. I cannot tell you how many men asked me to call them *Papa*." She laughed. "I learned to say whatever they wanted—*papa, darling, sweetheart*. In English, French, Spanish—even German! Yes, I learned many useful things over those years." She leaned back, seemingly resigned to the way her life had gone.

"Was there any chance of escaping?"

"I thought so. Secretly, I believed myself indomitable, that no one could hold me forever. I was sure that since I had got the better of my uncle and my mother, I would now win my life back. I was so very naive and optimistic. That was something we always had in common, you and I. Not like Daniel. I think he was born knowing damnation, which is perhaps why he fell in love with me."

At that moment, I felt the urge to confess how I'd betrayed him. I knew this was my chance, but when I tried to summon the right words, I found none.

"John, we do not have to speak of these things," she said, sensing my discomfort.

"No, I wish to. More than anything. It's what I've most wanted since my arrival."

"Twice I tried to run. I was beaten so badly by my pimp that I could not walk for a week each time. The second time, he tied me down to my bed and invited men in to use me—chimney sweeps, dustmen..." She wrinkled her nose. "I will tell you a secret—I didn't care so much that they were having their way with me, only that they left me crawling with vermin. After that, I stopped believing in the story I had told myself, of winning against the odds. I wrote a new one, in which triumph lay in making the best of my circumstances. Destiny had made me a whore. So for five years, until I was twenty-one, all I aimed for was to please the men of London. We each need a simple goal, I think. You know, an

English general once told me I had a very soldierly attitude toward my work." She gave a short, brittle laugh. "He meant it as a compliment, John," she added, annoyed that I'd not found it amusing. "Poor sweet John, always trying to protect Violeta. Please, have no regrets on my account—I was good at my work. You know, it just occurs to me that I never once looked up into the night sky in all those years in England. I even came to wonder why I'd made such a fuss about my uncle. And why I'd dreamed of America." She stood up. The candlelight cast an ominous shadow on the wall behind her, as though she were being followed. "No, being a woman was not what I'd thought it would be. But what ever is? And it was better than being a child—much better. You know, John, I can't even say why I murdered him. That seems to me unforgivable. A murderess ought to have a very good reason, don't you think?"

"Murdered who? I don't understand."

"I need some whiskey," she said, licking her lips. "May I fetch you some?"

Once she had filled our drinking glasses, she sat curled over hers, sipping at it like a cat. I said nothing, waiting for her to speak. "Five years after I'd come to England," she began again, "I woke to find a man lying beside me in bed." She gazed down into her glass, then swirled the whiskey with her finger. "He had skin like milk. And fine blond hairs on his arms." She licked her fingertip. "Many Englishmen are like that. But when I awoke beside him, I couldn't remember anything about him or how he came to be there. I believed I was living in Porto and that my uncle had stolen into my room. I grabbed his walking stick. I hit him with it as he slept. I hit him too many times." She raised her imaginary weapon over her head and brought it down with a whack of her hand to the table. "The blood trickled out of his mouth and I kept on hitting him, until his wife was a widow and his lads orphans. When I knew I had killed him, I did not regret it."

"You thought it was Uncle Tomás and that he—"

"No, no, when I saw his blood, I knew he was not my uncle. I remembered his name was Frederick, and that he had a wife and two sons. But I kept on beating him. His death was pleasing to me."

She leaned back and gnawed at her thumbnail. "My pimp took me to Liverpool to escape investigation. I changed my name, and I worked for another two years there—mostly at the docks." She jumped up to refill her glass and mine.

"How did you get away from him?" I asked.

Sitting back down, she said, "Patience, John. I'm just getting to that. One rainy day in early spring, an elegant young woman disembarked from a ship and asked me where she might hire a hackney cab. She spoke with an accent that I recognized, so I answered in Portuguese. We laughed at the coincidence and I ended up accompanying her to her hotel. Her name was Manuela Silveira Dias. She was exactly my age—twenty-three. Her husband was English and they had just moved back from America. He was already living in Newcastle-upon-Tyne with their two children. She'd been obliged to linger behind in Boston and now wanted to contract a governess. Before we separated that evening, she asked if I wanted the job, without even inquiring as to how I made my living." Violeta looked at me incredulously. "Unforgivably irresponsible, don't you think? What did I know of rearing children?"

"She sensed something in you—something kind and purposeful. It's what we all sense."

Violeta scoffed. "No, she just believed in the goodness of people—a bit like you, John. She was Jewish too, you know. Her ancestors had fled Lourenço Reis and his friends."

"What did you tell her?"

"I told her I'd be her governess. She gave me her address. The next night I took a hackney from Liverpool all the way to Manchester. From there, I caught a series of coaches to Newcastle. With only the clothes on my back, I moved into Manuela's home. My room was next to the children's." Tears welled in her eyes. "I had my own bed, and the sheets—Remember when Daniel moved into Senhora Beatriz's home? 'The sheets are smooth as moss!' he told us."

I reached out for her hand, but she pulled it away and sat up stiffly. "I was never found by either the police or my pimp, though I worried constantly they'd discover where I was. John, tell me this—where does remorse live in you?"

I believed she meant to ask me what my deepest regret was. "I wish I'd given solace to my father. It might have changed everything."

"No, *where* is it inside you? Where, John?" To my confused expression, she said, "Mine is in my eyes. When I gaze into a mirror, I see all my regrets staring back at me, as though they are all that I am made of. I tell you this—innocent blood never dries. And I'll tell you something you can tell Midnight about hunting—guilt is the best hunter of all! Living with Manuela's children came to mean everything to me. I could disappear into their world. That is what I have always been trying to do, in one way or another—blend into someone else's life."

"Do you still correspond with them? Have they visited you here?"

"I wrote letters, even though I was told not to. But I never received any reply. Manuela must have burned them."

"Why would she do that?"

Violeta sighed. "When the children were older, Manuela sent them to boarding school. I might have stayed on in her home, but I risked confessing myself to her. We'd been like sisters. I did not tell her all I've told you, but I told her about how I'd earned my keep and intimated that I'd done other wicked things. When I was done, she told me I was to pack my things and leave her home immediately. I rushed to her husband for help, but he locked his door to me. I went down on my knees and begged, but he would not open it."

"He must have been a hard man—to refuse you like that after all your service to his family."

"Hard? He was only protecting his family from a whore and murderess."

"You are much more than that."

"Am I?" she shouted. "Am I really?"

"To me, you are."

"You!" She spit her words at me. "You see me with eyes clouded by a past that is long gone. It is gone, John. And the girl I was is dead! See that clearly before it is too late for you."

She rushed to the doorway to her garden, then turned back, her whole body shaking with urgency. "Do not dare try to comfort me!" She shook her fist at me. "Let me finish, John, so I never have to speak of these things again." Running a hand through her hair, she regained a measure of calm. "Two months later," she said, "while I was working at a brothel near the river in Newcastle, Manuela's husband sent word that he'd arranged work for me as cook and housekeeper to an old American widower named Lemoyne. I could have the job only on the condition that I never seek out their children. Lemoyne owned a dozen apple farms north of New York, along the Hudson River." She gestured around the room. "This was his town house. I worked for him for four years till he died, a little over two years ago. In his will, he gave his farms to his sons. To me, he left this house and a small pension."

"He must have valued your help."

"Yes, my help." She frowned. "And many other things besides."

"When I first arrived, Violeta, you looked frightened. Why was that? Was it because I'm a man?"

"No, John. I thought the police had caught up with me." She shook her head disconsolately. "A part of me has always hoped they'd catch me and punish me for all the evil I've done. I felt that very hope beating softly beneath my fear when I first saw you."

"Violeta, you deserve so much more than you have." I stood up and went to her, but she pushed me away. "You were forced into prostitution," I pleaded. "You were violated and brutalized. Have you forgotten the way they sheared your hair?"

"Only because I told. If I had kept silent . . . It was my fault."

"That's not true," I said. "I'll not let you say such things about—"

She reached up and slapped me with all that was left of her strength. "Get out!" she wailed. "Before it is too late, leave here! I do not want you here. Do you hear me? I've no place for you in my home!"

Knowing I would not leave her, she fell into my embrace, sobbing. I walked her up to her room. As we passed through her doorway, she asked, "Can someone contemptible earn the right to be happy—or to find peace?"

"You are not contemptible. Please don't say that."

She traced her fingertip across my cheek where she'd slapped me. "I am only speaking the truth."

"The man you murdered might be one of the generous dead, like Daniel. Can't you believe that's possible?"

Her eyes opened wide. "John, he had two children. Would you forgive a woman who separated you from *your* two girls?"

IN HER ROOM, I tucked her into bed. When she turned away from me on her side, I gathered up her hair to begin braiding it.

"No, don't touch me. Just tell me a story."

"Is that why you sent Daniel and me away that day in New Square? Did you regard yourself as unworthy of happiness?"

She made no reply. Perhaps because she was not looking at me, I found the courage to confess my betrayal at last. "Then I am unworthy too. Because I betrayed Daniel. I . . . I told him you might leave for America without him. The day we left you forever—the last day of his life. He became distraught. And he was drunk. He ran off to the river."

Violeta turned over to face me. "I tried to save him," I moaned. "I've never tried so hard in my life to do anything. But I let him drown. I wasn't strong enough."

"Is that what you've thought all these years?" she asked, sitting up.

"Yes."

"Oh, John, of all the people who loved Daniel, you did him the least harm. By the time you told him about my leaving for America, I'd already given him fair warning. He knew that I intended to go someday—with or without him."

"But then why did he look so shocked when I told him?"

"Don't you see? He must not have guessed that you knew. He must have felt that I'd betrayed him by telling you. It was my fault, not yours."

"Then I didn't push him into the river?"

"No, John, Daniel jumped. And there was nothing you could have done to save him. Only I . . . only I could have done that."

I closed my eyes and shivered, feeling years of hidden shame leaving me. The world had changed; Daniel had not despised me before his death.

Gratitude for this made me more determined than ever to unburden Violeta of her remorse. "We all deserved so much better," I whispered. "You, me, and Daniel. But we had so little choice back then. There was nothing you could do either—nothing."

She kissed both my cheeks and said, "You're kind, but I cannot go on speaking of the past. I am too tired. Forgive me."

I SLEPT FITFULLY and descended into a dark, shuddering nightmare in which I was locked in the Lookout Tower during a frantic rainstorm. Midnight was nowhere to be seen, but he was speaking in his clicking language from inside my head, as though we had become the same person. When I awoke, I realized that he seemed to be progressively disappearing—at least in body—from even my dreams.

Near five in the morning, I again spotted Violeta in her garden, but I did not go down to her; I did not wish to make parting more difficult for either of us.

At breakfast, I found that I could not eat a thing. I sipped cup after cup of tea and nibbled at some toast and jam simply to make Violeta happy. She tried to make light conversation about the cool weather and other trifling matters. My boat was to leave at the tolling of eleven o'clock. At ten, my agitation was such that I wished to shatter all the windows in the house. Instead, I stood up to take her leave.

"But I shall accompany you to the wharf," she said anxiously, as though there were no question of her remaining behind.

Even her wretched white bonnet was dear to me now. "I could not bear to wave to you from aboard ship," I confessed. "Please, let us say good-bye here."

I held her close until she could smile when I tickled her chin. Her last words to me were: "John, my fondness for you is so deep that I shall save you from myself. You must not fall in love with me. And if you already are, then I beg you to use this voyage to turn your heart away from me."

They say that suffering hardens us to life, but I felt then, looking into her jade eyes, that we had both been broken by it.

XXXVIII

WE MADE SLUGGISH SAIL AND TOOK FIVE DAYS to arrive in Alexandria. The town was more rustic than I'd expected, though it did boast many handsome residences and countinghouses. I had never seen such a concentration of black people before, and though many wore ragged clothing while working as shop assistants and laborers, several individuals I passed were smartly dressed. I believed this boded well for Midnight and was pleased to see such signs of prosperity.

I found lodging at Harper's Boarding House, a wooden mansion on Fairfax Street, not far from the port.

My first destination after depositing my things was King Street, a busy main road running east–west through the city. According to the letters from Captain Morgan, it was here that the apothecary named Miller who had purchased Midnight maintained his shop prior to his death from yellow fever. I was hoping that a son, daughter, or wife might be able to give me some information.

On finding the address in question, I learned it was now Reading's Estate Agency.

I sat by Mr. Reading's desk and told him my story. Hoping that any added information I could give him might bring me closer to my goal, I mentioned that my friend might have been known in Alexandria as Tsamma, which had been his original name. "Tsamma is a kind of melon that grows in the desert," I observed. "During the droughts, the people and animals of Africa drink its plentiful juice."

Mr. Reading lit his cigar. From within a cloud of smoke, he raised his furry eyebrows and said, "A kind of melon?"

"Aye, that's right."

He fought to restrain his mirth, then, failing in this Herculean effort, laughed with such force that he nearly toppled from his chair.

Seeing my displeasure, Mr. Reading sat up straight and said with renewed seriousness, "I do apologize, Mr. Stewart. It's just that a melon . . ." He cleared his throat. "Now, returning to your inquiry, I must tell you that the Africans are generally given good Christian names when they arrive at our market. Your Midnight may be called Washington, Adams, Jefferson, or Jackson by now."

As for the Miller family, the estate agent had never met them. There had been an interim owner of the house, a ship's carpenter by the name of Barrow, but he had no idea where Mr. Barrow lived or if Mr. Miller had had children or a wife.

"Now," said he, funneling the smoke through his fleshy lips toward the ceiling, "did your nigger have any scars or marks?"

He used this word *nigger* so easily that I started.

"None that I recall, except for a small nick on his brow."

"Was he branded?"

"Good God, I hope not."

"Well, could you describe him?"

"He was a small man, five feet or so in height, with handsome bronze skin, and a broad flat nose, very dignified, with—"

"A broad flat nose, you say?"

When I confirmed this, he grinned. His rudeness was bringing out the Highlander in me. "So, Mr. Reading, what have I said this time to cause such hilarity?" I snarled.

"All the saltwater niggers have broad flat noses, Mr. Stewart."

" 'Saltwater'?"

"From Africa."

"Mr. Reading, they are all from Africa, I would have presumed."

"In that you are quite wrong, sir. Some are bred locally. Most, in fact, as the slave trade was halted by a damnable act of Congress some fifteen years ago. Most of our niggers were born right here in the United States. And I'm afraid, sir, that you'll have to arm me with a better description of yours if I am to help you spook him from his hole."

SICKENED BY THE ease with which Mr. Reading spoke so crudely about Negroes, I thanked him and took my leave. I spent the rest of that morning on the sagging mattress of my hotel room drawing Midnight. This proved much harder than I would have thought, no doubt owing to the stifling heat, which obliged me to strip off my clothes and sit panting by my window for the frail wisps of breeze coming in from the ocean.

My sketch captured his puckish side, which is why, I suppose, so many of the people I showed it to later that day said, "Oh, you've got quite a rascal there, haven't you!"

At first, I took this as an endearment. Only slowly, when several frowned disagreeably, did I begin to understand that they meant something akin to ne'er-do-well. I was forced to conclude that a great many people in Alexandria had such feeble imaginations that they could not conceive of a high-spirited African as anything but an affront or threat.

To no avail, I spent the rest of the afternoon showing my sketch to more than twenty shopkeepers along King Street and Washington Street.

A quick-talking carpenter named Friedlander did finally recall that Mr. Miller had a daughter named Abigail. A half hour after our talk, he tracked me down at Hall's Dry Goods and said that he now remembered that Mrs. Abigail Miller Munson lived on Queen Street. Indeed, he had already confirmed that she was presently at home. Taking the address and giving my thanks, I rushed away.

MRS. MUNSON'S WOODEN house was painted in pleasant tones of cream and pink. Upon answering my knocks, she smiled with endearing modesty and led me through double doors into her sitting room, offering me the place of honor at the end of her rose-colored sofa.

Abigail Munson was thirty, I would have guessed, though the worry lines on her forehead made me consider that she'd had a hard life. Her eyes were clear and kind, and her movements—quick but careful—indicated that she was probably the mother of little children.

Large, colorful maps of the American colonies hung on the walls in gilded frames, which I admired while she poured coffee into cups of crimson-glazed porcelain. When I lifted my cup to have a closer look, she said worriedly, "I do hope there's nothing wrong."

"No, no—it's just that I'm a tile-maker and potter. And your porcelain is lovely."

"What a kind thing to say, Mr. Stewart, thank you," she said in her lilting voice. "My husband imported this set from France for me. It was one of my wedding presents."

Mrs. Munson took a dainty sip and then explained to me that Mr. Friedlander had been less than honest with me at first, owing to my manners and accent, both of which had been described to her as downright vexing. Thinking better of his judgment, he had then sent a clerk to her home to ask if he might give the Scotsman her name. She had agreed to see me, since she welcomed the chance to meet a foreigner and had nothing to hide. "Of late, we in the South have been so vilified in the Northern press that you will have to forgive us if we are less than fully hospitable."

"Most understandable, under the circumstances."

I explained the purpose of my visit and thanked her for seeing me. She was eager to have a look at my sketch. When I unfurled it for her, she said, "Why, I do indeed remember that face! Midnight, you say. I do not believe my father called him that." She looked out her window to the garden. "Though I cannot recall just now. Samuel—might it have been Samuel?"

"In Africa, he was called Tsamma. Perhaps it was changed to the European name most phonetically similar."

She leaned toward me, her eyes radiant. "I am sure now, it was Samuel. But it must be at least fifteen years ago."

"Seventeen, I believe."

"I was a girl when he came. My father needed an assistant. A friend of his suggested this man Samuel. As I recall, he was a mute. That was a shock to us all."

"Mute? No, the man I'm searching for spoke quite well. At least, when—"

I might have continued, but the possibility of his having had his vocal chords cut by slave-traders chilled me to silence.

"I can see this is difficult for you. Would you like more coffee?" she asked.

"No, thank you. Mrs. Munson, when your father passed away, Samuel was sold. At least, that was what I was told. Do you know where he was taken?"

"I'm afraid not."

"Or who purchased him?"

"I don't believe I was ever told."

"Would anyone recall?"

"I have two brothers, sir, but they are both considerably younger. They were just boys. I don't think either would know. But I will ask."

"I'd very much appreciate that." Though I smiled, I was unable to hide my disappointment.

"Mr. Stewart, I'm sorry I've been of so little help," she said sweetly. "I wish there was more I could do."

"Is there anyone else you know who may have taken an interest in Samuel?"

"I do not think so. He worked in the back room of Father's workshop. No one saw him."

"And was he in good spirits, you'd say?"

"Yes, I believe so. Though he kept to himself. He was able to write and often did so in a memorandum book. I remember that clearly. Once, he wrote me a poem. Though I cannot recall what it said. It was most unusual to see a Negro writing, as you can imagine."

"And the book he wrote in, do you have it?"

"No, I'm afraid I must disappoint you again. I cannot imagine where it's gone."

"I . . . I taught him to write."

"Did you?" she beamed. "How clever of you!"

"He was the clever one." I shaded my eyes with my hand to hide my emotion.

She came swiftly to me as though to comfort a fallen child. In imploring tones, she said, "Oh, Mr. Stewart, no matter what you have been told, no matter what you have read, not all of us are dead to feeling with regard to the slaves. I myself have two good friends of the Negro race, more valuable than any other property I have ever owned. They have been of incalculable help to me in raising my children. Mr. Stewart, I beg you to understand. Many of us can plainly see that slavery is wrong not only for the Negro but for the white race as well. It is an evil."

When she dabbed at the corner of her eye with a lace handkerchief plucked from her sleeve, it struck me that she was acting—and had been from the very beginning.

"The slave trade is a terrible thing," she declared. "I believe that with all my heart. But it is too late for us." She hung her head in sorrow and took a deep calming breath. "Slavery has been with us these past two centuries. It would be suicide to end such a tradition. In the North, there is industry and all the wealth it provides. Here, with our tobacco farms and small port, we could not make do without the labor of the Negro. That is what the editors of the North fail to comprehend." She clasped her hands together as though to recite a fervent prayer. "We would perish without our traditions and our values. They are the ark we ride in. And yet the Northerners would wish to see us drown in a sea of blood. I do not believe that a Scotsman, of a race that has suffered for so long under the English, can see that as fair."

MRS. MUNSON AGREED to send word to my boardinghouse of any helpful information that might be given her by her brothers. I left her house confused, wondering whether any of what I'd seen and heard had been genuine.

That evening, rain came down in dark, thunderous sheets, fanfared by lightning. Closing my eyes and recalling the first time Midnight left our home in Porto to follow a storm, worry consumed me. I spent the next hour hunched over my desk, writing again to my children. I told them that Alexandria was a beautiful city with a handsome wharf and that I was doing well. I also apologized again for leaving them and said that I would be back as soon as possible. I wrapped up two pairs of filigree silver earrings that I'd purchased at a jewelry shop that afternoon—roses for Esther and bells for Graça—and placed them carefully in the envelope.

After picturing them wearing my gifts, I began another note, this one to my wife:

> *Dearest Francisca, I am in a land where I know no one and am besieged by doubts. The Americans mostly either lie to me or ridicule me, and I sometimes have no idea what their intentions are. In my nightmares I am unable to understand Midnight—or even myself. You once told me that you would come with me anywhere, and I wish you were here with me now. But we are so powerless to protect those we love. I see that now more clearly than ever, and it is what most scares me when I wake in the morning. Then, I feel...*

As I dipped my pen in my inkstand, it seemed pointless to add any more lines to a letter that would never be posted or read. I crumpled what I'd written and set my flint to it, then threw it into the fireplace and watched the flames separate me from Francisca again.

THE NEXT MORNING, the proprietress of the boardinghouse, Mrs. Van Zandt, suggested that I take my drawing of Midnight to the Slave Pen, where thousands of blacks were transported to Charleston and other Southern cities each year. "Though if you are looking for a nigger yourself," she confided, "then you'd be better off at a private auction—the prices are much more reasonable."

I was expecting a prison of colossal proportions, but it was only a three-story brick building painted a dusty tan. Its side yards were enclosed by high whitewashed walls that were spiked on top with nasty-looking shards of glass. Though unable to see over, as they were a good ten feet in height, I could hear the subdued conversations of the Negroes awaiting shipment and the morose clanging of heavy chains.

A slender, gray-haired man in striped trousers was standing in the doorway to the countinghouse, slicing a golden apple with a short knife. I introduced myself and learned his name—Coleman. He generously offered me a piece of his fruit, which I accepted. I then invented a story about Midnight designed to elicit a more positive reaction than I'd received from Mr. Reading: I was looking for a former servant of mine who had just inherited several hundred dollars from his father, a freed Negro who had been employed at my New York household. The man I wanted to find had been a slave in Alexandria but was sold elsewhere some seventeen years earlier. There would be a reward of fifty silver dollars for any person who might lead me to him. I asked if I might show Mr. Coleman my drawing.

He pointed his knife toward one of the side yards. "Ya know how many nigger bucks I've sold in Alexandria over the last seventeen years? I'd wager fifty thousan' or more. So Mr. Stewart"—and here he squinted at me as though peering into a beam of light—"ya don't truly think I'm fool enough to remember your Midnight, do ya?" He smiled maliciously.

"I was only hoping you might recognize—"

"We ain't runnin' no asylum, ya know."

"If you would do me the favor of just taking a look," I said, unscrolling my drawing.

"Ugly rascal," said Mr. Coleman, cutting another slice of apple. Then he looked up into the sky, in no particular hurry to comment. "Don't look like it, but we'll have sun today. That's a good thing." Mischief was dancing in his eyes when he looked back at me. "Know why?"

When I shook my head, he said, "You know anything 'bout turkeys, Mr. Stewart?"

"Our neighbor had a turkey named Marigold when I was a lad. She was—" I was about to say *a sweet thing* but realized he would only mock me. I said rather foolishly, "She was large."

"Well, Mr. Stewart, when it rains, your Marigold and all her friends point their heads up toward the sky and open their beaks. They're so goddamned ornery and bone-stupid that they can drown that way." He pointed toward the yard. "Niggers ain't got any more sense than turkeys. You can quote me on that. Yesterday, with all the rain, we had one buck drown in the mud. Don't ask me how. That's how stupid they are. He lost me six hundred dollars or more. So, Mr. Stewart, it's better for my business when we have sun. And it'd be better for you if you forget about your Noonday Bell. He's long gone. Prob'ly drowned in some mud somewheres."

XXXIX

MY ENCOUNTER AT THE SLAVE PEN SO UPSET
me that I marched away in my rage toward a horizon of
trees in the distance. I soon reached a neighborhood where
Negro families were living on their own, in squat houses
separated by overgrown lots. Two young lasses—no more
than four and seven, I would guess—were playing up ahead,
the larger rolling a rusted metal hoop, the smaller skipping.
Both wore pretty pink ribbons in their closely cropped hair.
I realized with a jolt that I had not seen a white person in
several blocks. Furthermore, I was being stared at by several
blacks sitting on porches, and now even by the girls themselves.

I walked toward the *kelpies.* Smiling, I said, rather too eagerly, "My, you two are lovely girls. Are you sisters?"

They looked at each other, startled by my accent, most
likely. The littler of the two dropped a smooth ivory pebble
that had been hidden in her hand. Then, without warning,
the larger girl shrieked at the top of her lungs. I jerked my
hands up to protect my ears while she grabbed her sister's
hand and raced off. They ran to an old tilted house partially
hidden behind a broad oak, fifty paces ahead. Once they'd
reached the safety of the porch, the older one leaned over the

railing and gave me a hard look. Her tiny sister, sucking her thumb, looked curious.

After a moment, a wide-hipped woman wearing a blue head scarf charged out the front door. The older girl pointed at me as though I were a bandit.

"Madam," I called, "I was just asking the girls if they were sisters."

She made several furious hand gestures. Then she gathered up her children and marched into her house, banging the door closed.

"YOU'S MADE AN enemy of Aunt Carolyn Gold, so you's in a right bit a twisted trouble."

When I turned toward this voice, my mouth dropped open: Standing on the rickety porch of a whitewashed house was an elderly woman in trousers and a waistcoat of homespun. Since she wore no shirt under the waistcoat, her bare shoulders and belly were plainly visible. I should have guessed her to be about seventy years of age, as her hair was gray and her posture stooped, yet her glassy black eyes were youthful and her cheeks as smooth as velvet. I found her stunningly beautiful, but alarming as well, rather as though she had materialized out of a long-forgotten dream.

"She's gonna work a deep spell on ya, chile—so deep ya gonna look up to look down. She once sank a ship in the harbor, and four men ain't gonna tell us what it felt like 'cause their mouths ain't never come up to the surface."

"I expect I ought to apologize to her."

" 'Pologize? To that varmint?"

She frowned and flapped a hand by her ear to chase away a fly. "Come on up here, chile," she said, taking pity on me and waving me over. "Ya gonna need my help."

After kneeling to pick up the polished stone dropped by the younger of the two girls, I made my way up her stairs to her patio. She whistled and gazed on me admiringly. "You tall, young man—darn tall! I'm Mary Wright. But most ever'body jus' call me Moon Mary. 'Cept my chil'ren."

I told her my family name was Stewart but asked that she call me John.

"If ya don' min', I'm gonna keep the devil from snappin' at me and call ya Mr. Stewart."

I placed the white pebble on the railing of her porch and asked if she'd mind returning it to the younger sister, explaining that she had dropped it.

Moon Mary picked it up and sniffed it. "You saved this for her? Why ya carin' what that girl leaves on some nigger street?"

"Little girls drop things and invariably wish to have them back. I know—I have two daughters of my own."

"You's in trouble, chile. 'Cause I don't need much eyesight at all to tell me you's a long ways from home, and you's got that varmint Carolyn Gold conjurin' powerful on ya, and she don't take kindly to no one fright'nin' off them princesses a hers. Now, I don't us'ally meddle in nobody else's business, but seein' as how ya got youssful in a fix, and seein' as how you returned that pebble . . . Wait right where ya are, chile." She pointed a crooked finger at me. "And don't you go fright'nin' nobody else."

She stepped into her house, waddling a bit like a duck, and returned momentarily with a brown and white jug containing a pint of green liquid.

"Drink this," she said, handing the jug to me. When I asked what it was, she snapped, "Jus' ya drink it, chile. 'Tain't poison. Or would ya prefer helpin' Carolyn Gold by doin' nothin', 'cause she don't mind none if ya make her spell set inside ya easier."

I lifted her brew to my lips. It tasted sour. She snorted at my reticence. "Stubbornness done taken ya pris'ner, chile. Now, that's just lemon and mint and a few other things b'sides. No spell can beat my med'cine once it's grabbed a holda ya."

It was sugary, and there might have been pepper in it as well. It burned my throat.

"Now, that wa'n't so bad, was it, Mr. John?"

"No, it was good in a way," I croaked out of politeness.

When I remarked that she was now using my first name, she snapped, "Never min' that!" Snatching my hand, she spun me in circles four times, mumbling to herself in what must have been an African language. Finally, she had me bend down in front of her and pressed a finger into my forehead. Later, I discovered a dot of ashes there.

"You's lost, ain't ya, Mr. John?" she said, squinting. " 'Cause ya sure as hell look lost."

I told her what had happened at the Slave Pen, which obliged me to explain my hunt for Midnight. When I'd finished, she licked her lips as though tasting something good and said, "You's gonna find him. I'm right sure of that." When I asked why, she said, " 'Cause ya got a hole in ya. So ya ain't gonna give up."

"And what if Midnight is long dead himself?"

"I'll tell you this, Mr. John, people find whatever's there for them to find, if ya know what I mean. That's the way this life works." She slapped her belly and said, "If ya don't mind me sayin', you's goin' at this all wrong, chile—asking on King Street and at that hor'ble Pen. Them white folks ain't gonna know where your friend Midnight is at. So ya gotta ask us right here where we live."

"This neighborhood of yours . . . do your owners let you live here in exchange for caring for their houses?"

"We's free here. This is the Bottoms." To my bewilderment, she replied, "It's simple, chile. Some of us have bought our freedom. Others were given it by their masters."

"Bought it how?"

"From the work we do on Sundays."

"And this house of yours, do you own it?"

"I bought it from the Quakers. They's the ones that help us here."

"And you're completely free?"

"Well, I don' know nothin' 'bout *completely.* I got the papers, sure enough, but how can I be completely free when my babies ain't? You know a Negro mother who's ever that free?"

She told me that of her three children, only her eldest son, William, had escaped slavery. He'd run away to Boston, where he worked as a cooper. She had not seen him in forty-three years and had not heard a word from him in fifteen. Her younger children, a girl and a baby boy, had been sold to a local slave-trader, who'd taken them to Charleston.

"Might be as far away as N'O'leans by now," she said.

"If you haven't been able to find them, then what chance do I have to find Midnight?"

"Ya listen up, Mr. John. A white man with a mem'ry . . ." She whistled loudly and shook her head. "A white man with a mem'ry is a pow'ful creature. I can see now that you got Midnight right inside ya. He's there. He's protectin' ya against the likes a Carolyn Gold and ever'thin' else. I see him plain."

I thought of Midnight giving me his body heat when I had been made ill by Hyena.

Then she said something I'll never forget: "Don' ya worry, Mr. John.

Midnight left part of himself in ya. And you's on a holy journey to find him. As sure as you were goin' to Jerusalem to see Jesus Himself."

SO IT WAS that I ended up showing my drawing around the Bottoms neighborhood that afternoon. The residents I spoke to were friendly, but no one recognized him. Hot and sweaty, I made my way back to the boardinghouse, where I doused myself from head to toe and shaved.

After dozing off, I woke to flies buzzing in circles by my head as though searching for a way into my ears. The light outside was hazy. Sunset was settling in gold and pink. Bells soon tolled eight o'clock. I wondered if I would always feel so alone in America. Then I drank the water left in my glass and stumbled out to visit a tavern by the port, hoping that the cool breeze there might give me back my energy. In front of a clothing shop on Prince Street, two white men approached me, the older dressed in a fine ruffled shirt. The more youthful of the two was pale and blond, with bright blue eyes. He was just a lad, surely no more than twenty.

"You must be Stewart," the older man said confidently.

With relief, I realized they must have been sent by Abigail Munson with some information about Midnight. Smiling with gratitude, I replied, "Indeed I am, sir. And you must be one of dear Mrs. Munson's younger brothers."

I reached out my hand, but he did not take it.

"Have you made plans to leave Alexandria yet?" he asked gruffly.

"No, sir, I have not. And if you will excuse me..." I tipped my hat.

The older man put out a hand to stop me. "Jim, you best have a go at him," he said to the youth.

At that, Jim punched his fist into my gut. Badly winded, I fell to my knees. A harsh blow to the back of my head introduced my face to the cobbles. I cannot say how long I was lost to the world, but I remember that a kindly white gentleman came to my aid and helped me to stand. My attackers had long since fled. Though my head was throbbing, I denied being in any discomfort, and I was grateful that no permanent damage had been done.

Despite a certain dizziness, I trudged on to a tavern at the port, where I downed a bottle of poor-quality Madeira. After that, I staggered back to my hotel, hoping that sleep would rid me of my thoughts of defeat.

* * *

IN THE MORNING, still feeling fragile, I ate bread and warm milk at a nearby coffeehouse. Upon returning, Mrs. Van Zandt informed me that I had two visitors waiting in the garden.

"One is a nigger buck, so you will have to meet him outside. I am sorry, but those are my rules." She glared at me, plainly incensed.

Standing on a brick patio at the back of the house was a broad-shouldered black man in a handsome green velvet coat. Talking in hushed tones with him was a thin, elderly white man in a worn linen shirt and trousers. They smiled as I approached, as though heartily relieved to see me. The black man was missing an earlobe, and his eyes were like yellow moons. He introduced himself as Hussar Morgan, and he had a very powerful handshake. The white man was named John Comfort.

They knew my name already.

"I'd ask you to my room, but Mrs. Van Zandt will not allow it," I said apologetically.

"We are aware of her rules," Mr. Comfort replied. "Patience is an important virtue in Alexandria, as thee hath surely learned by now."

Seeing my surprise at his antiquated vocabulary, he explained that he was a Quaker.

"May I see your drawing of Samuel?" Mr. Morgan requested. "I believe I may know him."

After retrieving my sketch from my room, I opened it for him eagerly. He studied it for only a few seconds, then said with assurance, "Yes, sir, that's Samuel all right."

"Did he ever speak of me? Of John?"

"No, I'm sorry, the man I knew was mute."

"You are the second person to tell me that, sir. But unless he suffered some terrible accident, it would seem impossible."

"Mr. Stewart, I assure you he never spoke in my presence."

"I believe you. It's just that . . . Might a slave-trader have cut his vocal cords?"

"No, I don't think so. There was no scar on his neck."

"Thank God for that. Tell me, was he in good spirits?"

"I did not know him well. He seemed—how shall I put it?—he seemed resigned. He was not sad, but if I were a religious man," he continued, looking at Mr. Comfort, "I would say there was a piece of his soul missing."

"And do you know what became of him?"

"After Mr. Miller passed away, Samuel was sold to a slave-trader—a local man named Burton, who worked for a dealer from Baltimore by the name of Woolfolk. Mr. Burton died . . . well, it must be over ten years ago. I was told at the time that Samuel had been forced aboard a ship bound for Charleston."

I asked, "How did you come to know him, Mr. Morgan?"

"I was a gardener at the time for a wealthy family. Samuel would help me on Sundays. He was most fond of plants and flowers. And then, when this happened"—he flicked his finger at his missing earlobe—"he treated the wound for me."

"Did you meet with an accident, sir?"

Mr. Morgan laughed and said it was a trifling story not worth repeating. His Quaker friend replied cryptically, "Alexandria is a town of many accidents," and would say no more.

"And if you will excuse my curiosity, how did you learn of my presence in your city?"

"It was Moon Mary," Mr. Comfort replied. "She asked that I help thee. And Hussar is an old friend."

Mr. Morgan handed me back my sketch. "If I may speak plainly, sir, you are not safe here. People are saying that you are an English mischief-maker and a fervent opponent of the slave trade."

When I explained my ancestry, Mr. Comfort said, "Scottish or not, I have taken the liberty of booking thee a berth on a ship leaving this very morning for Charleston. And I would beseech thee to consider departing sooner rather than later."

"If Midnight is not here, then there's nothing to keep me. Thank you for looking out for me." I handed both Mr. Morgan and Mr. Comfort cards on which I'd written Violeta's address. "In the event you learn anything more of Samuel, please send a letter to me care of this friend."

"May thee find Samuel in Charleston," Mr. Comfort said gently.

Mr. Morgan seconded this wish, shook my hand, and added, "And may you find that he is no longer mute."

XL

You's Dead Even If
You's Alive

AFTER MY PAPA DISAPPEARED AND MASTER
Edward Roberson had me abducted from River Bend in
March, he had some white men take me to his brother's infernal cotton plantation. It was up-country a ways, near Co-
lumbia, and I worked my fingers bloody there for seven of
the slowest months in history. Those days and nights were
made of warm molasses. And they had everything wrong
stuck to them, including me.

I worked right on through the first three weeks of harvest
time, up till early September. I was smelly as a skunk most of
the time—addlebrained too—because Papa was gone and
Mamma was dead. And caring for cotton is even worse on
your spirit than it is on your back.

I learned then that sadness can get so powerful that it
owns you even more than the Master does.

Master Edward took me up there because he thought my
papa might wait a couple of months for tempers to settle,
then sneak back into River Bend to rescue me.

I guess I couldn't rightly see how bringing me to that
plantation was going to foil Papa's plans forever. Presuming
he was still alive and had any. Because he'd surely find out
where I was if he snuck into River Bend and asked any of the

slaves. But I hadn't given Edward enough credit for wickedness. What he did just about outdid even himself. Because he called all the house and field slaves together and told them in a solemn voice that I'd been rushed out of the Big House in the night to a hospital in Charleston shivering *like a poor little cricket.* Then, three days later, with worry creasing everybody's brows and Lily squeezing on that brass cross around her neck like it had my life inside, Edward put on the most grief-stricken face he'd ever made and told everyone I was dead from the ague.

It might have been nice to have some soft velvet on the interior of my coffin, but I had to settle for a pine box. My friends put me in the ground in the slave cemetery down by Christmas Creek. Inside my coffin, Master Edward must have stashed my weight in dirt wrapped in cloth, and maybe some old cheese too, because everybody told me later that I'd stunk so bad that Crow and some of the others had to hold their noses. Edward refused to open the lid, which was nailed closed, because he said my body was eaten up something horrible by disease.

This plan worked just like he hoped, because about two months later a mulatto man stole into River Bend one night when Master Edward was gambling in Charleston and asked after me. Two of the field slaves told him that I was dead from the ague and already buried.

The mulatto crept in and out real quick, like a shadow at sundown.

I hoped that my papa was still somewhere nearby and might have sent someone there to get me out, or, if he was up North and earning wages, paid someone to come rescue me.

MASTER EDWARD HAD me brought back to River Bend in the middle of September. He reckoned that my father, if he was hiding somewhere, had heard by now that I was dead. You could see in his flashing eyes how much evil pleasure it gave him to think that he had fooled everyone.

After a couple of weeks at River Bend, he even let me start going again to Charleston to do our marketing and buy plants.

You ought to have seen the faces on everybody when I came back to River Bend and got out of the carriage in front of the piazza. Lily ran out shrieking from the kitchen. "Morri girl, Morri girl!" She fell to her knees mumbling prayers, thanking the Lord for delivering me from death. Then she wrapped me in her big old hug, taking turns kissing her cross and me. When she let go, Weaver stared at me as if I was a ghost. I took his hand, and he let out one of his big laughs, lifting me up onto his back like I was a little girl wanting a horsy ride. When he finally let me down and I stopped laughing, he asked me what heaven was like, and if it was pretty up there. "Heaven?" I said. "Heaven ain't got nothing to do with Middle Country South Carolina, best I can figure out. If it does, then I just as soon go to hell next time."

Later, when we were alone on the piazza, Weaver said something I thought pretty darn intelligent: "I guess when the white folks say you's dead, you's dead even if you's alive."

I RECKON THE truth can kind of sneak up on you slowly, just like tragedy. Because it took another four months back at home for me to see that getting clean away from River Bend wasn't all I wanted. No, ma'am. Not when Master Edward could decide that any of us was dead, any old time he liked.

I got some much bigger notions once we celebrated Lily's sixty-fifth birthday. That afternoon, Edward the Cockerel bit into the slice of cake we'd saved for him and cracked a tooth on a ceramic shard. From his hollering and stamping around, we knew he was going to make good on his threats and find another cook. "I always said she was gonna poison me, that prune-faced nigger!" he kept on shouting. He might have had Lily whipped, but she ran off and hid down by Christmas Creek till he calmed himself down.

When I asked her about her clumsiness the next day, she pointed to her eyes.

"They're getting worse?" I asked.

"Morri baby," she said, chomping on her gums, "I can jes' see shapes outta de lef' one. But de right one's still pretty darn good, I think. You go on an' test me now."

I stepped five paces from her and asked her how many fingers I was holding up. I wasn't holding up any, mind you. She squinted for a while, then said, "Dree."

"Looks like that good right eye is doing all the seeing for you, sure enough," I replied cheerfully.

So it wasn't much of a surprise when the new cook arrived one day. Her name was Marybelle. She was about twenty-five, I'd have guessed, skinny as a blade of grass, with a big smile that made you tingle. I liked her right away. True, she talked too much, but she was right observant.

She came to the conclusion that all Lily needed was a proper pair of spectacles and she could go on cooking for another ten years at least. Marybelle had a good heart, and she put up with all our meanness over those first weeks without a single complaint. We treated her bad because of her coming to replace Lily, you understand.

When you consider that she'd already had two children and that both had been dragged off to God knows where, you knew how strong that girl was just to keep on waking up every day. We never questioned her about where her husband was. Something in her face told us not to.

When I asked Master Edward if I could take Lily to Charleston to purchase the spectacles she needed to keep from killing us with bits of pottery, he glared at me like I'd lost my senses. "Buy Lily spectacles? Morri, I ain't gonna spend a penny more on that old sow now that Marybelle's here. Not after all the money I just spent without any guarantee."

No guarantee of what? I wanted to ask, but he was angry and I kept quiet.

Crow and I pieced together the answer to that question from all he overheard in the sitting room. And what we learned was that there was a sticky complication to Marybelle's purchase. We might then and there have suspected something bad was going to happen, but I guess because she was still so new to us we weren't considering her well-being just yet.

Master Edward had paid five hundred and fifty dollars for her to a planter named Philip Fiore, but Mr. Fiore had the sale stamped without what Edward called "any warrant as to her soundness." This was owing to his having bought her without such a guarantee himself. Not that he thought of her as damaged goods. No, sir. He swore that she was in darn good health except for the rheumatism in her left shoulder.

But not six weeks after Marybelle started work in the kitchen, just about the time we stopped being cold to her for coming along to replace Lily, she began complaining of aches in her belly. I treated her with teas that helped some, but not enough. Lily thought she might have been with child, but she denied lying with a man over the past six months.

I looked at Weaver when she told us that, because he was right sweet on her. He shook his head real quick to say that he hadn't been with her in that way, though I could see he was intending it. He was a born rogue, that one.

Marybelle moved in with me, into my little side room by the kitchen, so I could care for her. She was suffering most of the time something terrible and hardly ever slept. I don't know how, but she kept on cooking the whole time for Master Edward, Mistress Kitty, and the children. She was a whole lot stronger than she looked, I'll tell you that.

Edward the Cockerel finally figured he'd better do something drastic if he was to save her. So he took Marybelle to Dr. Lydell over in Charleston. He brought her around to another physician, and then another. By the time all those white men were done poking and probing, two days of misery had passed and she was begging to come home to drink some more of my teas. Finally, after more pressing and pulling, those physicians told Edward she had two *schirrous* tumors in her ovaries the size of oranges.

Nobody around here knew what a schirrous tumor was, but if they were as big as oranges we knew that Marybelle wasn't going to be with us much longer.

Dr. Lydell told Master Edward that Marybelle's tumors must have been growing in her for at least a year, judging from their volume. What that meant was that by the time she'd been bought from Philip Fiore, she'd already been carrying them in her belly for a good long while.

"That bastard Fiore!" Master Edward exploded. "I'll get my money back or I'll kill him."

No, he wasn't about to stand for paying five hundred and fifty dollars for a nigger cook with rotting oranges inside her.

But when he demanded his money back, Mr. Fiore insisted on taking poor Marybelle to see two more physicians of his own choosing. They came to River Bend after examining her up and down to tell Edward what they'd found. Since Mr. Fiore was the one paying them, nobody was much surprised to learn later from Crow that they swore her tumors were brand-new. Even if that wasn't the case, they held that no one could be sure how long they'd been in Marybelle without what they called a "pathological dissection." And so Master Edward could not justly ask for his money to be returned. Unless . . .

"Unless," Edward the Cockerel went on to suggest, "you go ahead and do your dissection. Then you'll see I'm right."

We listened to Crow tell us about the heated quarrel that they all then had and the decision that was reached. They were going to settle the matter by cutting open Marybelle's belly and peering inside. Then they'd sew her up and send her on her way.

Maybe we weren't evil enough to understand. Because it turned out that they couldn't leave the oranges inside Marybelle. No, ma'am, they had to take them out to inspect them.

Instead of having to operate while Marybelle screamed and made a general fuss, they decided it would be much better to "put the poor nigger-girl out of her misery."

We only learned what they'd done after they'd murdered Marybelle. Likely it was arsenic, since that's a word Crow heard Dr. Lydell use, though Crow called it *senick,* not knowing what it was.

They dissected her still warm, according to Dr. Lydell. One surgeon from each side of the quarrel worked away at her belly with their knives. Marybelle had to be warm, you understand, so they could get the tumors out in a good state. Anyone who knows anything about doctoring would know that, they told Master Edward.

In the end, both sides agreed that the tumors taken from Marybelle were too well-formed and had created too many other littler growths in her belly to have been there only for a couple of months. So in the end Mr. Fiore had to return to Master Edward his five hundred and fifty dollars, though he was allowed to deduct the dollar and a half it cost to haul away the shredded body. It had to be disposed of in a special place, because by now it was filled up with arsenic.

Master Edward was right pleased with himself and walked around River Bend with a smile all that day, fanning the bills against his hand.

A week later I asked him again if I could take Lily to town to purchase new spectacles, and this time he agreed. But I wasn't going just for that. Not now. Because after we found out that Marybelle had been cut open still warm, I'd had myself what Papa used to call a Mantis-dream. That very night. In it, I saw what had to be done and why everyone had to come with me.

XLI

Just Like Mamma and Papa

I STILL DIDN'T KNOW HOW I WAS GOING TO do what I was going to do, and who I might ask to help me. Maybe I'd still have done nothing at all, but the next evening on the piazza, Weaver sat with me.

"What dey done to Marybelle was pow'ful wrong, Morri girl."

"It sure was, Weaver."

We fell into silence after that, both of us pondering justice, I reckon. I've always felt comfortable with Weaver, like he's an uncle. He patted my thigh and said, "You know, girl, if I had me a pistol in my hand right now, I'd use it. I swear to heaven 'bove, I'd use it good."

"I can see you would, Weaver."

"First I'd put Cousin Edward under the ground. Fifty feet under. Second, I'd walk right to Charleston and put balls in all dem doctors. I'd tell 'em, 'Dis here is a gift from Marybelle.' I could do it too. Yaw papa'd tell you dat if he was here. He knew how good I could shoot. One ball is all I'd need for each of 'em."

"I believe you, Weaver."

I didn't add anything to that, because he looked like he was making himself feverish. He must have thought I was nettled by his angry talk, because he stood up then and said, "I'm right sorry to put dis on ya, Morri girl. I needed to talk to someone and you's always been easy for me to talk to. Jes' f'get what I told ya, girl."

I tugged him back down. I explained that what bothered me wasn't what he said, it was knowing that I wanted to kill them all as much as he did and that we'd be mighty justified. I also said he was looking tired to me and if he wanted I'd make him some special tea. His tears started then, like they'd been held back for months, though it was more likely years. I'd never seen Weaver cry. No one had. I knew he'd been sweet on Marybelle, but I didn't know how much.

"She was a good and brave girl," I told him. "And real strong."

That only made him shake. He was a broad-shouldered man, but I managed to put my arms around most of him. That big strength of his had melted into despair.

"I's right sorry," he whispered, wiping his eyes.

"No need. We're family. You cry if you want to. You cry on me."

"No, it's enough." After he'd wiped his eyes again, he made a fist and said, "I'm gonna do it. I'm gonna do it dis time."

"Weaver, I dreamed the other night that a big flood was coming. Everything at River Bend was going to get covered with water."

"Even de Big House?" he asked.

"Even that. Now, what would you say if I could get us some guns? And maybe swords. You reckon we could fight our way to Charleston and get aboard a ship? One from the North. Or from England. You reckon you could teach some of us how to load and aim a gun?"

Weaver looked at me, biting his lip, considering hard. Then he nodded. And that's when we started planning for real.

ONE THING I knew right away: If we were going to fight our way to Charleston and make it out to sea, it had to be with the help of an old friend named Beaufort. For three reasons: He worked at a dockside warehouse in the city and got to know ship crewmen and even captains; he was a free-born mulatto and could come and go more easily than any Negro; and he was fatherly fond of me. I'd known him practically all my life, because part of what Papa and I always used to do on our marketing trips was collect new plants and supplies stored in the warehouse Beaufort guarded.

Beaufort once taught me something important too. One day, when he was bouncing me up and down on his knee, he sighed real long and said, "Morri, it's a right shame you's a slave girl, 'cause you's a clever little thing and could make somethin' of youssel."

I wasn't more than six years old, but what he said stopped my heart for a beat. Because I hadn't known I was a slave girl before that. I knew my parents were slaves, but I hadn't yet thought of myself that way. *I was Morri, and I was a slave, just like Mamma and Papa.*

I suppose I felt I could trust him because, unlike most of the rest of the mulattos in Charleston, he didn't consider himself just about white. He always said that a whipping he'd got as a boy from his own white papa had taught him that being *almost white* was an impossibility— pretty much like black folks in Maryland saying they were living *nearly* in the North. Lily heard that once when she went to Baltimore with Big Master Henry, and it always used to make us laugh.

So it happened that I took Lily to town for her to pick out some spectacles, but mostly for me to talk to Beaufort. The coachman, Wiggie, didn't have to come, since it was his day off, but he agreed to take us. Weaver too, since I told Master Edward that he needed to buy some things for the hens. Edward would never normally let us all go, but he was nothing but calm breezes of late because of getting his money back for Marybelle and fooling my papa.

The first stop for the four of us in Charleston was the eye doctor. It looked like it was going to take a while because there were two black men already sitting in the colored waiting room, so I gave Wiggie the five silver dollars that Master Edward had entrusted to me and asked him to stay with Lily. Then Weaver and I walked to Beaufort's warehouse.

Charleston used to make me right muddleheaded, there being so much commotion everywhere you looked. But as we walked through those shimmering streets that day, my thoughts were clear. It wasn't hard at all imagining what all those fine mansions would look like as charred wood, crumbled brick, and ash.

Weaver leaned down and put his mouth up to my ear. "So where's all de white folks at?"

"Which white folks you referring to, Weaver?"

All of dem, he mouthed. "We's more dan dey is," he said, raising his shoulders like it was strange.

"Weaver, keep moving," I said, grabbing his arm and leading him off. "And listen up: Now, every house you can see for half a mile around has got a handful of slaves cooking and cleaning and everything else. Some got twenty, thirty, or more. Must be ten or fifteen thousand Negroes in Charleston. I tell you this, the white folks are swimming in one big dark sea."

He was quiet for a while, thinking that over. Then he said, "Morri, dey must know dey doin' wrong. Even dem men who killed Marybelle must know it."

"Well, if you think that, Weaver, then you need spectacles more than Lily ever will."

WE FOUND BEAUFORT sitting at the front of his warehouse, behind an old wooden secretary. His hair was mostly gray now, and he had on a fine pearl-white waistcoat and scarlet cravat. He gave me a big smile of welcome and held out his arms. I introduced him and Weaver to each other, then asked if any of my plants or seeds had come in, which was Beaufort's chance to lead us to the back windows.

Now, before I tell you what I said to Beaufort, I got to explain one last thing. I'd asked him months earlier if he could find out if there was any British sea captain who might take kindly to a Negro girl hiding on his ship. And to get me the date of when he'd next be calling in to port.

Two weeks before, he'd given me the name of such a captain— Timothy Ott. He usually sailed out of Liverpool, bringing fabric from the British mills to America and taking giant bales of cotton back across the sea. Beaufort had asked a few sly questions and had come to learn the Englishman's views on slavery, which were mighty critical. In fact, he called Charleston an abomination, especially since he had to keep his black crewmen aboard his ships, because the city had a special law that said they'd have to stay in prison if they came ashore.

My heart was beating loud inside my ears as I whispered, "Any news from Liverpool on when the cotton prices might rise again?"

Beaufort looked skeptically at Weaver.

"He's family," I said.

"I ain't heard nothin' yet, Morri. I'll get word to you one way or another, don't you worry. You seem a bit jumpy t'day. You not sick?"

"It's because I got something else to ask you, Beaufort. Something bigger."

"You go ahead, Morri, I ain't gonna bite you."

"It's this," I said real soft. "Beaufort, you must meet a fair number of freed black folks down here—who have shipments coming in. You think that any of them might be sympathetic to me?" When he gave me a puzzled look, I added, "You know, about cotton prices in Liverpool. And maybe about sending some other things there too—other plants."

I hoped he understood my meaning without my having to talk any plainer. But he said, "What you mean, *other things*?"

He cast another dubious glance over at Weaver, so that he was the one who answered: "We're talkin' 'bout sending more dan jes' one."

Beaufort stood up real straight in shock. I told him, "All I'm asking is the name of a freed black man in Charleston who might help us send some plants up North or to England." My legs seemed to buckle and I thought I might pee on myself right then and there. I reached out to Weaver to steady myself. "Beaufort, you're the only one who can help me. You know I wouldn't ask you otherwise."

He was biting his lip and looking down at his feet. He was one pretty obvious conspirator, I'll tell you that. My heart was racing worse than ever, and that's how I knew everything was going wrong even before it had started going right.

"I don't know, Morri. We have to see 'bout that."

He wouldn't even look me in the eye. Weaver put his hand on my back. "Come on, girl, let's get goin'."

At the door, Beaufort gave me a quick kiss on my forehead. "Rollins—Henry Stansfield Rollins. He lives on Bull Street," he whispered.

"Beaufort," I whispered back, "I don't know Charleston real well. Where's—"

"Morri, Mr. Rollins might help you send your things off to England. But if he don't, I can't help you with your other plants," he snapped. "I'll tell you 'bout cotton prices in Liverpool, sure enough, but that's all I'm gonna do."

I DIDN'T WANT to stop to talk to any Negroes on the street to ask for directions to Bull Street in case anyone was keeping watch on us. So I decided to ask at Apothecaries Hall. One of its owners, Dr. LaRosa, had been a friend of my father's. After my papa found out that he was Jewish—this is back around 1814 or so—he used to go there to learn what he could about the local herbs he could give folks for scarlet fever, worms, and everything else that cast us down. They used to sit together in Dr. LaRosa's office and talk about Torah stories too. And once my papa even got invited for Sabbath supper on Friday night, though he couldn't go because Big Master Henry wouldn't allow him out after sundown—and especially not with some know-it-all meddling Jew, as he put it.

Most of the Jews in Charleston—including Dr. LaRosa—had ancestors from Portugal. Some even came right from the city of Porto, where Papa had lived. That always made him feel that coming to South Carolina wasn't so odd at all. Not that some of the apothecary's customers didn't complain about Papa being allowed into his office. One man even told him once that no niggers ought to set foot in a white establishment, "even if they could quote Genesis front to back."

Unfortunately, Dr. LaRosa wasn't in when Weaver and I stopped by. But a young clerk treated us kind and gave us directions while pointing out landmarks on a map of the city hanging on the wall. Bull Street wasn't all that close, and I was getting worried by now that we'd be gone too long from Lily and Wiggie.

"I tell you what," said Weaver, once we'd reached the street, laying his big old hand on my shoulder. "You head on back to be wid Lily while I go talk to Mr. Rollins. You get de carriage and meet me dere, den we'll all go home."

I argued awhile, but in the end I did what he said. I ought not to have worried so much about Wiggie and Lily, because they were still waiting to get her spectacles when I arrived.

At the time, I didn't consider that Weaver might have any hidden reason for wanting to see Mr. Rollins alone, but now I wonder if he wasn't trying to keep some of the risk just for himself. He likely thought he owed it to Papa to keep watch over me. I'll never know about that. Unless we can get the dead to speak, of course.

XLII

WE REACHED CHARLESTON ON THE MORNING of Tuesday, the Twenty-Sixth of August, after three days at sea. Having heard in New York that it was a handsome city cherished by its residents, I was surprised that the neighborhood close by the harbor was filthy with refuse and patrolled by packs of mongrels.

When I stopped a well-to-do man near the port to ask about these things, he told me that its impoverished appearance was due to the decline in prices paid for both cotton and rice on the Liverpool Exchange.

In the hope that Midnight had been able to find work dispensing medications in Charleston or somewhere nearby, or was still practicing this profession even today, I decided to first ask after him at apothecary shops.

I was as jittery as could be by now. I believed I might spot him at any moment—driving the carriage turning the corner, buying trousers at the clothing shop I was passing...

What stunned and pleased me most as I rushed toward King Street and the central shopping district was to discover that Charleston was an African city. Blacks performed every task around me that required physical strain and sturdiness—from the hauling away of refuse in carts to the ringing of church bells. For every person of English or Continental extraction I saw, I'd have estimated three Negroes. More than a few wore fine clothing and jewelry, having plainly achieved their freedom. The majority, however, were dressed either in soiled livery uniforms or in the rough wool and cotton called Negro cloth. Many were barefoot.

Once, I spotted two elderly white men riding horses and armed with both pistols and swords, which greatly surprised me; I didn't yet know that I was hunting for Midnight in a city under siege.

THAT FIRST MORNING I showed nearly a dozen clerks my sketch of the Bushman, and though three of them were only too happy to comment disfavorably on his so-called rascality once again, they all assured me that there were no Negroes handing out medicines in their city. "Only a Northern fool wanting to meet his maker would ever accept a powder or syrup mixed by a nigger," one guffawed.

By the time the noon bells had rung, my confidence in eliciting any helpful information from any of the white residents was all but vanished. I decided to take Moon Mary's advice once again and hail black tradesmen and merchants on the street. To do so, I approached them on the Negro side of the walkways.

Though my Scottish accent proved a difficulty, the first blacks I asked for help were able to follow me if I spoke slowly, but none could help me. Then I approached a handsome gentleman in a gold waistcoat and black trousers, perhaps forty years of age. After showing him my sketch, he informed me in the best King's English that he had never seen Midnight, but he added, "You will find a Negro apothecary named Mobley on Queen Street, sir. Caeser Mobley is his name. He is not the proprietor, but he is indeed employed there." After giving me directions, he then astonished me by adding, "If I may be perfectly frank with you, sir, it is plain you are a stranger here. I wish only to give you one small piece of advice: It is a trifle insulting for you to walk on the Negro side of the sidewalk, as you are only too plainly of the white race."

MR. MOBLEY WAS so thin that he looked as though he were made of wire. Begging his patience, I explained my purpose, adding that there was a fifty-dollar reward for any assistance that might lead me to Midnight.

Sadly, my interview ended abruptly, as he was certain he had neither seen nor heard of him. It never occurred to me that he might be lying. Nor did it enter my mind that from his point of view, I—a white stranger altering his voice to sound more Southern and tracking a black man—must have appeared a threat. Indeed, no one who might have been loyal to Midnight would have trusted me; I might have been a slave-trader or legal authority out to hurt him in some way.

IT WAS FIVE o'clock when, sweating like a soldier in a losing campaign, I made my way back to my hotel. Despite my determination to remain resolute, my heart sank to new depths when I passed a Negro youth loading heavy crates into the back of a wagon. He couldn't have been more than twenty, but his nose and one of his eyes were so afflicted with oozing sores that flies were feeding mercilessly at him. I spotted lice not only in his hair but also in his eyebrows. Our glances met for a moment, and I saw in his despair that he knew he was dying.

Rushing ahead, I found a churchyard where I could rest for a while. Sitting among those headstones, I could not understand how any of us had a right to live while abominations such as I had just witnessed were allowed to happen.

I took off Daniel's talisman and read it aloud to myself: *Divine Son of the Virgin Mary, who was born in Bethlehem, a Nazarene, and who was crucified so that we might live, I beseech thee, O Lord, that the body of me be not caught, nor put to death by the hands of destiny . . .*

Closing my eyes, I then spoke one of two protective prayers Benjamin had taught me, imagining myself reflected in the silver eyes of Moses. My old friend had told me that we were—all of us—his *pupils,* and therefore also silver in our essence.

Then I repeated—ten times, slowly—the other prayer that he'd given me. And I whispered a verse I'd recently read in Ezekiel: *I am against you, Pharaoh king of Egypt . . . and I shall fling you into the wilderness.*

I ended with two Hebrew words: *Hesed,* love, and *Din,* judgment.

I could not say what the purpose of any of this was, but it was all I had to help me in these dark moments. None of what I spoke or did calmed me much or cheered me. Cold sweat was cascading down my brow, and I felt that I was being emptied of all that made me who I was.

But I did not believe that an immediate lessening of my anguish was the point. For that, once I could stand, I took my disheveled self to a tavern, where I downed several ounces of a reasonable whiskey and smoked greedily at a pipe that I pulled from its hook on the wall. After shuffling back to my hotel, I washed my face, collapsed facedown in bed, and pretended I was a boy in Porto, with Fanny by my side. Breathing together, my arm around her belly, we drifted off to sleep.

XLIII

I AWOKE IN THE MIDDLE OF THE NIGHT, drenched in sweat, but I dared not open my window to allow the sea breeze to sweep inside lest the mosquitoes follow suit. I lay naked on my bed, imagining Midnight as he must have arrived in Alexandria and then Charleston. Manacled and beaten, he was shouting my name. He could not have been prepared for the otherness of this world, where they knew nothing of the First People nor of the hunters that rose into the sky as stars. Hyena had taken Charleston and made it his own.

Here in America, he must have clung to silence as a shipwrecked man to his island. I recalled how, in confiding his stories to me, he had prevailed upon me to keep several of them secret. This had been owing to his belief that his own health, as well as that of his people, would be put in grave peril if such tales fell into the hands of evil-minded people.

Silence must have become his only hope and power. He had made himself mute.

THE NEXT MORNING, I made up my mind to question every apothecary in Charleston and nearby towns in the hopes that Midnight had at some time been permitted by his master to pay one or more of them a visit. Though none of the first people I spoke to could help me, several clerks advised me to stop by at Apothecaries Hall, the most well-known dispensary in the city. I could not miss it, they said, because it had a large mortar and pestle painted on its facade.

I reached there near noon and waited for over an hour to speak to the proprietor, an elderly man with a kind face and voice named Jacob LaRosa, who questioned me at length. To my solemn disappointment, he told me that he had never met such a man. Hearing a catch in his voice that I took for a sign of mixed emotions, I begged him to be truthful with me, as this was the most important mission of my life. He assured me he had never met the Negro whose drawing I'd shown him. I did not believe him, but I could do nothing.

ON MY THIRD day in the city, Mrs. Robichaux, who owned the boardinghouse where I was staying, questioned me about my Portuguese heritage over breakfast.

"Why, I wouldn't be surprised if you had kin in Charleston, sir!" she exclaimed.

"Excuse me?"

"Some of the Jews of Charleston are able to speak Portuguese. I have been told that they come from that country."

She explained that there were hundreds of Jews in Charleston and that their church, as she called it, was on Hassell Street.

I ran most of the way there and found the Beth Elohim Synagogue to be an impressive structure in the Georgian style, surrounded by a metal fence of upraised pikes with a high ironwork gate.

The gate was open when I arrived, and a wizened old man wearing a large dark hat and a prayer shawl answered the door. His name was Hartwig Rosenberg and he was the hazan, responsible for singing the liturgy. He was suspicious of my motives until I mentioned that I, too, was a Jew.

Handing me a wide-brimmed hat, he led me into the synagogue proper. The shafts of light, spangled dust, and echoing of our footsteps afforded me the first moments of peace I'd experienced since arriving in Charleston. I did not feel alone at all; there were people here who'd understand me—and sympathize with Midnight's plight.

To my questions, Mr. Rosenberg explained that there was no one by the name of Zarco in Charleston, but there were at least two hundred Jews of Portuguese descent. When he told me what the most common names were, I learned there was even one Pereira, which had been Grandmother Rosa's maiden name. The family here spelled it Perrera.

What wonderful luck, I thought, as though entering through a gate of fellowship long locked to me. Yet when I explained my mission to the hazan, I was disheartened to learn that there were many slaveholders among the congregation. The community's elders—in keeping with the laws and traditions of the Christian majority—saw nothing wrong with the practice, as long as the Negroes were treated with respect. As to what might constitute respect, I asked if it might be the removal of only four toes from a *rascal* and not all five. To which Mr. Rosenberg glared and replied, "I need no lessons in morality from the likes of you, sir. For the Jews of Charleston, it is a question of survival. Standing apart would be a tremendous risk."

His harsh and condescending manner left me furious. "So you not only wish to betray the spirit of Exodus, sir, but also to become honorary Christians? Is that what you are telling me?"

"Very clever, Mr. Stewart, except that you do not live here and therefore do not know the pressures we are under. If you'll permit me, you might read the Torah again. If you do, you'll see that the survival of our people is its most important theme. While I serve our community, we shall not betray it."

Though I would have dearly liked to continue this quarrel, I said nothing more about my feelings, since I needed his help. I could fairly hear Mama saying, *John, winning this argument means nothing; finding Midnight is everything.*

I even apologized for my rashness, though I admit I regretted doing so as soon as I had spoken.

The hazan, pacified now, promised me he would ask the congregation this Friday night if anyone had seen or heard of my friend. "Perhaps," he said, smiling to ease the awkwardness between us, "one of them even owns him. Wouldn't that be good fortune?"

"Aye, good fortune, indeed," I replied, unable to disguise my disgust.

I left Beth Elohim armed with Mr. Perrera's home address and place of daily business. He apparently owned a clothing shop on Meeting Street, not two blocks away, and lived just outside the city. He, too, was a slave-owner.

*   *   *

ON LEAVING THE synagogue, I knew now that Midnight would not even have been able to appeal to the Jews for help. Charleston must have seemed to him a desert of the spirit. If he was still alive, where could he have found a place in this world to be himself?

When I reached Isaac Perrera's clothing shop, I was led to an office at the back, where an olive-complexioned, dark-haired man of perhaps thirty years of age was working over a ledger book. Placing his pen in its holder, he looked up at me and smiled.

"How may I be of assistance to you, sir?" he asked.

"I shall come right to my subject, sir, as I would not wish to take up your valuable time. I'm Portuguese and half-Jewish. I am alone in Charleston and in great need of a trustworthy person who might help me with a problem."

In awkward Portuguese, he replied, "And where are you from?"

"I was born in Porto, though my father is Scottish. My grand-mother's name is Pereira. She still lives in Porto, though most of my family is in London now."

"Yes, I have been told that there are many Pereiras in Portugal," he replied.

In his chilly gaze, I could see he wished to discount any common ancestry we might share. In his own way, he was telling me that I had no right to expect his assistance. To confirm this intuition, I said, "Indeed there are, sir—thousands. And it was presumptuous of me to come here to see you based on a similarity of family names."

"But understandable, sir," he acknowledged.

"I beg your pardon for the interruption. I shall leave you to your work." I paused to give him time to protest. As he simply nodded, I added, "Thank you for seeing me. It was most kind."

Humiliation obliged me to proffer a small stiff bow.

It was Thursday, August the Twenty-Eighth, and with every new day in America it was becoming ever more obvious that I was never meant to be a hunter.

XLIV

We Were on Our Own

MR. ROLLINS TOLD WEAVER THAT HE KNEW OF a man who might get us our muskets and pistols. I'll call him Mr. Trevor, since he's still in Charleston by all accounts. It was another six weeks before I got permission to go to town to do our marketing and try calling on him. Master Edward refused to make do without Weaver that day, but I knew how to handle the horses well enough and went alone.

Mr. Trevor's wife welcomed me into their small home and sat me down in a study filled with more books than I'd ever seen. She told me her husband would be with me right away.

Mr. Trevor always scared me, to tell you the truth. He was light-skinned and tall, and his eyes were always burning with awareness, as if he could see straight through you to your thoughts. His profession, which I'm not going to reveal, required a whole lot of learning.

That first day, I told him about the dreams I'd had of a city where it was always snowing. I told him about Papa having his heel-strings cut. I told him about Marybelle being dissected still warm.

"What makes you think a frail and uneducated girl like you is going to be able to succeed in this rebellion?" he said in a skeptical voice. "Because make no mistake, young lady, a slave rebellion is what we are discussing here, even if it's only a few individuals."

I do not know what gave me the ornery strength to say what I said: "It's you who ought to make no mistake, Mr. Trevor, because I'm getting out of River Bend one way or another. And I'm taking my friends with me. I swear that on my mamma's grave. You can help me if you like or not. But I *am* getting out!"

I don't think I made any impression on him at all. He looked at me with amused eyes. "Little moths usually fly straight into candle flames," he told me. "They think they're flying toward some eternal light, but they just burn up to nothing."

IF WEAVER HADN'T come to our next meeting with Mr. Trevor, I'm sure we'd have been given no help at all. But getting him permission to go to Charleston proved an uphill battle and the only way I could get it was by convincing Mistress Anne that she was in need of a chicken coop for her town house.

It took me three whole months of nagging to wear her resistance down. So it wasn't until June of 1822 that I could get Weaver into town to build her coop and meet with Mr. Trevor in secret. He told us not to come into his study this time, so we sat in the parlor, studying the framed pictures on the walls, which were all of Negro heroes. He even had one of a black man crucified on a desert hilltop. Mrs. Trevor told me it was Christ.

"Was Jesus a Negro?" I asked. "I thought he was Jewish."

"He was one of us in spirit," she replied, which made me want to laugh at first, but then later I felt something tingly in my fingers and toes while thinking about it—almost like my papa had said it.

Looking at that painting, I knew that if the white militia from the Citadel ever raided this place, they'd burn it and everything else in here to ash regardless of anybody's spirit. They'd never let a black Christ be crucified in Charleston. No, sir.

Mr. Trevor must have been persuaded by something Weaver said, because he told him that he could get us some of the arms and ammunition that had been stored by Denmark Vesey and his friends before they were arrested and hanged for trying to make an uprising.

Weaver and I weren't sure how we would smuggle everything up to River Bend. That put some cold worry in our hearts. And worse, it had

never occurred to us before that we had to pay for the muskets and pistols, but Mr. Trevor told us, "Guns don't come free to any man." Then,
laughing, he winked at me and said, "Or girl."

ALL THAT SUMMER, while Master Edward's family lived over at
their town house in Cordesville, I took advantage of their absence to
steal everything silver I could wrap my little fingers around. Throughout
the fall and winter too. Every two months or so, I made my way to town
with what I'd robbed, all those trinkets and pieces of silverware shrieking
at me from inside my pockets and my bag. Throughout those first
months of 1823, robbery, guns, and waiting to get out were all I was
thinking about.

It sure does take ages for a ripple to reach the shores of slavery in the
rice country of South Carolina, and by May, after a full year of me robbing my hands raw, Mr. Trevor said we still had given him only enough
silver to pay for five muskets, two pistols, and three swords. Though he
would also add an extra musket and sword with his own money.

I figured that wasn't going to be nearly enough for the twenty or
more slaves I was hoping to take with me. We were planning to give
everyone at River Bend a choice of coming or staying the week before we
left. Weaver would train a few of the men at using a musket or pistol. We
reckoned we'd make our escape on a Sunday night, since that was the
only evening when Weaver's wife, Martha, and their children could get a
pass to come to River Bend, and we'd get on our way in July, August, or
early September, because it was then, during the sickly season, that the
countryside would be nearly empty of white folks and patrols.

We were planning on leaving from Petrie's Landing, a little-used
wharf along the Cooper River for folks living in the town of Belmont.
Beaufort had been braver than I ever could have hoped and had gone to
speak to Captain Ott. The Englishman had not only agreed to help me,
Weaver, and anyone else who could reach his ship, but he would have his
crewmen take three rowboats to Petrie's Landing a day or two before the
night of our departure. We would take the boats and meet his ship in the
harbor. He would be captaining the *Landmark* and flying the Union Jack
and a small blue flag. He told Beaufort he'd shine a great big lantern on
that flag of freedom all night if need be.

Captain Ott told Beaufort he'd be returning during late August or
the first half of September, most likely. As soon as he docked, Beaufort

would hire a carriage out to River Bend. He would tie a red ribbon around a plank of the front gate and also leave a plant of some kind just inside the fence. If anyone saw it, I was to say it was a present for my garden from a friend in Charleston. But it was our signal to get moving toward Petrie's Landing that Sunday.

Sometimes I was so frightened things wouldn't work out that I'd need to run down to the river and sit with my legs in that ice-cold water just to keep my heart from exploding.

I said nothing to Beaufort about our guns. The less he knew the safer he'd be. Weaver and I promised him that if we were taken prisoner we would never name him. But I worried that if they were to cut off some of my fingers or put burning coals on my eyes, I'd name everybody I ever knew and even a few I ain't never met, black Jesus included. I prayed they would just hang me. Yes, sir, I rightly hoped they'd send me off quick as a cotton worm's sting.

ON SATURDAY, THE Fourteenth of June, we learned that we could go get the guns and swords we'd paid for. Mr. Trevor had left them under a blanket in a cove hidden by rushes, one mile south of Petrie's Landing, at a place called Farmer's Rock. We were told to never visit him again or try to contact him. Under no circumstances were we even to stroll by his house. So from that moment on, we were on our own.

WIGGIE TOOK ILL at much the same time with some stomach pains that kept him out of his carriages for nearly two months. If I were to say that I caused his problems with some teas I worked up with a bit of jimsonweed greens, claiming it was for his rheumatism, would you think me evil?

Maybe it was a bad thing to do, but I had to get permission to drive myself to Charleston every fortnight, because I was sure Wiggie would never agree to carry guns. Keeping him attached to the privy much of the time was the only way I could think of.

Weaver and I stored the weapons in a space under the piazza—all but one, that is. I sneaked a loaded pistol into my room and kept it under my bed. Ever since Big Master Henry had stuck his snake up inside me, I'd been waiting for Edward the Cockerel to try the same. This time, I was going to be ready.

Our overseer, Mr. Johnson, was our only sticky problem, but we always waited till he was away from the Big House with the field hands before taking the weapons out of the carriage. Likely Crow or one of the other house slaves guessed after a while that something peculiar was going on, but none of them was about to betray us.

Then, near the end of August, something happened to give us a scare: A white man with a strange accent started asking nearly everyone in Charleston about my father. I found that out from Caeser Mobley, a Negro apothecary Papa used to visit from time to time. He told me what happened in a note he sent to me with a Negro coachman. Though he couldn't write so well, I got the gist of it. The curious stranger was tall and wild-looking. Caeser guessed he was a slave-trader trying to trick Papa out of hiding. Or maybe some policeman trying to track him down and get himself a fat reward from Master Edward. The man had done a pretty fair imitation of a Low Country accent, but he must have been from up North. Mr. Mobley denied ever knowing my papa.

Whoever he was, he sure as hell was looking into things that weren't any of his business, and at the worst possible moment. So I was praying it was the last we'd ever hear of him.

But that wasn't what happened, don't you know. No, sir. Because the very next day, near about time for the noonday bell, who comes riding up to the Big House, with a fancy black woman driving him, but the nosy stranger. I couldn't know then that it was the same man who'd been asking after Papa, of course. But later, after the Negro woman left, he saw me, and his eyes popped so wide open with recognition that I knew it must be him.

XLV

A N HOUR OR SO BEFORE SUNDOWN, AS I SAT panting at my desk in the infernal heat, writing another letter to my daughters and Mama, there was a knock at the door. Slipping on my trousers hastily, I eased it open and discovered Mr. Perrera.

"Mr. Stewart, Mrs. Robichaux permitted me to come directly to your room. I apologize for surprising you."

"No, no, come in, sir. I'm pleased to see you." I moved a chair away from my desk and placed it opposite the bed. "Please, sit, Mr. Perrera. I would offer you something to drink, but I have nothing at all. In this heat, I am unable to drink whiskey or even wine for fear of fainting and waking in an even hotter place ruled by the devil."

We were both aware that I was trying to win him to my side with humor, but he did not seem to begrudge me this strategy and smiled as he sat down. I grabbed my shirt and said, "To what do I owe the pleasure of your visit?"

"I came to apologize, sir. I was rude to you today."

I dropped down on my bed opposite him. "No, not at all. An unkempt and sweaty stranger walking into your office and speaking a foreign language... I must have been a sight."

"No, it was not that. It was—how can I say?—I keep to myself. So when you arrived, I was startled, that was all. And if I may be frank, I find that I do not always have so much in common with the other Portuguese here, so I tend to limit my interactions."

"Indeed, sir, I am sure you are wise to do so."

"So, Mr. Stewart," he smiled again, "you mentioned a problem for which you needed help. Would you mind telling me what it is?"

I cannot say why I told almost the entire truth about Midnight, but I unburdened myself of it with alarming ease. I had not been aware of my own need to confess my kinship with him. The small death in my gut eased a little as Mr. Perrera listened attentively, and I began to see that the only relief I would find in America was in the arms of the truth of what I felt for my old friend. "Indeed, I have loved him over these seventeen years of separation no less than if he were my brother—or even a second father," I concluded.

"Love comes to us unbidden," Mr. Perrera replied. "Do you believe in destiny, Mr. Stewart?"

When I said I was not sure, he gazed out the window. "I find I only trust what has not been tainted by our history."

I found Mr. Perrera a rather cryptic and unhappy man, one of those souls always looking for answers to large questions.

When tears came to his eyes, he wiped them away roughly and said, "I am sorry for this terrible display."

"On the contrary, I think you are the first white person I have met in Charleston who has a heart."

"Will you give me the pleasure of accompanying me to my home for supper tonight?" he asked. "I should like you to meet Luisa, my wife."

"Now?"

"Yes, we live five miles from town. But it will take less than an hour to get there in my gig. It's out front, waiting for us." He seemed worried now. "You could stay the night with us," he added. "And I think, Mr. Stewart, if you will accept some advice, we ought to leave with some haste. One never knows in Charleston who might be watching."

MR. PERRERA HAD a fine chestnut mare that carried us swiftly across the country roads north to his home, a whitewashed house with a large piazza out front, just a hundred yards from a gentle tributary of the Cooper River. A broad oak tree and two smaller palmettos offered shade.

Luisa was seated on the stairs when we arrived. By then, dusk was descending quickly, but even in the failing light I could plainly see that she was a black woman.

ISAAC'S TWO CHILDREN were Hester, who was called Hettie, and Reed, who went by the name of Noodle. They ran to meet their father, begging him with squealing voices to lift them up. With the boy clinging to his back and the girl giggling in his arms, he kissed Luisa. She had deep-set, secretive brown eyes, high cheekbones that seemed to catch the last rays of sunlight, and a slender neck. She appeared irritated by my presence.

A hot supper was waiting for us, and to my apologies about creating a confusion, Luisa scoffed, saying that she was pleased to have a guest. She said that to be polite, however, and the stilted nature of our conversation over the meal convinced me to leave after supper. I would walk to the nearest town and ask for a room.

After the children were put to bed, I said, "Perhaps it would be better if I left. You are both very tired, and the nearest town must have an inn of some sort."

"No, no, John," Isaac said. "Trust me. Tell your story."

Unsure of myself, I began by speaking matter-of-factly. Yet when I mentioned how Midnight had trumped my mother's rudeness at our first supper together by saying that "Africa is memory," my voice could not help but express my admiration for him. Luisa gave a noticeable start, as though she had been hit on the back.

"You see?" Isaac said to his wife in triumph.

Gazing at me sternly, she said, "Go on, Mr. Stewart, tell me more."

She listened to talk of my early life rather as though I had something to prove to her. I resented this but said nothing. Afterward, she explained: "There are many white men in South Carolina who feel affection for their Negro servants. Particularly their black mammies. But you are only the third white man I have ever met who speaks with love and respect—and kinship too."

"I knew you would see it that way," Isaac said with a smile, standing up to give her a kiss on the top of her head.

"The other two?" I asked.

"Isaac and a minister from Charlotte I once met. His passion for a Negro maid was such that it changed all his ideas about slavery. He was obliged to give up his ministry to marry her."

I'd kept for last the story of how Midnight had saved me from Hyena. Recounting it to them was to change everything.

I was speaking of how the Bushman had funneled pipe smoke in my ears when Luisa exclaimed, "But I know that man! I've seen him do just that. He was well-known throughout the Low Country. His name was not Midnight when I knew him, but Samuel."

I jumped up. "You know Samuel? Is he alive?"

Luisa gazed up at me hopefully. "If it is the same man, he used to live at River Bend—a plantation near here. He was renowned as a conjurer and healer."

"River Bend lies up the Cooper River," Isaac said. "About ten miles away, I'd guess."

"He was a wonder," said Luisa, her eyes shining. "Every black person around here knew of him. I even visited him once with a friend who had been taken ill. I do not know if he is still alive. Last I heard of him, he'd disappeared."

"Disappeared?"

"Completely vanished. I would guess it was about three years ago. They say he may have escaped. But his daughter still lives at River Bend, I believe. I cannot recall her name. She—or someone else there—will be able to tell you if there's been any word of him." She paused for a moment to think. "He was just as you described, though older, of course. And he walked with a limp, occasionally using a cane."

"And he spoke—he was not a mute?"

"No, no, he was quite well-spoken, as I recall."

My heart was pounding so loud that I could not hear what my hosts were saying. My head seemed enclosed in glass. When I came to, I was sitting in a chair before a low fire crackling in the hearth. I'd nearly fainted, Isaac told me. He forced a glass into my hand. "Drink this, John."

I did as he said. It was brandy, and it burned. He and Luisa stood whispering behind me. Getting to my feet, I asked, "How do I get to River Bend?"

Isaac turned to Luisa. "If I were to walk to Charleston tomorrow, would you take John in the gig?"

"I could not oblige you to walk to Charleston," I interrupted.

"I don't mind. Honestly, I do it sometimes. It's good for my legs. I'd accompany you myself, but I must go to my store every day."

Luisa took my hand, gripped it hard, and gave me a hearty smile. "It will be my honor, Mr. Stewart, to take you to see where Midnight lived."

THAT NIGHT, SLEEP would not meet me halfway. I was remembering too many things of long ago. Indeed, on that night, *unlike any other night,* as we used to say at Passover, I could not fathom how I had reached the present. It seemed as though I had fallen all the way here in a single instant.

I went to the parlor and found Luisa seated at the dining table, drinking a cup of tea.

"You could not sleep either?" I asked.

She started, reaching a hand to her heart. I apologized for frightening her.

She laughed. "Your stories," she said, shaking her head as though perplexed. "I've been thinking about them and their similarities with my life."

She poured me a cup of tea. I said, "You mentioned that Samuel was well-known in the Low Country. How is it that no one knew of him in Charleston? I asked in scores of shops and churches. I even asked a Negro apothecary."

"The Negroes you asked were undoubtedly protecting him. You are a white man, and you were asking after a black man who has disappeared, who might be in hiding. There are runaways hidden for years in attics, in root cellars. . . . We've had two here ourselves. So anyone loyal to Samuel would have lied to you. The others may genuinely not have heard of him."

"Then his daughter may lie to me as well—particularly if Midnight spoke badly of my family."

"But after all you have said, I'd expect him to be eternally grateful to see you. You intend to try to purchase him, I presume."

"Aye, but I have not told you everything. Something terrible took place between Samuel and my father."

"John, you must tell her the stories you've told us—they will change her mind. She will hear her father in your voice. And you must speak to her when she is alone. If she is with others, even other slaves, she may feel constrained in her reactions to you."

"It may take some time to get her alone—and to convince her. I shall need to invent some reason to stay for a week or two at River Bend."

Luisa and I bandied suggestions back and forth, but none seemed right. After a time, I asked, "How did you meet Isaac?"

"Oh, I've known him forever, it seems. Once upon a time, there was Isaac and Luisa. . . . His parents purchased me when I was fifteen, as a laundress and seamstress."

"But didn't they have the same opinions as Isaac? I mean, weren't they—"

"Their change of mind about slavery came later. The odd thing is, just like you and Midnight, Isaac taught me how to read. Isn't that astonishing?"

"Aye, it's a strange coincidence at the very least."

I believed my reply then. But now I can see the obvious—that the act of teaching a friend to read is intimately tied to love. As a matter of fact, I can think of nothing more natural.

"Please excuse a stupid question, but are you a freed woman?" I asked.

She gave me a hard look. "John, that is surely not a stupid question. It's the *only* question, as far as I'm concerned. I was given to Isaac by his father as a birthday present when he turned twenty-one. That same day, he set me free." She cupped her hands around her mouth and whispered, "Though he hates for me to say that. He says I make it sound as if he did something for me, when he was only rectifying an abomination."

"Yet at the synagogue, I was told that Isaac was a slave-owner."

She frowned. "Some of those folks—even his aunt and uncle—they don't want to see what we are to each other. They prefer believing that I'm still his slave than knowing I'm the mother of his children and that we are common-law man and wife." Whispering again, she added, "Not only am I not white, but I'm not Jewish!"

LUISA FED ME a bowl of her pumpkin custard and told me a curious thing about River Bend: Its previous two owners—Big and Little Master Henry—had each been found dead with a knife buried in his neck. Locals believed they had been murdered by a ghost, perhaps the grandfather of Big Master Henry's wife, Mistress Holly. Apparently, he had vehemently opposed her choice of husband.

"The moral of the story," Luisa said with an amused pucker to her lips, "is you best get Grandpapa's blessing before you marry around the Low Country of South Carolina."

Looking at her shining eyes, I imagined stars peering through dark clouds. I could see she spent a good deal of her time protecting her family. I suspected she could be fierce. I tell you this: I would not have wished her angry at me.

XLVI

I MANAGED ONLY AN HOUR OR TWO OF SLEEP and woke abruptly at dawn. Midnight had lived only a few miles from here. Thinking of that, I knew that hope had found me. It played inside me like a fanfare, making me vibrate with the need to get to River Bend.

Sitting on the piazza, watching an ivory-billed woodpecker hammering on the trunk of an oak tree, I had an idea for how to convince the owner of River Bend to let me stay on his plantation. I retrieved my sketchbook and got quickly to work.

LUISA AND I left as soon as we were dressed, with Isaac and the children waving good-bye to us from the lawn. The road north was pitted and muddy. She and I spoke of her childhood on an island off the South Carolina coast. She missed the ocean, most of all at sunrise, and said that it was her dream to have a small cottage by the beach. When the children were grown, she and Isaac would travel to Europe, perhaps even to Portugal.

Hours into our journey, with the sun nearing its noontime zenith, a creaky wooden bridge permitted us passage over a marshy river. Soon we reached a gate from which dangled a wooden sign of black letters on a white background: RIVER BEND. I released the latch and swung it open. All around us were fields of rice, shoulder-high and swaying in the breeze. Four black men and two women were stooping in a field a hundred yards away. Up the dirt road, a half mile away, stood a large three-story house on a small hillock.

Luisa gave a deep whistle and shook her head at having to enter a plantation.

"I apologize for making you do this," I said. "If there was another way—"

"I'm pleased to do it for you. I'm just glad I'm not staying."

We rode up the muddy drive. Beyond the house was an endless horizon of pine, and on its south side was a large garden with hydrangeas, azaleas, and other flowering bushes.

We were met at the piazza by an old black man with closely cropped gray hair and one eye dimmed by a cataract. He wore ancient black velvet pants and what must have once been a white shirt but was now just tatters sewn together. He walked with a noticeable limp. The man told us hesitantly that his name was Crow. Luisa spoke for the two of us and asked if we could please meet with the master of the plantation. I looked around to see if I might get a glimpse of Midnight's daughter, but there were no other slaves in sight.

Before Crow had a chance to announce our arrival, a white man in blue satin pants and leather slippers rushed out to the piazza. He looked down at us, hands on his hips, as though we were trespassing.

I had expected Luisa to take the lead with him, but she raised her eyebrows and whispered, "Go on, John."

"Sir, I . . . I do indeed beg your pardon," I stammered, "for the unexpected nature of our visit. My name is John Stewart, and I am a stranger to this lovely land of yours, having recently come from across the sea, from far-off Britain. It is my intention to draw and paint the magnificent birds of South Carolina and to later publish these in a volume in London. As I have not yet had the pleasure of sketching the birds of this particular area of the lowlands, I . . . I was of the . . . of the . . ."

Owing to the impatient glare of our prospective host, my words faltered.

"You've caught me at an awkward moment, sir," he said irritably.

"But if you will give me a few minutes, I shall meet you in the tea room." Turning to the old black man, he snapped, "Crow, take care of Mr. Stewart."

I took my sketchbook from the gig, since I wanted to show him my drawings. Luisa told me she would wait for me on the piazza. "My presence will only make things more difficult," she observed.

Earlier, we had agreed that I would say that she was a friend's slave from Charleston and that her name was Dorothy. The less that anyone at River Bend knew about her the better, as far as she was concerned. "If they get my name, they might get me," she had said.

WHEN CROW ENTERED the room with a pot of tea and a platter of butter biscuits, I thanked him and asked for the names of the women portrayed in the various portraits that crowded the walls. He told me that the young lady with the defeated look was Mistress Holly.

"May I put to you a rather intemperate question?" I asked him. Upon receiving his agreement, I said, "Was this painted before or after her husband's untimely death?"

Thoughtful fingertips played over his lips. Crow's one good eye had a clear awareness. "Oh, that would ha' been long befaw he died, suh. Le' me see," and here he gazed up toward the ceiling and wrinkled his nose. "I reckon it was painted in 1800—that'd be twenty yea's befaw Big Master Henry passed on."

It was the same year I had met Daniel and Violeta. "And which of these men was her ill-fated husband?" I asked.

Crow pointed to a sandy-haired ox carrying a musket in one hand and a Bible in the other. His eyes were dull, and he looked rather like he might enjoy nothing so much as sleeping.

EDWARD JOINED ME a short time later, apologizing profusely for obliging me to wait. Then, over the next half hour, he made it his aim to convince me that he was a simple man of modest needs. Given that the silver in his sitting room alone must have required two days of labor each week for a slave to keep properly polished, this was a rather pointless ruse. Nevertheless, to give a sop to Cerberus, I pronounced him most manifestly a man of simple but elegant taste. "These are perfectly charming surroundings," I added.

Primped by my compliments, he consented with an eager smile to take a look at my sketchbook. He took time over each drawing, discovering some detail—a beak, a tail-feather, the glint of an eye—at which to marvel. This was not so much to praise my skill, though he did that often enough, but rather to draw attention to his own powers of observation.

I was about to ask him delicately about the possibility of my staying at River Bend, when the door to the parlor opened and in walked a skinny lass in an old white dress. She had dark, oval eyes, and her skin was bronze-colored. In her, I could see Midnight as he had been on that wondrous day of his arrival at our home in Porto. How lithe and handsome he had been! I had an overwhelming desire to run to her. My skin was tingling with the need to ask her about her father—to speak my heart to her as well.

Knowing that my father was responsible for the life of poverty and humiliation that this girl had inherited, my shame seemed to fix me in a snare; how could I even speak to her when she was sure to have spent her childhood cursing me and my family?

She carried biscuits for us on a platter, though we hadn't yet finished the previous batch or asked for more. Edward explained to me that she was always engaged in some foolery or other, like bringing in sweets when there wasn't any need. He winked at me as though we had established an intimate complicity, then said to the girl, "Morri, I used to think you had yourself a good head on them bony shoulders, but you are one silly girl. You think you can do anything you like, don't you? But you can't. You're going to see that one day, sure enough—one day soon, I reckon. Now, get your troublesome black behind out of here 'fore I box your ears."

"I's real sorry," she replied, but she did not seem perturbed by his reproach in the least.

I, however, should have liked to crash my fist into his face, which is undoubtedly why I thought of Midnight telling me: *You are just a gemsbok, so do not let yourself be provoked so easily. . . .*

Likely mistaking me for a friend of her owner, Morri gave me a disdainful look as she turned to leave.

I then summoned my courage and asked Edward if I might stay at River Bend for a week to draw the local birds. I held my fingers locked together on my lap as I spoke; I had noticed by now that white Southerners, like the English, regarded hand gestures as vulgar.

"But, Mr. Stewart," Edward said, looking puzzled, "I do not believe we could offer you the conditions you are used to in Britain. It is a modest household, as I've said, and my wife is away at present. I myself am only here two or three days a week. I'm quite sure you would find River Bend a most primitive place."

"I would need only a room and a single meal a day, Mr. Roberson."

"Yes, but the niggers, they are likely to be troublesome at this time of year. The hot moist summers create a sort of frenzy in them. They'd dance all night were it not for the whip."

"To tell you the truth, sir, I never even notice the Africans. None of their damned fool rascality will nettle me," I said, giving what I hoped was a convincing performance.

"Yes, I imagine you find woodpeckers and wrens more appealing," he said, grinning.

"Indeed so," I said, laughing.

Edward then scoffed at my insistence on paying for my stay, saying he'd never allow it. He called for Crow, who had waited at the parlor door, and instructed him to help me move my bags into Mistress Anne's old room. Before heading upstairs, I went outside to rejoin Luisa. I told her that all was well and returned with her to the gig to fetch my bags. I whispered that I had seen Midnight's daughter and that her name was Morri.

Luisa gripped my hand, then thought better of showing her feelings. Looking around to confirm we'd not be heard, she said, "Oh, I'm so glad, John. Did you speak to her?"

"I could not. I shall try later."

"You will convince her, I'm sure of it."

"If only I had your confidence."

"Confidence doesn't cost anything," she said with a grin, "so I've got bales and bales."

I thanked her and Isaac for their help.

"I'll not kiss you here," she whispered. We shook hands. "Now, you be careful, John. I'll leave you with what my mama used to tell me whenever I was up to something risky. I don't rightly know what it means, but it used to encourage me." She placed her hand against my chest and pressed. "You eat the night, child. Eat the night deep inside you."

LATER THAT DAY, I took my sketchbook outside, then rushed around the perimeter of the tea room toward the kitchen building, which was joined by a walkway to the main house. I could hear soft voices coming from inside. I knocked, and an elderly black woman wearing spectacles, in a loose white tunic, came to the door and bowed deferentially.

She soon told me she was Lily, the cook. When I asked if there was someone who might wash and iron a shirt and trousers, she hesitated for some time, rather as though deaf. Then, when I repeated my request, she said, "I get Morri right on it, sir."

"And might I talk to Morri herself?"

"Yes, you shawly can, sir. Ya jes' wait right here, please."

Morri appeared after a minute or so, her eyes filled with alarm, holding one arm straight down, her other hand grasping it at the elbow. She remained two long paces from me, wary. "Morri, I have a favor to ask you," I said.

"Yes, sir."

"The clothes I left on my bed are very, very soiled. Would you please make the shirt . . . you make it as white-white as the sky."

"White as the sky? I'm 'fraid I don' und'stand, sir."

"I have been told that that was the color of the sky at the time of the First People."

She took a step back.

"We are the First People," I added. "You and I . . . and everyone else. Though that is a secret only few people know."

Before I could explain myself further, she fled, groping her way along the kitchen wall as though blinded.

XLVII

Why Can't Midnight Talk?

WHEN THE STRANGER CAME TO THE KITCHEN door asking for me, Lily fetched me jumping like a toad, because she couldn't understand half of what he was saying. Sure enough, there he was at the door, all six foot of him, trying to trap me inside those blue-gray eyes of his.

He asked me in a real careful voice to do some washing for him—like I could refuse without risking a whipping. Then he said some peculiar things: that his clothes were *very, very* soiled. And that the sky was *white-white*. Only my papa ever talked like that.

That sure got me muddled good. Then the obvious came to me: The bastard already had my father prisoner! This was his devilish way of telling me. Likely, he and his kind were torturing Papa in some secret location. Maybe they'd had him there for years.

What he was doing here at River Bend, I couldn't say. Though being a white man, he probably just wanted to see me suffer with knowing that my papa was a prisoner.

But then why had he been asking in Charleston after my father like he didn't know where he was? And if Papa had been captured, why hadn't they returned him to Master Edward, his owner?

Looking at that man standing just outside the kitchen doorway made it hard to breathe. I felt my way out of the room and ran. I didn't know where I was heading, but I had to get out of the Big House before it choked me to death.

I DASHED AWAY as fast as I could and found Weaver fixing the chicken run. "Whoa, slow on down, girl. Wha's goin' on wid you?"

"We have to cancel what we planned," I whispered. Then I explained about the stranger who'd caught my father.

"No, baby, i's way too late to stop what we duhn started."

"I think he's kidnapped Papa."

I started to cry then, because I'd been hoping so much that my father had got away and was up North. If he hadn't been able to escape, then what chance did we have?

"We're going to die, Weaver! They're going to catch us."

"Calm yousself, girl. Calm yousself down. Tell me wha's goin' on in dat head a yaws."

I said that I couldn't understand why the visitor was asking about my papa when he must have taken him prisoner already. Weaver considered that while chewing on a stalk of rice, then said, "He's gonna find out who done helped him escape. You papa ain't sayin' and he wants to know real bad."

That made good sense. "If he talks to you, just say you never knew my father," I instructed.

"I can't likely say dat, girl. I been here all mah lahf."

"Then say you weren't here the day he disappeared. You were down in Charleston."

"Whatevuh ya say, Morri. Where ya dink he got yaw papa?"

"I don't know," I answered, but I knew then that I had to find out.

I STAYED AWAY from the house for a few hours, walking in Porter's Woods, hoping real hard that the stranger wouldn't stay too long. If he was here when Beaufort left his signal that the boats were at the landing, waiting to take us to freedom, then we were going to have to do some big killing at River Bend. It made me sick thinking about that, and I didn't know if I could really do it, but I figured that I'd only know for sure when the time came for me to squeeze the trigger.

On the way back to the Big House, I stopped by to see Weaver again, and he told me he'd had a right pleasant conversation with the stranger. He'd even taken him to see the slave cabins.

"Well, I sure as hell hope you didn't go showing him my room. And you better not have told him anything about Papa."

"I didn' say nuttin'. You in one of yaw ebil dispositions, ain't you, chile?"

"Well, I got a right to be."

I marched back to the house, determined to find out what kind of secrets this visitor was keeping. Crow told me that he was outside somewhere, so I snuck up to his room.

I found his leather travel bags sitting on the bed. I opened them up and discovered two things that got my heart jumping: a long white feather and a homemade arrow in three sections, each fitting perfectly into the next.

I sat there, stunned. Because the arrow was just how my papa had described the way his people made them back in Africa. The feather . . . well, it might have been plucked from any old hen, except that it was longer than any I'd ever seen. It made me remember that mysterious white bird Papa told me about, the one he'd tracked for years and finally caught a glimpse of over in Portugal.

The strangeness of this man just got worse and worse, don't you know. Because while flipping through his sketches of birds I discovered a drawing of Papa himself. He had talent, I'd give him that, assuming he was the one who drew it. He'd been able to put something of my father's spirit right on the paper. But it wasn't the man I'd known. Because staring at his face through my tears, I realized that this was my papa before I'd come into the world. He might have been only thirty years old. He could have outrun a deer back then.

Not only that, but there was a note scribbled at the bottom: *Why can't Midnight talk?*

I couldn't figure how this mud-minded slave-trader had a drawing of my papa that must have been made twenty or more years ago, maybe even before he reached River Bend. Most peculiar of all: How could he have known Papa's name wasn't Samuel when he lived all the way across the ocean?

XLVIII

A Whole House of Memories
Just Got Too Filled Up

I WAS WORM–STUPID NOT TO UNDERSTAND sooner that the stranger with my papa's arrow was a little boy turned into a man and come from a long ways away. But when I did, I ran out of the house and across the cornfield and through the slave gardens and along the path to the river. I found him sitting on a rock, and he turned to me like he was scared of what I might do. Maybe he thought I had a knife.

"You're John, aren't you? You're John the gemsbok!"

His eyes glistened and he stood up. "Yes, I've come from Portugal. And, Morri, you don't know how glad I am that I've found you."

I held up his sketch of Papa. "You have his arrow too."

"I've come to find your father. And to take you home if you'll come with me."

He walked to me, slowly, tears falling down his cheeks, but looking worried, too, like he was afraid of hurting me. He hadn't much of a voice left. "May I touch you, Morri?" he whispered.

I nodded, but I wasn't sure if I ought to trust him. He put his hands on my shoulders, then rubbed them down my arms. He was feeling the shape of me, like he was making sure I was real. He was real gentle—too gentle. It scared me.

He smiled then, quick, and wiped his eyes. He looked older now than I'd first thought. He must have been near to thirty-five. I did some calculations in my head and that seemed about right with what Papa had told me.

"What . . . what can I do for you?" I asked, real cautious.

Then he brought my hand to his lips, kissed my palm, and closed it into a fist, like my papa used to do now and then. That convinced me more than anything else that this *had* to be John the gemsbok.

"You keep that with you always," he said.

"I will," I said, my feelings all tangled up and tussling with each other. I kept thinking that this was John, and I ought to trust him because my father had, but the truth was that he was a white man and I didn't.

WE SAT BY the river talking for nearly two hours, and I ended up telling him all I knew about my father disappearing, which was near nothing, and about Master Edward sending me away. I confused him with how quick I spoke, because my heart was hopping around with nervousness, so I had to go back and tell him how everything had started—about my father coming to River Bend and his heel-strings being cut, and the murders of Big and Little Master Henry after their terrible spells. I didn't want to, but everything just sort of tumbled out of me, as if a whole house full of memories had just got too filled up. I even spoke about things I ought to have kept secret—like seeing Big Master Henry soaked with blood, with my empty glass of lemonade on the floor by his hand.

John excused himself real politely and ran off a ways by the river when I told him about my father being crippled for trying to run away before I was born. I thought he was relieving himself, but then I heard gagging sounds. He called to me and asked me if the water was safe to drink, and I told him it tasted mean but didn't do any harm. When he returned, he apologized for leaving me alone.

Sometimes while talking to him I wondered where I was. Because it didn't seem like this could happen at River Bend. I mean, a big tall white man listening to me as if what I said might change the world.

When he asked me who I thought had done the murders, I said I'd suspected Little Master Henry of killing his father, but then when he'd been murdered the same way . . . Well, it was a long time ago and nobody knew.

I wanted to put that subject behind us, so I asked about his journey from Portugal to South Carolina. Pretty soon, he figured out that I was mostly interested in hearing about Papa before I'd known him, so he started to tell me everything he could, which was a whole lifetime more than any white man I ever thought would remember about an African. He began with their first supper together and ended with the trip our papas had taken to England.

Then it was his turn to get all careful. He asked me if Papa told me what his father had done to him in London. I told him what I had heard. He said that that wasn't the way it happened, that Papa may not even have known the whole truth. Then he told me how his father had arranged for him to be kidnapped and sold as a slave to Mr. Miller in Alexandria. Before he told me, he said, "I only hope that you will not hate me when I have finished this terrible story."

I'm not sure what I felt after hearing it. I didn't hate him, no. And I told him that. "If my papa hadn't come here, I wouldn't have been born. And he'd have never met my mamma. He loved her something fierce. I reckon nothing of the past can be changed now. So I don't hate you or even your papa. I rightly ought to, but I don't."

"Morri, how do you think good men do evil things?" he asked. "Because what I haven't yet said about my father was that he was a generous and kind man. And I would not want you to think he didn't love your father. I know he did."

I tried to think of what Papa would say but couldn't come up with anything good enough. When I said I didn't rightly know, John stood up, all determined like. "Morri, I cannot go home till I find your father—or discover what happened to him. If he is a slave somewhere, I shall buy him his freedom. But with all you've told me, I still don't know where to start looking for him."

"I think he must be up North. You might have to go back to New York and start looking there."

"Will you come with me?"

"Me? Master Edward isn't about to let me sail on up to New York just now. Maybe after supper," I said, laughing.

"You don't truly think I'd leave you here now that I've found you? I shall offer any price to Edward for you. Though I apologize for speaking of you like that."

His intentions rightly scared me, don't you know, because any day now Beaufort was going to be leaving a ribbon at our gate. Not that I could tell him that, so I said, "I can't go with you. I have to stay here—in case my father comes back for me."

"But if he were, he would have by now. You said yourself that he must think you're dead."

"I was just saying that because . . . because I get scared sometimes being here without my parents. But he's going to come for me one day. You can be sure of it."

I wasn't saying what I really thought, which was that even if Papa was alive, Master Edward had outfoxed him. My lying got all mixed up with my fear and made my voice snarl. John looked at me as if I'd put a bullet in him. Then I remembered the letter my papa had left for him. But I couldn't very well give it to him without making him want me to go with him even more.

"You *are* angry at me," he said, like he was a little boy who'd just done something bad.

"No, I'm not, but I can't go with you." I stood up, thinking of those guns hidden under the piazza. "I've got to get back to the house now. You don't want to see Master Edward furious with me. He might just do something terrible this time."

"No, Morri," he replied, speaking like there was years of hate in him, "I think I would like to see him furious at you. I might like to see him just try to cut your heel-strings, because I tell you this: I'd put a knife in his neck and twist so hard that he'd be dead before he could even start making an apology to you!"

XLIX

AFTER MORRI LEARNED MY IDENTITY, WE HAD a long talk by the Cooper River. But nothing I told her could do away with her reticence to talk to me. Frustration made me cry. I let myself believe that once she knew who I was she would inherit all of Midnight's old fondness for me. I'd forgotten there was no magic in the world.

I despised my awkwardness in front of her and my inability to convince her to come away with me. Then I truly ruined everything by letting my Highland temper go and declaring that if ever Master Edward tried to cut her heelstrings, I would slit his throat.

Morri spoke to me after that as though I were dangerous—as indeed I might have been. She begged me not to say anything to Master Edward about my having known her father previously. Of course I had no intention of doing so, and her obliging me to swear filled me with disappointment. She also requested that I not mention to Master Edward my desire to purchase her. It was simply out of the question, she said, and would only raise difficulties for her. If I truly cared for her well-being, then I would leave her be.

*   *   *

IN MY ROOM that night, I lay in my bed picturing the slave gardens I'd seen that day—thinking, too, of how Midnight had cleared the land behind our house just after his arrival in Porto, enabling the long-dormant roses there to bloom. This coming spring, his rhododendrons here would be clouds of pink and red.

In the dark of my room, his disappearance left me tossing and turning. One man and one cowardly act could cause damage to so many people, over twenty years or more. The evil of what my father had done might even go on for many generations, because here was Morri, forced to live as a prisoner, isolated from all the rest of the world. Her children would be born and die here as well—or worse, might be sold to new owners living hundreds of miles away.

Risking an invasion of mosquitoes, I opened my window to look for the Archer, but I could not find him. I wished to eat the night and all its stars, just as Luisa had suggested, so that I might gain the prowess of those hunters.

L

My Vengeance Is Here

NOW THAT I'D MET A WHITE MAN WITH A MEM-ory for black faces, I wasn't so sure it was a good thing. Because what did I really know about him?

That's mostly what I was thinking about when I rushed down to River Bend's main gate before dawn the next day. But no plant or ribbon was in sight.

By the first rays of sunlight peeking through the pines, I was already pounding Master Edward's washing on the scrubbing rocks at Christmas Creek. I was hoping that John would leave. I figured I didn't owe him anything just because he'd been friends with my papa. He was only a boy then anyway. Maybe the man he was had nothing to do with the boy he'd been all those years ago.

A little later, Wiggie came to tell me that Rosa's baby, Cullenn, was coughing and I was needed. I was worried it was the croup, so I went out to Papa's garden and mixed up some chamomile and cassena for him to breathe in. The air in his cabin was stale as molded bread, so I took him out to Porter's Woods myself and built a fire there, because Rosa was a field hand and couldn't be spared from weeding the rice.

So that was where I next saw John—sitting at the edge of

the woods. He asked if Cullenn was my baby, which made me laugh, since anyone could see that he didn't look anything like me.

"Some babies take after the father," he said, his face getting all long and sad. "Like you, for instance."

I looked away, because his eyes were softening up my anger and I needed each and every bit of it if I was going to have the courage to pick up my pistol and march out of River Bend.

"Morri, I have to take you away from here," he told me.

"I thank you for thinking of me," I said coolly, "but it's useless talking about these things. I can't go."

He took a couple of steps toward me. "Don't you understand what I'm telling you?" he pleaded. "You don't have to stay here any longer."

"You're the one who doesn't understand. I'm likely to be punished if the overseer catches me talking to you. You're just making life difficult for me. So let me be." When he wouldn't move back, I hollered, "I can't be seen talking to you! Go away."

I saw I'd hurt him bad, but I knew it was for his own good and didn't say another word. Even so, I felt real guilty.

I didn't catch another glimpse of him all the rest of that day, Saturday. Weaver said that he saw him a couple of times sitting on a rock by the Cooper River, looking all worried, drawing in his sketchbook like his life depended on it.

John had supper with the family in the Big House on Saturday evening. Mistress Anne had come up from Charleston, and Master Edward and Mistress Kitty had arrived from Cordesville. They'd all heard there was a Scottish artist staying here, so they just had to stop by to get a good look at him. Crow told me later that Mistress Anne flirted with John something shameful nearly the whole supper.

I stayed most of that night with Rosa in her cabin, since Cullenn was still coughing and needed my constant attention. His nose was awful stuffed, so I did one of my father's tricks and covered it with my mouth to suck out all that muck.

Sunday was our day free, and Cullenn was better, so I told Rosa how to care for him, then went with Weaver over to Comingtee so he could meet his wife and children. We got bad news there right away. Martha and his two sons were having second thoughts about our running away. But Weaver said that it was too late to change our minds, that we had to go because too many folks knew about the plan and we already had the guns. Martha told us that a washing girl named Sarah was going to come with us, too. She and Weaver's son Frederick wanted to get married.

I passed the day watching the cotton barges drift on by, embroidering the sleeves on my Sunday dress, and singing some with Weaver's other son, Taylor, who had an old guitar. No one said another word about escaping. Weaver did a little fishing and caught us some carp, which tasted good for supper, though we all nibbled at the fixings as if we were going to be hanged in the morning. It's funny how nightfall can make you think about death.

We returned home late on Sunday, near midnight. In the morning, while I was hugging a few last minutes of sleep to me, Wiggie drove John to a house near Stromboli where that fancy black woman lived who'd first come with him to River Bend. I thought he'd given up on helping me, and a whole lot of feelings about that mixed together in my mind. I guess I even felt hurt. But then Crow told me that John had spent a good part of Sunday putting nosy questions to him, Lily, and even Mr. Johnson. He wanted to know all about the murders of Big and Little Master Henry. He had them describe everything in detail, down to what their spells had been like. He even asked Lily for her lemonade recipe!

After hearing that, I was mighty relieved he'd left us. Having him off the plantation meant there was no chance of any of us having to harm him.

Cullenn was just about all better by Monday. No fever and no cough. I figured that at least one good thing had happened. One good thing a day is all I generally ask for, though someday I plan on working myself up to two.

I AIN'T NEVER ever going to forget Tuesday the Second of September, 1823. Because on that morning I found a red ribbon tied to the gate and a pot of pink carnations. I can't say how I carried them back with me to the Big House, because I don't remember a single thing.

I went to see Lily. I do remember that. She sat me down and fanned me, because I was burning up. "Baby, you's scarin' me somet'in' fierce."

"I'm scaring myself," I told her.

*   *   *

WE WERE PLANNING on getting the muskets, pistols, powder, and swords out from under the piazza on Sunday at nightfall. We'd go out the front gate and make our way to Petrie's Landing, where the boats were waiting for us. We'd row them downriver to Charleston Harbor and Captain Ott.

We were going to bind Master Edward and Mr. Johnson with rope and lock them in the First Barn. We'd tie up the two Negro foremen too, since we'd never been able to trust them. By the time someone came along to let them out of the barn, we'd be safe on the *Landmark*. Or dead.

THAT NIGHT, WAY past midnight, I crawled under the piazza to get one of the muskets. It was dark, and I was afraid of a rattlesnake clamping its jaws down on my hand. I was shaking like a little girl. But I got it. Its barrel fit into the palm of my hand like death itself.

I gave it to Weaver at his cabin door. He woke Saul, Sweet-Pea, and Drummond, the field hands who slept in the same room as him. Sweet-Pea and Drummond were twins, just twenty years old, and Saul was their uncle. Weaver told them what we were planning. Sweet-Pea would come. Drummond said no thank you, it was a fool plan, but he wouldn't say nothing to the overseer or Master Edward. Saul said he wasn't sure if he'd risk it. Weaver stayed up that night by the light of two candles and showed Sweet-Pea and Saul how to put in the powder and take a shot. By dawn, Saul was damned certain he could fire the gun, so he agreed to come as well.

At the same time, I told Lily what we were planning. She grabbed a hold of the brass cross she kept around her neck like it might fly away and said that she was powerful afraid for me. She didn't seem to understand that I was telling her that she could come too. She just shook her head and said, "Not me, baby, I's gonna die at River Bend, don' ya know."

Nothing I could do could make her come along.

"I's gonna miss ya, baby," she said, starting to cry, "but I's gonna pray ya makes it up Nawth." She took my shoulders. "Ya bettuh jes' send me a lettuh when you gets there, 'cause I don' wanna be worryin' none 'bout ya. I'll ask Massa Edwood to read it to me. He's gonna be right relieved knowin' you's safe up Nawth."

She winked at that, and we burst out laughing. Then she held me to her breast like she was my mamma.

So now there were four of us from River Bend agreed to escape—me, Weaver, Sweet-Pea, and Saul. Four more from Comingtee made eight.

BACKBEND AND HOPPER-ANNE, Lily's grandchildren, said on Wednesday that they'd come, along with Backbend's wife, Lucy. They'd be taking their baby boy, Scooper, as well. Grandma Blue said she was too old to go traipsing about the countryside with dogs hankering after her old African hide. But her son, Parker, and his wife, Christmas-Eve—who was born on December the Twenty-Fourth, of course—were coming, along with her grandson Randolph, and his children Lawrence and Mimi. Rosa and her husband, Langston, said it was too risky. We didn't tell Wiggie yet, since we couldn't be sure he wouldn't pass on that information to Master Edward or the foremen.

Crow . . . We pleaded with the lean old buzzard, but he wouldn't change his no to yes. When we said we were going to lock all the white folks and the black foremen in the First Barn, he grinned like he did when he was young and said, "Someone got to stay behin' and make sure they don't get away. That'll be me."

"Please, Crow, I'm begging you. Come with us. We can't leave you."

"You 'member when they whip me so bad my ribs showed like teeth? When they did that, girl"—he squeezed my hand real tight—"I says to myself, 'Crow, you got to get back at 'em and make them bleed.' This is a chance for me, baby girl. You leave me here and I'm gonna make sure they ain't goin' nowhere. Their eyes gonna bleed when they sees River Bend empty and you long gone. And I want to see that for myself!"

"But you can come! There's freedom out there. Crow, you've got to come. I can't leave you."

"No, baby girl, my vengeance is here."

SO IT WAS decided by Wednesday at suppertime that thirteen of us from River Bend—including one newborn baby—were going to close the gate to our plantation forever behind us. And then there was Weaver's family from Comingtee: Martha, Taylor, Frederick, and Sarah.

Lord, I hoped that we could get seventeen persons on the three rowboats that Captain Ott was planning on leaving at Petrie's Landing.

*　　*　　*

LATE WEDNESDAY NIGHT, Weaver snuck across the bridge to Comingtee, where he told his family to make their way to River Bend by six o'clock on Sunday afternoon. Martha was sure now she had no courage for the escape, but Weaver told her there'd be a feather bed waiting for her in New York. That was a little joke between the two of them, since Martha was always saying that just once in her life she wanted to sleep on a downy mattress with a pillow that wasn't made out of old clothes. Weaver had always said the first thing he'd do with any money he ever made was buy her a proper bed.

THURSDAY MORNING, ALL of us except Weaver were as jittery as fish out of water about what was going to happen. We were all thinking the same thing: that if even one person said something stupid to Mr. Johnson or one the foremen, we'd all be neck-high in night soil. I was so close to fainting half the time that I had to keep dousing my head with water.

Then, around about noon, John walked in the front gate carrying a leather bag and his sketchbook. Weaver saw him before I did, because he was helping flood the rice fields about two hundred yards from the entrance. I only heard him when he reached the piazza, because he called for Crow. I'd been sweeping out a ragged troop of ants from the kitchen and ran to see who it was. He looked at me like he had some polished secret inside him that was going to change everything.

LI

ONE SEEMINGLY HARMLESS REMARK FROM Mistress Anne at our supper on Saturday evening, along with one of my own observations, combined to give me suspicions about the origin of the spells suffered by both Big and Little Master Henry. If I had not discovered their cause, then I believe that Morri might never have grown to trust me.

I was close to despair when the meal began, as Morri had again refused to even consider coming away with me. I'd seen her caring for a sick baby that afternoon and spoken to her gently, but she shouted back that I was making her life even more difficult than it already was. I simply couldn't seem to say anything right to her.

Mistress Anne spoke viciously at first about her dead father and brother, calling the former a brute and the latter a weakling. In the end she softened, however, and she improved my mood when she asked Lily to prepare fresh lemonade for us all, as in the days of her youth when Samuel had given a glass every night to her father and brother for health reasons.

"You know, Mr. Stewart," Mistress Anne said, "my father and brother were subject to the most terrible spells of fever and dizziness. To be totally honest with you, I occasionally fear my children have inherited this propensity, but so far we have been most fortunate."

To my subsequent questions, she replied that she had never asked Lily for her lemonade recipe but that it must have contained some of the herbs Samuel grew in his garden. "We all benefited considerably from his presence. Though he vanished into nothing three years ago. I tremble for the fate of the poor little man. I truly do. By now, dogs have probably eaten him down to the last bone."

As Lily entered the room with drinking glasses and a jug of lemonade, Anne requested that she tell us her recipe. It consisted of lemon juice, water, honey, ground mint leaves, and a powder made from several other herbs. Which ones precisely, she could not say. She told us that only Samuel had known, though Morri had come up with a recipe nearly as good.

By now I understood that the herbs were irrelevant, however. This would not have occurred to me if, during my childhood, Midnight and I had not read together on dozens of occasions Strabo's account of the victory of King Mithradates of Pontus over the Romans.

What *was* relevant was the honey.

I questioned Crow and Lily further the next day. Each was hesitant to speak to me, but through the accumulation of small details I was able to bring the dark treasure I sought to the surface.

Crow told me that Big Master Henry's spells had started before Midnight's arrival at River Bend, but he also dated that to 1809, which—from what Morri had told me—I knew to be a lie. He confirmed that only Mistress Holly and the Master had had keys to the bedroom in which his body had been found.

I questioned Crow at the door to his small room, just off the study. To change the subject, he showed me some of his knickknacks, including two molds he had made by pressing scallop shells into riverbed clay. He said he'd once had many others, some of which had been fired in an oven by his recently deceased younger brother, who'd been a blacksmith over at Limerick Plantation. And not just shells—he'd made molds of coins and Samuel's flowers as well.

Later, Lily told me that when Big Master Henry was under the power of the spells, it was as though he were soused to his eyeballs. Little Master Henry had been just the same, she said.

She also assured me that Samuel's medical knowledge and care had always returned Big and Little Master Henry to health. She started when

I asked if the particular lemonade she made during their spells was in any way different from her daily brew. She denied any difference.

I knew I would also hide the truth if I were in her position. To alleviate her fears, I said that I was quite certain she had never done anything wrong to either of her masters. Then it was my turn to lie. In a confessional voice, I said that one of my daughters back in England was subject to similar spells. I explained that I was merely hoping to learn the secret of her recipe so I might alleviate my child's suffering.

Thinking of my girls in faraway London, it was all too easy to let my eyes fill with tears. Softening, Lily whispered that when the Master was feeling a bit under the weather Midnight would sometimes ask her to secretly use what she called the curing honey—a powerful and dark variety that he extracted from the combs of a particular hive in Porter's Woods. Only he knew its location, though he had passed that secret on to Morri. Lily assured me that Morri would surely give me a jar of it for my daughter before I left River Bend.

I kissed her for this kindness, and glimpsed her rubbing her cheek as I stepped out the door.

SO I LEARNED how Midnight had brought on the spells. As to his motivation, it didn't seem that a slave would need a particular reason to give *mad honey* to his master. Yet Morri had provided me with one earlier, when she told me that her father had earned her the right to read, as well as gardens for himself and the other slaves, by curing Big Master Henry of the worst of his spells and then threatening never to help him again. Little Master Henry had likely granted further concessions for the same reason.

Lily always thought the spells got worse by themselves and that the curing honey was all that stood between her master and the grave. She had no reason to doubt Midnight, whose talents as a healer were renowned. He told her when to start using it and when to stop.

Of course, it might have been possible that the very first spell had been real and had given Midnight the idea for his gambit. In any case, once he had seen how easy it was to produce a grave illness and then effect a cure by withholding the cause, he understood the usefulness of this ruse. He had planted his rhododendrons to have access to the mad honey made from their pollen.

It was, in fact, a brilliant strategy. Likely he'd regarded it as unfortunate but necessary. And sanctioned by history through the victory of King Mithradates. It would have also been a reminder of the power that honey held in the Bushman culture.

DURING MY VERY first talk with Morri, she told me that Big Master Henry had had his way with some of the slave girls for a month prior to his falling victim to a terrible spell. A sudden spark in her eyes—which she tried to hide from me by gazing down—led me to believe that she had been one of his victims. Even if she had kept this a secret from everyone, her father would likely have guessed from some subtle change in her bearing.

This was motivation enough for Midnight to commit murder, as I saw it, as was the cutting of his heel-strings. Yet I didn't believe he had done either killing. For if he had sought to end either Big or Little Master Henry's life, he merely would have had to increase the dosage of honey or add a more potent poison to Lily's lemonade.

When I mentioned the possibility that Mistress Holly had committed the murders to Crow and Lily, they replied that it was impossible. They assured me that she'd cowered in front of her husband like a whipped dog. Lily also told me that the Mistress had been so fond of her ne'er-do-well son that she would have laid down her life for him without a moment's hesitation.

It seemed possible that up to three different people were involved in the murders: Midnight to bring on the spells with the mad honey and one or two others to plunge knives into Big and Little Master Henry.

If, in the first case, the perpetrator had been Mistress Holly, then her husband would not have cried out upon seeing her in his room. Though likely the murderer had stabbed him at the height of one of his spells, when he was delirious, and he therefore might not have been able to cry out the killer's name, whoever he or she was.

Unless he was already dead prior to the use of the blade and it had been used merely to divert suspicion from poisoning. That seemed to me likely, except that Crow had said that a great deal of blood had soaked into the victims' shirts. If they had been dead for even half an hour, I did not believe this would have been the case.

Perhaps the second murder had been the handiwork of Mistress Anne, who seemed to me a lady of thwarted hopes and vengeance, carrying all the rage her mother had never dared to express.

*   *   *

I'D HAD LITTLE reason to seek out Mr. Johnson previous to these discoveries, but I now went to him in the fields to see if he might have any ideas on the matter.

"I've nothing to tell you, sir" was all he would answer with regard to the murders. In the stern compression of his lips I could see he might have liked to thrash me for questioning him about such a delicate matter. The obvious had yet to occur to me—that he regarded himself as partly responsible, since the day-to-day running of the plantation was under his command.

"Do you believe one of the slaves capable of having committed the murders?" I asked.

"I would believe none of them incapable."

"And Mistress Holly?"

He bristled. "What are you suggesting, Mr. Stewart?"

"Only that she was gravely unhappy."

"I can't rightly see how that concerns you. No, I can't see that at all."

His stance had changed to one of defiance, and I could plainly see that I had made an enemy. I apologized quickly and walked back to the Big House.

FROM MY WINDOW, I spotted Morri returning home late that night, near the stroke of twelve. As she whispered good night to Weaver on the gravel driveway by the piazza, I realized what I'd previously refused to admit—that speaking with her would prove useless. She had told me so much in passing the day before, but I saw now, in the way she gazed slowly around the plantation, how hard it would be for her to leave this place without her father. Particularly as it was the only home she had ever known.

Sitting on my bed, listening to the ratcheting sound of the crickets and the hooting of a far-off owl, all the night seemed to be telling me, *Several lives are depending on you. You can work things out if you go slowly....*

I decided then that it would be best for me to join Isaac and Luisa for a few days. This would give Morri an opportunity to consider her destiny without my wishes playing havoc with her emotions. Also, I would prevail upon Luisa to return with me and speak to Morri. I was sure that she would have a much better chance of convincing the girl to leave River Bend than I did, that no argument I could ever come up with would be nearly as eloquent as Luisa's freedom itself.

STAYING WITH LUISA and Isaac—having time to think in congenial surroundings—only made me realize that I had no choice but to defy Morri's wishes and offer Edward every penny in my possession for her, even if she did not want to be bought. If he refused to sell her, I would find a way to steal her. I would undoubtedly need help, but Luisa had already mentioned that she and Isaac had hidden runaways before, and I felt certain that I could count on them.

I remained with Isaac and Luisa for three and a half days, and on the last morning Isaac proposed a way to get Morri away from the plantation without arousing suspicion—so I could talk to her calmly and wear down her opposition.

"Just lease her," he said.

"I don't understand."

"Slaves are leased out by their masters to do all sorts of work—as stevedores, seamstresses, cooks... Tell Edward that you want to lease Morri for a week or two to help you travel around the plantations of the Low Country. Offer him fifty dollars for her and another fifty for use of one of his carriages. He will accept. Then you will have plenty of time to convince her and you'll not have to force her to do anything. You can bring her to our home and Luisa will talk to her about the differences between slavery and freedom. It'll be quiet here, and we can all get to know one another."

Luisa was in agreement. We even dared to regard it as a foolproof plan.

L I I

Seventeen Lives
in My Hands

MASTER EDWARD CALLED ME INTO THE TEA room with a nasty shout just before noon on Thursday. His voice was so loud I thought maybe he'd crack some of the crystal I'd just dusted. John, who'd come back late that morning to River Bend, was with him.

"Morri, I have a rather exciting proposition for you," the Master said. "Mr. Stewart would like to lease you for a week or so, to help him orient himself in the Low Country. It would involve some travel. There would be a five-dollar wage in it for you. I daresay that we could spare you without too much suffering around here." He smirked at me. "What do you say to that?"

He was so full of himself that you'd have thought he'd won election to the State Legislature. He looked too happy for this to be good for me, and I ought to have known that some cold-as-death plan was hiding inside him.

"I ain't got no desire to leave, Master Edward. I'd shawly prefuh to stay here at River Bend, if it's all the same to you."

"You know I can order you, but Mr. Stewart and I would both prefer that you agree to go."

"Would you mind my saying a word?" John asked.

"No, no," Master Edward replied, "go right ahead, sir."

"Morri," he said, "I assure you that I truly want your help. I believe you might even appreciate the adventure. And Edward and I both agree that you are the person most qualified."

"Mr. Stewart would like to set out with you on Saturday," the Master added. "But you'll have to come up to Comingtee on Sunday because there's a supper we've planned. It's going to be a big party. I'm sure you'll like being there."

It was plainly the first time John had heard about the fete. Master Edward explained to him that some planter families were getting together. "We're counting on you coming," he said.

"I'd be honored."

Edward the Cockerel turned to me and gave me a stern look. "So, Morri, I'm expecting you to travel with Mr. Stewart on Saturday. Then on Sunday afternoon you'll come up to Comingtee with us all and help in the kitchen. Monday, you'll be back with Mr. Stewart, this time for a week or so."

"I ain't sure."

"What aren't you sure about?"

"If I's going with him."

"I don't mind telling you that I'm mighty disappointed in you, girl. I rightly thought you'd be pleased to get this opportunity. If I have to, I'll order you with the lash. How'd you like twenty? You hear that, you silly nigger girl?"

I SAT IN my room trying my best to think what to do, but it was like I was stuck in a big old chimney without any light—no way up and no way down. I couldn't think of how to make John not take me along with him without telling him about us running away. Just for once I wished I had the power to say *no*. When I got the right to say that one simple word up North, I didn't know if I was ever going to say *yes* to anything ever again.

JOHN CAME TO me an hour later, while I was ironing in Lily's room, just upstairs from the kitchen. He apologized for Master Edward's rudeness and said that he had hoped I'd be pleased to leave the plantation for a week or so.

Holding tight to all my years of anger, I said, "You don't know anything about me or River Bend. You're just a stranger here. And you come in meddling and everything, thinking you know what's what. But you don't. You don't know what an infernal mess you're making just by being here. Now, I'm not about to change my mind, so don't you go trying to make me. Because even if you have me whipped, I won't agree to leave with you. I'm not about to go traipsing across the countryside with you or any other white man. And now," I said, picking up my iron and sliding it along a collar, "I got plenty of work to do. So just you let me and everybody else be. I know you were fond of my papa, and I know he was fond of you, but he's long gone. He might even be dead. And I'm not him, so just leave me be. Just leave me be right now!"

I made myself as mud-mean as I could, because he'd proven himself more stubborn than I'd thought he was. With only three days and nights till Sunday, I had no time left to talk nice to a white man, no matter who he was. I had seventeen lives in my hands.

When he wouldn't budge, I screamed like a banshee at him. "Don't you understand what I'm saying? We don't want you at River Bend. *I* don't want you here. Get out and find yourself someone else to buy!"

THAT NIGHT, AFTER supper, Master Edward had Crow call me into his study, where he asked for my decision. "I ain't goin' nowhere. I gots to get my work done here at River Bend and that's what I aim on doin'."

"And what if I were to call Mr. Johnson?"

"Then you go on ahead and do your callin'."

He stomped out of the room like he was trying to push his big ugly boots straight through the floor. I ran to Lily, because I was frightened.

Next thing that happened was that Copper, one of the black foremen, rushed into the kitchen behind Mr. Johnson, murder in his eyes. Lily was standing in front of me as a shield, but Copper threw her into the cabinet where she kept her pans and grabbed me by the wrist. I tried kicking him, and so did Lily, but he caught my leg and lifted me right up over his shoulder.

Lily was screaming now, but Mr. Johnson slapped her so hard she fell to the ground with a shriek. While she was lying there, he kicked her twice in the gut. "You don't defy me, you useless nigger sow!" he shouted.

Copper hauled me out to the yard, where he and the other foreman tied me to the whipping barrel.

"Are you going with Mr. Stewart on Saturday?" Master Edward snarled.

"I ain't goin' nowhere with nobody!" I shouted.

In that moment before the lash cuts into your hope, you think you've got the strength to defy it. You think your righteous anger is so rock hard that it's going to make you invincible. And you think you ain't your body. No, the *you* that's important is deep inside, where nobody can reach it. But what you forget is that even the biggest wall of determination crumbles to dust when it's pounded enough. When it does, you find you ain't so deep inside your body as you thought. No, you're right there on the surface, where your skin is coming off in burning strips. You're nothing but the pain itself and you hate it more even than you hate the white man doing the lashing.

"Give her twenty to start with, Mr. Johnson," Master Edward ordered.

I gritted my teeth. The first stroke cut the air. It didn't hurt so bad— just stung like a wasp. I thought I could make it to twenty without peeing all over myself.

"Two..."

That one singed. I let out a shriek.

"Three..."

I felt my anger running clean away, hopelessness rising up to meet the next lash.

"Four..."

I let go all over the barrel and my legs. I couldn't help the tears from coming now. And I couldn't catch enough breath.

"Five..."

The whip hit bone. I pictured Lily hanging on to that cross of hers. I thought of God. I begged Him for help. I began to recite a verse from one of my favorite Psalms: *... the snare is broken and we are escaped ... the snare is broken—*

"Six..."

"Please stop, Master Edward," I moaned. "Please stop."

"Seven..."

I imagined my whole self was coming off—in bloody bits.

"Please let Morri go, Mastuh Edwood," Crow shouted. "You whip me instead."

"Eight..."

I was weeping now. Then I shrieked for help as loud as I could. And I hollered what he wanted: "I'll go with Mr. Stewart!"

Mr. Johnson stopped, but Master Edward ordered him to pay me no mind and keep on going. What I didn't realize is that he wasn't truly punishing me for defying him at all. No, sir, he had another, better reason for hurting me good and he was enjoying this.

"Nine..."

By now I was tugging something fierce at my bindings and crying out to God and Mantis and Papa. And I kept on shrieking for them, but no one would come.

"Ten..."

Crow begged again for Master Edward to lash him instead of me. I knew he was offering himself not just for me, but out of loyalty to my papa. But his voice was far off. Then I heard him grunt. I think Master Edward must have kicked him in the belly. I couldn't get enough air to scream so loud anymore. Which was damned good, because it meant I'd faint soon. I was hoping that Copper wouldn't throw water on me to wake me up.

"Eleven..."

Eleven didn't fall. By turning my head, I could see Mr. Johnson on the ground, his face in the dirt. He was getting to his feet real slow, but revenge was in his eyes.

"Whoa there!" Master Edward shouted. "Just wait a minute, Mr. Johnson!"

I could hear a scuffle and men yelling. When I faced forward again, I saw a shadow crossing in front of me. I thought it was my papa's.

I MUST HAVE fainted sure enough, because when I woke up I was facedown in my own bed and Lily was smoothing some fat onto my back.

"Ya gonna be jes' fine, baby," she was saying.

I turned to look at her. Her left eye was puffy and nearly closed.

"Can't see nuttin' outta mah left one anyways." She lifted a glass of water to my lips. Crow was there too, standing back from the bed. In a voice hopping with righteousness, the likes of which I hadn't heard coming out of him in years, he explained to me that Mr. Stewart had dashed down from his bedroom when he heard me screaming and run straight for Mr. Johnson and knocked him hard in the dirt, threatening to kill him if he ever touched me again.

"Ooh, baby," Lily said, "dat man was rattlesnek mad!"

Crow added that Mr. Johnson had wanted to fight a duel with Mr. Stewart right then and there, but Master Edward had calmed him down and sent him to his cottage. As he was leaving, he apparently gave me one more lash just to be spiteful.

"And Mr. Stewart?"

Lily replied that he'd been here to see me already, had been right where she was sitting. He'd wanted to make sure I was still alive. He had already spoken to Master Edward and was back in his bedroom now.

"What did Edward the Cockerel say to him?"

"He bawled him out at first, for hittin' Mr. Johnson," said Crow. "Then they drank some whiskey and ever't'ing was jes' fine."

"And nobody's told about us?"

Lily smacked my hand playfully. "Now, you hush up and stop frettin' yousself, chile!"

I WOKE UP Friday morning wishing I could slip out of the skin on my back like a snake and leave it to holler at someone else. One thing was for sure—I was going to have to figure a way out of going away with John the next day and of taking him to Comingtee on Sunday. If I couldn't, Weaver and the others were just going to have to escape without me. And I sure as hell didn't intend to get left behind in Egypt with Pharaoh. No, sir.

An hour later, I was already running a fever and slurring my speech like my tongue was made of glue. Crow reckoned it was the whipping. Lily took care of me in her room.

Master Edward had gone back with his family to Cordesville by now. He'd be returning Saturday morning by nine and had told Mr. Johnson that if I hadn't left with Mr. Stewart by the time he got here I was to be given thirty more lashes. Lily ran to fetch John, who was sitting down by the river, sketching the slaves in the rice fields nearby. She said we owed it to him to tell him how I was doing since he'd clobbered Mr. Johnson something good on my behalf. He came in looking all glum and sat by my bed, with his arms crossed over his chest, not saying a word. I was too weak to say anything mean-spirited to him. Truth is, I liked him looking at me with those clear, sad eyes. I guess everybody likes to feel sorry for themselves once in a while.

He asked Lily if he could be alone with me for a few minutes, so she went back to her cleaning. He felt my pulse and found it racing, then wet a towel with water and laid it cool across my forehead. He said my papa had done that for him once, almost twenty-five years ago, just before making Hyena leave him be. He said he would never forgive himself for getting me whipped.

"You've got to stop saying you're sorry all the time," I said, smiling.

"In any case, I would never want to force you to come away with me."

"So you'll go?"

"I don't know what to do. I suppose I'll stay through Sunday, when I have to go to that dinner party at Comingtee with Edward. I pray that you'll change your mind by then. This is no life for you. You must know that."

"I know it, but I still can't go," I said.

"I don't think I'll ever understand that. Morri, I know it's a big decision, and I'm willing to wait for you for as long as it takes. I can go back to Charleston and wait there for a few days, then come back here. I can keep coming back. Don't you see, I can't just let you stay here."

I figured that John would hear about our escape soon enough. Whether we got away or not, he'd be freed from his need to help me. "Just wait a week for me," I told him. "If I don't send you word, then leave without me. I know it makes no sense, but just do what I ask."

"Very well, I'll do as you say—for now. But what'll you do about Edward? He's sure to be angry with you for not leaving with me."

"Don't worry, I'll handle him," I said convincingly, but the truth was I didn't know what to do to get him to ease up on me. I didn't want to think about him, so I asked, "What about you? Will you go back to New York when you're done here?"

"Yes. Your father may be up North, like you said. There has to be a way to find him. And, Morri, when I've found him, if he's still a slave somewhere, I will see him to freedom. Then, if you've decided to stay here, we'll both come back for you. I promise you that. I only ask that if you receive any news of him you write to me. I'll leave you my address. And there is one other thing I would ask—though I have no right to do so."

"What?"

That's when he asked if he might kiss me. I'd never gotten a kiss on my cheek from a white man before. It felt dangerous, but delicate too— like something that children did when no one was looking.

SATURDAY MORNING, THINGS started going wrong right away. Weaver came in to wake me at dawn. He said that Backbend, Lucy, and

Hopper-Anne had changed their minds about joining us. They said my getting whipped and then going feverish was a sign that it was the wrong time. Sweet-Pea and Saul were also near to quitting. To keep Edward from sending folks to the Sugar House, they were talking about letting something slip to Mr. Johnson before things went too far.

If I didn't get up and talk to them all, Weaver said, then we were maybe going to have to give up on everything. But when I stood up, the world started twirling and I nearly fell over. So I told Weaver I'd meet him at the noonday break and talk to Backbend, Saul, and Sweet-Pea. It was a risk, because Mr. Johnson would wonder why I'd gone into the fields, but it couldn't be helped.

I had Lily make me some strong chamomile tea, but that didn't help much with the aches all over my body. Around about eleven o'clock, Master Edward came home and was hopping with fury when he saw me still there. He came into my room and threw off my blanket, saying that I was to be dressed and out of River Bend in a half hour or he'd have me whipped again. On his way out, he spit on the floor and told me he'd never met a nigger girl as stubborn as me.

I couldn't understand why he was being more mud-minded than usual till later. Then I realized that he liked his revenge served up before the main course.

Lily ran off to fetch John again. I hoped he'd ask Master Edward to go easy on me. I was feeling as if my life was turning around this day. If I left with John now, I'd be stuck forever at River Bend. Likely no one else would escape either, because if Weaver was thinking about failure, then things were coming apart good.

When John stepped into my room, I asked Lily to leave us again, then told him to close the door. Praying to Mantis that I was doing the right thing, I whispered to him about us escaping. And I said that he had to make certain that I didn't leave River Bend today because I had a good deal of convincing to do.

Telling a white man all this was one of the hardest things I'd ever done. I expected him to turn me in to Master Edward. I even said that I'd understand, him being of the same race and all, but that for the sake of my papa's memory I surely hoped he wouldn't.

"Morri," he said with a powerful sigh, "if I haven't told anyone about the mad honey your father gave to Big and Little Master Henry, then why would I say anything about you escaping?"

My heart almost popped out of my chest when he said that. I made him tell me again, since I wasn't sure I'd heard right. He explained then how he'd figured things out. I was quick to say that Papa hadn't done the killing. "He told me about the curing honey, sure enough—in case I ever needed to use it to defend myself. But he also promised me that he didn't do it."

John said he'd guessed that too. He had his money on Mistress Holly for the first murder and Mistress Anne for the second.

"So you'll make sure I stay at River Bend?" I said.

"I'll talk to Edward and invent some reason. Now, what weapons do you have?"

I explained about the muskets, pistols, and swords.

"You know how to use them?"

"Weaver does. He trained some of the men. He showed me too."

"And powder?"

"Plenty," I assured him.

"Where are you storing everything?"

"Under the piazza. Except for one pistol with me here."

"Here? Where?"

"Under the bed."

"That's insane! If they find it here, you'll be hanged. Give it to me."

I just looked at him. He held out his hand. "Give it to me. I'll say it's mine. Don't worry, I shall leave it in my room, under the bed. You can collect it there before your escape."

I still wasn't sure. He wriggled his fingers. "It is much safer with me. I'll not betray you. Everything of value I've ever done in my life has led me to you. I swear upon your father's memory. Now give me the gun!"

I crawled under the bed and handed it up to him. In that gesture, I knew I was placing my life in his hands. And I didn't like it.

WATCHING HIM SQUEEZE that gun in his hand, I knew I'd also have to give him the letter from my father. It was his, after all. So after he'd left my room, I slipped out of the house and made my way to its hiding place in Porter's Woods. Digging there with my hands, I started crying. Digging things up is a bit too close to remembering, I guess. I didn't give it to him right away because I knew that afterward we'd always be linked by whatever my papa asked of him. I wasn't sure that was such a good thing and only got the courage to do it that evening. After he'd read it, he couldn't speak. He sat with his head in his hands. When he handed it to me, I read it over. I ought to have been pleased that Papa trusted him so much, but the way my father wrote made me go all cold. Because I knew now that he wasn't up North. I'd never see him again. I was an orphan. And I didn't want any other father, even one my papa had picked for me.

We sat next to each other and he touched his long white feather to both our brows. Then he put his arm around my shoulder. I felt a quiet power in him that I'd only felt before in my father. I could almost hear his belly drumming. But all that did was make me more unhappy, because he wasn't him.

LIII

MY DEAREST JOHN,
We saw you from afar and we are dying of hunger.

    If you are reading this letter, then you have come to River Bend at long last. But I can no longer greet you in person. For that I am very, very sorry. How good it would be to walk hand in hand with you down by Christmas Creek. I stumble along like an old Bushman now, with a wee limp, so you would have to wait for me to catch up to you from time to time. But I do not believe you would much mind. It would even do you some good to go slower than you usually do!

    Try not to be sad that we shall not meet. What is left of me is still in you. And what was joined so long ago in Porto cannot ever truly be separated. You know that or you would not be here. Thank you for coming.

    The lass who has handed you this letter is my daughter, Morri. We call her that, but her true name is Memoria. She is what I have made of my past. And she, too, carries what remains of me. I know you will be as kind to her as you would be to me. We look alike, do we not?

    I have done what I can to push the evil that lives at River Bend as far away as I can. As Benjamin might say, I have tried to restore some of the silver that lingers inside this village of darkness. I can see now the nature of this evil, though it eluded me for years. It is a forgetfulness of all the stories of the world. But we remember the Bushmen stories, you and I, and we shall triumph in the end.

Remember how the Olive Tree Sisters would tell us to surround ourselves with beautiful things? You will see how I've tried to follow their advice with the gardens I have planted, particularly if you are fortunate enough to walk through them after a rainstorm. The rain here reminds me of where I was born, and that has been a good thing. Though I should have wished to walk for many miles and hunt.

You must play the gemsbok here. What you will see will make you wish to become a Scottish lion, but that would only bring you trouble. They understand nothing-nothing of Lion, Ostrich, Giraffe, and Zebra at River Bend. They understand nothing of the Torah. The Time of the Hyena is eternal here. So I beg you not to remain too long. We both know how Hyena has tried to fool you in the past. He will try again. Hold tight to the white feather I gave you when your spirits are failing. It will protect you. Have no fear—I can see Mantis still riding between your toes.

You will find many birds to imitate in the Low Country, many of them beautiful-beautiful, and they, too, will help you. They will remind you of all that is inside you and that cannot be damaged by this place.

Years ago I told you how Mantis stole Honey from Ostrich and how I would steal you a treasure if you ever needed it. I did not lie. For even though I cannot be with you, that treasure stands before you. I entrust Morri into your care. You will need each other to move safely into the future. Take her from this place and give her a home. Raise her as your daughter. I can think of no one who would make a better father, and I know that she will love you. If you are still the John I knew (as you must be), then I know what you felt for her the moment you saw her.

I shall tell you a secret: You never knew it, but you are the greatest hunter I have ever known. Your being here is proof of that. Perhaps you are not the bravest or the strongest, though those qualities are more present in you than you believe. Or even the swiftest, though you ran like the wind when you were a wee thing and likely still do. No, the greatest hunters are the most loyal and loving. So you will not fail. I know this.

Give my fondest regards to Benjamin. Tell him I have been working hard and that there is no place that needs our Jewish alchemy more than America. If I have been able to restore a little of what had been broken and forgotten, then perhaps it is not so bad that I have been sent here. Send a kiss from me to the Olive Tree Sisters and tell them that they have helped me do what I needed to do. Hug your mother for me and tell her I remember her only with fondness. I hope that she is well. Embrace your dearest father for me as well, and tell him that he is forgiven. I hope that he has pardoned the wrong I did him.

John, please forgive me for not being with you while you grew to adulthood. At this moment, that is my most painful regret. Know that I am eternally proud of you.

Midnight

Midnight signed his name with a snout on the *M,* tall ears on the *d,* and a frilly tail on the *t.*

I was touched by his faith in me in a way that went far beyond words, but I was left staggered by the impression that he'd known he was going to die. That possibility burnt all my other thoughts to cinders and left me facing a desolate landscape.

How much better and more worthwhile my life would have been had I had him near me, I thought. *How much more we all could have been had none of this ever happened.*

Was there any abomination greater than enslaving a man who could write such a letter to an old friend he had not seen in nearly two decades? It was a crime against everything that men and women ought to be—and everything we imagined that we could one day become.

After reading his letter, Morri must have come to the same conclusion about her father's demise. When her teeth began to chatter, I pleaded with her to sit with me. I curled my arm tight around her shoulders, just as Midnight had done with me so many times.

I knew that wherever he was, he was counting on me, and the knowledge gave me strength.

AFTER MORRI LEFT me, I sat wondering if I would have to kill someone to free her. Yet when I took out her pistol to feel how death fit in my hand, I noticed that the touchhole—which conducts the spark from the pan into the barrel—had been soldered closed. I picked at it with a sewing needle to no avail. This weapon was useless. Worse, it might have injured anyone firing it. I was about to go to the kitchen and request a gimlet from Lily in order to force the hole open when I realized the obvious: The hole had been purposely sealed. Someone involved in Morri's conspiracy, perhaps whoever had sold this gun to her, had wanted to foil her escape plans.

She had been betrayed.

I carried the weapon beneath my sketchbook into the hallway, then rushed down the stairs. Master Edward, hearing my footsteps, called to me from his study. I told him I could not join him at that moment. "I wish to sketch one more tree in this marvelous light," I explained.

I then hurried outside and slipped around to the kitchen. Morri was upstairs ironing. When I presented her with the evidence of treason, she gave me a look of hopeless agony. I explained that I needed to see the other weapons. We agreed that she would duck into her hiding space and have at least a few of them waiting for me in her room after supper. It was a risk, but it had to be taken.

It was plain to both of us that her own morale was failing. Yet I felt stronger than I had in weeks, owing, I think, to her trust in me.

I had already begun to think of another plan, and I told her not to be too concerned about the soldered touchholes, that we would not need firearms to reach Petrie's Landing. I said that I would need more time to think it through and would reveal all to her later that evening.

AT SUPPER, I forced myself to talk about trifles with Edward. Following our port wine, I went outside, telling Crow I wished for some air. It was a warm and humid night. He was of the opinion that a storm might be coming.

Stealing off to Morri's room, I tapped lightly on her door and called to her. I discovered her with two muskets and a second pistol. She was weeping; she had checked them already and they were equally ruined.

"I don't know how Weaver didn't see this," she moaned.

"Was it nighttime when he showed the men how to load and fire?"

"Yes."

"It would be easy to miss by candlelight. I presume he never fired one of the guns himself."

"No, never."

"The same would have happened to me. It's not his fault."

Then the worst possible revelation came to me: Master Edward and the owners of Comingtee already knew of Morri's plan. That now seemed clear. They had organized a party for precisely that reason. The patrols would gather early Sunday evening at Comingtee and ride into River Bend to trap the slaves. We were acting even now in a play of their authorship. Edward had invited me to Comingtee so I might enjoy the dogs going after the runaways.

"That sure enough explains the mud-mean things he's been doing lately," Morri said when I outlined my reasoning to her. "My God, I guess we're done for. And there ain't a blessed thing we can do." She slumped in her chair. "I don't know how this could have happened. Poor Weaver. Though maybe...maybe there's still time for one of us to get away," she said excitedly. "Would you take him with you, somewhere, anywhere—to your friends near Stromboli?"

"I don't think that's going to be necessary."

I spoke with confidence, because I had read enough military-history books to know that surprise was the most powerful weapon of all. The important thing was that Edward was not aware that we knew he had discovered the slaves' escape plans. He was still expecting them to flee tomorrow.

"We must leave now," I told Morri.

"Now?! We can't do that—it's too soon."

"No, what we cannot do is wait for them to catch us."

I told her then to tell Weaver and the others to get ready. As she had originally planned, we would first take Mr. Johnson, Master Edward, and the two black foremen prisoner and lock them in one of the barns. I believed I'd thought of everything essential until she said, "Martha, Weaver's wife, is at Comingtee with their children. They expect us to leave tomorrow. We can't go without them."

AS THE CURFEW bell had already rung, Weaver was back in his cabin. Morri and I found him there and she asked him to slip outside with her. He took the bad news stoically and went back in to make a plea to Saul, Sweet-Pea, and Drummond for their help. Regretfully, they refused. Nevertheless, Weaver, Morri, and I agreed on a plan. We would go to Mr. Johnson's cottage and take him prisoner. Using his keys, we would fetch rope from the First Barn or the Big House and tie him up, then proceed to take the two foremen prisoner. Lastly, we would restrain Master Edward and carry him to the barn as well. Then Weaver would run to Comingtee to bring back his wife and children.

Morri fetched us two swords from under the piazza. While she waited outside the kitchen, Weaver and I crept along the path to the overseer's house, which was between the Big House and the wooden bridge over the Cooper River to Comingtee. His door was locked, but a side window was open. It squealed when I eased it up. With our hearts pounding, Weaver and I awaited the sound of Johnson stirring from his bed. Hearing nothing, I eased inside over the sill. Weaver held a lighted candle, but a lamp on a table inside already cast a yellow light through the barren parlor. A staircase led up to the open door of the bedroom. Weaver joined me.

Mr. Johnson had to have heard the creaking of our footsteps on the bare planks of his floor. I gripped my sword in both hands as hard as I could. When he appeared on the stairs, I would run for him and slash my blade across his legs. He'd likely get a shot off at me, but Weaver would be able to take him before he could load a second ball.

So tight was I holding my sword that my wrists were aching. Despite the heat, I felt chilled to the bone. Surely a minute had passed by already without a sound.

My sword upraised, I went up the stairs and peered in the doorway. The bed was empty. It was too dark to tell for sure if Johnson was standing in a corner waiting to put a bullet into my head. I slashed my sword before me and jumped inside the room.

No one was there.

Weaver then had the good sense to go to the window. About two hundred yards away was the bridge to Comingtee. By the light of the moon we could see two men seated there. One appeared to be Johnson. Both men had muskets.

MR. JOHNSON AND his colleague were plainly standing guard between the two plantations. Obviously, Master Edward had been told by whoever had betrayed Morri that Weaver's family was hoping to join us. On this last night before our scheduled departure, they undoubtedly intended to prevent any communication between the two plantations.

As we rushed down the stairs, I was convinced that our hopes rested on Master Edward being as overconfident as he had always seemed. For if more than these two men were concealed around the plantation, waiting to spring on us, then all was truly lost.

A change of strategy was required. We would first have to subdue the black foremen and make quick work of them; if they succeeded in screaming, they would alert Johnson and his friend on the bridge to their plight. We needed a numerical advantage. Weaver would have to risk waking the slaves in the next cabin: Backbend, Parker, and Randolph.

Morri ran into the Big House to fetch Crow. They returned together with a length of rope. Weaver and Crow then went to the second slave cabin to get the other men. Morri and I remained outside. As her resolve seemed to be failing, I assured her we still had surprise on our side and that it would see us to victory. She said she hoped hanging was a quick way to die.

The two black foremen were given the privilege of sleeping alone in half of the ground house cabin. Weaver was the first in. He, Parker, and I dove for Copper, the stronger of the two, while Backbend, Randolph, and Crow went for Nighthawk. It is a difficult thing to subdue a frightened man who knows that he is despised, and I received a nasty kick in the jaw from Copper. Parker had to punch him twice in the gut to take the fight out of him.

When we had his massive hands tied behind his back, he strained at his bindings with such ferocity that I feared he'd kill us all if he were to break free. A towel was forced in his mouth and tied tight around his head with twine.

Nighthawk gave up much quicker and accepted the gag without a fight. Crow told him he would not be killed, and he plainly put his faith in that vow.

Morri had been standing guard. She did not believe that Master Edward or Mr. Johnson could have heard our struggle. We carried the two foremen back behind the First Barn and left them there, bound tightly together on their bellies, their feet tied back to their hands.

Wiggie, who slept in the Second Barn with his beloved carriages, must have been roused by our struggle and trudged to the door in just a nightshirt, rubbing his sleepy face. When we told him of our plans, he said it was madness and that we ought to confess ourselves to Master Edward immediately, which prompted Weaver to insist on tying him up. Wiggie assured us that he would not tell, but we could not risk it. While Weaver and Parker were at their work, tears ran down the coachman's cheeks. Morri apologized for us. We left him with the two foremen.

I asked Weaver to go now to the boat landing and row across the Cooper River. From there, he could make his way on foot to Comingtee without being seen by the men on the bridge.

Weaver assured me he would be back with his family in less than two hours. Morri, Crow, and I then walked to the Big House to take Edward prisoner.

Crow had informed us that the Master was likely still in his bedroom with Joanne, the young cook who'd replaced Marybelle. "He's playin' hide and seek with her," he'd said.

When we barged in, we found him standing behind the girl. At first, they looked at us in horror. Then Joanne reached for a blanket and covered her modesty.

"What's the meaning of this?" Edward bellowed.

"Put on your trousers. We are going for a walk to the barn, where you will remain for a time. You will not be hurt."

"But this is preposterous! A white man like you helping the niggers . . . You will be hanged." When I shrugged, he said, "Stewart, you are completely and utterly mad!"

"Put on your trousers." It made me giddy to give him orders.

"This is treason."

"Aye, it is, but nevertheless you will do as I say."

"You are betraying your race."

"My race?" I laughed. "Sir, it is a trifle more complicated than that. You see, I am a Portuguese–Scottish Jew who was raised in an atheist household believing that he was a Christian by birth and whose most beloved friend was an African Bushman."

"Still, you are a white man."

"Your trousers, sir—put them on."

I instructed Joanne to clothe herself. Petrified, she didn't move.

"Joanne," Morri said sweetly, "we are leaving here—leaving River Bend. You are welcome to come. Do you hear me, girl?"

"I's . . . I's staying with Massa Edwood," she stammered. "I's stayin' where I belong."

"Then you grab a hold of that dress of yours and come with me. You won't be hurt. Come on. Just do as I say."

Joanne rushed away with Morri.

"You will hang too, Crow," Edward said. "You are aware of that, I suppose?"

"I reckon so, sir."

"I might just cut off your balls too." He made a fist. "How would you like me taking those from you? I'll have Lily prepare them as oysters. What do you say to that, nigger?"

Suffering Edward's threats the entire time, Crow bound his owner's hands tightly behind his back.

"You're hurting me, nigger!" Edward shouted when Crow tightened the knot.

"Open yaw mouth, Master Edward."

He had a polishing rag ready to stuff inside. But Edward clenched his jaw closed.

On his dresser there was a repulsive ceramic statuette of a Negro child being peed on by a dog, with the inscribed motto: *The Rainy Season Down South*. I am not proud of what I next did, but I picked up the statuette and said, "If you don't let Crow gag you, I shall use this to convince you. Mind you, I shall break it either way, but it can either be on the ground or over your head."

If he had not smirked and told me to be damned, I do not know if I would have carried out my terrible threat.

"Step back, Crow. Now open your mouth, Edward!"

He would not. Hence, with all my force, I brought the statuette straight down upon his head. Shattered pieces flew in every direction. It was of harder clay than I had imagined, and Edward's legs buckled. Blood trickled at his temple. I had opened a mean gash.

I was immediately ashamed of my actions. But I did not wish to betray my regret. I ordered him to get his mouth open as wide as it would go. Groaning, he complied.

"No matter what you are thinking," I said, "you will not be mistreated if you obey me. We shall only lock you in the barn, nothing more."

WITH EDWARD'S KEY, Morri unlocked the door to the First Barn. Once we had the Master, the two black foremen, Wiggie, and Joanne bound so that they would not be able to stand or crawl, we locked them inside.

Weaver came panting back to us. All of us were standing there outside the barn by now—every slave on the plantation. Those who had decided to remain behind at River Bend were too restless to wait at their cabins.

"I can't get 'cross," Weaver moaned. "Dey's taken de boat."

He explained that the boat had been rowed to the opposite bank.

"Why didn't you just swim across?" I asked.

He hung his head and told us he didn't know how.

"Can any of you?" I asked.

When no one spoke up, Weaver said, "I gots to stay behind."

"No, you're coming with us," Morri declared.

"Ain't no way. You-all gots to go wit'out me."

"You goin', Weaver," Lily said. "Dey all know you's involved. You stay behin', you gonna hang."

"I can't leave Mart'a and my sons."

Parker suggested that all of us ought to rush the men on the bridge at once, but his wife, Christmas-Eve, said they'd likely put balls in at least two of us and she didn't want to risk one of them being her husband.

"None of us wants to die," Morri noted. "But we have to do something—and quick."

It seemed to me now that I had always known I would have to enter the water again one day. I was surprised, in fact, it had taken so long. A part of me even wanted to.

AT THE RIVER'S edge, I slipped out of my shoes, socks, trousers, shirt, and waistcoat. Blades of moonlight reflected off the hard dark surface of the water. I imagined that it was deep, muddy, and cold, and that its arms would receive me greedily.

Weaver and Morri were with me. The others had stayed back at the barn.

"Is the current generally a swift one?" I asked, handing her my white feather.

"It can be. But tonight"—she looked across the water—"tonight it doesn't look so bad. You say you can swim pretty well?"

"I haven't had a swim in twenty-five years. We shall see," I said, smiling.

A rush of fear overwhelmed me as my foot met the chilly surface. The river was thick with resistance as I took my first strokes. Then I imagined Daniel calling to me from the other shore: *Stop thinking, goddamn it, and just swim, you little mole!*

Which is what I did. Anxiety kept me afloat and moving fast. On reaching the other shore, I shook myself off like Fanny. Daniel laughed at me, but I was happy to have him on my side.

Then I rowed as best I could back to River Bend, forty paces downriver from where I'd started. Weaver and Morri rushed through the woods and marsh grass toward me.

Weaver crouched into the boat as I dressed in my dry clothes. We agreed to meet at the piazza in two hours, at a quarter to midnight. He told us to leave without him after that, for it would mean he had failed to reach his family—or been caught on the way back to River Bend.

ON CHECKING THE carriages in the Second Barn, we found that Master Edward had further outmaneuvered us. Each of the back wheels had been locked with two thick chains. None of Master Edward's keys opened them.

When we entered the First Barn to remove Wiggie's gag and question him, he told us that only Mr. Johnson had the key. We knew then we would all have to walk. Morri estimated that it was twelve miles to Petrie's Landing. We could reach there in three to four hours if we made good time.

Fifteen Negroes and a sopping-wet white man traipsing down a rice-country road were sure to raise hot suspicions in any passing carriage. But forging through the woods or proceeding along the river's edge would be impossible, according to Morri, since the overgrowth was woven thick and the swamps impossible to cross without being able to walk on water.

She went to her space under the piazza and got the last of the swords. We also took pikes, spades, and flails from the Second Barn and handed them around. As we would have to wait now for Weaver, we lumbered back to the Big House. The fear of death that I saw in Lily's face made me think of my daughters. I would not have wished them to think I'd simply vanished, as I sometimes believed about my father. Turning to Morri, I said, "If things end up going wrong... After I have been hanged, I would like you to write to my children at that address I gave you in New York. I would like you to tell them that I did indeed die. You must tell them you are absolutely sure of it."

"Me? John, I'm afraid you're not thinking right. Don't you know they're going to hang me too? And long before a white man."

CROW LED ME up to Master Edward's bedroom, then went with Morri to keep the other slaves calm. From the window there, I had a clear view of the bridge leading to Comingtee. Mr. Johnson and his colleague had not stirred. From the way they sat, I believed they might even be sleeping. Watching them, I understood that we would have to capture them as well. For if they were to discover our absence before dawn, they might blow the alarm and set their dogs after us—and alert the patrols too.

I went to my room and packed my feather, arrow, and sketchbook, along with Midnight's letter to me and the scrolled illustration done by Berekiah Zarco. They could bury me with those if I was caught.

Weaver returned at twenty minutes before midnight, with Martha, his two sons, and the girl Sarah in tow. They were all frantic, but Weaver believed they'd not been seen. All was quiet at Comingtee, he assured me.

I set off with them to join Morri, Crow, and the other slaves, leaving Lily behind at the Big House. But before we reached the cabins, two white men, each carrying a musket, appeared from out of nowhere. One of the men was Mr. Johnson. I didn't recognize the other, but I later learned he was Mr. Davies, an overseer at Comingtee. They must have slipped away from the bridge during the two or three minutes I'd spent talking to Weaver and his family. They'd probably heard—or spotted—them rowing over to River Bend.

"And where might you be headed, Mr. Stewart?" Johnson asked me, grinning. It was plain that he would enjoy shooting me.

I sprang for him. I remember hearing his shot and feeling a thud in my left shoulder, as though I'd been hit with a plank of wood. In my rage and fear I did not hear the second shot, fired by Mr. Davies.

When I bulled into Johnson, I sent his musket flying. I had taken the breath from him too, and while he was doubled over, I dove at him, clouting him twice upon the jaw, as hard as I could. Helpless, he covered his face with his hands and groaned that he could not breathe. I stood back from him and retrieved his musket. As I rubbed my bloody knuckles, he begged me in a quavering voice not to kill him.

Gazing to my side, I then discovered that Weaver lay dying on the ground. The ball from Mr. Davies had pierced an artery in his neck. The blood was spilling over him, and Martha was wailing. Frederick and Taylor had managed to overpower Mr. Davies and had already speared him with his bayonet. He, too, lay dying.

Working quickly but silently, we moved the body of Mr. Davies into the Second Barn; we would not have wanted our prisoners to see his blood-soaked corpse. We gagged Mr. Johnson, causing him so much pain in his broken jaw that he begged us not to through his tears. I am not proud to say that I cared nothing for his comfort at that moment.

For with his popping eyes he plainly wished to tell me that I would be a dead man if he had me in his power for but a moment.

BY NOW I had been alerted to the seriousness of my wound by an incessant throbbing in my shoulder and elbow. My left hand had grown cold and my shirt was drenched with blood, but I couldn't think about that now. We had to get away.

Parker, Crow, Frederick, and Taylor carried Weaver's body to the gate of River Bend. Martha had said that she would much prefer for him to be buried outside the grounds of the plantation. The men took turns digging. By the river, the soil was easily dislodged. We buried him in his clothes, without a shroud. I said the Jewish prayer for the dead over him—the *kaddish*.

With the rope we had left to us, we then bound the wrists of all the escapees. We started with the men and ended with the women, tying them tightly together, so that anyone seeing us on the road would believe that they were my prisoners.

I walked at the back. We would tell any patrols we met that I was marching them to Charleston for sale. I apologized to Morri for binding her, but she said, "If it gets me up North, you can put a bit in my mouth and brand me."

Martha's sobbing would not cause any suspicion, Morri told me, as it was not uncommon to see women crying on these forced marches to market.

AND SO WE made ready to walk away from River Bend forever, leaving Crow, Lily, and Grandma Blue behind. Crow shook my hand and said, "Be very careful now, Mr. John."

"And you go slow," I told him.

In a solemn fashion, he closed the gate behind us, then headed back to the Big House with his arm over Lily's shoulder.

AFTER THREE MILES, I was too depleted from loss of blood to go on. I remember Morri standing over me, but I could not take another step. My spirit had fled. I must have been delirious as well; I was sure I could hear Esther playing Bach on her violin.

Morri began speaking, but I could not understand her. I realized from her gestures that she wanted me to untie her, which I was only barely able to do.

There were many things I should have liked to tell her about her father just then, as I did not want to leave her with any unanswered questions after I was gone. But I did not have the strength. Instead, I told her about Mama's gold coins sewn inside the lining of my waistcoat. She was to bribe whomever she had to in order to escape.

I instructed her to please apologize to my daughters and my mother for me. She was to simply leave me where I sat in the dirt, because I could not go on. And she was to take her father's feather and not let it go.

She was begging me to keep going, but I told her that it did not matter. I was not sad. True, there was much I still would have liked to do, but I would make do with dying as well as I could—lying on my back and looking up at the Archer. All that concerned me now was that she find freedom.

After that I remember being seated with Benjamin and another man in his cellar. This other man had a long beard. He was reading to me from the Jewish mystical book, the Zohar. And what he said was this:

These are the high colors, hidden and glowing...

I asked him his name. He said it was Berekiah Zarco and that he had journeyed across three centuries to find me. All would be well. He would see me safely to the Promised Land.

Then he held his hand over me and began to whisper prayers, including the protective ones that Benjamin had given me when I'd last seen him in Porto.

LIV

Everything Had Always
Been Waiting

AN HOUR AND A HALF INTO OUR JOURNEY, John started talking to himself. It was in Portuguese, so I didn't get one darn word of it. Then he seemed to be speaking to his father, because he said the word *Papa* several times. He kept touching the feather my papa had given him to his eyes, like it was the only thing keeping him awake.

Later, when he stumbled, I discovered that his face was all sweaty and his eyes dull. Even just by the light of the moon, I could see him fading fast. I asked him if he wanted to stop for a while. I'd fetch him some water from somewhere. He didn't hear me. He looked past me, and whatever he was seeing wasn't anywhere near to South Carolina.

Then, after another mile, he fell on the ground, panting like there was a hole in his lungs. He said he couldn't go on, that he was heavier than the whole rest of the world. I told him he was going to live if he'd just keep on going. Maybe I didn't exactly believe that, but there are some times when you just got to give other folks encouragement. He said that he was not afraid of dying. He wished to just look at the sky and see my papa's hunters. That would be enough. That and me making it up North.

The last thing he did before losing consciousness was

thank me. It took me a whole day to realize that he was thinking just like my papa, and he wasn't thanking only me. No, sir, I think he was thanking the world for everything he'd ever lived.

SOME OF THE slaves were ready to leave him there, but I said I wasn't taking another single step without him. "He may be a white man," I told them, "but he's got a memory. And that's a precious thing I don't aim on losing tonight."

I undid everyone's ropes, since that ruse was useless as dirt to us now. Frederick, Taylor, Parker, and Lawrence lifted John up and took turns carrying him two at a time. I don't know how they did it, but those good black men carried him another seven or eight miles down the road.

No nigger fate blew the wind the wrong direction toward the patrols. No, sir. Not a single staring white face gaped at us from a gate or doorway. The planters were all either snoring away in their feather beds or upcountry avoiding the sickly season. And sure enough, Captain Ott had kept his word. At Petrie's Landing, three rowboats peered out of the marsh grasses at us like they'd been waiting forever for us to make up our minds to leave. Mimi ran to them and nearly fell in the water. I guess she wanted to make sure they were real. We all did.

We lay John on his back in the largest of the boats. His pulse was as weak as a whisper. I wished Papa was there to help him. Or at least to hold his hand while he died.

WE ROWED AS fast as we could. Twice, our boat and one of the others got stuck in some mud. Then the boat that Backbend, Lucy, and Hopper-Anne were in hit something, popped a leak, and started sinking. They were screeching something awful. We rowed to them and pulled them in our boat before they drowned, but it was close. And maybe someone had heard them too.

Fifty yards from the *Landmark,* one of the British sailors spotted us. Then they lowered down a couple of rope ladders that we had to climb up. They were forced to tie John under his shoulders with ropes to haul him onto deck. Captain Ott met us there and shook each of our hands like we were coming to his house for Christmas dinner. I begged him to get the ship's surgeon for John. I handed him the coins from the lining of

John's waistcoat. But he patted my shoulder and told me to keep them for our new lives.

While the surgeon was operating on John in a small room below deck, we headed out to sea. John's screams made me feel sick. Pacing outside the door where they were sewing him up, I had to sit right on the ground or risk falling over. A black sailor named Richardson, from a place called Hull, took me up to the deck, where I could breathe freer.

I guess those British folks had never seen so many black men, women, and children all together. They stared at us as if we'd been shipwrecked on a desert island our whole lives. And maybe they were right.

I SAT BY John's bedside that night. I slept some, but I preferred being awake, because my dreams all seemed burnt at the edges.

He didn't stir from his slumber, and I didn't dare touch him, but I thought that if I whispered to him it might pull him back to us—back to life. So I told him some of the stories that Papa had entrusted to me and that he might have even heard before, when he was a boy. I was hoping that Mantis could save him, even if the surgeon and I couldn't.

I THOUGHT THAT being free would fill me with joy, but I don't think I was ever so tired as I was over those next days heading up to New York. I was weighted down with all the muddy soil of River Bend, clinging to every part of me.

In the early afternoon of our first full day at sea, John woke up, but he was real groggy. I made him drink a glass of water and eat some bread, since those were the surgeon's orders. That evening his pulse started racing and his face was so hot I thought he'd burn to ash. At times, he got the chills too. When we were left alone I did what my papa used to do with me and spooned up behind him in his bed.

On our second day out to sea, his left arm grew *gangrenous*, the surgeon said. When I got a look at Dr. Brampton's saw, I knew I hadn't the stomach for what they were going to do to him, but there was no other way to save him. John's screams could have shattered all the glass in all the churches of South Carolina and still flown over the border with enough force to break all the crystal bowls in Georgia too.

I wasn't allowed to see him that day, so it was only the next morning

I could go in. From the way he looked at me, I could see he was back with the living. "Are we free?" he whispered. He spoke as if he didn't dare believe we'd made it.

He made me cry—because there he was without an arm and he'd used the word *we*.

JOHN WANTED TO talk after that, as a way of forgetting what had happened to him, I think. So while he lay back in bed, we spoke about all sorts of things, including who might have betrayed us. I told him about Beaufort and the two men who'd helped us get our arms, Mr. Trevor and Mr. Rollins. He had a hard time believing that a Negro or mulatto would betray us.

"I don't know about that," I replied. "There's plenty of us who just want to look good in a white man's eyes."

John said that Mr. Trevor might have needed to confide in a good many folks in order to get us our guns. Any one of them might have betrayed us and earned a few coins for his trouble.

One thing was for sure. Master Edward must have known for at least a few days what we had in mind. Maybe even for weeks. That was why he enjoyed having me flogged so much. He was getting revenge before the fact.

WE REACHED NEW York Harbor two days later. John was fighting the pain as best he could but still couldn't walk by himself, so Captain Ott had sailors carry him off the boat and put him in a carriage bound for his friend Violeta's house. The rest of us walked behind. We had no bags, no money, no map. The folks in New York stared fierce at us, worse even than the British, and they whispered too. We were looking at them—and at the brick buildings, and at the carriages, and at the low gray sky, and at the church spires, and at one another—as if this was all impossible.

But it was possible, sure enough. By this time, the astonishing thing wasn't that we'd made it up North, but that New York had been here the whole fifteen years I'd lived at River Bend, just waiting for me to come. Everything had always been waiting.

LV

WHEN I WOKE TO MYSELF, I TUMBLED INTO A panic so wide and deep that I thought it would swallow me whole and never give me up. How would I go on without an arm?

I kept very still, but I knew that wishing to be the man I had been was useless—there was no magic that would take me back to that time.

The ache of not being whole made me so sick that I had to reach for my basin. Thankfully I was alone, so no one heard my sobs. I muffled them with my pillow, rocking back and forth like a child.

Morri came to me while I was in this fragile and confused state. I gripped her hand and asked if we were truly free, since that was the only thing I could think of that might make my loss worthwhile. She said we were, and she lifted my hand to her cheek. I was moved that she had come to trust me, but I was so envious of her completeness of body that I could no longer look her straight in the eyes.

After she left me and I had another good cry, I decided to try to imitate a man with two able arms. Over the next days at sea, despite the constant waves of pain breaking over my shoulder, I smiled while conversing with Morri, Captain

Ott, and the amiable crew, as though my stump were but a superficial wound. I lifted my glass to the surgeon and thanked him heartily for his swift work on my behalf. I knew this was a lie I'd pay for sooner or later, but I could not show them my true feelings for fear of going mad with grief.

It was a tremendous relief, of course, that Mother would not have to visit my grave, that my girls still had one of their parents. Yet I knew I should have to rethink a great many things about my life. And though I expressed my heartfelt thanks to Morri and the others when she told me how I had been carried by the slaves to the rowboats for the journey downriver, a shadowy part of me cursed everything and everyone.

Whenever any of the refugees came to visit me in my cabin, I wondered what being out of River Bend meant to them. Most spoke in happy voices, but they were plainly frightened of the prospect of a life where their own choices would command their destinies. Morri dropped my gold coins into my hand, saying that she'd not been obliged to offer any bribes.

Martha and her sons were disconsolate about having lost their beloved Weaver, and they only appeared in my cabin twice, to express their regret at my having been wounded and to join the celebration hosted by Captain Ott on our last night at sea. At our party, little Mimi asked if my arm had been given a proper burial. I did not know, I told her, but I hoped it was at peace wherever it was. Later, the surgeon told me it had been tossed overboard.

SITTING WITH MORRI, I often pondered the mystery of Midnight's disappearance. "We will start looking for your papa as soon as we get to New York," I assured her.

"I'm afraid he's dead, John. We have to face it."

"No!" I shouted, letting my emotions escape my rigid control for a moment. "If he's dead . . . if he's dead, then why have I lost my arm? It can't be!"

I was screaming so loud that Morri called for help. The surgeon came in and forced two spoonfuls of medicine into me. I fell into a slumber in which my regrets seemed to seep into everything around me. In one dream, Daniel and I were at the bird market in Porto. He said that my having only one arm was why I'd been unable to save him from drowning. When we returned to my home to eat supper with my parents, we realized we'd made a mistake: Our house looked more like a dank cave. We didn't know where we were. Then Daniel said we were in the belly of a giant beast—half-lion, half-bird. We heard the wind howling outside, and we knew we were flying, but we could not see where we were going.

MY SHAME MADE me wish to lock my door the closer we came to New York, for I'd soon have to face Violeta. I regretted now not having made love with her before, as a whole man.

There are some women who are all efficiency when faced with the difficulties of others, and Violeta proved herself to be one of these gifted individuals from the moment I appeared on her doorstep. After her first gasp of horror at my misfortune, her great jade eyes awash with tears, she transformed herself into my nurse. "You are home now," she said, bending down to kiss my brow, "and I shall see you well if it is the last thing I do."

It's difficult for me to speak about the initial relationships Violeta established with the former slaves of River Bend, since over those first three weeks I was largely confined to my room. I could not help but notice, however, that Morri became taciturn and fidgety whenever she and Violeta found themselves with me at the same time. I could see in the girl's worried face that she had sensed the clash of emotions inside our hostess.

Whenever she or Violeta would ask about my feelings, I would lie, speaking of the amputation as insignificant compared with the suffering of those in slavery. Morri was reluctant to give her opinion but finally said, "I don't reckon miseries can be compared, John. When I was at River Bend, it didn't make me feel any better knowing there were white families that were also dirt-poor and stuck living in places they hated. I made believe it helped, sure enough—we all did—but it didn't help at all."

FOUR LONG AND intimate letters from Mama, Fiona, and my daughters were waiting for me upon my return. Thankfully, all was well in London. Seeing their handwriting made me tremble with longing, and I assured them that I was well in my replies. To avoid later criticism from my mother, I did note that I'd had a *wee mishap* in South Carolina. I said nothing more, since bad tidings would only act as a summons, and I could not face my mother in my present state. As soon as I decided my next move, I wrote, I would send instructions to Esther and Graça. I warned them that I might soon be asking them to join me in New York.

THERE WERE TIMES over the next fortnight of loneliness and physical discomfort when I was one heartbeat from begging Violeta to hold me or let me see her without her bonnet. But she never descended to her garden in the night as on my previous visit. If she had, I might have hobbled down the stairs to her and settled at her feet like Fanny. Outside, under the stars, I think I'd have been able to speak the truth.

WHAT STARTED ME on a healthier road was a startling correspondence I received from Isaac and Luisa. Aside from news of their family and colorful drawings of woodpeckers done by Noodle and Hettie, it contained an article from the *Charleston Courier* that characterized our flight to freedom not as an escape but as a *foul and grotesque* series of murders committed by the *ghost* of River Bend, who had been discovered—after all these years—to be Mr. Johnson the overseer! The reasoning behind this bold conclusion went as follows:

The body of Edward Roberson, Master of River Bend, had been found in one of the barns at River Bend, a knife in his neck. This was, of course, precisely how both Big and Little Master Henry were killed. Hence, the same villain must have been responsible. Additionally, Mr. Davies, an overseer at Comingtee Plantation, had died from a deep bayonet wound in his chest. It was written in the article that his presence at River Bend had been requested by Edward Roberson, as he had suspected his own overseer of plotting against him.

Mr. Johnson's body had been found outside the First Barn, a bullet in his temple. This wound was apparently self-inflicted, since he gripped a pistol in his hand. His jaw had been broken, as though in a struggle with his employer, Mr. Roberson. Both men had scrapes on their elbows and knees, possibly resulting from a fistfight. Mr. Roberson also had a nasty gash on his head, likely the result of a pistol-whipping given him by the murderous overseer.

The article affirmed that Mr. Johnson had undoubtedly taken his own life after killing Edward Roberson and the other overseer. Two Negro foremen had also been killed, likely for remaining loyal to Master Edward.

"Their affection to him was as to a father," Mistress Anne had told the *Courier.*

As to a motive, it was suggested that these were crimes of mad passion and greed. Mr. Johnson had been rumored for many years to be in love with Mistress Holly, the wife of Big Master Henry, the former owner. He had apparently sought to do away with Henry and his son in order to take control of both River Bend and its mistress. In his maniacal and unbalanced mind, he had imagined Edward Roberson as the last impediment to his plans to take control of the plantation.

There was no mention made of Joanne, Wiggie, and the other slaves we'd locked in the First Barn. Presumably, their lives had been spared.

In his letter to me, Isaac asked whether any of what was written in the article was true or if it was a concoction of the white authorities.

I found it all a tangled confusion and read it over many times, as though it were in a foreign language. Morri showed greater insight, telling me that the authorities would never have wanted it known that there had been a successful escape from a plantation. Such tidings would have struck fear in all the white residents of the South. In consequence, the planters and police had fabricated this story. Better have it known that it was a simple crime of passion and avarice than a successful Negro flight to the North.

"But how can they keep our escape a secret?" I asked her.

"They can't. But if they don't admit it happened, then the slaves will think of it only as a rumor and the white folks as a damnable lie. I'd reckon that's how all our history is going to be written."

It occurred to me then that similar unreported rebellions must have happened many times before, on plantations across the South. To this, Morri said, "I don't expect there will be any record of any group of slaves having beaten them. Not a single printed page."

SO ALERT OF mind did she prove on this and other occasions that I often shook my head in amazement at her being only fifteen years old. In my talks with her over the next few days about River Bend, I began to think of her as a friend—and truly her father's daughter. Her presence, more than anything else, gave me back my true smile and voice, and I was pleased that when she looked at me now it was with affection.

We talked quite a few times about what she wanted to do with her life. I favored finding her a private tutor in history, philosophy, music, and other essential subjects, with the end goal of preparing her for a university education. But she believed I was getting far ahead of myself. She said she wished for something simple: to earn her keep. She'd always enjoyed embroidering, and together we thought of the possibility of her making clothing on consignment, as Francisca had.

I saw in her eyes that that would not have pleased her much. Thinking like Midnight, I said, "Just walk around the city. See what there is to see and it will come to you. I know it."

Then, while I had her fond attention, I risked yet one more tumble with my heart and told her that I was hoping to adopt her. As she might have agreed to this simply to thank me for helping her escape from River Bend, I took both her hands in my one, squeezed them tight, and said, "It would ease my mind to know I have followed your father's instructions. As I think you know by now, I am not only greatly fond of you, but I admire you as well. But, Morri, you must not say yes unless it is truly what you want, even if your father would have desired it. I hasten to add that I shall never try to replace him in your heart—never. Think on it and tell me what you've decided in . . . let us say, a month."

Morri agreed, but in her eyes was the despair I'd provoked by speaking of her father as in his grave. I knew, however, that he himself had given me no other choice.

THERE STILL REMAINED the question, of course, of who had committed the murders at River Bend. Separately, Morri and I came to the same conclusion: Crow.

It had become clear to me over the course of my few days at River Bend that his spirit was not truly broken but hidden at most times deep inside him. After the slaves had escaped from River Bend, Crow must have taken his revenge.

Yet the doors to the bedrooms of Big and Little Master Henry had been found locked after they'd had knives plunged into their necks. Without the key, how had Crow entered?

Neither Morri nor I could answer that at first. But then I remembered the impressions of shells in clay he had shown me. I began to believe that he must have taken the bedroom keys from Big Master Henry or from Mistress Holly just long enough to make impressions in his molds, then had them fired by his blacksmith brother at Comingtee. Without my pressing him for information, Crow had told me that he'd also made impressions of silver dollars. I think he wanted me to guess the truth, so that those of us who escaped would know he had avenged himself.

After murdering Master Edward and the others, Crow had probably put a pistol into Mr. Johnson's hand in order to fool the white authorities. It seemed equally possible that he had left the bodies bound and bloody, just where he had murdered them. Whoever was in charge of the investigation might have concocted the version of events that had been printed in the newspaper to prevent fear on the part of the white citizenry, just as Morri had said. In that case, Crow would be hanged, and most likely in secret.

But if he had planted all the clues and convinced Lily and the other slaves to say nothing, then the police might have believed him innocent. He might even have comforted Mistress Kitty in her grief.

LVI

PUZZLING OVER THE ARTICLE AND THE EVENTS at River Bend with Morri did wonders for my sense of having some choices in life—and of having the strength to plan for my future.

Violeta's downturned glances in my presence gave me to understand, however, that she feared my newfound vigor. That she, too, might have preferred our relationship to take a friendlier and more honest course—that she was at the mercy of emotions she did not well understand—never occurred to me.

Despite the evidence from my previous visit, I failed completely to understand that Violeta simply did not speak her mind. If I'd reflected carefully on our days together as children, I'd have seen this as consistent with her character. Likely, the desire to unburden herself to others had been beaten out of her, first at her home in Porto, and later in England.

THE NEED TO secure productive labor for the River Bend refugees soon eclipsed my personal concerns. To be of help to them, I gathered my courage to leave my room for more than a few hours at a time at the beginning of our fourth week of freedom. It immediately became plain to me that most of them were in need of a routine. Parker in particular had taken to drink and often came home cursing. Morri took me aside on my first day downstairs and told me how once, after an evening at a raucous tavern, he'd clouted Christmas-Eve right across her face, blackening his wife's eye. I realized that I had to act swiftly and that to help them find work it would be necessary to show my empty coat-sleeve in public. That Morri and the others had—in some vague but determined way—been waiting for me to come down and offer my help from the very start became only too obvious to me. I gained considerable respect for their patience and tact with me.

I passed the next days taking our River Bend guests around to shops and warehouses, endeavoring to find them steady work. Nearly always we received the same false smiles and swift refusals. I remember in particular the owner of a dry-goods store on Wall Street whom I tried to convince to offer work to Hopper-Anne, whose English was exceedingly good and clear. Not only did he stare at my missing arm, but he also had the cheek to say, "My customers do not expect to be waited on by a Negress, no matter how fair her skin might be or how nearly white she can talk."

For better or for worse, losing an arm had diminished none of my Highland temper, and I roundly lambasted him for his hypocrisy.

After a time, it became only too apparent to me that my finding all the former slaves honest work was going to prove impossible. Fortunately, they understood this sooner than I did and took matters into their own hands.

Through the friendships that Hopper-Anne, Lucy, and Christmas-Eve made at St. Philip's Protestant Episcopal Church, they were soon able to find work for Parker, Randolph, and Backbend, as stevedores for Harkness & Co., a private shipping concern on South Street. Hopper-Anne was contracted soon afterward at a black-owned bakery on Chambers Street, and Christmas-Eve and Lucy started as scullery maids at Spear Tavern on Broadway.

Violeta offered invaluable assistance to the rest. She sat at her desk in her sitting room and composed a moving letter soliciting advice from Francis Lemoyne, the eldest son of the old man she had cared for. Though he harbored a lingering resentment over her inheritance of the house we were encamped in at present, he nevertheless contacted some

Quaker farmers he knew and succeeded in obtaining offers of work for all the former slaves of River Bend who wished for a life in a rural setting.

In the end, all but Morri and Randolph seized this opportunity. Randolph decided to remain as a stevedore in New York with his children, and we were soon able to find them a suitable flat on Bowling Green.

"No way I'm ever going back to a life of field work," Morri told me. "You know, John, life doesn't get much better than getting away with saying no."

SEVERAL DAYS LATER, Morri came home singing and panting at the same time. She was so electric that she went hopping around the sitting room. While I puffed on my pipe, she told me that on one of her walks through the city she'd met the headmaster of the Church Street School for Negro Children, a former runaway named William Arthur. "He told me I could start giving reading and writing lessons right away! He doesn't mind that I don't speak so perfectly. Or that I'm not much older than the children. He doesn't mind one drop!"

After we'd drunk a wee glass of port wine to her success, she sat on the arm of my chair and squeezed my hand hard. Her face was scrunched up tight, as though she had a big secret to tell me.

"What?" I asked.

"I'd like for you to adopt me, John, but only on the condition that if my father returns, he can adopt me back."

I RECEIVED THE first of my mother's replies to my letters during our seventh week in New York. *John,* she wrote, the nib of her pen having scratched through the paper with irritation, *if you do not tell me precisely the nature of your "mishap" in South Carolina in your next letter (to be written today!), then I promise you I shall show up on your doorstep uninvited and give you a lecture of a kind that you have never heard, but plainly ought to have!*

A few days later, while I was still pondering how to write of my injury to my mother, Backbend, Lucy, Hopper-Anne, Scooper, Parker, Christmas-Eve, Frederick, Sarah, Taylor, and Martha boarded carriages in front of Violeta's house for the journey sixty miles north to two Quaker farms located near the town of Southeast. They would earn good steady wages and their children would be able to attend a local school-house. The Quakers—who by now seemed to represent to me the possibility for goodness in our world—had generously agreed to help them build cottages as well.

As their carriages departed, I heard Morri humming "Barbara Allen" to herself. I joined her for a verse. Thankfully, this was to set me thinking seriously again about how to find Midnight.

LVII

IN ALL MY WEEKS OF ANGUISH I HAD HARDLY forgotten Midnight, but rereading his letter in New York had convinced me that he must have had a vision of his own end—a Mantis-dream.

I see now that—even more than the loss of my arm or Violeta's distance—this passive acceptance of his death had made my weeks of solitude so grim. I have discovered that my times of greatest misery have always been related to a feeling of defeat, and I have nearly always found my way back to health by beginning a new campaign.

So, with Mother's gold coins and what was left of my savings, I decided to publish a request for Midnight—or anyone knowing of his fate—to write to me. I would place these advertisements in newspapers all over the United States, from New York to the western territories, every week for as long as it took to receive a reply. Of course, even if he was still alive, I could not be sure that he was in the habit of reading news of any sort, but there was every likelihood that he knew someone who was.

Morri was eager to help write our announcement, which we finalized as follows:

Seeking Midnight, Samuel, or Tsamma. We saw you from afar and we are dying of hunger.

Anyone with information, please write to the Gemsbok care of Senhora Violeta, 73 John Street, New York.

I have found a beautiful feather that you thought was lost to you forever and have it safe with me. Go slow.

We did not wish to put anything in the announcement about River Bend or mention Morri's name, fearing the attention of slave-traders who might wish to kidnap her.

The second part of my plan was to become my most important work in America. I decided to compile a list of slaves and freed blacks in South Carolina, along with their residences. Later, I would add the other states of the South. This seemed essential to me, for whenever the great destruction of slavery finally came, in five years or fifty, those who had been in bondage would face the near-impossible task of finding brothers, sisters, mothers, fathers, and children who had been lost to them for many years. They would desperately need such a list.

It was a huge undertaking, and I knew it would take many years and enormous effort to be even close to complete. Even so, the more I thought of the plan, the more exciting it became.

To create my list, I knew I would need hundreds of correspondents from all over South Carolina—people willing to survey the slaves, freed blacks, and mulattos in their vicinity and write down their full names and locations, as well as those of their kin.

The Quakers would help, I was quite sure, as indeed they have. And among the congregation of Jews in Charleston, I have so far found several industrious and generous souls as well.

My first correspondents were Isaac and Luisa, naturally enough. I wrote to them shortly after I received their letter, giving them an account of our escape, and they have so far provided me with one hundred and twelve names and locations.

Census reports have indicated that at least two hundred and sixty thousand Negroes are held in bondage in South Carolina alone, and so I plainly have much work in my future. But I am neither deterred nor daunted. The list will grow exponentially as more people learn of it. All of nature itself is on my side in this battle, I am certain.

*　*　*

ON NOVEMBER THE Fourteenth, a week after the former slaves departed for upstate New York, I signed Morri's adoption papers. As I was not an American citizen, this procedure was handled through the British Embassy. She decided to register herself as Memoria Tsamma Stewart, which I thought a splendid and unique name. To celebrate, she and I took a ferry boat to Brooklyn, where we dined at a waterfront tavern that admitted Negroes. I drank a wee bit too much whiskey to celebrate, but Morri guided me safely back to our ferry boat.

I had kept away from the Church Street School till then in order to avoid embarrassing her, but I now decided to make a fatherly inspection of her place of work. Sitting at the back of her classroom, the pride I felt in seeing her free and useful confirmed to me that I had not been wrong in going to watch her.

While listening to her children read aloud a fable by Aesop, I felt Midnight's presence next to me. I could see him grinning like a mad fool.

After visiting Morri's school, I ceased questioning whether losing my arm had been a just sacrifice for her freedom. Seeing the little ones flocked around her, tugging on the bright crimson dress I'd bought for her, I stopped comparing miseries, as she herself had advised. I am grateful for that, for at one time I thought my selfishness would be my undoing.

OTHER EVENTS ALSO conspired to restore me to full and honest vigor, the first of which was completely unexpected.

I still had not written back to my mother explaining my injury. This cowardice, combined with my longing for my daughters and my uncertainty as to what would now be best for them, plunged me into a sudden spiral of despair and insomnia. I locked my door and would allow neither Morri nor Violeta inside. I smoked too much and made myself sick. What I did not know was that Violeta had another key. She let herself into my room before dawn on the Nineteenth of November, while I was smoking Papa's pipe like a fiend, and announced, "I can bear our struggle no longer, John. If you promise to say nothing afterward about what has taken place between us or what you wish to happen in the future, I shall lie with you now."

"Are you sure?" I asked, sensing both our destinies turning around this moment.

"Yes," she replied.

I walked to her, hope and gratitude in my heart. Kissing her lips—as I'd wanted to for more than two decades—sent such an electric charge through me that I felt myself tugged out of my own body.

To be with her meant everything to me; I was at the center of the world. There, deep down inside our union, my lost arm was not so burdensome a handicap as I had thought.

Afterward, she lay her head against my shoulder and drifted off to sleep.

At length, I thought of Francisca. She seemed so very different from Violeta; they were women born under constellations guarding separate territories of the night. Perhaps it was that, more than anything else, that made me believe my wife would not begrudge me any happiness I might now find in my new life.

I stroked Violeta's hair while she slept, as I'd always desired. The simple movement of my fingers calmed me, and the soft feel of her made me believe that I'd finally reached home. I knew now that all would be well between us.

Indeed, over the next weeks, our relations were everything I'd hoped they'd become. We went for long walks into the northern wilds of Manhattan Island, watching blue jays, kingfishers, and other birds more unfamiliar to me. She collected fire-colored oak leaves, and I bought her flowers. We munched chestnuts in the parks and chased each other up the staircase. For the American holiday of Thanksgiving she prepared a turkey with cranberry preserves. For a sweet, she made me *rabanadas,* as my mother had taught her. We never discussed what had taken place between us because there was now no need. In the silence of our bed at night, it seemed to me we'd finally made up for Daniel's death. Our union was a triumph over betrayals, madness, gravestones, and forever good-byes. It was proof that resurrection was possible. Perhaps it was even another miracle.

I was not sure if Violeta could have a child at this late date, but when we merged in the night I desperately hoped that she could.

THE SECOND EVENT to spur my personal renewal was my decision to begin making tile panels and pottery again, and for this purpose I had the small shed at the back of Violeta's garden cleared. I purchased a secondhand potter's wheel and tile-making tools.

Centering a pot with one hand proved not nearly so difficult as I had imagined, and within a few days I was able to make modest bowls, plates, and jugs. I also finalized my sketches for a tile panel of field slaves I wished to make, though I found that without my arm I did not yet have the stamina for such an ambitious project.

I FINALLY SENT a letter to my mother and daughters explaining that I wanted to stay in New York and requesting that Esther and Graça come as soon as possible. I apologized for disrupting their lives yet again and would explain all upon their arrival. About my arm, I said only that I had received an injury while in the South, but that it was nothing to be concerned about; my American physicians had pronounced me in fine health. I had not yet found Midnight, I said, but I was now fully engaged in the hunt once again.

BY NOW, I understood that I was fond of Violeta in a way that went far beyond declarations of passion and gestures of affection. In a vague way, I knew we were made of different elements, but that seemed all the better, as though our alloy would prove stronger than any purity.

One day when we were out walking, I broached the subject that had been consuming me for so long. "Violeta, I'd like to have a child—to start a new family with you in this youthful country."

She went pale. I sat her down on the nearest stoop and squatted next to her. "What is it? I thought you'd be pleased."

"I am, John. It's just a shock. Give me a moment."

"If you're worried about my daughters, I'm sure they'd love having a baby brother or sister. Though we mustn't allow them to choose the name," I said with a laugh. "They prefer all the worst ones."

She reached up with her hand to touch my mouth, and I kissed her fingertips. She said, "Enough, John, let us talk about it later. I'm just too stunned right now to speak."

I REASONED I'D give her a day or two to adjust to the idea before speaking of it again. The next evening, however, Morri and I were obliged to dine at the home of William Arthur, her headmaster. Violeta had asked to be excused, as relations between her and Morri were still a bit tentative. We returned home much earlier than we'd expected, as Mr. Arthur was an early riser and was always in bed by ten o'clock.

Finding Violeta absent from the sitting room, I took the stairs two at a time to our bedroom, planning to dive upon her, but she was not there. On intuition, I went to the window of the room in which I'd previously slept. I discovered her sitting in her garden, swathed in a black Portuguese mantilla. In her hands was the tabletop Daniel had carved for her just before his death. She was sobbing.

I ran down to her, but nothing I could say or do would stop her tears.

"Please tell me what's wrong—is it Daniel? I often think of him too, you know."

Looking away from me, speaking in Portuguese, she said, "I do not love you, John. Not as you would wish. Not like I loved Daniel." She reached a trembling hand to her mouth. "I never shall, you see, so we must never have a child."

"Then why . . . why did you come to me?"

"It was the only way to rid us both of the angry resentment that had developed between us. It was the only way to help you." Gazing up at me with eyes full of sorrow, she said, "I warned you that you ought not to fall in love with me. I did everything I could to show you that."

I understood then that she had kept so much distance between us because she did indeed wish to save me from herself. In an odd way, she had been more generous through our weeks of disappointment than she had been in sharing her bed with me. There had been no true complications between us from her point of view; she had simply never loved me.

I stood up, sensing my life spinning slowly to a stop. But I was not angry or even sad. Though it was a paradox, I felt both hollow and very heavy. I felt that I was composed of all the thoughts I'd had of her over the last twenty years—all my prayers and wishes. I was very tired—of myself most of all.

"You did indeed warn me," I told her in a voice of stone, unwilling to break down. "I genuinely thank you for that. And for trying to help. I see now what a dilemma I put you in."

I pressed my dry lips to her cold cheek and glided up the stairs as a specter. From my room, I watched her sitting in her garden for more than an hour. Then she went inside, leaving the tabletop on her bench. Staring at it through that forest of dark weeds, imagining my face as

Daniel had carved it, I saw how I'd never wanted to understand the plain truth of our relationship. Even as a lass she had told me that I could hope for nothing more than friendship.

When she returned to her garden, it was with a long knife. My heartbeat jumped and my eyesight dimmed; I was sure she was about to take her own life.

When I reached her, she was defacing the portrait Daniel had carved of her, slashing at it with a violence so deep that I stepped back without knowing it, nearly toppling. I would have liked to still her hand, but I knew by now that she did not want or need my protection.

THE NEXT DAY, I did without breakfast and took a lonely walk along the Hudson River, thinking of the child we'd never have. I met Morri after school and explained solemnly what had taken place between Violeta and myself. I told her I intended to spend a weekend outside of the city so that I might think out my future—and that of my daughters.

MORRI AND I took a long boat ride on Saturday morning to the colonial town of Roslyn, at the bottom of a slender inlet on the northern shore of Long Island. On our first afternoon there we took a walk through the woods, up a rather steep hill and far into a desolate distance of leafless trees. It was as cold as I'd ever known it, and I felt as though I were walking through an old landscape that had frozen inside me. I expected to see Violeta's body on the ground, as she had been after her uncle's attack.

Morri walked faster than I and would often wait for me to catch up. It pleased me the way she looked back for me.

On Monday, sometime before dawn, the snow began to fall. It was the first snow that Morri had ever seen. Dashing outside, she promptly fell on her bottom, bruised but laughing. I sat down beside her. Tilting my head back, I watched the flakes falling, feeling their tickling chill on my cheeks. She and I lay together for a long time, letting ourselves be covered.

WE GOT BACK to Violeta's home early Monday evening, as Morri had the day off from school. She met us at the door with kind words and kisses, offering to make us hot coffee and *rabanadas* as a treat. I could not bear her generosity and rushed back out of the house. By late the next afternoon, having passed the night in a decrepit boardinghouse overlooking the Hudson, I'd found a small three-bedroom house in Greenwich Village that I could begin leasing in a week. It was old and plain, and the garden was nothing but frozen mud and filth, but its walls were sound enough to the taps of my fist and it was not expensive.

When I informed Violeta of my intentions, she gave me an encouraging smile and said, "I ask you only that you keep your studio here. So that we might remain friends. Do me that one favor, John."

For the first time in my life I said no to her. A single word had never come harder to me.

I WROTE IMMEDIATELY to Mother to tell her of my new home, and I changed the address in my newspaper appeals. On my last night at Violeta's house, she slipped out to her garden before dawn. Gazing up at the stars, contoured by moonlight, she seemed again that nymph of the night I'd previously imagined. When she spotted me, I stepped back into the shadows like a criminal. She began tossing a ball up in the air. It was Fanny's. In my mind, I could see my beloved dog jumping for it and barking. I stumbled back to bed. A little while later, I heard the sound of pebbles being tossed at my window. I covered my head with my pillow. When finally I removed it some minutes later, she was still tossing her stones. She continued until sunrise, but I dared not go to her.

ONE MORNING IN mid-January there came a thunderous pounding at the door of our new home on Waverly Place. Running to answer it, I found my mother raising her hands to her mouth, already in tears. Behind her were Esther and Graça. At least a score of stuffed bags were being unloaded from three large carriages.

Our reunion was somewhat hysterical, as they always are in my family. It was rather like a mad Italian opera played at too fast a tempo, with four characters of wildly different temperaments searching for an equilibrium lost somewhere between tears and laughter. I kissed my children all over and took turns holding them.

The girls were wearing the filigree earrings I'd purchased in Alexandria and told me with pride that they hadn't taken them off in weeks and had no intention of doing so for many more. On touring our house, I told them that they would have to share a bedroom, but they claimed that it was better that way, since they always slept more soundly when together at night. Like Morri, Mama had her own room and pronounced it perfectly charming, though it contained not a single piece of furniture or even a rug. Conditions were obviously very cramped and modest, and despite their smiles I suspected that they found it depressing after so long a journey. When I showed them how I'd encamped in what had been the pantry, in preparation for their arrival, I could feel my courage tiptoeing away from me.

"Just keep breathing," Mama told me. But I could not laugh. She tapped my forehead as though to knock some sense into me. "Stop worrying, John," she said, plainly intending it as a command. "We've all faced much worse than a bit of crowding and dust in our lives, even Graça and Esther."

I TOOK MY children and my mother on separate walks down Broadway over the next two days, as in the light and air I could talk more freely of the loss of my arm and my experiences at River Bend. I apologized immediately to Mama for losing my arm, since I had come out of her complete and it seemed an affront to both her pain of childbirth and years of care. She hushed me up and kept saying, "You ought to have told me much sooner, you know. You needn't always suffer alone. You've been doing that since you were a tiny lad, and I think it's about time you stopped."

I kept reassuring her that my difficulties had long passed. But she could not reconcile the image of her son in her mind with the man before her. In the early morning, while still half-asleep, I sometimes caught her standing in my doorway, watching me with troubled eyes.

Mama has always been a creature of unexpected moods, and after this initial period of disbelief and sorrow, she turned playful with me once more. Though this in itself was a heartening relief, I knew it would take many more months for her to be able to look at me without comparing me with what I'd been.

Each of my daughters reacted differently to the loss of my arm. Graça, ever thoughtful, was given to wary silence on the subject, until I realized in a moment of revelation that she was awaiting reassurance that I was much the same man I had always been. I had forgotten my own lesson from childhood, that separation was more difficult for the young. So it was that for a fortnight I doted on her from morning till bedtime, reading to her for an hour or more each night after tucking her in. When she lost her cautious manner with me, when she could pass a day exploring the city with my mother without even remembering my existence, I knew she would be fine.

Esther decided to play nurse at this late date, and for a time I suffered with good humor her helping me down the stairs and fluffing my pillows in bed. Then it began to irritate me, and I once made her cry with my blustering. It was Mama who told me that the girl was not so different from her sister as I thought, and that she was calling for my reassurance in the way most suited to her own character. So I allowed myself to be pampered by her for several more weeks and asked only in return that she let me listen to her practice her violin. This pleased her so much that she even became my morning reveille, serenading me awake each morning with minuets and gavottes by Bach. I knew she was well when she began to snap at me occasionally without worrying that I might go away again or that another limb of mine might just drop off.

RELATIONS BETWEEN MY family and Morri were awkward at first, as I might have expected. Her solution was to withdraw deep into the protective solitude of her upstairs bedroom when she was not teaching. One afternoon, when I dared to knock and step inside, she cried in my arms. She was sure the others all hated her. "I'm so different from them. You've been so kind, but it's a mistake my being here."

Mama entered the room then, having heard the commotion, and knelt by Morri, who sat up in alarm. She held the girl's shoulders. "Morri, now listen to me. Your papa was the truest friend I ever had. He saved John's life, as you may know, and he therefore saved mine." She dabbed at the girl's tears with her handkerchief. "At that time I made a pledge to him—that I'd always treat him as though we were kin. So it was not John's adoption of you that brought you into our family." She kissed each of her hands and made them into fists. "You, my child"—she smiled—"were part of my family before you were even born!"

They looked into each other's eyes for a long time. Then Mama slapped her thigh playfully and said, "Now, come with me into the kitchen. We can get to know each other while we prepare supper."

That evening saved the day. The girls took their cue from their grandmother and, over supper, began to think of Morri as an older playmate. Indeed, they vied shamelessly for her attention that very night, Esther with her violin and Graça with her maps and almanacs. Their first major decision as a threesome was reached the next morning: As soon as they were a bit older, they would voyage to Scotland, Italy, India, and China. "On the way back, we'll visit Africa, to see where your father comes from," Graça told Morri with great seriousness.

They were seated on our small sofa, and I squeezed down with them, sitting Esther on my lap. "Well, if you go by sea, do not count on me coming along," I said, sighing mightily.

Mama laughed till she cried. On regaining her breath, she said, "John, you never understand, do you? The three of them have absolutely no intention of inviting you or me along."

ONE EVENING SHORTLY after their arrival, I felt strong enough to explain to Mama what had taken place between Violeta and myself. She went to see her once or twice a week after that, and on occasion brought Esther and Graça along. The children came to be very fond of her and often talked to me of their games together. Mama confirmed that she was gentle and doting with them. I remembered how much she had cherished the children in Newcastle whom she'd raised, and she was plainly finding joy again with my two girls. I begrudged her this only at my worst moments.

When my mother and my children would walk to Violeta's house, it began to seem to me as though they were visiting a ghost. She became not so very different from Daniel in my mind. It was reassuring in a way, since I suspected that I might soon begin to remember her only with fondness.

And so it was that Mama, Esther, Graça, Morri, and I began our life in New York, awaiting word of Midnight.

John Stewart, April the Fourth, 1824

LVIII

They Embraced the Knowledge
of What Was Coming Next

S TANDING ON THE STREET AND WATCHING
those carriages roll off with near half the people I had ever
known made me feel all broken inside. Only Randolph and
his children, Mimi and Lawrence, stayed behind on
Manhattan Island. They became my only links to River
Bend, which wasn't much good since I'd never been right
close to Randolph.

I stayed put in New York because I knew from the moment I reached here that it was the place for me.

Here, everybody runs around trading and building. New
York is things exchanging hands. It's movement. And I like
being part of it. Not that I didn't miss the slow routine of
River Bend. We all did, I'd reckon. Though none of us
would ever just come out and say that to any white person
except maybe John, because they'd take it the wrong way
and use it against us. Even the ones up here who weren't
much fond of slavery didn't seem to think we were good for
anything except carrying boxes and cleaning chimneys. I
never thought I'd see a person in the North nearly so miserable as the field slaves were at River Bend, but watching the
Negro sweeps in their filthy rags, I knew better.

The secret truth was that I missed following Lily around

the kitchen and licking her spoons. I missed Crow telling me in that tricky voice of his what silliness he'd overheard Master Edward say. I even missed sitting on the piazza after everyone was asleep and wondering when the hell I was going to get myself out beyond that dark horizon of pine.

I guess because of living in my mind somewhere between River Bend and New York, I stopped knowing who I was for a while. I wanted to talk to John about that just after we got here, and I even came close once or twice, but he was stuck deep down in the sands of his own misfortune and I wasn't about to add to his worries. Violeta, the woman he loved, struck me at first as someone too secretive for anyone's good. I sensed a big slice of anger in her too, like she might just be concealing guns in her room. You never saw anyone do as much as her, and act so kind, and help in a hundred different ways, all without ever letting you see what she was feeling. She was a giant question mark all wrapped up in a high-brimmed bonnet. But she couldn't hide from me that she feared John wanting her so much. Whether this had to do with him having only one arm, I couldn't tell.

It was during this period that I started writing down things about my life at River Bend and how we all got to New York. Later, John read some of it and told me to keep on going, that I had a gift for telling my story. When we spoke like that, just the two of us, I began to see a whole lot of my father in him—in little things he did and said, like the way he some-times sat on his haunches or said things were *very, very* this or that, or the way he'd write an *A* with a tail attached or a *B* with paws. It was like we were both living out what my papa had left behind.

IN EARLY NOVEMBER, maybe a week before most of the other River Bend folks left New York for their farms, I was strolling on Church Street when I saw a group of Negro children funneling out the door to one of those thin brick buildings they have up here, all of them shrieking like steam. While I was watching and smiling, out stepped a young black man smoking a pipe. That reminded me of my papa, so I guess I was staring, and he said to me, "What you looking at, girlie?"

I wasn't too happy with that *girlie,* so I corrected his grammar: "What *are* you looking at."

"What's that you're saying?"

He seemed to be another one of those puffed-up Northern Negroes we'd met, who thought we were all just wormheads—and who claimed not to understand our Southern accents.

I started to walk on. "You know how to read and write, young lady?" he called after me.

I turned and sized him up. He was not half bad-looking if you squinted.

"If I know how, what's it to you?"

He laughed at that and said, "Where are you from?"

"The moon." Imitating the nasal way the blacks around here speak, I said, "That's why I got my peculiar pronunciation, don't you know."

"What's your name?" When I told him, he said, "Well, Morri, how'd you like to put your reading and writing to good use at teaching?"

"I've never taught anyone anything."

"Good," he said, laughing. "Then you won't have to unlearn any bad habits."

"What would I teach?"

"Reading and writing. This is a schoolhouse. Allow me to introduce myself—I'm the headmaster, William Arthur."

He came down the stairs to me and shook my hand.

"You're the headmaster? Why...why, you can't be more than thirty years old!"

"I'm twenty-seven. I never knew there was any age requirement, you see. If there is, you had better tell me about it, since this is my third year."

"Will you pay me?"

"A regular wage every month. Can you start later this week?"

"Why not today?"

He laughed again. "Because I don't need you today. I need you in two days. All you have to do is be here every morning at nine o'clock sharp and show the children how to read and write. Four hours a day. Two different classes of thirty. Think a young lady from the moon can do that?"

"Well, I guess we're going to find out, aren't we?"

I WAS SO happy about my new job that when I got home I told John we ought to get the adoption papers ready. It was what he wanted, and what my papa had wanted, and I was in the mood to make everyone in New York as happy as I was. Then John spoke about Papa as if he were dead, spoiling things good. I forgave him only because I saw in his eyes that we were the same in a way—since we'd likely wonder all our lives what had happened to him.

I GREW FOND of the children at my school right away, and they all flocked around me like I was made of sugar crystals. Maybe because I gave them things to read that they liked. Reading for them is different than it is for us. Adults love surprises and new things all the time. Children love repetition. They embraced the knowing what was coming next.

When I told Randolph about the school, he enrolled Mimi and Lawrence. It made me smile like a loon just seeing them there—like all of us were made of moonlight. Pretty soon I had them and nearly all of the children—even the tiny ones—well on their way to knowing their ABCs. We had some poets among us too. There was a boy named Charles who wrote a whole epic about an ant, a mouse, and a rat who took a boat all the way to Africa. It was real good work.

John came to my classroom after he adopted me, and it was real encouraging to have him there. He'd found good work to do—making a list of slaves and freed Negroes in South Carolina, so that all those folks could find one another when slavery finally ended. And we wrote a message to my father that John had printed once a week in more than a hundred newspapers.

I realized I liked him more and more. I trusted him too, which was more important, the way I saw it. I could see why Papa was so fond of him.

Pretty soon after I started teaching, William Arthur asked me and John to supper with him. That opened the gate between us as friends, and he invited just me to his rooms from time to time. John gave me his permission but said to be careful, since though I acted older I was still just what he called "a wee lassie." Nothing happened between us though. I thought it might not ever happen.

By the end of December, things got badly twisted between John and Violeta, because she finally told him what he might have guessed long before—that she'd never love him like he wanted. He and I went out to a tiny town on Long Island for a weekend, to escape from her and talk things out, and I saw how disappointment was taking all that man's strength.

It snowed on Monday morning, just before we headed back to the city. I slipped on the walkway when I ran to greet it. Lying there, watching those unstoppable flakes falling to the earth, opening my mouth to taste their wetness, I knew I'd never live anywhere it didn't snow ever again.

In January, John's daughters and mamma came over from London to stay with us. You never saw so much commotion. Mrs. Stewart scared me at first, but I liked her iron affection for her son. And I liked that she wore her spectacles only when nobody was looking. That used to make me laugh when I was in my room alone. She said some real nice things to me right away and taught me how to cook, though a few of her recipes for codfish were just about inedible as far as I was concerned. She reminded me of Lily. I guess because she was a lot older than me and fierce as can be in defense of the folks she loved. I thought that John was real lucky to have her as a mamma.

At first I thought those daughters of his weren't much alike. Esther was always rushing around and giggling. You never saw a child's fingers move so fast as when she was playing her violin. It made me all nervous sometimes that she might hit a lot of wrong notes. She talked fast too, so that you couldn't understand half the words she was saying and had to ask her to start all over. Esther brings me back to when I was just little. We have secrets and giggle all the time. Graça is slower. She studies her maps and most everything else as if there's something there that's going to change the whole wide world. I grew fond of her right away, because we both liked silence and observing things. Esther took more getting used to, but like I say, she ended up tugging me all the way to fondness with her excitement. I like it when they knock before coming into my room. It's like we're family, but I still have my rights to be alone and not always be so friendly. They've got plans for going away with me, all the way to Africa. I told them I'd take them, and maybe I would, but the truth is it's enough for me to stay in one place that's safe.

IN EARLY JUNE of 1824, after being courted real sweet for months by William Arthur, I found myself in his rooms on Chambers Street one evening, fiddling with a silk cushion on my lap while we talked about the school. When he took the cushion away and kissed me, I just about fainted.

There were some things about him I wasn't too sure of. And I liked having the power to say no more than just about anything else. I tried to go slow. But he just loved doing things quick. So sometimes after that night in June I'd lie with him for a time in his bed and then rush on home before John and Mrs. Stewart would begin worrying about me. William and I were as fond of each other as two people can be who are a bit unsure of what their lives together are going to mean. The only thing missing from my life were the people who were dead or stuck back at River Bend. I missed Crow and Lily and Weaver and Grandma Blue. And Mamma. I wondered if my papa was with her now, or if he was still somewhere in our world. I wondered if they could see the good things that were happening to their Memoria. I wondered that nearly all the time and knew I always would.

Memoria Tsamma Stewart, June the Twenty-Seventh, 1824

POSTSCRIPTS

LIX

IT IS NOW THE SEVENTEENTH OF OCTOBER, 1825, and more than eighteen months since I last wrote of my life. For nearly two years we have been placing our requests for Midnight to write to us every week in one hundred and twelve newspapers. All the plates, vases, and ewers I've glazed and sold have gone into having them printed.

Mother contracted an agent in Portugal to rent out our home in Porto and sell our lands upriver, and with the proceeds we were able to purchase a comfortable Federal house in Greenwich Village with a view over the Hudson River. We moved there in August of 1824, and as there was room for Mama's pianoforte, she had it shipped over from London that very month. By the end of September, she already had secured seven students, two of whom are gifted. She's talking seriously these days about founding the music school she had first envisioned in London. She's even trying to convince Aunt Fiona to come to New York and help her.

Morri still finds her teaching rewarding, though she had herself something of a shipwreck with the headmaster, who seemed for a time to have really fallen for her. After some weeks of tearful trouble, she reached land healthy and contented, however. She's got better balance than anyone I've ever met—except for maybe her father.

Lawrence and Mimi are in one of Morri's two classes. When I saw them there recently, Mimi said she hoped that I did not miss my arm too much. I let her and the other children touch my stump, which they found rather scary and marvelous. How they love being frightened when they know they're perfectly safe!

Esther is studying violin and music theory with a demanding but kindhearted professor from Cologne. Graça has proven herself something of a minor sorceress with languages and is already speaking beautiful French, thanks to the tutoring of a fine young man from Strasbourg.

Over the past several months, Violeta has taken all the Church Street children, as well as Esther and Graça, down to Castle Garden on moonless nights to learn the constellations. She is eager and patient with them, and it is doing her good to be able to teach them, my mother tells me. I am slowly doing my best to develop a new sort of relationship with her. Though we do not see each other, we send greetings and news through my daughters. Mama calls it a "paper-and-ink friendship," guided from afar by what can never be. She says that that is sometimes all one can hope for. I am trying to rid myself of all expectations.

At the time we were suffering together, I did not realize that much of my urgency and desperation was prompted by the sudden absence Francisca's death had created in my life. I see now what a brave effort Violeta made in trying to save me from my own foolishness.

I NOW HAVE thirty-nine correspondents and a list of one thousand seven hundred and eighteen names and locations of blacks in South Carolina, Georgia, Mississippi, Alabama, and Louisiana. My scroll reads not infrequently like the Old Testament: *Moon Mary, daughter of Augustus and Angola Mary, mother of William, Sawmill, and Linda, sister of Tina, Claude, Merchant, and Picker Stephen* . . .

FREQUENT LETTERS FROM Isaac and Luisa have given us news of River Bend, where Crow was indeed hanged shortly after our escape, at least if the rumors they heard in Charleston are to be believed. Shortly after our *sudden departure,* as Luisa so nicely refers to our escape, Mistress

Anne invested in new *stock* straight from the auction block. She had the rice fields back to full production within months.

Lily, Grandma Blue, and the others who had remained behind were still in bondage. They are, of course, at the top of the list I am putting together. Morri has written to Lily to say we are all fine and that we miss her. We hope she has found someone to read the letter to her.

On realizing that I was not likely to return to Porto anytime soon, I began writing long letters to Benjamin, Gilberto, Luna Olive Tree, my father-in-law Egídio, and even Grandmother Rosa. Luna often sends sketches of fruit and flowers to me, and I return the favor with my drawings of the inhabitants of New York.

One day in September of 1824, there arrived in the post a slim manuscript written by Benjamin, entitled, "On the Hidden Meaning of Slavery," whose dedication was made to me. In it, he gave readings of verses in the Torah to demonstrate that slavery was the last gasp of a dying world. The Lower Realms were shedding their skin like a snake, he theorized, in preparation for rising closer to the Upper Realms. The true and lasting evil of this practice, he wrote, *is that slavery keeps our spirits from fulfillment and realization, from soaring into the firmament inside each of us, and therefore from union with the Lord. As such, it is an abomination that must be abolished if we are to create a world fit for the Messiah.*

In his accompanying letter, Benjamin told me that though the political situation in Portugal has calmed, he foresees a civil war before too long between those who favor a constitution and those who prefer an absolute monarchy.

In one of my letters back to him, I told him that I had seen Berekiah Zarco while fading from life on the road from River Bend to Petrie's Landing. He told me that there was little beyond the scope of a powerful Jewish mystic—even traveling across time—and that he wouldn't be surprised to meet Berekiah one day himself! He was certain that my illustrious ancestor had helped to save my life by reciting secret prayers over me.

I learned of Benjamin's death just four months ago from Luna Olive Tree and can still not bring myself to write more than a few words about its significance to me. It is as though an eclipse has set not simply over our life together but over the hopes he had for a better world to come. I wonder sometimes if there is anyone left to take over his mystical prayers and alchemy—who is endeavoring in a secret cellar somewhere to find the meaning in every moment.

Too weak to write me a last letter, the old apothecary had asked Luna to tell me that he was proud to have counted me among his friends and that—after I brought Morri to New York—he had seen me seated at the right hand of God in one of his visions. I was to always remember that each and every one of us was silver in the eyes of Moses.

Mama and I spoke a *kaddish* prayer for him, of course. And on the evening we received news of his passing, I set my flint to the seven candles of her menorah and let it blaze in my bedroom window all night long. It seemed essential to commemorate his departure from our world with light.

SO IT WAS that we reached October of 1825.

Three days ago, on the Fourteenth, at five in the afternoon, there was a knock on our door. Esther, who was practicing her violin in the sitting room, answered it and shouted, "Papa, you'd better come inside!"

I was in the garden, putting in some autumn bulbs—not an easy task with only one arm. With my fingers filthy with dirt, cursing the disturbance, I stomped into the sitting room.

He was removing his shoes in the doorway. I guessed it was him from that wee gesture and from his silhouette. No one else could have had that form.

He took a step inside the house. His eyes held the rains of the desert.

For a time I could not speak. My body seemed to be merging with everything around me. "We saw you from afar and we are dying of hunger," I whispered.

He repeated my words. Then, in a delicate and lilting voice, he began to sing "The Foggy, Foggy Dew," changing the lyrics for our reunion:

And every, every time I look into his eyes, he reminds me of the olden days...

In my broken whisper, I joined him: *He reminds me of the summertime. And of the winter too. And of the many, many times I held him in my arms....*

I ran forward and fell at his feet, hugging his beautiful belly, breathing in the scent of him, which I now knew I had dreamed of all these twenty years of separation. I was sobbing and shaking. But I did not wish to regain my composure; my spirit was simply too full to be contained, and there was no need to restrain it any longer. In his arms, I could be what I most desired.

He ran his hands over my head, then bent down and kissed my brow. I reached up and gripped his hand, as if to assure myself that he was real. "Yes, I am here," he said.

Esther came and knelt beside me.

"It's Midnight," I whispered to her.

"I know."

I stood up then and asked the question that I had been afraid to voice all my adult life. "Can you forgive me?"

He grinned. "There is nothing to forgive, my wee gemsbok. I am very, very glad to see you. Thank you for coming to find me." He reached up and touched my cheek. "You look the same as when you were a lad. Just a trifle taller," he said with a laugh.

"I lost my arm while escaping with the slaves from River Bend."

He patted the stump. "That's a very bad thing. I'm sorry. We shall dance for your loss. But truly you will be just fine without it. I expect you've discovered that by now, as you were always so quick to learn."

I nodded. I held his shoulder for support and began to weep again. I must have been quite a sight.

As I had not been able to think properly, Esther said to Midnight, "Morri is alive and is at her school. She has been waiting for you."

AND SO IT was that Midnight and his daughter were reunited at our home that very afternoon. After they had cried together, I gave him his old rattle and the hug sent to him by Benjamin. He was overjoyed to receive them, but distraught at the news of the apothecary's death. We spoke of Benjamin and the Olive Tree Sisters for a time, and I told him how Graça was killed. Morri had already told him about Weaver's sad fate. Of Father, all I told him for now was that he was long dead, killed during the French occupation of Porto. Midnight wept silent tears upon hearing that and shook for a time as I held him, reassuring me that he did not either hate him or remember him with anger. Then he smoked his pipe by our hearth and spoke to us of his disappearance and how he had come to find us.

I had been concerned about his seeing my mother for the first time, of course. And things were indeed difficult between them initially. I imagined that they would have much to talk about and would need many weeks to ease themselves into a new form of friendship. But there was time now.

I suppose I shall never be absolutely certain of what I desire for them. And sometimes when I see them together I still think of my beloved father and all that might have been.

I COULD NOT bear to be apart from Midnight that first afternoon as he spoke to us of his vanishing from River Bend. I sat close by his side and draped my arm over his shoulder. He kept his hand on my leg, which was a great comfort. Morri sat at his feet. All around was my family.

To our astonishment, the Bushman told us that the Indians were responsible for his disappearance. Way back in 1814, five Creek men had ridden in to River Bend, and in exchange for a fortune in hides, Big Master Henry had permitted Midnight to try to cure their dying healer. In this effort he was wholly successful, and this had, naturally enough, won him renown among the Creek clans in the South. Then, in December of 1820, the pregnant wife of a chief in the mountains of Georgia took gravely ill. This clan head was the son of the mighty chief whose healer had been cured six years earlier by Midnight. He dispatched a party to River Bend immediately, to exchange more hides for permission to bring the Bushman temporarily to Georgia. Times had changed, however. The Indians were losing power and territory every day. Dealing with them in a civil manner was no longer regarded as a necessary evil by the settlers and planters. Master Edward ordered the Creek emissary off his plantation and said that under no circumstances would he consider losing Midnight for even one day.

At this point, the Indians asked no more favors. Four warriors on horseback took Midnight on the Twenty-First of January from Porter's Woods, as he was chasing honeybees flying to their hive. The men covered their tracks carefully and raced with him off to Georgia. They met no opposition along the way, particularly as they were heavily armed and rode across back trails used infrequently by whites.

Midnight stayed by the ailing woman's side for more than two months, from her fifth to seventh month of pregnancy, treating her with essences and teas. Though he was unable to save her, he successfully delivered the baby, a boy. For this, the chief agreed to grant him safe passage out of slave territory.

First, however, Midnight insisted on rescuing his daughter. Wearing Indian garb, he was escorted back to River Bend by a party of twelve warriors. A scout of mixed black and Creek blood, who spoke fine English, stole into the plantation one evening and asked after Morri. This was the man who had been described to her as a mulatto.

As Master Edward had intended, the scout learned that Morri had died recently of illness. Midnight himself insisted on seeing her grave. Fooled by her wooden marker into believing that she was truly dead, possibly killed by Master Edward as revenge, he had the Indians take him beyond the borders of slavery, far into the wilderness that lay west of the Arkansas Territory. He no longer wished to live in the United States.

Midnight spent the next four years following the rains and the lightning in the mountains and deserts of the American Southwest, living as the Bushmen had for millennia.

"I went slow," he told us. He smiled down at his daughter and caressed her hair. "And I grieved for my Morri in silence, without speaking for many months. But I went far. Then Mantis joined me, and together we rode between the toes of Eland, and it was very, very good."

In the spring of 1825, longing again for companionship, he made his way to a ramshackle settlement of traders, trappers, and prospectors some forty miles west of Independence, Missouri, along the Santa Fe Trail. A Jewish hunter and fur trapper from Cincinnati named Mordecai Levi was astounded and pleased by his knowledge of Torah stories and invited him along on his excursions. Midnight had been living with Levi in a wooden cabin for four months when the old adventurer noticed a curious announcement in a copy of the *Cincinnati Gazette* sent to him by his elder sister. He had heard the Bushman greeting many times—*We saw you from afar and we are dying of hunger*—and knew immediately that an advertisement including these words could only have been intended for Midnight. He showed him the newspaper.

"You are a clever lad," said the Bushman to me now, patting me on the knee and grinning. "I understood quickly-quickly just what you meant by the beautiful feather. I began walking that very day."

"You walked the whole way here?" Mama asked.

"Indeed," he said, grinning.

"It must be more than a thousand miles. In how many months?"

"Three. I walked slowly because the land is very, very beautiful and I knew that Morri was safe with John. As always, Mantis kept repeating to me, 'Go slow.'" He laughed. "And I did. I wasn't about to risk another twenty years of troubles getting here."

*　　*　　*

NEITHER MIDNIGHT NOR I could sleep that first night of re-union, so we sat together long after the others had gone to bed. When I asked him about his experiences as a slave, he considered his words for a long time.

"It's something like a stone a day, John," he finally said.

"I don't understand."

"I don't think I can explain all it meant to me, but for now I'll just tell you this: The master hands you a stone every day, and you take each one from him and put it in your pocket. You do it very, very carefully, because you don't want to make him angry." Midnight pretended to receive a stone, then placed it in my palm. "But, John, pretty soon you run out of pockets. And you aren't allowed to put them down, so what do you do?"

"I don't know."

"You start swallowing the stones. Soon your stomach gets all filled up and you start feeling sick, so you lie down." He rubbed his belly. "Just one day of rest, you think, and everything will be better. But the master keeps on handing you stones. Because he's got his money invested in you and he's decided he doesn't want to wait even one day for you to get your strength back. You say no, because you think you can. So he whips you, which makes you confused-confused, since you don't know how to live a life where you can't decide anything. Not even Mantis can tell you how to do that. After a few months your spirit is so heavy with stones that it can no longer even stand up. So, being kind, you lie your spirit down. And you let it be covered by the stones, till it can't breathe or move."

"So you're buried alive," I said.

"That's right, John, but only one stone at a time."

WHEN, LATER THAT night, I told Midnight that his being betrayed by my father seemed to make him different from the other slaves and his imprisonment even more cruel, he replied, "No, John, that's not the way it was. I was exactly the same as them. Every slave has been betrayed. By his chief in Africa, who sold him for a few yards of cloth or a musket. By the white men who shackled him and brought him across the sea in the belly of their ship. By the plantation owners who purchased him and set him to work in the fields." He spread his hands wide, then brought them together as though to gather in the entire world. "Even by this age we are living in, which permits these things to happen."

"Is that why you do not hate my father? Why you can forgive him?"

"In part, though *forgive* is not the right word."

"What is, then?"

He made clicking noises in his own language, which made me frown.

"John, you've always wanted clear answers, and sometimes there aren't any." He grinned, patting my leg. "Your father did not only betray me, but all the world—all men and women and creatures of the forest— even himself. And Mantis most of all. But it was only possible because of forces and powers that went far beyond him. It took me years to see that clearly and to see my own betrayal of him in that light as well. You wish, I think, to hear that I despised him. I shall not disappoint you—I did, and for many years. But I also remembered him fondly. That made what took place between us even harder to live with." He drew in deeply on his pipe. "We have all paid for our errors, over many years, and now I only wish your dear father were still alive. What a good man he was and how wonderful it would be to see him!"

He left me speechless, and when he smiled at me reassuringly, I knew he was telling me that we would never need to speak of these things again. I knew I would forever owe him a great debt for that alone.

Yet his insights soon turned my thoughts to how Violeta had also been betrayed by the world. His eyes, squinting, began probing me for the cause of my sudden distance, and I told him how everything had gone wrong between us. I tried not to sound heartbroken, but he detected it plainly enough and told me a story I'd never heard before:

"Once," he said, "there was a shepherd in the north of Portugal who took his flock to the greenest pastures he could find. At night he slept in a wee stone hut nearby. But in the morning, he discovered that one of the sheep had been shorn. He was not happy. And he was very, very bewildered. The next night, the same thing happened."

I got off my chair then and sat on my haunches to listen more comfortably to his tale. Midnight did the same. We faced each other, only a few feet apart. I felt as though we were in his desert homeland and would never be separated again.

"The shepherd was furious. Being clever, he remained awake on the third night and watched the Women of the Sky descend from the stars along a cord they'd woven from the air. He saw them grab one of the sheep and take shears to her coat. Whereupon he jumped out from his hiding place and ran after them till he had caught the loveliest maiden of all. He took her as his wife. And from that moment on, he had no more trouble from the Women of the Sky."

"He must have had some or you wouldn't be telling me this," I said with a laugh.

"Thank you, John, for pointing that out," he replied, his eyes radiating joy.

"Now, there was only one problem," he resumed. "His wife was in possession of a beautiful woven basket, and he could see nothing of its contents because of the lid. Before she would agree to marry him, she obliged him to promise that he'd never lift the lid and peer inside—at least until she had given him permission to do so." Midnight shook his fist at me. "She warned him that if he were to disobey her wishes, a terrible destiny might await them both. Yet as the summer passed, the need to know what was inside made him restless. One day when his wife was not at home, he—"

"He removed the lid," I said.

The Bushman pursed his lips comically, wrinkled his nose, and gazed around as though fearing watchful eyes. Then, after peering inside his imaginary basket, he breathed in longer than seemed possible on his pipe, as though to inhale the words of the story. Wisps of smoke curled from his nose and ears.

"When his wife returned," Midnight said, "she knew what her husband had done. She began to cry, accusing him of having looked inside the basket.

"The shepherd said to her, 'How silly you are to shed tears over such a trifle. There was nothing at all in the basket. It was empty as can be.'

" 'What do you mean, empty?' his wife said.

" 'That is precisely-precisely what I mean. There was nothing there.' "

Midnight clapped his hands together, so that I jumped. "And that, John," he said, "was the very last word the shepherd ever spoke to his wife, for she reached up into the descending sunset of red and gold, took the end of a heavenly cord, and climbed back into the sky."

"And . . . ?" I asked.

"And nothing." He grinned.

"That's it?"

"Yes, that's the end."

While I struggled to work out what it meant, he tapped the floor between us with his foot. "John, do you know why she went away?"

"To punish him for his curiosity?"

"No, no, no," he scoffed, twisting his lips into a frown. "That is the Jewish story of Adam and Eve. This is a Bushman story."

When I shook my head, he said, "Not because he had broken his promise. Nor because of his curiosity. The Woman of the Sky was aware of our nature and had expected him to look, of course. Just like the God of the Torah always expects Adam and Eve to take the apple he leaves for them. No, the Woman of the Sky turned her back on the shepherd because he had found the basket empty and laughed."

"But it *was* empty."

"No, in point of fact, the basket was filled with the beautiful-beautiful things of the sky, which she had placed there for them both. The shepherd simply did not see them."

Midnight made a circle in the air with his hand. "John, Mantis was once lost," he continued. "And he walked all over the African desert to try to find his home. Finally, exhausted after many years, he gave up. It was only then he recognized his tree and his leaf."

"Midnight," I begged, "I am out of practice, so will you please tell me what you mean or I shall scream and wake the entire household."

He pointed two fingers at me. "The lid of the basket is your eyes. When I look inside, I see beautiful-beautiful things—all that you have put there in your life. Even the Violeta you knew as a lad is there. She is there for you whenever you want her. But the secret is, she cannot come out into this world. Her destiny is to remain only inside you. In fact, whenever you try to make her come out, she dies."

THE NEXT DAY, I told this story to Mama. I think it put her in the mood to speak to me of Midnight for the first time. But before that, she played the second movement of Beethoven's "Appassionata Sonata" with incomparable fragility and thoughtfulness, as though she were creating a new and delicate form of life with the notes—an ethereal being made of music.

I sat down next to her to turn the pages. When she was finished, I was so overwhelmed that I told her she was a genius. She laughed. "John, you are sweet, but you have mistaken me for Mr. Beethoven."

"No, Mama, you're wrong. His genius has come through you to me, so there is no difference."

Her eyes moistened and she said, "That is, without doubt, the nicest thing anyone has ever told me. You know, sometimes I think if we just listened to Mr. Beethoven and Mr. Mozart a little bit more, things would be so much better. But we don't really hear what they want to tell us. Not really." She brushed some hair off my brow. "I don't think I knew what they were saying until I was your age at least."

"And what is it they're saying, Mama?"

"It's a secret," she whispered, grinning girlishly.

"I'll not tell a soul, I promise."

"Well, John, I'll only tell *you*, since the others would think me mad. All the great composers are telling us with their chords and melodies— and even the silences between their notes—that life is long, but not nearly as long as we first believe. It's going to be much harder than we ever imagined too, so we must make as much beauty as we can while we are here and help all the people we love to do the same. We must listen to one another as we would listen to their music too—that's very, very important. And we must have the courage to fight against anything that would compromise our own beauty or in any way do it harm. All the truly great composers are preparing us for living correctly, and giving us encouragement to go on with our lives as best we can, even if we've made the most unforgivable errors—like me and Midnight and your father."

I wiped away tears, explaining, "It's just that with Midnight here . . . and what you just said . . ."

"Yes, we've had a hard time of it, all of us. But we've been very lucky too. You know, it occurs to me more and more that despite all the death we've known, we've had a chance to meet the most wonderful people— and to be with one another, of course. And now, with Midnight back, it is as though we can finally close an old rusted door behind us and step ahead together into the future, whatever it brings us. That was your doing, John. Thank you. I'm enormously proud of what you've accomplished."

"Do you think sometimes about what happened between you and Midnight?"

"Oh, yes, of course. I was such a fool to go about things the way I did. I didn't understand myself, let alone your father or him. And I know your father didn't understand himself either—I see that now. Not, at least, till it was too late. John, would you like to know what troubles me the most about my life?"

"Of course."

"We learn so many things as we age. And yet all that knowledge . . . all of it just disappears when we die. That seems to me a terrible waste."

"Unless you pass it on."

"Yes, unless we do that, but it's not so easy. Perhaps it isn't even possible. All of the most important lessons we probably have to learn ourselves."

"But if what you say about the greatest composers is true, then your music lessons may make all the difference in your students' lives."

"I like to think so, John. At least, that's why I keep giving them."

"Have you spoken to Midnight yet about what took place between you and Father, and . . . and what Papa did to him?"

"Yes, we've already had a few chances to speak seriously. Midnight has grown older as well, and I think we both see the mistakes we made. But we cannot return to the past to change the way things happened, so we must just keep walking. That's what he told me, and I think he is right." Mama asked me to hand her a Mozart score. "And as for me, John, I shall also keep on playing and listening, and teaching as best I can."

LX

Giving of Ourselves
to the World

IT IS ONLY THREE DAYS SINCE HIS ARRIVAL, and it's just about impossible to believe he is here. He lies on a straw mattress in my small room. He sleeps peacefully. And just like yesterday, he'll wake this morning wanting to see every last inch of New York. I sit by him sometimes, my hands on his sleeping chest. Last night I stared at him through the pearly darkness of the light of the moon that long ago told our people we were eternal beings. I believed it was true while watching him.

I CAN'T KEEP up with him as he races through the city. I don't know how he goes so fast with his crippled heel-strings. He turns around to me and laughs as we walk. I moan and wave him ahead.

WE NEVER GUESS how strange life is before we suffer some real sadness and confusion. I was an orphan, and then I was adopted by John, and now I have my papa back. It almost makes me believe that all things are possible. Papa says this is the most powerful belief of all.

I put the *almost* there because things got real fouled up with William Arthur when I stopped having my time of the month about ten weeks ago. He hollered at me something evil and started telling me what I had to do with the baby growing inside my belly. He accused me of having "robbed his seed."

I let him just go his own way. Because I know what robbery is, and I never robbed anything from him.

These days he's barely polite to me at our school. But that's all I want from him now. I've got the children in my classroom to educate, and I've got John and his family, and I've got Papa, and that's enough for me.

I guess I'm not willing to push and pull on myself till I'm all in a knot just to stay with a man. Even a good one. I need a whole lot of hours for myself, anyway. What happened between us is maybe not even his fault. Or mine. But I didn't escape from River Bend and see Weaver die in his own blood so I could start taking orders again.

After I stopped seeing William, I started liking being on my own— liking it more than ever. I suppose I'm one peculiar young lady.

GEOGRAPHY, TOO, IS important. I have to remember to tell that to the children. If we were living just two hundred and fifty miles south of here, we would all be slaves. I guess one of our goals ought to be to make maps and borders less important—for everyone everywhere.

THERE IS SO much I don't understand. But I'm only seventeen years old. Papa says many things still ought to be mysterious to me because they're mysterious to everyone. John told me that it is a Jewish tradition for some dangerous secret teachings only to be taught to people over forty.

What I want to understand most is how all this was waiting for me in New York and I didn't know it. We cannot predict the future, that's true enough, but I didn't have even the tiniest notion of the life I'd have one day.

Because of that I've come to believe we all have thousands of possibilities stored inside us, each one like a caterpillar inside a giant cocoon. Lots of folks don't want to admit it, but the life that comes out of us is shaped more than just a little by circumstance. Not that I wouldn't have the same wings, spots, and colors even if I was still living at River Bend.

I think I'd probably be pretty much the same as I am now. But I'd be mighty diminished. For one thing, I wouldn't be teaching, wouldn't be giving back to the world, which now seems to me the most important thing.

I think that that is the saddest thing about slavery: We aren't allowed to give of ourselves to the world. I read that in the book John gave me about the hidden meaning of slavery. It was written by the Jewish conjurer in Portugal, Benjamin. And I think he's right.

I'm grateful to have that chance now. I am grateful to Mamma, Papa, and so many others. To Lily too. And Crow, of course—my brave, beautiful Crow. And Weaver, who died for me to be here. And John.

In the oddest way, I am even grateful to Master Edward, Mistress Holly, and even Big Master Henry—to all the white folk at River Bend, for they helped to make me who I am.

I will go slow, like Papa is always saying. I will take every last thing I can and then give all I have back to my children—the wee one growing inside my belly too.

Memoria Tsamma Stewart
New York, the Seventeenth of October, 1825

LXI

MIDNIGHT . . . I LIE AWAKE AT NIGHT, ALONE IN my bed, and know that I have done one very, very good thing in my life. Perhaps that is enough for a man.

No, I am no hunter in the way it's usually meant. But we found each other. Violeta told my girls to tell me that we did so by the light of the Archer, and I think she's right.

There is still so much I don't understand about her. I hope that our life apart can work out as we would both wish it. When I wrote her a note about Midnight having found us, I told her a bit of what he'd said about slavery. She wrote back: *A single act of cruelty can take a lifetime to undo—and sometimes not even a lifetime is enough. It's as though we have one chance to be good and if we deviate by even half a foot, we're lost. We've learned that the hard way, you and I.* As a postscript, she added, *Do you suppose some people even get to like the taste of stones?*

Not just Midnight, but Berekiah Zarco found me too, journeying across three centuries to help me as I fell into darkness. It might just have been a vision resulting from my delirium, but it is also true that he, as my ancestor, lives inside me. In that very real sense, he has indeed journeyed into the future, and I am his vessel.

Thinking of him now, I wonder what it is I'd like to leave behind after my death for my descendants, just as he left his illuminated cover page for me. Perhaps I would choose the sketch of Midnight I made in Alexandria in order to find him. I think that anyone looking at it would recognize that I had done the best I could to capture the beauty of one person with my modest skills.

The Olive Tree Sisters would say that I'd succeeded in inhabiting my sketch. Perhaps I am indeed good enough now to execute the tile panel of the field slaves. We shall see.

When I was seven, I learned from *The Fox Fables* that *He that pursueth evil pursueth it to his own death.*

But what about good? Might it somehow be able to restore life?

I cannot say, of course, but I've begun to suspect that goodness is the only miracle within reach of human hands: *He that pursueth good may join together what has long been separated.*

I knew that the moment I saw Midnight standing in my doorway.

And what of that generous old fox who wrote down his fables so that a mischievous seven-year-old lad from Porto might one day find them? Might he have meant to tell me all along: *He who has been snared and hunted, when set free, may accomplish so much more....*

I do not wish to leave behind my daughters, Morri, Midnight, and Mother, but if I knew I was about to depart from this life, I would feel I had accomplished something. That is, I think, what we all need to know.

We believe we are creatures of time, space, and a specific place, when we are nothing of the sort. Over the last nights, I have sat in the dark, facing Jerusalem, and seen that plainly. I have felt myself falling free of this body, shedding it like a phantom limb. Borders open and I am outside myself, drifting like music. I do not know where I am. I am nowhere. And I know I am no different from Midnight.

Indeed, I am every pitch and every chord. We all are, or we could not hear them in our ears when no music is being played. Everything out there has a cognate inside. Every last atom.

Hope has made full use of me. Not that I am finished. No, I think I've a further journey to make. Though I am not yet aware of its nature, I can feel the pulling on me of forces greater than myself. Of the world, if you will. Or of my daughters, who carry their mother and me inside them and who no doubt wish for me to remain with them for a while longer.

I do not believe that there will be life everlasting to follow, nor that we shall rise on the Mount of Olives when the Messiah comes. For the secret is this:

The Messiah is here now and we are already living on the Mount of Olives.

That is the most important lesson I learned on my journey, while hunting Midnight.

And so, life is written in the present tense, out of ink bequeathed to us from the past. Death too. Genesis and Exodus are taking place inside us all at this very moment. Even Christ's Passion. And it is a good thing that they are, for we would not want to wait. Why would we?

Eat the night!

It was the angel Raphael who said to Tobit, "Write down all these things that have happened to you."

And to give thanks, just like Tobit, that is what I have done.

Father, you may come back to us now. We shall journey forward together and you may take hold of my hand. We shall beg forgiveness from Midnight. I know you are a good man, just as I know you committed a monstrous act. I have the letters you wrote to try to make amends, and I am aware that you regretted what you had done. I do not know what the lesson of your life and death may be, except that we may all do terrible things when the Time of the Hyena is on us.

Perhaps evil such as you have done cannot be forgiven, not even by the one you have wronged, since it is an abomination against life itself. But if we are very lucky, then we may banish it from the present tense and consign it forever to the past. Midnight reassures me that we have. He remembers you fondly.

If you are dead these many years, Papa, as must truly be the case, then I still say this to you, since you have always dwelt inside me:

We have seen you from afar and we are dying of hunger.
You are redeemed and may go now in peace.

John Zarco Stewart
New York, the Seventeenth of October, 1825